PRAISE FOR HEROIC

"A roller coaster ride filled with thrills and intrigue

– Alma Boucher, Reader's Favorite

"A powder-keg combination of military, medical, and techno thriller. Buckle in for a wild and suspenseful ride."

–Meg Gardiner, #1 New York Times bestselling author

"Both a military thriller and a medical thriller, which rips and races through twists that will make you dizzy as a medical examiner discovers a plot going back decades and burrowed into the depths of his own history."

– Lisa Black, New York Times bestselling author

"This story is a burning fuse from page one! It launches with heart racing speed from the starting block and sprints the whole way through. If you want a fast, heart-pounding thriller that you can't put down, make Heroic Measures your next read."

-- Jennifer Graeser Dornbush, Crime Author.

"A high-octane blend of action and intrigue. . .that's a delight to read from beginning to end, Heroic Measures is an unreservedly recommended Golden Quill read!"

– Book Viral Reviews

"This is a great step into military and technothrillers for fans of Patricia Cornwell and other forensic crime authors, and an equally perfect introduction to more relationship-based novels for military fiction buffs."

- firstCLUE Reviews

Also by Joel Shulkin, MD:

Adverse Effects

Toxic Effects

HEROIC MEASURES

Book 1 of the Death Benefits series

Joel Shulkin, MD

Zero Dark Publications

Miami, FL

Zero Dark Publications
382 NE 191st St #815734
Miami, FL
www.zerodarkpublications.com

Book Layout © 2017 BookDesignTemplates.com

Cover design by Abigail Simmons, The Killion Group

Heroic Measures/ Joel Shulkin, MD. -- 1st ed.
979-8-9900188-1-5

Dedicated to those who risk their lives
to defend our freedoms.

And, as always, to Geiza, without whom I wouldn't be
brave enough to write this story.

Show me a hero and I'll write you a tragedy.
—F. SCOTT FITZGERALD

Courage. Honor. Loyalty. Sacrifice.
You're braver than you think.
—CAPTAIN AMERICA

PROLOGUE

The first thing US Marine Corporal Mark Greenwood noticed when he woke up half-buried in a sand dune was the intense heat. He hated the heat. He hated the desert.

So, when he realized he was on fire, he was downright pissed.

"Shit!" he shouted, and patted his burning arms. He rolled in the sand until he managed to douse the flames on his head and shoulders.

When he was sure he was no longer burning, he stood and assessed his situation. He was outside the ruins of what looked like some kind of medical building. Chunks of rubble lay scattered around him, half burying the broken and charred bodies of what he assumed had once been human men. A smoke trail rose from inside the building and twisted away on a dust devil. The interior walls glowed amber. Mark sniffed the air. Odors of propellant, charcoal, and blood assaulted him. An air traffic control tower loomed over him, and beyond it, an air strip stretched toward the horizon.

Pain shot through his skull. Electric.

He jammed one palm against the back of his head—it felt wet, sticky. He gnashed his teeth.

"Relief," he whispered. "Relief, damn it."

A cool wave washed over his body. The pain subsided.

The corporal lowered his hand. Blood covered it. Blood and some kind of grayish stuff.

The world around him shimmered, like a mirage. He squeezed his eyes shut and counted to ten, then opened them again. Blinked several times. No more shimmering. Better.

It'd been a long time since he'd felt pain like that. Something must've hit him hard. But he didn't have time to figure out what it was.

"Foxtrot team," he said into his radio, his voice deep and raspy. "What's your position?"

The radio crackled and hissed.

"This is Greenwood. Hostiles are down. I repeat. Hostiles are down. Awaiting orders."

Still no response.

"Sergeant, where the fuck are you?"

Automatic rifles popped in the distance. Mark scanned the ground. Where was his M27?

More gunfire. Well, he didn't need a rifle, anyway.

Pebbles kicked up in a wake behind him as he sprinted across the sand.

Something felt off. His right leg wobbled with each footfall. He had to fight to keep his six-foot frame balanced as he ran. After a few seconds, he stopped and looked down.

A jagged piece of white bone poked through his Combat Utility Uniform below the knee. The camouflage was stained black.

"Shit on a stick." Mark bent over to push the bone back into place. Pain shot up his thigh. Gritting his teeth, he kept his fingertip pressed on the bone and started counting. He could feel the bone weaving together, and when he reached sixty, he let go. The bone still felt unstable, but it would have to do. He resumed his sprint.

The Humvee stood perched atop a dune half a klick away, the front passenger tire flat. He spotted Lance Corporal John Kirby inside the armored turret, manning the M2 cannon. He couldn't see Sergeant Grant or the others.

Movement caught his eye. Off to the left.

Two soldiers holding rifles raced toward the Humvee.

A fly buzzed by his ear. Mark swatted it away and focused.

Hostiles!

Something popped inside his skull. Tiny shocks jolted his brain, forcing him to stop running. He pressed both palms against his head and roared in agony.

"Relief. Relief. Relief."

The pain washed away. He lowered his hands.

Eliminate all resistance.

The voice came from inside his head. Toneless. Genderless. Commanding.

Adrenaline surged through his body. The last remnants of pain vanished.

Mark squinted. The hostiles were only a quarter klick from the Humvee. Why wasn't Kirby shooting at them? It was almost like . . .

Eliminate all resistance.

With a grunt, Mark ran. Harder. Faster. He closed the distance in less than five seconds.

The hostiles turned and raised their rifles.

He ripped their weapons away, snapping their wrists. The hostiles screamed.

He tossed one rifle to the ground and swung the other with both hands. The stock smashed in the face of one of the hostiles. The other tried to run. Mark shot him in the back, turned, and finished off the one he'd battered.

Another fly buzzed in his ear. He wiggled his finger in the canal until it stopped. Fucking desert bugs.

Someone shouted from the Humvee.

The M2 roared to life, fifty-caliber rounds whizzing through the air.

Mark froze. Why was Kirby firing at him?

A round slammed into Mark's shoulder, ripping a hole through the muscle. He screamed and forced himself to stare through the haze of white-hot pain at the Humvee turret.

No, it wasn't Kirby. Son of a bitch. That was why he hadn't shot at the hostiles. The man at the cannon *was* a hostile.

Another round grazed his thigh. Rage burned a swath through his body. He threw away the rifle and dashed toward the Humvee.

The cannon kept firing at him. He ignored the rounds pummeling his body armor, even the ones that managed to penetrate his side and abdomen.

Mark scrambled over the Humvee's hood and leaped onto the roof.

The hostile punched at him. Mark caught the fist and twisted, hearing and feeling a loud crack.

That earned a scream. Mark grabbed the hostile's throat with his other hand. He squeezed, and the neck snapped.

Mark hurled the lifeless body onto the sand.

"Greenwood!"

The voice sounded familiar. Mark looked down.

A US Marine stood next to the Humvee, aiming an SSW40 grenade launcher at him. It took a moment for the corporal to recognize Sergeant Gardner Grant. He was about Mark's height and build but lacked the hard edges. On the ground nearby, another Marine nursed her injured leg with one hand and leveled an M18 pistol with the other. Corporal Micaela Deodato.

Grant's eyes widened, his lips twisting into a grimace as he asked, "What the hell happened to you?"

Mark tried to process a response but couldn't. He'd just saved them from the hostiles. Why were they pointing guns at him?

"Why did you kill those men?"

Again, Mark stumbled over the question. But this time he was able to find an answer. "I was following orders."

"Not my orders. Whose?"

Eliminate all resistance.

The world shimmered. That fucking fly buzzed in his ear again.

Mark rubbed his eyes and squinted.

Something about Grant's face wasn't right. It looked like him—but it wasn't. Mark glanced at Deodato. Same with her. Their eyes were cold. Distant.

They'd flipped sides.

Mark swung the M2 around and locked on to Grant.

"You traitors!" he shouted.

"Corporal," Grant said, keeping the SSW40 trained on Mark. "Stand down."

Sweat streamed down the corporal's cheeks. His shoulders tightened. This was total FUBAR. His whole team couldn't have betrayed him.

Eliminate all resistance.

He tightened his grip on the cannon. It didn't matter. He had to complete his mission.

"Get down, Sergeant!" Deodato shouted. Her pistol fired.

Bullets streaked toward Mark. One grazed his cheek. The other buried itself in his arm. He roared and rotated the M2 in her direction. The cannon spat at Deodato, and she crumpled to the ground.

The SSW40 in Grant's hands made a heavy *thump-thump* sound. Grenades whizzed toward Mark.

The world exploded.

1

Regional Armed Forces Medical Examiner System Suite
Defense Department Hospital, Ramstein AB

As Lieutenant Colonel Stephen Englehart studied the ragged loops of intestines wrapped around chunks of shrapnel and draped over the autopsy table, he thought of the trash compactor scene in *Star Wars*. He tensed as if, at any moment, a tentacle would shoot out, snare his neck, and yank him inside.

Stephen donned nitrile gloves and adjusted his surgical gown before glancing at a tray holding all four of Sergeant Carlo Herrera's limbs, twisted and mutilated. His gut spasmed, his mind racing back thirty-plus years to another grotesque scene. Mangled flesh. Blood everywhere. And the screams...

He shook it off, taking deep breaths underneath his surgical mask until the moment passed. Grabbing his face shield, he prepared the straps.

"You okay?" Tech Sergeant Melinda Stewart stopped snapping digital photos of the body on the metal table and stared up at him, azure eyes peeking out over her surgical mask. At five-one, she was a head shorter than him.

"I'm fine." Stephen flashed a grin. "But that's the last time I have sausage for breakfast."

She rolled her eyes.

"Seriously," he continued as he positioned the visor over his eyes. "What the hell happened to this guy? Someone drop a cherry bomb in the toilet?"

Melinda snapped another photo and then glared at him. "Not funny."

"You're right. But humor is my defense against life's atrocities." He dropped his chin and gave her his best puppy-dog eyes. "Forgive me?"

She squinted at him.

Stephen lifted his mask and pouted.

The skin at the corners of her eyes crinkled, and she tucked a loose lock of blond hair back into her tight-coiled bun. "Fine. But please show a little more respect."

"I have nothing but respect for the Fallen. My heart goes out to them." He pulled up the soldier's Virtopsy scan on the monitor and began scrolling through images. "My mouth, on the other hand, doesn't know when to stop."

Melinda glanced over her shoulder before leaning close to him and whispering, "You can prove that later tonight."

His cheeks flushed. At the old Landstuhl mortuary building, he'd been more independent, getting his orders from the AFMES Dover office. But the military, never happy unless their thumbs crushed every pulse, insisted on establishing a local command structure. That meant the pathology chief could appear unannounced at any moment. Fortunately, that rarely happened. Still, he was glad Melinda knew to keep her voice down.

"So," he said casually as he flipped through the digital images. "What happened to him?"

"He and his partner were on foot patrol in Achin. According to the report, he stepped on a landmine."

"Ouch." Stephen scanned the soldier's uniform and spotted a patch on the shoulder. "He's Special Forces. Didn't he know not to wander around Afghanistan without keeping an eye out for unexploded ordnance?"

"One would think." Melinda leaned close to the soldier's face and clicked the shutter. "Search and Rescue swept for remaining UXO. In a nearby hut, they found three sets of remains. Looked like an animal attacked them."

"What kind of animal?"

"No idea. They were torn apart but not eaten. What kind of animal does that?"

Stephen froze. Images flashed in his mind. Yellow eyes. Swollen muscles. An officer saying: *The way he tore her apart…*

He shook it off. That was a long time ago. He'd only been twelve when it happened. It had taken years of therapy, but he'd gotten past that. Why was he dredging up those memories now?

Because you're weak, a voice said in the back of his mind. *You've always been weak. You couldn't stop it from happening then, and you're pretending to have it under control now. It's only a matter of time.*

Stephen tightened his jaw, breathing in and out through his nose. It wasn't so much an actual voice as it was his inner doubt, his self-loathing, his guilt. At least, that was what his therapist had told him. For three decades, he'd been able to keep that voice bottled up, transforming that guilt into productivity. Uncle Alex had told Stephen he was crazy for pursuing forensic pathology, but his course had been set the moment his parents died. Maybe he'd never know why Dad had done what he did, but Stephen could help others. So many took their secrets with them to their graves, but he knew how to get the answers their families needed. And in doing so, he could make it a little better for the servicemen and women fighting for the same flag Dad once served…

"Hey," Melinda said, waving a gloved hand in front of Stephen's face. "You sure you're okay?"

Taking one more deep breath, Stephen turned to her and forced levity into his voice. "Sure. Just thinking I could use a good butter schnitzel after this."

Melinda groaned. "Only you would think of food right before an autopsy."

"It's not how I appear, but what I do that characterizes me."

"Who said that? Ghandi?"

"Nope." He grinned. "Batman."

"Of course." Melinda sighed. "I'm beginning to think I need to dress like Catwoman to compete with your comic books."

"Make it Poison Ivy and you'd win hands-down."

"No, thanks. The thought of leaves touching my skin…"

Chuckling, Stephen changed the subject back to the work at hand. "So, this guy steps on a landmine a short distance from where three civilians get mauled by a mountain lion or something?"

"More or less." Melinda snapped another photo. "Don't feel too bad for them, though. Report is they were making bombs before they were attacked."

"Terrorists?"

"BTB." *Believed to be.*

"What about Herrera's partner? Did he get caught in the blast?"

"Nope. He's MIA."

"He disappeared?"

"Yep."

"Is that why the Army Criminal Investigation Division sent Herrera here instead of Dover? They're thinking foul play?"

"I guess so." She clicked the shutter again.

"And there were no witnesses?"

"Nope."

Click. Click.

Stephen pressed a knuckle against his chin as he shifted his glance from the monitor to the dismembered corpse. Closing his eyes, he visualized the scene, imagining an intact Sergeant Herrera striding down a dusty road, his partner by his side. He pictured him stepping on UXO. He saw the soldier's limbs flying in multiple directions. If the partner got injured too, where was he? And if he hadn't, why would he disappear?

He opened his eyes and scanned the corpse again.

"Any chem? Rads?"

"He's clean."

Stephen picked up one of the soldier's dismembered arms. "Flash burns. Fingers are burned to crisps."

"From the UXO."

"No, if he stepped on a landmine, there's no way the flash would reach his arms with enough force to blow them off without incinerating his pelvis." Stephen placed the arm back into the bin. "For this pattern, he would've had to be holding the device when it detonated."

Melinda stared, wide-eyed.

"What?"

"Damn, you're good."

"I love hearing you say that."

Hot electricity sparked between them as they held each other's gaze. She turned away, her skin flushed above her mask.

"It's obvious to anyone used to seeing these injuries. I can't believe the death investigators missed it." Stephen pointed out several white areas on the CT scan. "Prep him for post. If we can figure out whether these are shrapnel or fragmentation, we'll have a better idea of what killed him."

"You got it, ba—" Melinda caught herself, her eyes darting side to side. She took a deep breath and said, "Yes, sir."

As she began unfastening the straps on the soldier's body armor, Stephen mused on her near slip. If anyone happened to walk in and overhear—one of the other pathologists, security, a janitor—it wouldn't take them long to put two and two together. That observation would be promptly reported to his superiors. And then his career would be over.

The one thing the military couldn't tolerate was an officer fraternizing with enlisted personnel. Even though it was consensual, getting caught meant court-martial. Each moment they spent together, they had to watch over their shoulders. That meant no dates at local restaurants. No long walks in the park. They worked together during the day, and at night they stayed at her house. He'd never admit it to anyone, but the fear of getting caught sent a little thrill down his spine each time he was near her.

"Hey," she said, "you want me to prep that other bright spot?"

"What spot?"

"The one near the scapula."

Stephen turned back to the CT scan, squinting.

Son of a bitch. She was right. It was tiny, but clearly a foreign body.

"How'd you catch that?"

"I've been working with you for half a year." She tugged at the heavy breastplate. It held fast. In one fluid movement, she scooped up a pair of scissors and made two deft slices in the soldier's fatigues on either side of the armor. With a grunt, she ripped the breastplate free and dropped it with a clang onto a metal tray. Flecks of burnt cloth and skin flew up and settled onto the stretcher. "I'd have to be an idiot not to learn something."

Mingled odors of blood and gunpowder filtered through the mask and wafted into Stephen's nostrils. While the tang of formaldehyde was like an old friend, this combination still made his stomach twist. At least it wasn't as bad as that coppery-sweet odor of fresh blood, like when he and Sharon returned to the house that day…

You gotta stop this, he told himself. *The past is past. Nothing good comes from reliving it.*

As he helped Melinda pry off the remaining armor scraps, Stephen reflected on how easily she did what to most people would be horrifying. No, she wasn't an idiot. Or weak. Or any of his other initial impressions. When she'd shown up that first day, decked out in her starch-stiff Class As, he'd thought of the old movie *Private Benjamin:* a five-foot-four prom queen playing soldier dress-up. Two hours later, when she heaved a 250-pound cadaver that had fallen from a gurney off Stephen's trapped chest, he'd realized she was so much more. Their relationship had started out as a reckless fling, but over the past few months it had become something more. What exactly that was, he wasn't sure yet. Just being next to her, close enough he could smell the hint of jasmine on her skin, triggered a rush of memories of her body pressing against his, the light touch of her tongue . . .

"Well," he said, forcing away the daydreams as he set aside the last bit of armor and moved over to examine his dissection tools. "I hope they don't reassign you to a flight crew. The good ones always disappear."

"Nah, I'll take twisted forensic humor over frat boy pilot jokes any day." She paused while removing the soldier's helmet. "But I won't be the one to disappear."

Stephen stopped in the middle of testing the bone saw. "What do you mean?"

"Just some break room gossip." Avoiding his gaze, she finished removing the helmet and dropped it into a bin. "Something about you retiring."

His mouth went dry. "Oh."

"You weren't going to tell me?"

"This is my twentieth year of service. If I leave now, I get full benefits and can do whatever I want. But if I stay, I'll have to take a command position."

"So?"

"So, that means all my time will be spent doing paperwork during business hours and schmoozing after-hours. No autopsies. No on-site investigations." He glanced at the door and then whispered, "And no time for us."

Melinda squinted, her eyes dancing and bobbing as she studied his face. At last, she turned away to start cutting the remaining scraps of the soldier's uniform. "You could've discussed it with me."

"I was planning to, once I clarified all my options."

She side-eyed him. "Options? I'm an option?"

"That's not what I meant."

Her gaze dropped back to the soldier, and she started cutting away his underwear.

A ball of frustration formed in Stephen's stomach. He'd hoped to have this discussion over a bottle of Lambrusco, not like this. He liked her. He did. Maybe more than that. But was he ready to plan the rest of his life around her? Hell, the ink on his divorce papers was still drying.

He touched her wrist. She turned to face him.

"Nothing's been decided." Stephen lowered his voice. "I promise, once I have all the information, we'll sit down and—"

The *Superman* theme song started playing in his pocket.

"Damn it. I thought I silenced that." He checked his phone. Local number he didn't recognize. He turned the phone off and stuck it back in his pocket. Colonel Restrepo had strict rules about use of personal phones in the hospital. "Sorry. I—Uh, what was I saying?"

"Forget it. We'll talk about it later."

Stephen's cheeks burned. He was making it worse. "I think we should—"

"Don't stop on my account."

The floor fell out from beneath Stephen at the sound of the new voice. They'd been caught.

2

Stephen and Melinda turned to see Major Thomas Wilson standing in the doorway, wearing an Army-issued jacket over his Class A uniform and a cockeyed grin plastered on his chiseled face, perfect teeth practically glistening against his dark skin. Stephen tensed, wondering how long Tom had been hiding in the shadows, listening to their conversation, and then decided he needn't worry. Although Tom's arrogant swagger had irritated him when they first met, as the only other forensic pathologist on base, he'd defended Stephen several times against Restrepo's attempts to micromanage him. Besides, one night over drinks, Tom had bragged about barely dodging a court-martial over an affair with a wing commander's twenty-year-old daughter. Fortunately for Tom, he hadn't violated the Code of Conduct, merely pissed off a powerful man who was able to transfer Tom as far away as possible. Even if Tom suspected something was going on between AFMES staff, Stephen doubted he'd tell anyone.

"Did I interrupt something?" Tom asked.

"Other than this young man's autopsy?" Stephen answered, and snatched up his favorite scalpel. "No."

"Good. Because we've got a bird incoming. ETA thirty minutes."

Stephen lowered the scalpel. "From where?"

"Al-Hasakah."

"That's a forward outpost. It's a combat casualty?"

"No..." Tom ran his fingers through his hair. "It's *five* combat casualties."

Stephen's back muscles tensed. "Why the hell aren't they going to Dover?"

"Huge winter storm over the Atlantic, and another one over eastern Germany damaged the plane." Tom held his hands out in what seemed like a plea for truce. "I just got off the phone with AFMES in Dover. They're not happy about it either, but Captain Reinstein said to press on and do what we can."

"Press on? We're supposed to lighten Dover's load, not bear the full weight." Stephen swept his hand dramatically. "We've barely been in this facility for a year, and we're still trying to dig ourselves out of the backlog of missions they had to put on hold during the transfer from Landstuhl."

"We don't have to autopsy them." Tom shoved his hands into his pockets. "Their freezer shorted out. They want us to store the bodies until they finish repairs. But Reaper said we have to process them as if they were staying."

Tension rushed into Stephen's neck and arms. Colonel Luiza Restrepo, or "Reaper," as Stephen and Tom lovingly referred to her, was the chief of pathology. She had a proclivity for assigning short-notice projects, demanding hourly updates while she disappeared for hours at a time doing whatever schmoozing she could find to advance her career. "You've got to be shitting me."

"She said we could pull whoever we could find to help us."

"Great. You know how much the anatomic pathologists love forensics."

"Spencer and McNiven are on call. They still owe me for covering for them while they went to that beer fest." Tom scratched his cheek. "Look, you know Reaper wants to prove to the brass they were wise to expand our program, and this is her way to do that. We don't have a choice."

A familiar rage bubbled in Stephen's belly, a rage he'd fought for decades to keep under control. He glanced at Melinda, who seemed frozen, her eyes never leaving his face.

Stephen took a long, slow breath. He couldn't lose it, not ever, not after what happened to his dad. He would never let something like that happen again.

"Fine." He ripped off his surgical mask and goggles and tossed them into a bin. To Melinda, he said, "Let's get Herrera back in the cooler, and then you can go home."

"I'm staying to help."

"You don't have to do that. We'll meet the plane when it lands, tuck those soldiers in, and call it a night. Even if one of them shows signs of decomposition due to the freezer malfunction and needs an autopsy before transfer, they'll still be dead tomorrow."

"True." She folded her arms across her chest. "Unless Reaper calls again and orders you to finish all five tonight and I have to come back in after already taking a shower."

Stephen tried not to react to Melinda's use of Restrepo's nickname. Enlisted techs were supposed to show respect for commissioned officers. If he let it slide, it would imply favoritism, but after their conversation about his possible retirement, and now with this new assignment, he feared reprimanding her would stoke her anger. He hoped Tom wouldn't notice.

"All right. Thanks, Sergeant Stewart." He turned back to Tom. "We'll meet you on the flight line for the dignified transfer."

"Sure." Tom glanced at Melinda but didn't say whatever he was thinking. To Stephen, he said, "Hey, I have to tell you about something when we have time."

"Why not tell me now?"

"It's, uh, personal. Something you should know about."

Stephen blinked.

"Forget it." Tom waved his hand. "It'll wait until after we get these casualties checked in. See you in twenty."

After Tom left, Melinda turned to Stephen and asked, "What was that about?"

"No idea," Stephen said. "Maybe Reaper—I mean, *Colonel Restrepo*—has him more shaken that he wants to admit. Whatever, he's a big boy. Now, let's finish putting our big boy away." He lowered his voice. "And I'm sorry we won't get to talk tonight."

"Yeah, I'm sure you're heartbroken."

He looked at her sharply.

"Don't worry," she said. "We'll have plenty of time later."

Exhaling through his nose, Stephen nodded and tried to lighten the mood. "I know it's overkill, but you think we should shower before the dignified transfer?"

"Well, you should, anyway." Melinda flashed him a half smile. "You stink."

3

I want to tell you the truth. Here it is. I'm Spider-Man. Weird, huh? No, I'm kidding. It's Stephen and I can't answer the phone right now, but leave a message…"

Major Sharon Englehart sighed as she hung up the United Service Organization's public phone. She'd expected her big brother would be too busy to meet her at the RAB passenger terminal, even if she was a short distance away, on the same base as the hospital where he worked. Of course, he had no way of knowing her trip had been rerouted midflight to Ramstein instead of into Stuttgart due to the weather. But that fact didn't help her mood.

Grumbling, she pulled her cell phone out of her Army Combat Uniform pocket and turned it on for the eighth time. No service. She recalled the salesclerk explaining something about the Global System Whatever, and that some of the phones they offered were incompatible with networks in other countries, but the phone she'd bought was half the cost and a hell of a lot cuter than the bulky thing they wanted to sell her. So now she had a super-cute, hot pink, worthless hunk of plastic. Well, she could still play Candy Crush.

She opened the settings on her phone as she left the USO and searched for hot spots. Sure enough, one popped up: *USOFreeWifi.* As she waited for it to connect, she scanned the small but clean and well-lit terminal. A light rain had started to dot the window walls. She'd expected someone from her unit to meet her on arrival, but that would've been at Stuttgart. Her household goods had shipped separately, leaving her with one gigantic duffel bag to haul around.

Her phone pinged as it established a Wi-Fi connection. Sharon opened an app and typed an email to her brother, explaining what had happened and asking him to drive her to Panzer Kaserne. As she hit *Send,* she realized the effort might be futile. The last time she'd emailed him about a memorial service for their parents, he'd replied three weeks later, asking if it was too late. The guy had a heart as big as a blue whale but the attention span of a fruit fly. Clucking her tongue, she tucked away her phone. She'd need to find her own way to Stuttgart.

Hoisting the massive bag over her shoulder, she straightened her six-foot frame and began marching through the terminal, aware of the looks she was drawing. While Steve had inherited their mother's medical brain, Sharon got their father's physique and athletic prowess. That made it possible to become the third woman ever to complete Green Beret training, earning her command of a Special Forces company at Panzer Kaserne. If she managed to get there.

She made her way to an AMC customer service desk. There was no line, just one man in a ski parka, talking to the attendant. After taking position a respectable distance away, she pulled out her phone again and started searching the internet for local restaurants. After an eight-hour flight, she could have killed for a mushroom pizza.

"What the fuck do you mean it's canceled?"

Sharon's head snapped up, her body reflexively tensing. She leaned over to see Ski Parka flailing his arms. His haircut was high and tight, skin tanned and weathered—he looked like someone who'd survived a few tours in the desert.

Behind the counter, the attendant cowered, her eyes wide. She wore a sleek red dress over sand-colored skin. Black hair draped over her shoulders. AMC usually employed enlisted personnel, and the few civilian contractors tended to be old men. If this was a new direction they were moving toward, Sharon was all for it, but this woman seemed in over her head.

Another attendant, this one a young, buzz-cut airman in combat dress, intervened, holding his hands out in a conciliatory manner. Ski Parka screamed louder, his voice raising to such a high pitch that Sharon couldn't understand a word. He began pounding his fist on the counter. The two attendants jumped back.

Suddenly, Ski Parka stopped yelling. He glanced over his shoulder, mouth moving as if he were talking to someone, and then his head whipped back toward the attendants. He balled up his fist and started kicking the desk, ranting once again.

Sharon's blood turned cold. She was all too familiar with the signs of PTSD, having suffered years of therapy as a kid. If this man was untreated, or off his meds, things could escalate.

The AMC airman was picking up the phone, probably to call security. The man in the ski parka pointed a finger at him and screamed something. Sharon could only make out the word "regret." Whatever he said must've been convincing, because the airman returned the phone to its cradle. The woman in the red dress bit her lip and started typing, her hands shaking.

Sharon flexed her fingers for another second before dropping her duffel bag to the ground. She marched over and placed her hand on Ski Parka's shoulder. "Hey," she said softly, "we're all frustrated with the weather, but—"

He whirled around to face her, eyes wild, aiming a pistol at her chest. Sharon stiffened. His hand was shaking as much as the attendant's.

"I don't want to hurt anyone," he said, head twitching, moving his hands together in a sloppy cup hold. "But I will shoot whoever gets in my way."

Sharon clenched her fists but said nothing.

After a moment, his gun hand relaxed. His resolve was waning. He didn't know what to do. He probably expected Sharon to say something profound, to talk him down. But she didn't. She remained at attention, brow furrowed, waiting for him to make the next move.

"I need to get home," he said casually, as if they were chatting over a coffee. "I don't care if they have to get Air Force Fucking One, I'm going home. Today."

Red Dress pleaded with her eyes. Sharon gave a slight nod.

Ski Parka stared at Sharon, confusion obvious on his face. He swung the gun back in the airman's direction. "Don't try anything—"

Sharon charged.

Ski Parka turned back, raising the gun in a sloping arc. She jammed her palm against the gun barrel, and his eyes widened as his grip loosened.

Sharon grabbed his wrist with her other hand. She twisted in and down, bending the trigger finger until she felt a crack.

The man screamed. She wrenched the gun away and kicked him in the abdomen, and he doubled over.

"Call Security," she shouted, and backed away. She twisted the gun around and aimed it at his head. "Don't move."

He clutched his broken finger to his chest and looked up at her, eyes filled with tears.

Sharon kept the gun trained on him until three security police arrived. Two of them restrained Ski Parka and hauled him away. Sharon handed the gun to the third.

"He needs a mental health evaluation," she said. "You can get more information from the AMC staff."

The SP nodded and approached the service desk while Sharon went to reclaim her duffel bag. She glanced over her shoulder to see the airman wander off with the SP, leaving only Red Dress.

Sharon slung the bag over her shoulder and ambled over to the service desk. Red Dress stared at her with wide eyes.

"That was amazing," she said with a German accent. "I don't know how to thank you. How did you—?"

"Special Forces." Sharon pointed at the patch on her shoulder. "Green Beret."

"Oh. I've never heard of women in the Green Berets."

"There weren't. I'm the third to make it."

"Impressive." Red Dress seemed to catch herself staring and shook her head. "I'm sorry, but you're—I mean..."

"I'm what?"

"You're so tall."

"I know. I'm a half a foot taller than my older brother. He always calls me Amazon." Sharon chuckled. "Thinks I'm Wonder Woman."

Red Dress tittered. "He's right."

They held each other's gaze for two heartbeats. A warm tingle ran through Sharon's belly.

Then the woman ripped away and turned to her computer, leaving Sharon uncomfortably disappointed. "How can I help you?" she asked.

"My flight was diverted here due to the storm. I'm supposed to in-process at Panzer Kaserne for my first command position. Well, technically, it'll be my second, but I led a troop for less than a week before I got this new assignment, so this'll be my first real command and . . ." Sharon trailed off, her cheeks flushing. No matter how cool she was in a combat situation, whenever she met a pretty girl or a hot guy, her mouth got stupid. And this girl was smoking hot. She covered her eyes with her hand. "TMI. I'll stop talking now."

Red Dress smiled, displaying white teeth. "It's okay. I like hearing you talk."

Sharon's blush spread down her neck.

Stay professional, she told herself. *You know nothing about this lady, and you still gotta get to Stuttgart.*

"You said you're going to Panzer Kaserne, yes?" The woman's blue eyes sparkled.

"Yes."

"There is a shuttle, but it doesn't leave until tomorrow morning."

"Could I take a taxi?"

"Yes, but it's expensive, and the train can get confusing if you don't speak German." Red Dress wriggled her lips. "I recommend the shuttle."

"Okay." Sharon glanced around the near-empty terminal. "Do you know if they have any room at TLF?"

"The Temporary Living Facility is full due to the diverted flights."

"How about a local hotel?"

"I'm afraid they're full, also." Red Dress twitched her button nose. "Some sort of comic book convention in town."

Sharon rolled her eyes. "Even in Europe, I can't get away from those things."

The woman giggled and then scanned the terminal. She reached into her pocket and slid something across the counter.

Sharon picked it up. It was a thin white card with a black stripe. "What's this?"

"A key to a room at the Ramstein Inns. It's here on the base."

"I thought you said all the rooms were booked."

"They are, including this one." The woman's eyes glimmered. "As long as you don't mind company."

Sharon felt a warm rush as she slipped the card into her pocket. "Sure, as long as you don't mind that I like to sleep on top."

4

Six young soldiers in camouflage battle dress, black Army berets, and white gloves marched along the tarmac toward the C-130's massive cargo bay. Inside, five aluminum cases waited near the edge, draped in stars and stripes. Flight crew, wearing Air Force flight caps and forest-green jumpsuits, stood behind the caskets.

Freezing drizzle fell on Stephen's neck, but he remained at parade rest as he waited outside the plane. Whether in the rain, snow, or one-hundred-degree heat, the dignified transfer always took place for the country's fallen heroes, so long as the planes were able to land. It was a risk being out in the cold for too long, what with Stephen's medical condition, but his last blood draw had been reassuring. And orders were orders.

The flight line was silent, save for the *tap-tap* of the pallbearers' shoes against the tarmac. Tom Wilson stood on Stephen's left, his flight jacket zipped up snug, shoulders almost touching his ears. For once, he looked serious. Even a cocky son of a gun like him understood the gravity of the dignified transfer.

On Stephen's right stood Melinda, shivering under her Air Force-issued jacket. The flight cap topping her head offered little protection against the sleet. Stephen bit his inner cheek. As much as he wanted to put an arm around her, hold her hand, or at least move closer to her, he resisted the urge. Even though every eye was on those caskets, there was too much chance of getting caught, especially with the brass arriving for the ceremony.

"Company . . . halt."

The carry team, now split into two lines, stopped in front of the first casket. Their faces remained stoic. Eyes forward. Back straight.

Three officers stepped out from beside the plane and marched up the ramp. Two were in fatigues: the on-call chaplain and Mortuary Affairs Director Sumit Agarwal. Colonel Agarwal took his place with the flight crew, while the chaplain took position in the center of the cargo bay, clutching a copy of the Bible.

The third officer, wearing US Army service dress, sauntered up next to Agarwal and stood at attention. A full rack of ribbons and medals glistened in the lamplight on the left breast of his uniform. Three shiny silver stars adorned each shoulder. White sideburns protruded from under his well-polished service cap, in sharp contrast to his tanned face. A thin gray mustache clung to his lip like a caterpillar about to fall from a branch.

Stephen tightened his fists. Military custom demanded a general officer attend every dignified transfer. With Army European Command less than a half hour away in Wiesbaden, it was easy enough to make that happen. Most generals stayed in the background out of respect for the Fallen, but this one was different. His eyes were always moving, looking to see who was watching him, ensuring the Armed Forces Network cameras caught his good side. He never showed up when the parents of the Fallen denied media access to the dignified transfer. Disgust nipped at Stephen's chest. This general did not have heart.

The chaplain began reciting a quiet prayer. There were no families watching tonight, no mother's sobs drowning out the chaplain's words. For that, Stephen was grateful. When he performed an autopsy, he could forget that the body under his knife had once been someone's child, spouse, or sibling. He could forget that that body was once alive, that the soul that once inhabited it had dreams, loves, feelings, and thoughts. It was the only way to get through the day. But facing loved ones, seeing them grieving, shattered the illusion. It made it personal.

The chaplain finished her prayer. The carry team crouched, resting their gloved hands on the handles strategically placed around the caskets. In precise unison, they lifted the box.

"Present . . . arms."

The commands were not shouted but uttered solemnly, just loud enough that Stephen could hear them from outside the plane. Every uniformed officer in attendance raised their right hand in salute as the carry team proceeded down the ramp.

A cold mist kissed Stephen's face as he held his salute. A single AFN camera operator silently filmed the processional. Dignified transfers at Ramstein were still new. After a few dozen, the media would lose interest or, more likely, Command would stop working so hard to justify the expanded overseas operation. Stephen gnashed his teeth. He respected the men and women who fought for the country with all his heart, but his loathing for the system that took advantage of them grew each year.

As if reading Stephen's mind, the general shifted uneasily. Stephen watched out of the corner of his eye as the general tilted his head, studying the remaining caskets. His trimmed eyebrows met. His lips pressed into a thin line.

Stephen puzzled over the general's reaction. The flag officers usually remained stone-faced, as if they were too busy thinking about what they were going to buy for their significant other's birthday or what they would drink at the Officer's Club before the helicopter ride back to Wiesbaden. What was different enough to catch this man's eye?

The general caught Stephen staring. His forehead creased.

Stephen glanced away, but knew he'd stared for too long and called unwanted attention to himself. If he ducked out right after the transfer ended, he might be able to avoid the imminent confrontation.

The carry team reached the mortuary truck and halted. The truck driver held a salute while they loaded the first casket. When the team finished, they saluted the fallen soldier and then, in unison, turned on their heels and marched back to the plane, where four more caskets waited.

Back and forth, back and forth, back and forth. They proceeded with their silent duty, hoisting an aluminum box, carrying it to the truck, saluting, and then marching back for another. The rain intensified. Their feet tromped on the tarmac with a soft, slushy sound as they approached the plane for the final coffin.

The temperature plummeted as the carry team marched down the gangway. Stephen bit his inner cheek. It would be disrespectful to end the ceremony before the last soldier was safely aboard the truck, but the weather had no respect for the dead.

As the carry team touched the tarmac, a soldier in the back slipped on a patch of slush. He fell backward, his ankle twisting violently. The rest of the carry team shifted, trying to redistribute the weight of the casket, but the sleet was making it tough for them to keep their grip.

Stephen rushed forward while everyone else remained frozen in shock. He threw his shoulder underneath the casket, grabbed it with both hands, and hoisted. They managed to stabilize the coffin, keeping it from crashing to the ground.

The soldier next to him nodded approval, and then his eyes widened. Stephen turned his head to follow the soldier's gaze and blinked in surprise.

The general stood there, pale blue eyes scanning Stephen up and down. Before Stephen could speak, the general slid one hand under the casket and lifted it away from Stephen. He jerked his head to the side, indicating the soldier who'd slipped, then shifted the coffin onto his shoulder and nodded to the soldiers in front.

Stunned, the cadence caller said in hushed tones, "Forward . . . march."

The carry team stepped forward, now more vigilant for ice patches. The general's crisp service dress stood in sharp contrast to the camouflage worn by the rest.

It took another moment for Stephen to recover from his surprise, but he hustled over to the injured soldier and knelt beside him. As he rolled up the soldier's pant leg, Stephen's cheeks tightened. The skin around the young man's ankle was purplish.

Stephen glanced back at the carry team. They were sliding the casket into the last open spot on the truck. They stepped back, stood at attention, and saluted, holding their salutes as the driver closed the back door and returned to the front of the vehicle.

"How's it look?" the soldier whispered. His baby-smooth cheeks glistened in the illuminated rain. His eyes looked hopeful. "Think I'll be able to deploy to Kandahar next week?"

Stephen forced a smile. "Don't worry. Kandahar's not going anywhere."

As he slipped his hand under the soldier's armpit and started helping him to his feet, Stephen heard the truck drive away. Someone touched his shoulder. He turned to find Tom Wilson. Melinda stood two feet away.

"Here," Tom said. "Let me help."

Tom slung the soldier's arm around his neck. Together, he and Stephen helped the soldier hobble over to the waiting bus. They were halfway there when Stephen heard footsteps crunching on the frozen tarmac behind them. He looked over his shoulder.

The general stood with his hands on his hips, seemingly oblivious to the icy pellets bouncing off the brim of his service cap. His mouth moved as if he were chewing gum, which would've been against regulations. A name label over his right chest read *Ross.*

Stephen tensed. He'd been right about the confrontation. To Melinda, he asked, "Can you help Major Wilson the rest of the way?"

Melinda glanced at the general and then nodded at Stephen. She took the soldier's arm, and together with Tom continued the limping march to the bus.

Turning back to the general, Stephen straightened his back to match the general's height. "Hi, Uncle Alex."

5

Stephen and Lieutenant General Alexander "Blitzkrieg" Ross faced off as the freezing rain bounced off their shoulders. Wrinkles lined Ross's eyes and mouth. Whereas most generals vied for a spot at the Pentagon as soon as it came open, Ross had played the long game, staying active duty well past the time when most would've retired, and now he commanded the entire US military presence in Europe. Stephen wondered how many years taking care of Sharon and him had set Ross back from his goal. If the man hadn't adopted them after their parents died, would he be on the Joint Chiefs of Staff by now?

Ross tilted his head and scanned Stephen up and down. His lip twisted.

"I still can't believe you went Air Force," Ross said, acid lacing his words. "What happened, anyway? Boy Scouts wouldn't take you?"

"No," Stephen said, "but the Army had already commissioned a rock and filled their IQ quota for the year."

They glared at each other for three heartbeats. The rain lightened.

A smile cracked the general's stony expression. "That was a good one."

Stephen didn't return the smile. "Thanks."

Ross nodded as if answering a question Stephen hadn't asked while his eyes tracked side to side. "The upgrades look good. You enjoying your new digs? That was me, by the way."

"You built the hospital with your bare hands, right?"

"No, but I authorized the project."

"Oh, well thank you for that. I'm surprised they didn't name it after you."

Ross frowned. "Can we not do this?"

"Sure." Stephen turned to leave. "Bye."

"Hold on."

Stephen stopped and looked back.

"I'm sorry I haven't visited," Ross said, avoiding Stephen's gaze. "I'm not proud of the things I said the last time we spoke."

"The last time we spoke to each other was three years ago."

"Yes, it was." Ross looked back at Stephen. "And I can see you're still upset…"

"Upset?" Stephen barked a laugh. "I'm not upset. I feel betrayed. You hid the truth from me for thirty years."

"That was for your own—"

"You let me think it was my fault. That I pushed him over the edge, when the reality is, he was already toppling over it."

"Let the dead rest, Steve. What's done is done."

Stephen bit down on his tongue. If he hadn't become a pathologist, he might not have gained access to his father's autopsy reports. Then he would never have known Dad had an undiagnosed adrenal tumor, causing him to have rage attacks. As the stress of deployment and trying to hold his family together spiraled out of control, Dad couldn't hold it back any longer, and then . . .

Stephen shook his head. "How am I supposed to rest, knowing I failed him?"

Ross closed his eyes and lifted his head. Rain splattered on his face. He lowered his chin again and wiped water from his eyes. "I never blamed you, son. But you blamed yourself, and I knew if you ever saw that report, all those years of therapy would've been useless. Washed away. Because the truth is, we all failed him."

They stared at each other for another moment. Silent. Unmoving.

At last, Stephen said, "You always were good at pep talks. I feel awesome now."

Ross cleared his throat and jerked his head in the direction of the C-130. "Make sure no one touches those boys tonight."

"You don't want us to process them?"

"Do what you must, but don't disturb their bodies. They were killed in battle and deserve all the honor of Valhalla. I want everything intact when they arrive at Dover for autopsy."

"We can do combat autopsies here. That's why they built the expanded facility *you approved.*"

The corner of Ross's mouth twitched. "I know. But you haven't done any here yet, have you?"

Stephen said nothing.

"That's what I thought. This is a high-level case. No room for error."

Stephen studied the general's face. There was something Ross wasn't telling him. "What happened to them? New tactical weapon?"

"I'm not authorized to say." The man furrowed his brow. "Promise you'll leave this alone."

For the briefest moment, Stephen considered telling Ross exactly where he could leave it, but he decided he didn't want to spend any more time dealing with his estranged caretaker than he already had. Besides, the cold rain had seeped through his uniform and was starting to chill his bones. "Whatever. It was great seeing you, Alex. Let's do this again never, all right?"

Stephen turned and marched away before Ross could say anything else. He massaged the scar on his shoulder as he trudged through the thin layer of slush. It didn't matter that Ross could crush his career with a phone call. Stephen knew he wouldn't do it. Whatever else had happened between them, the man cared about Stephen. Even if Stephen no longer felt the same way.

6

Fifteen minutes later, Stephen entered the mortuary facility, rubbing his arms for warmth. A water fountain bubbled into a rock-walled artificial pond in the center of the room. Local plants and flowers were arranged in carefully landscaped clusters. The new mortuary mirrored the Carson Center at Dover Air Force Base, right down to the Wall of Fallen Heroes in the center of the room. Due to the newness of the facility, the wall listed only a dozen names. Stephen glanced at the wall as he rushed past, wondering if he would still be there when it started to fill.

A set of metal double doors opened after he swiped his badge, revealing a long, stark hallway. The cold blast from the air conditioning made him shiver—a necessary evil when keeping bodies from decomposing. He hurried down the hall until he reached the Explosive Ordnance Disposal room. Tom and Melinda were waiting for him inside while four mortuary technicians wheeled each casket one at a time into the specialized X-ray room to scan for bombs or other active devices.

"What was that about?" Tom asked.

Melinda was eyeing Stephen. He'd told her a little about his history with Ross, but not everything. Now was not the time for details.

"Nothing," Stephen said, removing his dripping-wet jacket and draping it over the back of a chair. "The general wanted to make sure we appreciate our new digs. And on that note, what do we have on these soldiers?"

"Meet Foxtrot Team, Force Recon," Master Sergeant Malcolm Booker said as he approached, swiping an iPad screen. Booker, the noncommissioned chief of Mortuary Affairs, was career military, no-nonsense, and by-the-book. At five foot nine and built like an Abrams tank, he knew every detail about every decedent that came through the mortuary. If he didn't know something, it wasn't meant to be known. "They were scouting an abandoned airfield when they surprised a sniper nest. Foxtrot Team fought back but got hit with a high-explosive grenade. Took out the whole team except one."

"Where's the survivor?"

"MIA."

Stephen chewed the inside of his cheek. A soldier missing in action after an ambush could be due to any of several reasons, none of them good. "Do we have photos of the scene?"

Booker handed the iPad to Stephen. The first set of photos showed a Humvee huddled on a dune, scorched on one side. The bodies of two US soldiers lay strewn in the sand. One was splayed out as if he'd been trying to make a sand angel. The other lay on her back, eyes wide open, a pistol near her open hand.

"So, this one fell off the Humvee," Stephen said as he enlarged each photo. "And this one got surprised by the explosion. Where are the other three?"

"Keep looking," Booker said as he leaned over a technician's shoulder to review the most recent X-ray. He nodded to the tech, who signaled for the others to move on to the next casket. "Everything's there."

The next photo showed two bodies lying three feet apart, twisted in awkward angles. Stephen noted their positions and frowned. Something wasn't right. He swiped through the next four images, all close-ups. Both soldiers wore the wide-eyed, gaping expressions of abject fear.

"How far were these two from the Humvee?" he asked.

"About twenty meters," Booker said. "Why?"

"That's outside the effective casualty range of a grenade." Stephen studied the images again. "No burn marks. These two were killed by hand."

"Maybe whoever fired the grenade went back and killed them later," Melinda said. "Tying up loose ends."

"Yeah, maybe." Stephen flipped back to the first image in the set again and zoomed in on an area past the bodies. He scratched the back of his neck.

"You've got that look," Tom said. "What is it?"

"The footprints in the sand. They're going the wrong way."

"What does that mean?" Booker asked.

"They were running toward the Humvee." Stephen looked up. "If the grenade caught them by surprise, why would they rush blindly into the fire instead of ducking for cover?"

Booker's mouth twisted. "I don't know."

The techs wheeled the fourth casket into the blast-proof room.

Sucking on his tongue, Stephen scrolled to the last set of photos. His gut wrenched as the screen filled with the blackened remains of what once had been human. More than half of the body was covered in burns, the uniform charred, and armor shattered. The face was twisted in a mask of surprise, jaw hanging unhinged on one side.

"Oh my God." Melinda covered her hand with her mouth.

A sour taste filled Stephen's mouth as he flipped through the last four images. He'd seen burnt remains before, but the look in this soldier's eyes was like nothing he'd seen. No, that was wrong. He'd seen it once before, a long time ago…

"Were they able to get a positive ID?" Stephen asked.

"From the dog tags, yes," Booker said. "First Sergeant Gardner Grant, team leader. They'll need dental records to confirm. His fingers were blown off. Couldn't even get a good set of prints."

"Might have to wait for the DNA match to know for sure." Stephen pointed at the dislocated jaw. "He lost half his teeth, too."

"Doesn't look like the grenade blast caused that." Tom leaned around Stephen to peek at the screen. "No scorch marks over that side of his face."

"And if he'd gotten hit with enough force to knock off his jaw, it would've incinerated his nose and eyes, too." Stephen nodded. "Looks like a mechanical injury. Was there anything on the scene to explain it, like a bloody tire iron?"

"No," Booker said. "The only things they found were the soldiers' weapons."

"They were ambushed and killed, but whoever attacked them didn't take their weapons?" Stephen frowned. "That doesn't make sense. What about the sniper nest? How was the rescue team able to get in and out without being attacked also?"

"Snipers cleared out. The airstrip was clean."

"Took nothing, left nothing," Tom said. "Doesn't sound like insurgents."

Stephen studied the photos again. Behind him, the techs wheeled the last casket into the X-ray machine. "Wounds on the torso are patterned."

Tom blinked. "You're sure?"

"Positive."

"What does *that* mean?" Booker asked.

"Grenade fragmentation causes random wound patterns. More concentrated injuries suggest the victim was close-range to the blast." Stephen traced a finger over the screen. "These wounds have a clear centripetal distribution, meaning this soldier was on top of the grenade when it detonated."

Booker's eyebrows arched. "You can tell that from the photo?"

Stephen shrugged.

"So, you think he threw himself on the grenade to save his friends?"

"If he'd done that, his hands wouldn't be burned. And since the blast didn't punch a hole through his body, it wouldn't have burned the Humvee or the other two." Stephen looked up at the others. "Someone wanted to make sure this guy was dead."

A siren blared.

"What's that?" Melinda asked.

"UXO alarm." Booker ran over to the monitors. "What'd you find?"

The X-ray tech shook his head. "I don't see anything."

Tom leaned over Booker's shoulder and pointed at the screen. "What about that?"

"Where?"

"There. Cranial."

Stephen came up behind them and stared at the area Tom had indicated, where he saw a tiny bright spot in the center of the skull.

"Too small to be an explosive," Booker said. "Probably fragmentation."

Stephen shook his head. "Too round."

"Doesn't look like a bullet," Tom said. "We should remove it to be sure."

Booker scowled. "You think it is explosive?"

"Well, no. But I—"

"If it's not UXO, it doesn't concern us." Booker motioned to the techs, who began wheeling the body out of the scanner. "Let's finish processing these soldiers and put them on ice."

Stephen exchanged a glance with Tom. He hated letting a mystery go, but Booker was right. Performing even a partial autopsy on one of these soldiers would violate direct orders. The last thing he needed so close to retirement was an Article 92 dishonorable discharge. He looked over his shoulder at Melinda, who was watching him expectantly. He gave her a *What can I do?* gesture.

The techs wheeled the five caskets out of the EOD room as Booker marched off to start paperwork. Stephen, Tom, and Melinda led the techs down a maze of corridors to a set of double doors. Tom swiped his badge through a card reader, and the doors swung open. They continued down another hall until they reached the medical examiner's office.

Once inside the antechamber, Stephen signaled to the techs to start reopening the caskets.

"This is a partial processing," he told them. "We need to make sure none of the bodies suffered additional decomposition due to the refrigeration malfunction. We'll take photos to document their current condition. Please make sure none of the personal effects were damaged."

"Don't forget to scan their bar codes," Tom said. "Command will want to know we gave them back the right remains."

Melinda crossed the room, dug in a drawer, and held up a bar code reader.

"Okay." Stephen donned nitrile gloves and rubbed his hands together. "Let's get to work."

One by one, they opened the human remains pouches. Melinda snapped photos of each body. The first two, one male and one female, had been the farthest from the explosion. No burn marks. Bullet holes riddled their uniforms, but what caught Stephen's eye was that the hands of both soldiers were bent backward at impossible angles.

"Broken wrists," he said to Tom. "Looks like they were snapped back."

"Both soldiers, both wrists." Tom scratched his chin. "That's new."

"Some kind of message?"

"I don't know." Tom motioned to Melinda. "Get some good close-ups."

While Melinda took more photos, Tom picked up the bar code reader and scanned the metal tag attached to the first body. He puzzled at the number on the screen, then shook his head and moved on to the next. Again, he tilted his head, studying the number he'd scanned.

"Something wrong?" Stephen asked.

"Uh, no." Tom shook his head and put down the reader. "Let's see the others."

As the medical examiners worked, the techs closed the pouches on the first two bodies and hoisted them into the cooler. The next soldier, a male, had a broken neck, as well as flash burns on one side. The fourth was a female sergeant covered in burns and bullet holes. Tom scanned the tags for each. Both times, he rubbed his upper lip as he read the numbers.

"You're getting twitchy," Stephen said, stepping over to look at the screen. "What's going on?"

"It's nothing." Tom turned off the scanner and tucked it away.

Stephen scrutinized Tom's face, trying to interpret the odd expression he wore. "Do you know them?"

"Of course not." Tom scoffed. "It's been a long day, and I want to get home. Let's check out the last one and icebox them so we can get out of here."

Stephen nodded, but he continued to watch Tom out of the corner of his eye. His partner had been acting strangely for the entire afternoon. Did it have something to do with whatever he wanted to talk to Stephen about? Maybe it would be better to tuck the soldiers in and leave so he could find out what was going on.

Tom unzipped the last human remains pouch. He backpedaled, his eyes wide. "What the—?"

Stephen peered inside the bag. His voice caught in his throat. "Is that . . .?"

Tom scanned the tag with the bar code reader. The screen lit up. He nodded. "Sergeant Gardner Grant."

"But that's impossible."

"I know."

They both stared at the body lying on the table. The photos they had seen showed a soldier 50 percent covered with burns. But this man, whose jaw still hung askew, otherwise had nary a scratch on him.

7

The fallen soldier had been close to six and a half feet tall, solid as a marble sculpture. His square jaw was dislocated, but his heavy brow and angular nose were intact. Tape held his narrow eyes shut.

"Did they switch the bodies by mistake?" Stephen asked in a whisper, glancing at the techs, who were closing the cooler doors on the last two pouches.

"Jaw's broken in the same place," Tom whispered back. "Too much of a coincidence."

"That would mean they faked the photos." Stephen's mouth went dry. "What if this guy's not dead?"

Tom gaped at Stephen.

"It's happened. Medics don't check vitals because the scene is so horrible there's no way anyone could've survived, and then the body arrives at the morgue barely alive, but alive nonetheless."

Tom pressed two gloved fingers against the soldier's neck. "No pulse. No breathing." He removed the tape from the soldier's eyelids and lifted the lids. "Pupils fixed and dilated. Skin's cold. He's dead."

Stephen sighed with relief. "A medical examiner's worst nightmare is the dead waking up on the autopsy table."

"That's not going to happen. But I think I know what did." Tom turned to the enlisted personnel. "We can take care of this last one, boys. Go home."

A senior airman said, "Sergeant Booker ordered us to make sure they're all securely stored."

"They will be. We need to collect data for a study on body armor resistance to explosives, and then we'll tuck him in." Tom flashed his best winning smile. "Besides, isn't the Mahoney fight on AFN in twenty minutes?"

The airman exchanged glances with the other techs, then said, "Don't forget to lock up, sir."

After the techs left, Tom indicated Melinda, who was still snapping photos of the other bodies. "Stewart, too."

"She won't be a problem."

"No, she won't, because she won't be here." Tom gave him a pointed look. "Trust me."

Stephen glanced at Melinda. She was going to be pissed, but he needed Tom to talk.

"Sergeant Stewart," he said, trying to sound authoritative. "You can go, too."

Her eyebrows rose. "Are you sure? I haven't gotten any shots of Sergeant Grant yet."

"We'll handle it." He smiled reassuringly. "You should go dry off and clean up. I'll never hear the end of it if I let one of my techs catch pneumonia."

Her gaze darted toward Tom. "Yes, sir."

Once she'd left, Stephen turned to the man "Okay, spill it. What the hell's going on?"

"That's a great question," Tom said. "One I've been trying to answer for the past five years."

"What?"

"General Ross ordered you not to autopsy these soldiers, didn't he?"

"How did you—"

"Look at this bar code." Tom activated the scanner, scrolled back to the most recent scan, and showed it to Stephen. "See the last seven characters?"

"PSP1986."

"Now look at this one."

Stephen blinked. "PSP1986."

"And this one."

Stephen's chest tightened. The same characters again. "What does it mean?"

"Last year at Dover, a C-130 arrived transporting casualties. Abrams tank fire. The wing commander ordered all four autopsies had to be done by the same medical examiner."

"Who?"

"Sidney Shores."

Stephen frowned. "I thought Shores retired years ago."

"He stayed on as a part-time contractor. Which made it odd he would take on four autopsies at once."

"Maybe not that odd. A couple of busy days and then he could take the rest of the week off. Sounds nice."

"Still, it seemed strange the rest of us weren't allowed to touch the bodies, and even stranger when I read the autopsy reports."

Stephen didn't like Tom's tone as he said that last part. "What do you mean?"

"They all had the same cause of death. Asphyxiation."

"That would make sense in a tank fire."

"It would, except the Army runs fire drills all the time. None of them tried to escape?"

"Well, maybe the fire was too strong. Blocked the exit."

"Shores didn't document any severe thermal burns." Tom's eyes took on a wicked gleam. "According to his report, they essentially lay down and waited for the smoke to kill them."

"You're telling me Shores faked the reports?"

"I didn't believe it, either. But when I tried to access the digital images, I couldn't. They set up a firewall to prevent anyone but Shores from accessing them."

Stephen considered this. "Okay, it does sound suspicious, but if you didn't see the actual bodies, you're speculating. Maybe Shores made a mistake."

"Yeah, I thought you'd say that, and I would have agreed, until I pulled all the cases Shores had done since he retired from Active Duty. Out of fifty autopsies, twenty-eight had bar codes ending in PSP1986. And all twenty-eight had the same diagnosis."

The heat drained from Stephen's cheeks. "You're sure?"

"Positive."

"Did you tell anyone?"

"I went to Reinstein."

Stephen nodded. Navy Captain Abe Reinstein had been the AFMES chief at Dover for the past five years. "What did he say?"

"That he'd look into it." Tom's lip twitched. "Next thing I knew, I was being offered the choice to face court-martial or transfer overseas."

"So, the affair . . ."

"Never happened."

Stephen reeled. "Why didn't you tell me the truth?"

"I didn't know you that well, and I'd narrowly escaped the death of my career. I didn't know who I could trust."

"But you trust me now?"

"Yeah, I do." Tom pointed at the soldier's body. "And, if these Fallen are part of that same cover-up, we can't let whatever happened to them get swept under the carpet. Their families deserve to know the truth."

Tom's words struck Stephen deep in his core. He understood the need for the truth better than most. And wasn't that why he became a medical examiner in the first place? To find the truth?

"Okay, but even if what you're saying is true, what are we supposed to do about it?"

"Autopsy them ourselves."

"Ross ordered us not to touch them."

"Fine, so we Virtopsy them. No one'll be the wiser."

The Virtopsy, or virtual autopsy, used CT scans to create 3D images that allowed pathologists to assess internal structures and look for mechanisms of death like organ damage or foreign bodies. They wouldn't be able to study tissue samples, but it wouldn't leave any external signs of intrusion.

"We need one of the techs to run it," Stephen said at last.

"I know how."

"You do?"

"Last time that Swiss consultant was here, he ran through it with me. He wanted to show how easy it was to use the machine." Tom grinned. "Even a moron like me can do it."

"All right, but if we find anything, we need to call Reaper."

"Of course. She wanted to build our reputation, right?"

Stephen groaned. "Let's start with Grant here. He couldn't have died from a broken jaw. Maybe we'll find some internal injuries to explain it."

Together, they loaded the body onto the scanner and retreated to the monitor room. As the machine lit up, Stephen pondered reasons military command would request fake autopsy reports. Concealing an embarrassing botched-up exercise? He could understand that happening once or twice, but on over thirty decedents? Maybe one of the new terrorist groups had their hands on a dangerous weapon. He could see the military hiding evidence to avoid causing a panic until they found a way to counter it. If that was the case, he and Tom could be tried for treason for exposing it.

Stephen dug his knuckles into his cheek as he studied the images that appeared on-screen. Yes, he wanted to know what had happened to these soldiers, but not enough to face prison time.

"No skeletal fractures in the lower extremities," he said as the scanner worked its way along the body. "All abdominal organs look intact. Keep going."

They continued scanning upward. The chest came into view.

"Lungs are intact. No obvious rib fractures." Stephen paused. "What's that around the heart?"

"What?"

"There." Stephen pointed at the heart. "There's a blur. Like a double image."

Tom studied the screen. "Probably an artifact of movement."

"Movement? He's dead."

"Maybe the body slipped when the bed slid forward."

"Isn't it designed to keep that from happening?"

"Sure, but nothing's one hundred percent."

"True," Stephen said as he considered that. For years, he'd been certain his father's death was his fault, and then he found the autopsy report showing it wasn't. If he'd been wrong about that, what else had he been wrong about? He focused his attention on the screen. "Image is clear enough to see the heart muscle walls are intact. Valves intact. Aorta and vena cava intact. Looks like he didn't die of heart failure."

"So, what killed him?"

"Maybe a poison or toxin."

"That happened to kick in while he was on a mission?"

Stephen didn't have an answer. "Let's finish with the brain."

The bed slid forward. Images of the brain came into view.

"Upper spinal cord looks good. Brainstem's fine. Broken jaw at the ramus. Looks like the condylar process is missing." Stephen scanned the next images. "Cerebellum's good. Midbrain . . . Stop." Stephen pointed at a spot in the center of the brain. "Foreign body between the frontal and parietal lobes."

"Must be what we saw on the UXO scanner."

"It's perfectly oval-shaped, and there's no tunnel through the tissue or in the skull."

"Maybe an older injury?"

Stephen pressed his lips together and studied the image for another moment. "The surrounding brain tissue is irregular. The damage radiates back to the midbrain."

"Midbrain injury could affect motor movement and brainstem control." Tom let out a low whistle. "It could knock out his whole autonomic system, causing his heart to stop."

"And his diaphragm." Stephen's mouth went dry. "He'd be fully awake while his body stopped working, unable to move, until he lost oxygen."

"Okay, so we've got mechanism of death. Now on to cause." Tom pointed at the object on the screen. "What the hell *is* that?"

"I don't know."

"Well, there's one way to find out."

Stephen stared at Tom. "Please don't say what I think you're going to say."

"We've come this far. And this mystery is going to eat at you until you solve it." Tom's eyes glimmered. "We have to open him up."

8

Sharon woke with a start. She pressed her palm against her forehead, as if she could force the nightmare she'd been having about her parents' funeral out by hand. She could still feel the cold wind blowing on the back of her neck, the sense of loss dragging at her heart. The feelings didn't dissipate like they tended to with dreams, because this wasn't a dream. This had been the end of her childhood.

Groaning, she buried her head under a pillow to block out the world spinning around her. She fumbled on the nightstand until she found her phone and pulled it under the pillow. She still needed to get a cell phone that worked on European bandwidth, but at least her battery was charged, and the hotel had free Wi-Fi. She opened her email app. No new mail.

The clock on her phone showed it was already nine. She dashed off a quick email to Steve, saying she was fine, staying overnight at the Ramstein Inns, and would catch the shuttle to Stuttgart in the morning. When she'd finished, she started to write about what she'd discovered three days earlier, the secret that would change everything between them. Halfway through the sentence, she stopped, reconsidered, and erased what she'd just written. This wasn't something she could put in an email. She needed to say it to his face, to see his reaction. It was the only way to know if it was true or not.

She reread the rest of the email and sent it with her usual sign-off: Church out. Sharon.

A sharp pain bit into her shoulder, right at the joint. She ran her fingers over her skin and found a small Band-Aid. Strange—she didn't remember hurting herself. But she was having trouble remembering the last few hours. Her head felt like it was wrapped in gauze, and her tongue was numb. It must've been all the Schnapps she'd had with…

Sharon shoved aside the pillow and sat up. The woman from the AMC desk. This was her room. The sheets were in disarray. Sharon's undergarments were on the floor next to a familiar red dress.

Images flittered through Sharon's mind, vignetted around the edges like old photos. She remembered meeting Red Dress at the hotel bar. They'd had a few drinks and then…then…

She pressed her palm against her cheek. Either the sex had been completely forgettable or so amazing it gave her partial amnesia.

Someone was talking.

Sharon held still, listening. It was Red Dress, talking to someone in German.

"... Ja ... Ja ... Nein, noch schlafen ... Ja, verstehen ... Scheiswetter ... Okay, frühmorgens ..."

Sharon massaged her shoulder. She understood the German words for yes and no, and something about sleeping and shitty weather. She shook her head. It didn't make sense and probably wouldn't, even if she kept listening. And it wasn't exactly gracious to eavesdrop on ... uh ... what was that woman's name?

With a groan, Sharon flopped back onto the pillow and closed her eyes. What would Uncle Alex say if he could see her now? Had he had any idea how things would turn out for her and for Steve when he took them under his wing?

She snorted. Uncle Alex never did anything without knowing every detail five months in advance, unlike her sorry, impulsive ass. Sure, her impetuousness had saved her platoon from walking into a trap. But she was going to be in command. She had to think before acting now, and not do careless things like jump into bed with strangers.

"Oh, you're awake."

Sharon opened her eyes. Red Dress was standing in the doorway, hair tied in a ponytail, wearing a sheer nightgown and nothing underneath. Damn, she was hot. Regrets about her impulsivity vanished from Sharon's mind.

"Yeah, I heard you talking on the phone." Sharon smiled. "Everything okay?"

The woman's eyes flashed, lips puckered, but then she returned the smile. "I arranged for the shuttle to pick you up here at the hotel. They will come very early. It's nothing urgent."

"Good." Sharon crooked her finger. "Because I have something that is urgent."

"I can help with that. But first, we need another drink."

"My head's already swimming. I'm usually not such a lightweight, but whatever was in that Schnapps kicked my ass."

"That was nothing." Red Dress opened a cabinet and removed a bottle. She filled a glass, which she held out to Sharon. "You need to try Polish vodka."

Sharon took the glass and sniffed it. Her nostril hairs burned. "You don't need to get me drunk. I'm all yours."

"This vodka contains wild bison grass. It's believed to have aphrodisiac qualities." Red Dress's eyebrows danced. "I'm curious to find out if that's true."

Sharon raised the glass to her lips.

"Wait." The woman placed her hand on Sharon's.

"What?"

"In Germany, you must toast properly." Red Dress poured another glass for herself. "You must look the other person in the eye as you clink glasses and say, '*Prost*.'"

"What happens if you don't?"

"Seven years bad sex."

Sharon laughed. "What's your name?"

"Anja."

Sharon stared directly into Anja's blue eyes, noticing the gold flecks in the irises, as they clinked glasses. "Prost."

9

"This is a bad idea," Stephen said for the fifth time as he studied the soldier's body. After unwrapping him from the remains pouch, they'd stripped off his uniform and set it on another table. The left uniform shoulder bore a Marine Corps Special Operations Command patch. The name patch over the chest was burned off except for the first two letters: GR. Yet the skin underneath was unharmed, aside from missing chest hair on one side.

"Do you have a better way to identify that foreign body in his brain?" Tom tied on a blue surgical gown. "Got some telekinetic powers I don't know about?"

"I wish." Stephen grunted as he donned a scrub cap. "But we do this, our careers are over."

"You're blowing this out of proportion. We're duly qualified to do this autopsy. And we're saving them time. We won't get more than a slap on the wrist."

"They shipped you here for digging where you shouldn't. Where are they going to send us this time? Alaska?"

Tom tilted a scalpel this way and that, then replaced it on the tray. "Look, I was going to tell you this later, but you need to hear it now."

"What?"

Tom glanced at the upper corners of the room. "Did you know Shores started working for AFMES back in the late '80s? Dude's ancient."

"No, I didn't." Stephen adjusted the GoPro camera. "So what?"

"So, before I got caught, I ran a search through the autopsy reports from his active-duty days, trying to find that same bar code pattern."

Stephen looked up. "Did you find it?"

"Oh, yeah. Seven had it. All from 1989."

The hairs on Stephen's forearms bristled. That was the year his life had changed forever. "The code is PSP1986."

"Right. Obviously, they died three years after it started."

"And the PSP?"

"Not sure, but whatever it means, it must've been put on ice for three decades. I didn't see it used at all between 1990 and two years ago."

Stephen's fingertips tingled, the way they did whenever he could tell someone was about to say something he wasn't going to like. He thought of it as his "Stephen-Sense."

"And this is supposed to matter to me because

. . ."

"One of those reports was for a young Army captain named Englehart." Tom locked his gaze with Stephen's. "Isaiah Englehart."

The floor fell away from beneath Stephen's feet. He leaned against the examination table to remain upright. "No."

"I'm sorry, buddy. It's true." Tom sucked on his tongue. "Your dad was part of this."

Stephen pressed his fingertips against the exam table, willing the cold metal to leech out his anger. "You knew this whole time, and you're telling me now?"

"I studied the names of all seven of those originals. There are a lot of Englehearts out there, so I didn't put you two together until recently, when you told me you lost your parents as a kid."

Stephen inhaled and exhaled through his nose, fighting the urge to tackle Tom. "What else did you find out?"

"I know about the adrenal tumor."

"Then you also know about what happened to my mom."

Tom nodded.

Stephen dug his fingers into the table. He stared at the body in front of him, remembering how his parents had looked when he found them, staring back with cold, lifeless eyes. His stomach heaved. "We're not doing this."

"C'mon, Stephen . . ."

"We're not doing this." Stephen gnashed his teeth together. "You're manipulating me, stirring up old memories and feelings for whatever game you're playing. But I'm not playing it with you. What happened to my parents was horrible, but it's in the past. I have to let it go."

Tom fiddled with a clamp. Satisfied he'd had the last word, Stephen started to rip off the gloves.

"It wasn't his adrenal," Tom said.

Stephen froze. "I said, stop."

"I found the slides in a storage cabinet. Reinstein always talked about scanning the old samples into the computer but never got around to it." Tom lifted his chin. "I didn't see any chromaffin cell tumors."

Prickly heat flushed along Stephen's neck and cheeks. Every time he tried to bottle up the past and tuck it away on a shelf, someone pulled the bottle out and smashed it on the ground, letting it all flood back in again. Removing his fingers from the table and wiping one hand against the other, he said, "I know."

Tom's eyes widened. "You do?"

"I mean, I suspected it. The autopsy report had things wrong. It didn't mention the scar on his right arm from a knife wound in the Persian Gulf. It listed fatty liver from chronic alcoholism, but Dad never drank." Stephen swallowed hard. "He had to be the sober one."

Shaking his head, Tom asked, "Then, why…"

"I confronted General Ross about it, gave him the chance to provide a good explanation." Stephen snorted. "He didn't have one. Chewed me out for reading the report and dodged the question, like he did out on the tarmac tonight. That's when I knew he was covering up the truth, and the fact is, it's for my own good."

"How can hiding the truth be for your good?"

"Because even if Dad didn't have a tumor, it's my fault he got so mad he lost control, and his rage caused a massive cardiac infarction. If I hadn't . . ." Stephen trailed off, unable to get the words out.

"Look, I get it. You don't want to uncover anything that might look worse for your dad." Tom pointed at the soldier's head. "That's why we need to do this. What if whatever is in this guy's head was in your dad's head, too? What if it caused your dad to lose control and not whatever you did?"

Stephen's cheeks cooled. "You're not serious."

"They have the same bar code number. If we learn what happened to Sergeant Grant, we can figure out what really happened to your dad."

Blinking, Stephen said, "Sergeant?"

"Yeah, Booker said he was Sergeant Gardner Grant."

Stephen grabbed a probe, leaned forward, and smoothed out the creases in the soldier's uniform.

"What is it?" Tom asked.

"Two stripes. This guy's a corporal, not a sergeant."

Tom let out a low whistle. "So, he's not Grant."

"Right." Stephen chewed his inner cheek. "Who the hell is he?"

10

I was right," Stephen said, stepping back from the examination table. The moonlight streaming through the four picture windows at the far end of the suite cast an eerie glow. "They got the bodies mixed up. No wonder he doesn't look as bad as he did in the photos."

"But he's got the same jaw injury," Tom said. "And how the fuck does one mix up cadavers? Where's the real Sergeant Grant?"

"I don't know." Stephen set his jaw. "We need to call Reaper."

"Are you crazy? We can't involve anyone else."

"If she agrees, we'll be following orders."

"And if she doesn't?"

Stephen picked up the Defense Switch Network phone and dialed. "She will."

After four rings, Stephen heard the three clicks indicating a secure line, followed by a familiar husky voice. "Who is this?"

"It's Englehart, ma'am. Sorry to bother you so late."

"Why are you calling me from the autopsy suite at nine thirty? What're you still doing there?"

"We've got a situation. We stayed as you ordered to process those Fallen." Stephen glanced at Tom, who gave him a worried look. Stephen assuaged him with a hand gesture. "But we think they mixed up the bodies."

"Mixed up?"

"Yes, ma'am. One has a different rank than the presumptive ID."

"That's why it's presumptive, Englehart. They get shit like that wrong all the time. It doesn't mean they sent the wrong body."

"No, it doesn't." Stephen cleared his throat. "Except the photos taken at the scene showed extensive flash burns and external wounds. This guy doesn't have a mark on him."

Reaper was silent.

"Ma'am?"

"I'm here, damn it. Just processing. Not a mark, you said?"

"Only a broken jaw."

"How'd he die?"

"That's the thing. We don't know for sure."

"Did you do a Virtopsy?"

"Yes, ma'am. No internal injuries. All we could find was a bright spot in the brain. We're not sure if it's shrapnel or something else, but it might be the cause of death."

Reaper stayed quiet for another moment. Stephen could hear her breathing. He and Tom stared at each other while they waited.

Finally, she said, "We need positive ID. Get blood spots for DNA analysis, and do a thorough external examination for tattoos and birthmarks."

"Yes, ma'am." Stephen took a deep breath. "And that spot on the brain?"

She hesitated again. "Do what you have to do."

Stephen glanced at the body. He could've left it at that and, if questioned, said they were following Reaper's orders and got confused, but he wasn't sure that would work. "General Ross ordered us not to touch the bodies."

"Ross? He was there?"

"Yes, ma'am."

Stephen knew she and Ross had butted heads in the past. She saw the general as a broken rung on her ladder to the top and contradicted him out of spite. It was a gamble playing them against each other, but one he hoped would pay off.

"I'll handle Ross," she said, her voice almost a hiss. "If the body you've got there isn't the one Ross thinks it is, his order doesn't apply, now does it?"

Stephen couldn't help but grin. "No, ma'am. It doesn't."

"Keep me posted on what you find. But it can wait until morning."

"Yes, ma'am. Good night."

Stephen disconnected and gave Tom a thumbs-up. "We're good."

After a few minutes of prep and donning face masks, the two pathologists began their visual inspection. Tom wore a GoPro strapped to his forehead and they both narrated as they went.

"Skin shows no discoloration," Stephen said as he ran a fingertip along the soldier's chest. "No birthmarks, scars, or tattoos. Either this guy never saw combat before the other day, or he's led one charmed life."

"Drawing blood samples." Tom filled a large syringe from the soldier's femoral vein. "I'll run a basic immunoassay and send blood spots for DNA matching. Anything . . ."

Stephen looked up when Tom didn't continue. "Everything okay?"

"The blood's bright red." Tom licked his lips. "This guy's been dead for two days. His blood should be as thick as pudding by now."

Wheels turned in Stephen's head. "Help me turn him over."

Together, they logrolled the body onto its side. Stephen ran a gloved hand down the soldier's back. "No livor mortis. Only early signs of rigor mortis. He's been dead less than a day."

"Maybe he wasn't even part of Foxtrot Team." Disappointment laced Tom's words. "He might not have anything to do with PSP1986. He probably choked on a chicken bone or something."

"Or they intentionally switched him," Stephen said. "And the real Gardner Grant is still out there."

The corner of Tom's mouth drifted upward. "Now, you're thinking like me."

Stephen laughed nervously. "Let's roll him back."

"Hold on." Tom pointed at the base of the soldier's neck. "There's something here."

Stephen leaned closer. Sure enough, there was a tiny bar code tattooed onto the soldier's neck.

"That's not AFMES." Stephen frowned. "Set him down."

They laid the soldier back on the table. Stephen crossed the room and found the bar code scanner. When he returned, he nodded to Tom, who responded by lifting the upper body enough for Stephen to scan the soldier's neck.

The screen flashed and then lit up. Stephen and Tom glanced at each other.

"PSP1986," Tom said. "Looks like we can rule out an accidental switch."

"Yeah." Stephen kept his voice level. "But if it was intentional, why?"

"Well, there's another option."

"What?"

"Maybe this is the same guy from the photos, and he got better."

They stared at each other for two seconds, and then they both laughed.

"Now who's reading too many comic books?" Stephen snorted. "We should go ahead and start the dissection. Chest and abdominal first?"

"A much as I enjoy a good mystery, I think we should skip right to the good part." Tom pointed at the soldier's head. "We know there's something there. Let's find out what it is."

"Fine." Stephen picked up the scalpel and handed it to Tom. "Clean incisions along the scalp line. If we're wrong, we need to give the morticians something to work with to cover it up."

With a nod, Tom began slicing a line from the soldier's right ear, up over the forehead, and down to the left ear, allowing them to peel back the skin.

"Aside from the jaw," Stephen said, leaning in to study the glistening bone, "skull looks intact."

"Agreed. No entry or exit holes." Tom jerked his head. "Flip you for the Stryker?"

"I'll do it." Neither of them enjoyed using the vibrating saw when there was a chance it might aerosolize infectious material, but it was effective. "As long as you buy drinks the next time we go to Lagerhaus."

"Deal."

Stephen fired up the saw and started cutting through the skull. Bone dust kicked up into the air. He made clean cuts around the frontal bone until he was able to pry it off, revealing a gelatinous mass of pinkish rubber.

"Looks okay so far." He used a probe to push aside folds of tissue. "No residue. No evidence of a subdural bleed. Frontal cortex looks intact. Mass appropriate for skull size."

"Any shrapnel or projectile tracking?" Tom aimed the GoPro into the skull cavity.

"No." Stephen retrieved the scalpel. "Preparing to remove the whole brain for inspection."

As Stephen slid his hand between one cerebral hemisphere and the skull, searching for the brainstem, Tom coughed. "So, you and Stewart are a thing, huh?"

Stephen froze. He looked up at Tom and whispered, "What?"

"Hey, don't worry. Even though I didn't really have an affair with the commander's daughter, I've been where you are. Your secret's safe with me."

Unable to blink, Stephen kept staring, wondering how Tom had figured it out. Worse, if Tom knew, who else did?

"That's great," Stephen managed to say at last, resuming his blind search of the cranial cavity. "Except there's no secret. There's nothing going on."

"Uh-huh." Tom nodded. "Sure."

Heat prickled up the back of Stephen's neck. They'd been as careful as was possible in a tight community like Ramstein, but he'd always known there was a chance someone could discover them. Maybe it was better that it had been Tom and not someone else. "How did you find out?"

A knowing smile crossed Tom's lips. "Are you kidding? The way you two hush up whenever someone walks into the room? The private jokes? Buddy, if you're going to play this game, you need to step it up. You'd make a lousy spy."

Stephen's fingertips brushed against what felt like a rubbery tube. He'd found the brainstem. "Thanks for the advice."

"So, is it serious?"

Melinda's face appeared in Stephen's mind. The way those blue eyes sparkled when she laughed, those lush lips. *Was* it serious?

"No," he said, returning his attention to the soldier's brain, regretting the words the moment they passed his lips. Melinda deserved more. But if Tom thought it was only a fling, hopefully he'd drop it and wouldn't let it slip to someone else. "It's one of those things that happens overseas, you know? Over before it even starts."

Tom pressed his lips together. "Yeah."

Stephen slid his fingers up the brainstem, preparing to pull back the cerebral tissue so he could sever the delicate lifeline. His fingertips grazed something hard.

"Hold on." Using both hands, he parted the cerebral hemispheres like they were the Red Sea and burrowed his way down until he spotted a glint of black metal. "Give me some light."

"Is that—?"

"Light!"

Tom switched on the GoPro's LED light and shone it into the brain cavity. He let out a low whistle. "That's not shrapnel."

"No." Stephen jabbed at the disc with a probe. It looked like a hearing aid battery with a thin two-millimeter projection off one side. It clung to an area of brain tissue with tiny spikes that reminded him of an old computer chip. "It must be one of those new implants. They're supposed to help people with seizures or severe paralysis or aphasia."

"This guy's Special Forces. I doubt he was a paraplegic."

Stephen studied the implant. "That projection looks like some kind of antenna. Wireless transmission, maybe?"

"Wireless has limited range, and RFID isn't much better." Tom clucked his tongue. "It probably uses LoRa. Long-range LPWAN has a range of over thirty klicks in rural areas."

"How do you know about that?"

"I used to do some amateur hacking back in the day." Tom grinned. "And maybe I still keep up on the latest trends."

"You're an odd duck, Tom." Stephen poked at the implant with his probe. "Looks like it's attached to the left temporal lobe with an extension into the frontal lobe. That places it over Broca's and Wernicke's areas, right?"

"Yeah. So, it has something to do with communication."

"Could be therapeutic, then. Maybe treatment for an older brain injury." Stephen studied the brain tissue and frowned. "This area's necrotic. Whatever this thing is, it must've burnt out and took part of the brain tissue with it."

"Can you remove it?"

"Hand me the forceps."

Stephen used the surgical tweezers to lift the implant, then delicately sliced the brain tissue underneath it. He lifted the sample out of the skull and laid it on the metal tray. Using the scalpel, he poked at the prongs until they pulled free of the brain matter.

"Let's mount this on paraffin." He dropped the tissue sample into a clear test tube. "We may get a better idea of what happened to it."

"Right." Tom took the test tube.

Holding the implant close to his eyes, Stephen turned it this way and that. A tiny red light at the end of the antenna started blinking. Stephen jumped, almost dropping the forceps.

"Jesus," he said. "It's active."

"It's still able to transmit." Tom's eyes danced behind his face shield. "You realize what this means? We can figure out what frequency it's using. It'd have to be one that's rarely used, which means there can't be many receivers in the area tuned to it, so—"

"Hold on, Scully." Stephen shook his head and stuck the implant in another test tube. The light went dark. "Not to interrupt your geek-out moment, but we told Reaper we'd find out who this soldier is and how he died, not chase down an alien transmitter, or whatever you think this is."

"Why does everyone always think the unexplained involves aliens?" Tom rolled his eyes. "Humans are far more capable of sadism to fuel scientific curiosity. Anyway, don't you want to find out what happened to your dad?"

"Dad didn't have an implant."

"Not that you know of."

"He didn't. I'm sure. This kind of technology didn't exist back then." Stephen set the tube aside. "I don't know why he shared the same bar code sequence with this man, but it's got nothing to do with that."

"All right, fine, fine." Tom held his hands up in surrender. "You're the boss."

Stephen mused as he checked the brain tissue once more. Was he really the boss? He had to answer to Reaper, to Ross, and to Reinstein back at Dover. And he disliked every time he had to seek their approval. What would it be like if he were in command? What would he change if he called the shots?

Nothing, the little voice whispered in his ear. *You're pathetic. In less than a day you'd curl up in a fetal position and cry for Mommy to come help you. You'll never be a leader, Stevie-boy.*

"Hey," Tom said, waving a hand in front of Stephen's face. "You okay?"

Stephen stared at him before remembering he was in the autopsy room with his hands still buried inside a man's skull. Shaking off the dark thoughts, he withdrew his hands and blinked. Was he imagining it, or did the tissue look less damaged now? He blinked again. Had to be the lighting.

"Yeah, I'm fine." He glanced at the test tubes in Tom's hand, full of blood. "Do we have enough to run screens and send a sample for DNA confirmation?"

"Should be, but it'll take them a few days."

"You got what you wanted." Stephen indicated the now-dormant device in the test tube. "Can we let him rest in peace?"

"We need to figure out what this implant does and why he has it. What if there are others like him? They're at risk of the same thing happening to them."

Despite his bulk, the soldier looked young, with hardly a wrinkle. The reason Stephen had joined the military wasn't out of some nonsense loyalty to his adoptive uncle but a desperate need to prevent any of the brave men and women serving the country and their families from enduring the same hell his family had suffered. Tom made a good point. How different might his life have been if a medical examiner had taken the time to uncover the truth about his father?

"All right," he said, turning away from the table to choose a fresh scalpel. As the blade glinted in the fluorescent light, he marveled at how something so small could hold the key to answering so many questions. He pivoted back to Tom. "Let's get that brain out of there . . ."

He stopped. Tom was gaping down at the body.

Stephen followed Tom's gaze.

The scalpel slipped from his fingers and clanged onto the metal table.

The soldier's eyes were open. And they were staring directly at Stephen.

11

The soldier's brain glistened in its exposed skull cavity. A level of clear fluid rose, bathing the tissue in nutrients. The skin flap lay partly folded over, covering the top half of his face. Peering around it were two pale blue eyes, darting in every direction as if they were balls in a toddler's pop-up toy.

"Whaaammmmaaah?"

The sound escaped from the soldier's lips like gas leaking from a pipe. Stephen stared at the soldier, his brain racing to process what he was seeing but couldn't possibly be seeing.

"Holy Flatliners," Tom whispered, eyes bulging. "He's fucking alive."

"Whaaaaaaaaapen?" Emotions ranging from fear to anger flitted over the soldier's face.

"I'm gonna be sick," Tom said, clutching his belly.

"Hold it together," Stephen said, more to himself than to Tom. A body that wasn't dead waking up on the autopsy table was bad enough. But this man's brain was staring back at him. There was no way he could've endured that without screaming in pain. If he were brain dead, he wouldn't respond, but no one had ever recovered from brain death. It wasn't possible.

The soldier jabbered nonsensically.

"What do we do?" Tom asked, scanning the room. "CPR?"

"If he's screaming, he's breathing." Stephen positioned two fingers over the soldier's neck. The artery pulsated beneath his fingertips. Stephen swallowed hard and withdrew his hand. The movement artifact on the CT scan—the soldier's heart must've been beating too slowly to detect. Now, it was pumping and picking up speed. "He doesn't need CPR."

"What about an IV?"

"I'm not Frankenstein. We don't even have a crash cart here." Stephen bit the inside of his cheek. This was bad. This was very bad. "He needs advanced medical care. Call the ICU and get a transport team here. We'll keep him comfortable until they arrive."

Tom stood frozen in place.

"Go!"

Tom spun and scurried over to the wall phone.

The soldier had stopped screaming and thrashing, taking deeper breaths as he eyed Stephen. Stephen returned his gaze, feeling his own heartbeat level off at a rate over a hundred. How he was able to keep from losing his shit, he wasn't sure, but he had to do something.

"Are you in pain?" He wondered what he would do if the soldier said yes. They didn't even keep acetaminophen on hand in the morgue.

The soldier's eyes bounced around in their sockets before settling on Stephen again. "Hoooodafagaroooo?"

It took a second for Stephen to puzzle out the meaning behind the slurred speech, at the same time deducing that the man's brain was trying to remember how to coordinate the oral muscles. Like a stroke victim, the soldier might have trouble both speaking and comprehending. Speaking slowly and deliberately, Stephen said, "I'm Lieutenant Colonel Englehart, one of the medical examiners at Ramstein Air Base. Do you know who you are?"

The soldier's eyes drifted apart briefly before snapping together again. An aspirated hiss passed his twitching tongue and lips. He scrunched up his face, apparently displeased with the result, and tried again. "Greh . . . Greeeee . . . wooooog."

"Greenwood?"

The soldier's head bobbed.

"Okay. What's your first name?"

"Duh . . . Muh . . ." He growled. "Muh-muh-na-guh."

"It's okay." Stephen laid his hand on Greenwood's arm. The soldier didn't even flinch, making Stephen wonder if he'd recovered peripheral sensory function yet. "You're going to need rehabilitation therapy for a while."

Greenwood scowled and probed his tongue against his broken jaw.

"I wouldn't do that," Stephen said. "There could be a nerve trapped—"

The soldier's hand balled into a fist. He swung his arm upward. The fist crashed into his own jaw with a crunch.

Immediately, his eyes bulged wide open. He howled.

"Shit." Stephen called over his shoulder to Tom, "How are we on that transport team?"

"They're in the middle of a code," Tom shouted. "ETA twenty minutes."

"Not soon enough. We need narcotics. Probably sedation."

The soldier shut his eyes and mumbled something that sounded like "belief."

Stephen ripped off his latex gloves and rifled through the dissection tray. He threw up his hands in disgust. There was nothing he could use to help this man.

Greenwood's eyes flew open, blazing. "Ssssnot woookin!"

"What's he saying?" Tom asked as he rejoined Stephen. "What do we do?"

"I'm lost on both accounts." Stephen spoke to Greenwood: "Help's on the way. I'm going to replace your frontal plate and tie some temporary sutures in the scalp until they can do it properly. I'm sure you'll need antibiotics."

The soldier's eyes rolled upward. He lifted his hand again and touched the skin flap. His eyes tracked back to Stephen. "Whadadaddoo?"

"You were dead. Or, at least, it looked like you were. We were in the middle of autopsying you. I know how frightening this must be, but—"

Greenwood's hand shot out and clamped around Stephen's throat.

"What . . . did . . . ooo . . . do . . ." Greenwood paused to inhale a wheezing breath. "To . . . me?"

Stephen tried to answer. No sound came out. He struggled against the soldier's grip.

"Get off him!" Tom grabbed at Greenwood's arm. "We're trying to help you."

The soldier backhanded Tom, who flew through the air. Tom's shoulders and back crashed against the wall. He staggered and slumped to the ground.

"Pain . . ." Greenwood pulled Stephen closer. The smell of death flooded Stephen's nostrils, but he couldn't gag because of the hand clamped around his throat. "Why . . . won't . . . it . . . stop?"

Stephen jiggled his head.

Greenwood loosened his grip. Stephen gasped, drinking in the life-saving air. He coughed. His stomach heaved.

"Cun . . . toll . . . uh," Greenwood said, looking up at the ceiling. "Do . . . ooo . . . copy?"

Stephen stared blankly. Greenwood wasn't talking to him. Was he?

The man's face reddened. He slammed Stephen against the wall. Colored spots floated in front of Stephen's eyes. Pain radiated from his occiput to his ears.

"What . . . did . . . oooo . . . do?"

Stephen managed to push through the gauze around his mind. Greenwood was trying to communicate with someone, and now he couldn't. Stephen's gaze shifted to the autopsy table, searching for the test tube holding the implant.

It was gone.

Heart racing, Stephen turned back to Greenwood. The soldier's eyes blazed.

"Look, whatever that thing was, it burned a hole in your brain." Stephen licked his lips, praying his words made sense. "We removed it. It's here somewhere. We can put it back if it's important to you."

Greenwood glared at him, nostrils flaring, studying him like a bear trying to decide whether to devour its prey. Sweat rolled down Stephen's forehead.

Then Greenwood released him and stepped back. "No. Don't want it."

Despite fearing for his life, Stephen couldn't help but marvel at how this hulking soldier, for all intents and purposes dead a few minutes earlier, now towered over him, moving as if nothing had happened. Stephen eyed the power saw on the metal tray. If the man attacked again, could he move fast enough to grab the weapon and defend himself?

"Where . . . are . . . the . . . others?"

"The others?" It took a second for Stephen to process the question. "You mean, the rest of your team?"

Greenwood nodded.

"They're in the freezer. You were all supposed to fly to Dover tomorrow."

The dark shadow passed over Greenwood's face again. "They're . . . dead?"

"Yes."

"How?"

"Ambush. Insurgents used some kind of IED."

Greenwood's scowl deepened. "Where . . . are . . . insurgents?"

"They ran off."

"No." He flexed and straightened his fingers. "I . . . killed . . . them."

"When you're recovered, you can help us sort out what happened." Stephen spoke in as soothing a voice as he could muster. "For now, I need you to sit down and—"

"There . . . was . . . no . . . IED." Greenwood took a step toward Stephen, fist raised. "Need . . . find . . . controller. Find out . . . why . . . teammates . . . are dead."

Stephen retreated, groping behind him for anything he could use as a weapon. He glanced past the soldier's shoulder and spotted Tom staggering toward them, clutching something in his hand. His partner stumbled and swung downward.

"Wait!" Stephen shouted, too late.

A whine cut through the air. Greenwood winced. Blood sprayed from his back.

Greenwood sank to his knees, doubled over, screaming. The bone saw was wedged between two of his posterior ribs, bobbing up and down with every inhalation. Blood streamed down his back.

"Shit," Tom said, still standing behind the soldier. His hands hung by his sides, shaking. "Shit, shit, shit."

"Tom, call security."

The man kept staring, mumbling, "Shit, shit, shit."

"Tom!"

Tom glanced down again at the writhing, moaning soldier, and then sprinted for the phone.

Stephen's head throbbed from the crack against the wall, but it had cleared enough for him to assess the situation. The smart move was to run, lock the door behind them, and let security handle Greenwood when they arrived. But now, thanks to Tom, a soldier was dying. True, they'd thought he was already dead, but this wasn't field triage of an expectant casualty. This man was going to die by their hand, and no jury would believe they were acting in self-defense. They needed him secure until his brain regained enough function for him to think rationally, but he had to be alive for that to happen.

Whispering a silent prayer, Stephen stepped over the soldier, who had stopped groaning. He crouched and wrapped his hands around the saw handle.

"What're you doing?" Tom shouted from across the room. "Don't—"

Stephen yanked the saw out of Greenwood's back.

The soldier's spine arched. He howled like a wounded tiger.

"I need to stop the bleeding." Stephen stuffed a roll of gauze into the wound. "This'll hold you until you get to a hospital."

Greenwood flipped onto his back. His bare foot caught Stephen by the chin. Stephen tumbled backward, crashing into the metal tray. The bone saw flew across the room. Surgical tools tumbled and clattered on the floor around him.

The soldier crouched, fingers splayed like claws, head rotating to scan the room. With two huge strides, he crossed the room and picked up his frontal skull plate. He held the bone in place, folded the skin flap over it, and stapled it.

Stephen gawked in horror.

The soldier winced with each clip. After six, he tossed aside the stapler. Rivulets of blood streamed from the borders of the skin flap as he searched the room again. His gaze fell on Tom. His mouth twisted into a snarl. He turned toward him.

The gaping wound on Greenwood's back was closing on its own.

"Tom, get out of here!" Stephen shouted. "Shut the door behind you."

Tom bolted for the door.

Greenwood bounded across the room. He grabbed Tom by the back of the neck and lifted him off the floor, slamming him against the nearest wall.

Tom beat at Greenwood's arm with his fist. "Let me go, you freak!"

The muscles in the arms swelled. Greenwood punched Tom in the face.

"Stop!" Stephen scrambled to his feet. He snatched a scalpel off the ground, compared its size to Greenwood's, and grabbed a hacksaw instead.

Tom rammed his elbow into the soldier's face in return. Greenwood blinked. His expression contorted into a mask of unadulterated rage.

Stephen charged, wielding the saw over his head.

Greenwood swatted him away. Stephen careened into an autopsy table. The metal corner of the table butted against his forehead. Bright colors swirled in front of him as the floor rushed up to meet him.

He heard shrieks of agony, coming from miles away. Dark streaks and rainbow stripes swirled all around him. He planted one hand on the ground, feeling the cold linoleum against his palm. He tried to push up. The room tilted and spun.

More shouts. Different. Not Tom. Not Greenwood.

"—hands where we can see them," a man was yelling. "Get down on the ground!"

A ferocious growl answered.

Forcing himself to lift his head, Stephen parted the darkness enough to see four security police by the door, guns aimed at Corporal Greenwood's head. The soldier still held Tom by the shirt. The medical examiner's head lolled back. Blood trickled from his mouth.

"Last warning," the lead officer said. "Set him down, and raise your hands over your head."

Greenwood glanced at Tom, then at Stephen. His animalistic expression faded into one of confusion. The veins in his arms bulged with a purplish hue. His eyes, icteric, asked a voiceless question.

Stephen stared back, an empty void filling his chest. He'd seen that look before. Many years ago.

"That's it." The officer stepped forward. "Put him down."

A low, guttural growl spilled from Greenwood's lips.

"No!" Stephen tried to stand, but the room tipped again. He tumbled.

Greenwood lunged for the SPs.

"Fire!" the officer yelled.

A flurry of gunshots sounded. Greenwood halted his forward charge and staggered backward. He looked down. Bullet wounds dotted his bare chest and abdomen. He roared in pain.

"Fire again," the officer said.

Greenwood whirled away from the police before they could reach their triggers, sprinting in the other direction. He dashed past Stephen and leaped into the air. Crashing through the window, he disappeared into the darkness.

12

Icy wind blew through the shattered window, carrying tiny snowflakes that disappeared as soon as they entered the room. Stephen remained sprawled on the floor, surrounded by broken glass, too stunned to move. He was aware of a dull ache in his shoulder and the back of his head. His mind struggled to process what he'd seen, but like the snowflakes, each thought dissipated as soon as he tried to grasp it.

One of the SPs approached and offered a black-gloved hand. Stephen studied it, afraid to touch it as if it might separate at the wrist like in a zombie movie. The SP, apparently mistaking his hesitation, crouched, slid his hand under Stephen's armpit and lifted him to a standing position.

"Can you walk?"

Stephen nodded.

The SP released him and marched over to a man wearing a black suit and tie. Stephen looked past them and spotted the third SP kneeling on the floor, checking Tom for a pulse. The medical examiner wasn't moving.

As Stephen staggered closer, he could see Tom's chest rise and fall, slowly. Too slowly.

Stephen shooed the SP away and knelt. Tom's lip was bleeding. One eye was swollen shut. One arm was bent in an impossible angle. Bruises blossomed around his elbow and on his neck.

"Hey, buddy." Stephen checked Tom's pulse. It was strong. "Hang in there. Help should arrive soon."

Tom's uninjured eye flew open. He started to panic.

"It's okay." Stephen tried to sound reassuring despite the sinking feeling in his gut. "He's gone. Escaped out the window."

A look of confusion passed over Tom's face. He opened his mouth, and a low groan came out.

"Save your strength. You need it to recover."

Tom's head lolled to one side. His gaze drifted past Stephen.

"What?" Stephen looked over his shoulder. Two of the SP's were conferring. The third, the one who'd been examining Tom, was searching the room. "They're doing their job."

Without warning, Tom lurched forward, threw his good arm around Stephen's waist, and hugged him tight.

"Whoa." Stephen patted Tom's back twice and tried to disentangle himself. "You're going to be okay. I promise."

The corner of Tom's mouth twisted into what might've been a smile. Then his eyes rolled back, and he slumped to the ground.

"Tom. Tom!" Stephen checked his partner's pulse: Still strong.

"Transport team is here," said the man in the suit as three more uniformed officers entered, carrying a stretcher and emergency bags.

"We could've used you ten minutes ago," Stephen said as he stepped back to give the team room to work. "If we had sedatives, we might've been able to knock that soldier out before he managed to hurt anyone."

The paramedic gave him an annoyed look and said, "File a complaint," before inserting an IV into Tom's arm.

The man in civilian clothes touched Stephen's elbow. "Sir, could I speak to you for a moment?"

Stephen followed him to the other side of the room. He found himself glancing over at Tom and realized the man in the suit had done the right thing to pull him away. As hard as it was to stand by, helpless, he had to let the experts do their work.

The man pulled out a notepad. "Sir, I'm Special Agent Marcus Wade from the Office of Special Investigations. Could you explain what happened here?"

"To be honest?" Stephen shook his head. "I'm not sure I can explain any of it."

"Could you try?"

Stephen summarized the events of the evening, starting with the C-130's arrival and proceeding to the moment Greenwood awoke. He omitted General Ross's order not to touch the bodies. While he'd have to deal with it at some point, it wasn't something this officer needed to know about. As he was wrapping up his description of Greenwood's attack on Tom, the paramedic announced that the team was finished and transported the injured pathologist out of the room. With their absence, the space felt even colder and emptier.

"So, this soldier was identified as Sergeant Gardner Grant." Wade skimmed his notes. "But he said his name was Corporal Greenwood?"

"No, he said his name was Greenwood. I deduced he was a corporal from his stripes."

Wade made another note. "Was there any indication he wasn't dead before you started autopsy?"

"No." Stephen replayed the events in his head. "Not exactly."

"I'm sorry, sir. What does that mean?"

"There were some things that didn't add up. He was supposed to have been dead for two or three days, but his condition didn't match. And photos showed he was badly burned, but when we opened his pouch, he looked unharmed. We assumed someone had switched the bodies."

"Why would anyone do that?"

Again, Stephen hesitated. Repeating Tom's paranoid suspicions would get him in hotter water. "I figured it was a mistake. It happens."

Wade looked dubious. "How often does it happen?"

"No idea."

After scanning his notes again, Wade said, "So, there were things that didn't, as you say, add up. But he seemed dead."

"Yes. There was no sign of brain activity."

"Okay." Wade made a few more notes. The other SPs were still searching the room, but Stephen couldn't tell what they were looking for. "Why did he have staples in his head?"

"We'd started autopsying his brain."

Wade's eyebrows rose, face paled. "You . . . were cutting into his brain."

"Yes."

Wade covered his mouth. His skin turned greenish.

Stephen suppressed his satisfaction at the tough cop's weak stomach, but then he noticed the other SPs pulling open and sifting through drawers.

"I don't mean to be rude," Stephen said, controlling his voice. "But what the hell are they doing? Why aren't they out searching for Greenwood?"

"We've already dispatched all available units, but I need to know how dangerous this guy is. He seemed like a wild animal."

Stephen noted that Wade had sidestepped his question. "Everything suggests he was brain dead. For whatever reason, it's like he rebooted. His mind's in a primitive state, driven by instincts. Pure fight-or-flight."

Wade tapped his chin with the pen. "That's why he bolted?"

"Once his brain finishes rebooting, if there's not permanent damage, he could regain higher cognitive processes and be more reasonable."

Wade lowered the pen. "Or more dangerous."

"What?"

"Nothing." Wade tucked the notepad in his pocket and called over his shoulder, "Find it?"

"Not yet," one of the SPs replied. The others began sliding out one of the freezer drawers.

"Hey!" Stephen started toward them. "What do you think you're doing?"

"Easy, sir." Wade held him back. "They need to check the other bodies. We don't want any more reanimated zombies tonight."

Stephen studied the officer again. Medium height and build. Herringbone suit neatly ironed. Shoes spit polished. Not the mark of someone working overtime on a high-tempo base.

"Your boys didn't seem surprised when Greenwood brushed off those bullets." Stephen chose his words carefully. "That doesn't concern you?"

"We've seen soldiers high on PCP and other drugs. Makes them think they're invincible. We figured that's all it was."

"In a morgue?" Stephen scoffed. "He was naked. What kind of party did you think we were having?"

Wade's thin smile faded. "Sir, do you usually conduct late-night autopsies?"

"No, this was a special situation. We were working under Colonel Restrepo's direction."

"And she'll back you up on that?"

"Of course. Why wouldn't she?"

"Sir, Colonel Restrepo called a half hour ago and asked us to sweep the area. She said she had reason to believe someone was trying to tamper with some of the Fallen. We were en route when we got Major Wilson's distress call." Wade scratched his cheek. "Why would she do that if you were here under her orders?"

The blood drained from Stephen's face. Had Reaper set them up?

"I don't know," he said, setting his jaw. "But I intend to find out."

"Agent Wade," one of the other cops said, approaching them. He was holding something in his hand.

"Did you find it?"

"No, but we found this."

The SP held out his hand and opened it. In his palm was a GoPro camera.

Wade took it and held it up to Stephen. "Do you recognize this?"

"Yes, Major Wilson was using it to record our autopsy. It must've fallen off when Greenwood attacked him."

Nodding, Wade pressed a button and waited. After two seconds, he held it up to the light and studied it. "It's damaged."

"Here, let me." Stephen reached for the camera.

Wade yanked it away and stuck it in his pocket. "Thank you, sir, but we'll have our tech team work on it. We've called maintenance. They'll come soon to board up that window before the storm surges again. I suggest you find someplace warm to bunk in here. They've got a Black Flag warning in effect. No unnecessary travel."

"That's it?" Stephen swept his hands, indicating the empty room. "You don't have more questions about what happened here?"

The officer's eyebrows raised. "Is there something you want to share... sir?"

As Stephen was about to mention the implant, he stopped himself. Reaper had betrayed him, and these cops seemed more interested in covering up what had happened than finding the truth.

Swallowing hard, Stephen said, "That's it. What will you do with Greenwood when you find him?"

"Don't worry, sir." Wade gave Stephen a thin-lipped smile that was neither friendly nor comforting. "We'll make sure he's not a threat."

13

As Stephen headed to the men's locker room, the starched fabric of his uniform grating against his skin like sandpaper, he tried to sort out everything that had happened. Tom was clinging to life. Reaper had backstabbed him. And there was a half-crazed hulk of a soldier on the loose who'd been dead an hour earlier. When he reached his locker, he removed the lock and tossed his phone and keys inside. He stripped off his uniform and stuffed it into the locker. As he reached for his spare clothes, he stopped and sniffed himself. Melinda was right. He did stink.

After a long shower, scrubbing with antiseptics and astringents, making sure to clean every crevice and orifice where the stench of death could hide, Stephen toweled off and changed into sweatpants and a black T-shirt. The soft cotton calmed his jangled nerves, but only a little.

Stephen stuck his wallet back in his pocket. As he picked up his keys, he remembered he wouldn't be driving anywhere that night and tossed them back in the locker. He wished he could get as far away from there as possible. A night at Melinda's would've been just the thing. He wondered what she was doing.

Probably sleeping, like he should've been. He turned on his phone. Christ, it was after midnight already. He had to wake up in less than six hours. And that was if he could sleep at all.

His phone chimed. A message appeared: *1 new email.*

Stephen was tempted to ignore it, save it for the next day. It was likely to be spam. But he could use the distraction.

When he opened the email app, it announced he had over a thousand unread emails. Melinda had gotten on him about that, as had his ex-wife, but he doubted he'd ever change. There were too many other things to do besides sift through all the junk and news blasts. And he didn't want to delete anything that might be important to him someday. That seemed to be true for most of his life—always holding on to things from the past, afraid to let go.

Dispelling the self-reflective thoughts, he clicked on his new emails. The top one jumped out at him. *Sharon.*

His mouth went dry. He'd known his sister was flying into Germany. He'd offered to drive out to Stuttgart to meet her and completely forgot. When had he become such a lousy brother? Or had he always been one?

As he read the email, Stephen felt worse. Sharon was a short distance away, on the same base. True, he'd been dealing with intense stuff, but after an eight-hour flight, she'd be entitled to some unforgiving thoughts.

He looked up the number for the Ramstein Inns. It was ridiculously late, but he had to at least call her.

After three rings, a sleepy female voice said, "*Hallo*, Ramstein Inns."

"Yes, this is Lieutenant Colonel Englehart. Can you please connect me to one of your guests?"

"Name?"

"Major Sharon Englehart."

"One moment."

While Stephen waited, he searched for a roll of breath mints to mask the taste of death lingering in his mouth. Realizing he must've left it in his pants, he reached into his locker.

"Sir?"

"Yes, I'm here."

"There's no Sharon Englehart registered."

Stephen stopped searching for the uniform. "Are you sure?"

"Was she scheduled to check in today?"

"Her flight got diverted here. I think she got a last-minute room with you."

"That's impossible. We're fully booked, with no available rooms."

Confusion hung over Stephen like a fog. "She said she was staying at the Ramstein Inns. Is there another hotel with a similar name?"

"Perhaps she meant the Air Force Inns at Vogelweh, but they're also booked."

"Do you remember seeing a tall, blond Army major around five or six o'clock?"

"My shift started at eight. May I suggest you call again tomorrow?"

Stephen wanted to make his own suggestion but stopped himself. It wasn't the clerk's fault. He thanked her and hung up.

Puzzled, he reopened Sharon's message and hit *Reply*. Trying to sound as apologetic as he could in text, he told her to call him in the morning before she left for Stuttgart. He started to write that he'd drive her there himself, but then he considered how he was going to have deal with Reaper and Ross and deleted what he'd typed. Instead, he wrote that he wanted to see her off and then they could schedule a more appropriate visit after she'd settled in. He reread it and shook his head. It sounded more like someone declining an offer for a new credit card than a brother speaking to his little sister. He erased the whole thing and simply wrote *Call me when you wake up*, then stuck the phone in his pocket.

As he dug in the locker for his uniform again, he wondered what could've happened. Maybe she'd already left? Or she could've found someone to stay with. A smile passed his lips. Now that sounded like Sharon.

He reached into the side pocket of his camouflage pants. His fingers grazed something hard and smooth. Curious, he withdrew it. His heart jumped.

It was a test tube. And inside was a tiny black cerebral implant.

He puzzled over it for two seconds, and then it dawned on him. When Tom had hugged him, he must've slipped it into his pocket.

As Stephen studied it in the incandescent lighting, his mind connected the dots. The implant had played a role in Greenwood's death, and maybe in his impossible recovery. If Special Agent Wade's tech team managed to access the GoPro's video data, they'd know about the implant.

Stephen replaced the tube inside his pants pocket and buried the uniform deep in the locker. In the morning, he'd call Sharon again and figure out what to do with the implant.

14

A horrible ringing sound awoke Sharon from a dream. She lifted her head and tried to localize the noise as her eyes adjusted to the darkness. It was the hotel room phone on the nightstand. She rolled over and covered her head with the pillow. Her head pounded like she'd been sitting front row at a Foo Fighters concert. What was in that Polish vodka?

The phone kept ringing.

She buried her head deeper and murmured, "Anja, get your phone."

The ringing persisted. Sharon sat upright. "Anja?"

The other side of the bed was empty.

Grumbling, Sharon picked up the phone receiver and said, "Hello."

"Guten morgen, ihr Pendelverkehr ist angekommen."

"What? I'm sorry, I don't speak German."

"Oh, I thought you were Frau Wagner. What is your name?"

"Sharon. Sharon Englehart."

"Very good. Your shuttle is here."

"Already?" Sharon blinked. "What time is it?"

"Five o'clock."

"Shit." Sharon threw off the sheets. "Sorry. I mean, can you tell them to wait ten minutes? I need to get dressed."

"Of course. I will tell them."

"Thanks."

Sharon fumbled through the darkness until she found the lamp and turned it on. Her undergarments and uniform were still on the floor, but Anja's red dress was gone. Sharon scanned the room. All of Anja's things were gone.

As she dressed, she tried to remember if the woman had said anything about having to be somewhere. There wasn't even a *Thanks for the one-night stand* letter, or whatever the Germans called it. Mournfully, she buttoned her top. She should've known it wasn't going to lead anywhere, but she still liked the idea that it could have.

After tying up her combat boots, she grabbed her duffel bag and made her way downstairs. The desk clerk gave her a sleepy smile as she reached the reception area.

"Is the shuttle still here?" Sharon asked.

"Yes, they're waiting outside." The clerk pointed to where a white van was idling.

"Thank you." Sharon started for the door, then stopped, and turned back. It was a silly waste of time, but she needed to try. "Did Frau Wagner leave anything for me? A message, maybe?"

"No, but she's staying with us for another four nights. You can always call, and we'll be happy to transfer you to her."

"But all her things are gone."

The clerk's forehead crumpled. "She did not check out. Perhaps she brought her belongings with her on a day trip."

"Yeah, perhaps. Thank you."

When Sharon went outside, she found a bulky German man roughly her height smoking a cigarette next to a Mercedes Sprinter. He looked up at her from under bushy eyebrows, took another drag on his cigarette, and tossed it onto the sidewalk. Wordlessly, he approached and reached for her duffel bag.

"I can get it," she said, withdrawing from his touch. He had thick, grimy fingers like he'd been changing the van's oil minutes earlier. "Sorry, but I never let this out of my sight."

The driver eyed her for an uncomfortable moment before shrugging and leading her to the rear door. He slid it open and waved her inside. She poked her head in to find two rows of seats, where four male soldiers were already seated. They watched her with the quiet study of trained fighters.

Sharon dropped her bag in front of the first row and squeezed into the empty seat on the far side, next to a dark-skinned man wearing a Navy Working Uniform. He acknowledged her with a curt nod and then redirected his gaze forward. The driver shut the door. An overhead light came on, which helped since the tinted windows allowed little sunlight to enter. After buckling her seat belt, Sharon leaned back and tried to relax, but she was still running on adrenaline from having to dress and depart so quickly after waking. She had no idea how long the ride to Stuttgart would take, so she pulled out her cell phone and activated it. There was a new email. She opened it.

A jolt of surprise struck her when she saw it was from Stephen. *Call me when you wake up.*

Pressing her tongue against her inner cheek, she hit reply and typed: *Had to dash. Taking super-shuttle to Stuttgart now. Will call when I can get to a working phone. Church out.*

She hit *Send* and watched the status bar freeze halfway. The display showed a weak Wi-Fi signal. Damn. She tucked the phone back into her pocket. It would send eventually.

The van's engine started. Sharon turned to the soldier next to her and spotted a patch depicting an eagle sitting on an anchor. He was a Navy SEAL, and a handsome one at that. Too bad he was enlisted.

"Think we'll get a movie on this flight?" she asked, hoping to chip away at his stony countenance. "Or is that only in first class?"

His eyebrows met. "I don't know, ma'am. I've never taken this shuttle."

Clearly, her sarcastic wit would be wasted on him. "Yeah, this is my first time, too. I thought the driver would be American."

"The bases employ German nationals for nonmilitary operations. If they pass background checks, it's cheaper than importing American contractors."

"Makes sense."

Sharon turned to look behind her. The three soldiers in the back row were also enlisted. Two wore the globe patches of Air Force Special Tactics, while the third wore the red-and-blue insignia of the Marine Raiders.

"You guys are all going to Stuttgart?" she asked.

"No, ma'am," the SEAL said. "We're going to Baumholder."

"Baumholder? Is that near Stuttgart?"

The Raider laughed. "Not even close. It's about forty klicks northwest from here. Complete opposite direction."

Sharon's neck muscles tensed. "Shit. I need to get off."

She unbuckled her seat belt and rushed to the door. She tried the latch. It was locked.

"Damn it." She moved to the front of the cabin. The divider to the driver's area was solid metal. No window, no door. She banged on it. "Hey! You need to let me out. I'm on the wrong shuttle."

The van lurched forward, tossing Sharon back onto the Navy SEAL's lap.

"Son of a bitch," she said, trying to disentangle herself from the other soldier. "What's wrong with this guy?"

The van sped around a corner. She clung to the SEAL until the centripetal forces stopped.

"What kind of shuttle doesn't have a way to contact the driver?" she asked.

Before anyone answered, mist began streaming from the overhead vents.

Sharon's nose wrinkled. The air smelled musty, like dirty sweat socks.

She leaped to her feet. "Gas!"

The others fumbled to unbuckle their seat belts. One of the airmen started coughing. The Raider next to him did the same.

Sharon's throat constricted. She gagged and tried to hold her breath. Her chest muscles tightened. A burst of spasmodic coughing erupted.

Two of the soldiers charged at the nearest window and began beating on it with their fists. The window made a dull thudding sound but held fast. Sharon struggled to her feet, held on to the back of her seat, and jumped into the air. She twisted and kicked the window behind her with her heavy boots.

Not even a crack.

The soldiers began hacking and choking. Two slumped to the floor. The other two doubled over, hanging on to the seats before sinking to their knees.

Sharon fumbled through her pockets until she found her phone. There was a weak public Wi-Fi signal nearby. Biting her tongue, she opened WhatsApp and dialed Stephen's number. Her head felt light, like it was wrapped in a cloud.

The phone rang.

Come on, Steve. She could barely form a thought. *If there was ever a time for you to answer, it's now.*

A noise indicated that the call had failed.

Sharon roared in frustration. She gripped the back of the seat, clinging to consciousness.

She managed to hold down the microphone button to record a voice message.

"Steve," she managed to mumble, her tongue numb. "Help . . . gas . . . Anja . . ."

The phone slipped from her grasp. It fell to the floor.

Sharon reached for it. The world turned gray.

She toppled against the seat, bounced off, and blacked out before her head hit the ground.

15

The alarm on Stephen's phone jolted him awake. Six already. Groaning, he threw off the blanket and stood up from the cot, his back cracking and knees popping. He always hit the gym three times a week to maintain fitness standards, but he'd struggled with his last PT test. While he could crank out the push-ups and sit-ups, he wasn't a fast runner and doubted he ever would be. All those years of boxing had helped him bulk up and work out his anger but done nothing for his endurance. Maybe if Uncle Alex had spent as much time with Stephen, teaching him unpronounceable martial arts skills, as he had with Sharon…

The thought of his sister snapped him back to the present. He dug through his pocket until he found his cell phone and a new email from her. His heart sank. She was already on a shuttle to Stuttgart. He'd missed her again.

He stuck the phone back in his pocket. At least she'd found transportation, and he could catch up with her later. Might as well focus on matters closer to home, like dealing with everything that had happened the night before.

As Stephen dressed in his Class A blues, he considered what he was going to say to Reaper when he saw her. Why the hell had she called the SPs to check the morgue when she knew Stephen and Tom were working there? She couldn't have known Greenwood was going to spring back to life and attack them . . . could she? No, that didn't make sense. Reaper was a schmoozer and an opportunist, but she wasn't part of some conspiracy.

Since he was still in the main hospital, he decided to check on Tom. It took ten minutes for him to navigate the hallways and elevators to reach the ICU. He followed the nurse's direction to Room Four. Through the window, he saw Tom lying in a hospital bed, hooked up to an IV line and a cardiac monitor. Bandages covered the left side of the man's face and neck. His right hand was wrapped in a splint. The EKG tracing showed a slow but steady heart rate.

Stephen's skin cooled as he entered the room. It hurt to see his partner like that, but at least Tom was breathing on his own.

Tom's right eye opened. It wobbled and then settled on Stephen. A thin smile spread across his face.

"Hey," he said. "You should've seen the other guy."

"I did." Stephen sat on the edge of Tom's bed. "He never stood a chance."

Tom's laughter eroded into a fit of coughing and groans. "I can feel my broken ribs grinding against each other. So much for laughter being the best medicine."

Seeing Tom like this brought everything that had happened slamming back. Maybe the autopsy had been Tom's idea, but Stephen should've said no. If he had, if they hadn't removed that damned implant, then maybe Greenwood wouldn't have woken up. Maybe he wouldn't have gone berserk. Maybe . . .

"You're blaming yourself," Tom said. "Don't. I'm glad this happened."

"You're glad you got used as a punching bag?"

"No, that part sucks." Tom coughed. "But now you know what we're up against. You need to find out what really happened to that soldier."

"That's not our job. He's not even dead."

"He was."

"No, he wasn't. He was alive. We just missed it."

"He was close. That's good enough in horseshoes, hand grenades, and death."

Stephen frowned. "That's not the saying."

Tom tried to shrug and winced, settling for a snort. "Close enough."

"Even if that were the case, it's not worth risking our careers, or our lives."

"Do you still have what I gave you?"

Stephen knew he meant the implant. "Yes. I'll give it to Reaper."

"Don't. It's our only chance of finding out where this all started. I have a friend in Erlenbach: Edmund Brubaker. Take it to him."

"Are you crazy? I'm not taking unidentified tech to a local."

"You can trust him. He's got information you'll find interesting."

Blood rushed through the arteries at Stephen's temples. He forced himself to breathe slowly before saying, "No. We shouldn't have done the autopsy, and we have no business meddling in whatever they're doing with those soldiers. The SPs were searching for something, like they knew what to look for."

"See? I told you: you can't give it to them."

"It'll get them off our back."

"You think they'll let us go?" Tom laughed, and then, quietly, he asked, "What happened to the GoPro?"

"They took it."

"And when they review it, they'll hear our conversation about PSP1986."

Stephen's cheeks burned. "Why would they care about something that's three decades old?"

"Do you know nothing about our government? They're still trying to cover up Kennedy's real killer." Tom glanced around the room as if he were searching for something before refocusing on Stephen. "Look, the military monkeyed with that soldier, and now they'll try to hide it. Like they did with your dad."

"I keep telling you, this has nothing to do with my dad. His wounds didn't close like Greenwood's, and . . ." He swallowed hard. "And he didn't come back from being dead."

"I know. I'm sorry. But there's still a connection. I saw your face when Greenwood's muscles swelled up. It wasn't fear. It was recognition."

Stephen pressed his lips together. There had been a pang of familiarity—those purplish, swollen veins, the jaundiced eyes. When he'd learned about his dad's adrenal tumor, he'd written off those signs. But if the autopsy report was faked . . .

"Okay, I'll admit I've got a lot of questions—but if, as you say, there is a big conspiracy, they'll make sure we don't find clues to what they're doing."

"That's why you need to be discreet. Don't discuss this with anyone. Not Reaper, not your girlfriend, not anyone at Dover." For the first time, Tom looked spooked. "Get Brubaker to help you. He's outside the system. And you need to run your own investigation. Were you able to hold on to those tissue samples we got from Greenwood?"

"They're in my locker."

"What about the samples I drew?"

"On their way for DNA identification."

Tom nodded to himself, his lips moving but saying nothing.

"What's wrong?"

It took a second for Tom to make eye contact with him. When he did, his mouth twisted into a lopsided grin. "My parents told me not to join the military. If anything happens to me, tell them I wish I'd listened."

"Stop it. You're going to be fine."

"Yeah, you're right." Tom's eyelids drooped. "Hey, I'm tired. I think I'll take a little nap, okay?"

"Sure, buddy." Stephen patted his arm and stood. "You do that."

As he left the room, he noticed one of the physicians sitting at a computer terminal. He walked over and asked, "Are you taking care of Major Wilson?"

The doctor looked up. "Yes. Who are you?"

Stephen displayed his hospital ID. "I'm his partner at AFMES."

"Ah, Dr. Englehart. Yes, he listed you as a contact."

"How's his condition? Is he stable?"

"He suffered severe physical trauma. Face and neck hematomas. Humeral fracture. Broken ribs with a small pneumothorax." The doctor flipped his hand. "But other than that, yeah, he's stable. He should be home in less than a week."

A wave of relief washed over Stephen. "Good. If anything changes, give me a call." He handed the doctor a business card. "Tom doesn't have any other close contacts."

The doctor smiled. "With any luck, when I call you, it'll be to take him home."

After exiting the ICU, Stephen returned to his locker. Everything was as he'd left it, including the uniform stuffed in the back. He found the test tube containing the brain tissue sample and pocketed it. As he started to do the same with the implant, he stopped and twisted it between his fingers. If the SPs found him with it, after he'd lied about it being missing, what would they do to him?

What kind of idiot are you? Just hand it over and then you can go back to planning your early retirement and never have to think about any of this again.

As Stephen weighed the tube in his hand, an image of his father flitted through his brain, giving him a reassuring smile, telling him that nothing gets handed to you on a silver platter. Sometimes, all you can do is hope.

Okay, maybe he'd read that in a Captain America comic book.

He buried the test tube deep in his locker. As he left the locker room, he arranged his thoughts. If Tom was right, he could trust no one. And that meant he had to be always on guard.

16

When Stephen entered the medical examiner office, his muscles relaxed. There were no SPs, no police tape, nothing to indicate a terrible attack had occurred a few hours earlier. It wasn't until he poked his head into the autopsy suite and saw the makeshift barrier covering the window on the opposite end of the room that the previous night's events hit home. The maintenance crew had cleaned the blood stains off the floor, but they'd tossed the surgical instruments into a bucket and left it there.

"Bit of a mess, isn't it?"

Stephen turned to find Colonel Restrepo standing behind him, wearing her service dress uniform, neatly pressed. Her hair was pulled into a tight bun and . . . was she wearing makeup?

"You could say that." Stephen wasn't in the mood for standing on ceremony, especially not with her. He decided to get right to the point. "Why did you call the SPs and tell them someone was tampering with the bodies?"

What might've been regret or amusement crossed her lips. "That's not what I told them. I said I had reason to believe someone without authorization was trying to access the morgue."

"Same difference. Why?"

"After I hung up with you, I started thinking about how anyone could've committed such a major screw-up like switching bodies." She paused to smooth her bun. "The only viable reason is it's not a screw-up. Someone knew the bodies were switched, which meant they would do everything possible to prevent discovery."

"You think someone was planning to break in here and attack us?"

"I guarantee they had someone keeping surveillance. Once they realized you two were here much later than necessary, they would've sent someone in to make sure you either didn't find anything or couldn't tell anyone." She sniggered. "But the shit hit the fan before they could act."

"So, you want me to believe you were trying to protect us."

"Of course I was trying to protect you. I always take care of my people." She adjusted her coat sleeves. "Tell me everything that happened. Not the abbreviated version you gave Special Agent Wade. Everything."

Stephen almost didn't tell her about the implant, but he remembered he'd already said over the phone that they needed to autopsy the soldier's brain. He told her about Greenwood waking and attacking them, and about Greenwood's confusion over what happened to his teammates. But he didn't mention PSP1986.

When he finished recapping the events, Reaper gave him a hard look. "Where's the implant?"

"Disappeared. Either Greenwood took it, or one of the SPs pocketed it."

She rubbed her chin as she continued squinting at him. He kept his jaw set, trying to look as relaxed and sincere as possible. At last, she jiggled her head. "Too bad. I would've killed to look at that tech."

Stephen ignored her choice of words. "I didn't peg you as a techie."

"Are you kidding? I spent a year working with DARPA before I went full-time Active Duty."

"Really?"

"Who do you think convinced them to green-light the Virtopsy project?"

"I had no idea." Stephen's respect for her tripled. "When you were there, were they working on implant technology?"

"Not that they told me about, but I only had Secret-level access. Conspiracy buffs love to speculate on what goes on there, but they don't have a clue."

"Like regeneration?"

She frowned. "No. That's science fiction."

"I saw that soldier's wounds heal on their own."

"Hadn't you just suffered a head injury?"

He hesitated. "Yes, but . . ."

"And the body you autopsied turned out not to be dead. Your adrenaline spiked; your mind was freewheeling. You would've believed that soldier could turn water into wine if he had a thermos and a tube of food coloring."

A prickling heat crept up Stephen's neck. "I know what I saw."

"Fine. I trust you do. But get a head CT, just in case."

"You're deeming me unfit for duty?"

"Of course not. I won't even file an official report." She gave him a pointed look. "As long as you go voluntarily."

The heat spread to his cheeks. He forced himself to take a deep breath, hold it, and release it. "It's time for my routine labs, anyway. I'll go over lunch."

"Thank you." She adjusted her lapel. "As for Corporal Greenwood's resurrection, the most likely explanation is he had catalepsy, probably drug-induced."

"You think he was using cocaine while on duty?"

"Antipsychotics can have the same effect, and they can also induce psychosis. I assume you're going to run a toxicology screen on the sample you obtained?"

"Yes. I can test it for the most common antipsychotics, as well."

"Check prolactin levels first so you're not testing blindly." Restrepo plucked a piece of lint off her sleeve. "Now that the storm is lifted, they'll be coming in a few hours to get the rest of the bodies for shipment to Dover."

"What about the coolant problem?"

"All fixed."

"But we should autopsy them, too. Their injury patterns are inconsistent with the field report, and the way Greenwood reacted to hearing they were dead—"

She cut him off with a wave of her hand. "I know this seems important to you, but it's out of our hands now. I gave you authorization to autopsy the one soldier because we needed positive ID. Now, he's gone. I'm allowing you to finish analyzing whatever samples you obtained from him, but that's it. Do you have any reason to believe the others were misidentified?"

His resolve deflated. "No."

"Then, as I said, it's out of our hands. Besides, you need to finish autopsying Sergeant Herrera."

Stephen opened his mouth to object, but it would be a waste of breath. "All right, but I'm going to need help with Tom out of action. He was going to run the histopathology while I handled the gross dissection."

"I'll send McNiven." Reaper ran a finger over her eyebrows. "In the meantime, I need to go. AFN wants to interview me about what happened."

"You're going to tell them the truth?"

"Don't be silly. As far as the base and surrounding communities need to know, one of our boys had too many Pilsners, stripped off his clothes, and wandered off during the storm. Most Americans can't handle German beer." She straightened the buttons on her service dress coat. "If anyone from OSI comes around, don't answer any questions. Call me on my cell and wait until I return. Understood?"

There was something she wasn't telling him. But he'd worked with her long enough to know she'd tell it on her own schedule. He nodded.

As Reaper strolled to the door, Melinda arrived, already dressed in scrubs. Their eyes met as they passed each other. Something was exchanged between them, some unspoken conversation, but Stephen couldn't follow it. His skin prickled. Melinda gave the colonel a curt nod and said, "Morning, ma'am."

Reaper's gaze flicked back at Stephen. The corner of her mouth twitched. "Morning," she said, and then she was gone.

"What was that about?" Melinda asked as she set her purse down on a desk. She shivered and rubbed her arms. "And why's it so cold in here?"

"You didn't hear?"

"Hear what?"

"About what happened last night."

Her eyebrows met. "I would know if someone hadn't dismissed me like a child."

"Believe me, I did you a favor."

He sat her down and told her the story he'd told Reaper. Her eyes widened to the size of grapefruits. When he finished, she shook her head.

"That's crazy. But Tom—I mean, Major Wilson—is okay?"

"He should be out in a few days."

"Thank goodness. But what were you two thinking? You rejected a general's orders."

"I know. It was foolish, but . . ."

The hint of a smile crossed her lips. "You enjoyed contradicting him."

He hesitated, not wanting to admit it, and then gave a small nod.

"Always the thrill junkie. I'm still angry at you, you know."

"If something went wrong—which it did—I didn't want you to get caught in the crossfire. An Article 92 would destroy your career. I had to protect you."

"No, you didn't." She sat up straight, shoulders squared. "I may be enlisted, but I can make my own decisions. It was my choice whether to take the risk. But instead, you chose to be my CO and made the decision for me."

A knot formed in Stephen's chest. Now he understood why the military discouraged fraternization. His order was appropriate as a commanding officer, but not as a boyfriend. What would happen if they were in a life-or-death situation, one that could affect others? Would he do what was right for the mission? Or what was right for their relationship?

"You're right," he whispered. "And we need to have a longer conversation about this. But when we're wearing these uniforms, we need to be professional. I am your CO, and that's what I must be. There are going to be a lot more eyes on us after last night."

Her gaze bounced around his face, as if she were looking for signs that he was impersonating Stephen Englehart. After a breathless moment, she looked away, smoothed out her uniform, and stood. "Yes, sir."

Stephen felt a pang of regret as he realized he may have driven a wedge between them, surprised that the idea of losing her hurt far more than he'd expected. The pain was as bad as when his ex-wife had left him. A spark of determination ignited inside him. He couldn't lose Melinda. At the first opportunity, he needed to set things right. But the medical examiner office was not the place to do it.

"I need you to prep Sergeant Herrera," he said, trying to sound authoritative. "We'll finish the autopsy at oh-nine-thirty. I need to finish something in the lab, and then I'll meet you there."

She looked at him questioningly. "Right away, sir."

As Melinda marched to the autopsy suite, exaggerating the lock-and-step of her natural cadence, Stephen crept off to the small lab in the back of the office. It was little more than a closet with a desk, a rolling chair, and a microscope. He sat and pulled the test tube containing Greenwood's brain matter out of his pocket. After flicking it to ensure the tissue was still moist, he pulled a glass slide out of a box. Using a fine-edged scalpel, he cut a thin slice off the tissue and mounted it on the slide.

Once the sample had been fixed and stained, Stephen set it under the microscope and adjusted the focus. The visual field filled with pink blocks of cells and tiny purple dots indicating the nuclei. The cortical cells appeared healthy, without inflammation or damage.

Stephen recalled the extensive burns to the brain matter and held the tube containing the remaining tissue sample up to the light. It was white and smooth. No scorch marks.

Confused, he returned to the microscope, centered on a dense collection of neurons, and turned up the magnification. He nearly fell out of his chair.

The neurons were dividing, almost twelve hours after they'd been removed from the soldier's brain.

17

As Stephen prepped for autopsy, he couldn't stop thinking about Greenwood's brain tissue. Rapid neuron replication ceased after the fifth year of life. No way could adult neurons be dividing that quickly. Add to that the fact that these cells had been out of the host body for nearly twelve hours. They should've been dying, not thriving. He began to think he hadn't imagined those wounds closing on Greenwood's back after all.

"Hey." Melinda, already wearing a face mask and surgical gown, waved a gloved hand in front of Stephen's face. "You in there?"

Stephen blinked at her. He hadn't told her about the brain tissue, torn between the urge to share what he'd found with someone else and the need to keep her safe. And he kept hearing Tom's voice, whispering: *Don't discuss this with anyone. Not Reaper, not your girlfriend…*

"Seriously, I'm starting to get worried." Melinda plucked a penlight off the dissection tray and shone it in his eyes. "Are you having seizures from that head injury?"

He took her wrist gently and smiled. "I'm fine."

"You don't look fine. What were you thinking about?"

Tell her, Steve. Tell her, like you should've told someone about your dad...

Stephen mentally covered his ears. This wasn't the same as what had happened to his family three decades ago. Melinda wasn't at risk. But she would be if he dragged her into this mess.

"I was thinking I owe you a bottle of Lambrusco." He tilted his head. "And a conversation."

She studied his face, her mouth puckering. Then she broke eye contact and handed him a scalpel. "Sounds good. But first, we should finish up with Sergeant Herrera."

Stephen nodded and took the scalpel, their fingers making brief contact. A warm tingle rushed through his body. He forced himself not to gaze into her eyes as he positioned the scalpel for the first Y incision. "Let's see what's going on inside our friend here."

Thirty minutes later, he held the soldier's stiff heart in his hands, turning it this way and that. A bucket sat on the end of the examination table, filled with the looped intestines and abdominal organs they'd already removed and weighed. As Stephen studied the thick ball of muscle, imagining it beating, ejecting life-giving blood, he glanced at Herrera's face.

The sergeant's eyes opened.

Stephen jumped back. The heart slipped through his fingers.

Melinda's hand shot out and caught the organ. She looked up at him sharply. "What was that?"

"I…"

He looked again at the soldier's face. The eyes were closed.

"You didn't see it?" Stephen asked.

"See what?"

Shaking his head, Stephen searched in vain for an excuse, at last saying, "I don't know."

Melinda lowered the heart onto the scale to weigh it. "I do. You're afraid it's going to happen again." Before he could argue, she gave him a nurturing look. "You're a strong man. It'll take time, but you'll get through it. I know you will." She glanced over her shoulder and then said in a lower voice, "I'm here to help you. If you'll let me."

Warmth flooded his chest. He was an idiot for locking her out. With all the madness going on, he needed someone sane, someone he cared about, someone who made him feel good about himself.

"Thank you," he whispered. "That means a lot to me."

A smile bloomed on her face.

"But you're right. This man is not coming back to life." He took the heart back from Melinda and held it up to the light. "Not without this, anyway."

Melinda focused the digital camera and snapped a few shots.

"There's some mild ischemia," Stephen said after cutting open the heart and running his finger along the inner muscular walls. "Most likely from blood loss. No significant myocardial damage. Looks like his gut took the brunt of the blast. Let's move on to the brain."

"Yes, sir," Melinda said, placing the heart in a specimen container.

Stephen examined the head, planning his incisions along the scalp to expose the frontal bone. As he did, he paused. Herrera's face wasn't frozen in the mask of surprise of being caught in an explosion. He bore a look of determination. Desperation. Like he knew what was going to happen.

Stephen hesitated, reluctant to get too close to the cadaver, but he had a job to do. Bending down lower, he inspected the soldier's face and cursed under his breath. Tiny capillary eruptions in the eyes. Petechiae scattered over his cheeks. His gaze continued to trail downward to his neck. There, in the skin folds ...

"Son of a bitch."

"What?" Melinda looked up in the middle of preparing the dissection tools.

"How did we miss this?"

"Miss what?"

"Hand me a probe."

Melinda handed him the thin metal strip. Stephen rolled the soldier's head to one side and used the probe to push aside the skin folds.

"There," he said, using the probe to indicate a series of purplish marks. "Bruises around the trachea. Five of them in a linear pattern." He held up one gloved hand and wiggled his fingers. "Like a hand. He was strangled."

"But that doesn't make sense."

Stephen set down the probe and stepped back. "Pull up his Virtopsy scan."

The images flipped by on-screen, transitioning fluidly like in a movie.

"Stop." He held up his hand again. "Go back two."

She stepped the scan back to an image of the neck region.

"Zoom in on the spine."

The image enlarged. Stephen's mouth went dry. He licked his lips. "Uh, skip ahead three. Slowly."

Looking puzzled, Melinda advanced the images. Stephen's skin prickled.

It took three attempts for him to speak, and when he was at last able to do so, his voice sounded small and shaky even to his ears. "C3 to C5 fractures, consistent with compression damage."

"What could cause that?" Melinda asked.

"Severe osteoporosis maybe, but his bones would have to be so brittle he'd have had other injuries." Stephen ran through a differential in his mind. "I don't see evidence of metastatic tumors. A motor vehicle accident could cause it, but it wouldn't explain the bruising pattern."

"So, what then?"

He swallowed hard, trying not to think about his own neck being held tight by strong hands. "He wasn't just strangled. Someone crushed his vertebrae with their bare hands."

Melinda's eyes widened. "But that's not possible."

Stephen stared down at Sergeant Herrera. The soldier had set off the explosion because he needed something powerful to stop whoever was killing him. "I think it is, now."

18

You think Corporal Greenwood did this?" Melinda indicated Sergeant Herrera's bruised neck. "But how? Greenwood was in Syria, and Herrera was in Afghanistan. That's thousands of kilometers apart."

"I can think of an explanation," Stephen said, feeling jittery. "But it's not reassuring."

"What do you mean?"

"It could be why someone switched the body. To cover up the murder."

Melinda tapped her gloved finger on the table. "That would mean someone either transported him to Al-Hasakah after he died, or they stopped in Achin, swapped the bodies, and then continued here. Wouldn't the flight crew notice something like that?"

"Not if they were in on it."

"That's a bizarre idea, even for you. Sir."

Despite the situation, Stephen allowed himself to grin. She was trying. "I know, it doesn't make a lot of sense to me, either."

"Besides, why switch a burn victim for someone unburned after photos were already taken?"

Maybe because he was burned, and got better, Stephen thought, but he didn't say it. "They didn't expect to stop here. I'm sure they didn't expect he would wake up."

Melinda stared down at the cadaver, lips twisting.

"What're you thinking?" Stephen asked.

"What if someone else killed him?"

"Someone else with superhuman strength?"

"Why not? If they made one, it stands to reason they'd make more, right?"

Stephen gaped in awe. She was right. "There's something else. Greenwood seemed confused about the deaths of his teammates. He kept saying 'I killed them' and 'There was no IED.' What if the rage didn't start after he woke up? What if it happened before? Maybe he did kill his teammates."

"Did you find anything suspicious on them after I left?"

"We didn't go back to them. We were focused on Greenwood and . . ." He stopped. "Two soldiers had both their wrists snapped. They would've had to be in direct contact with their opponent, and ISIS isn't big on hand-to-hand." Stephen stepped back from the autopsy table and stripped off his gloves. "We need to look at the other bodies."

"But someone's coming any minute to get them."

"Then we better move fast."

They searched the cooler for the drawers containing Foxtrot Team. Stephen slid one open, revealing a woman. The name tag read Romita.

Stephen donned a fresh pair of gloves and lifted the soldier's arm. The hand bent backward at a ninety-degree angle. He focused his penlight over the wrist.

"Bruising around the metacarpals." He tilted his head for a better look. "Could be patterned, but it's too dense to tell. Let's check the other one."

The male soldier's wrists were also bent in half and covered with bruising.

"We could x-ray them." Melinda chewed her lip. "See if they have crush injuries like Herrera."

"No time. We need to find something that's not supposed to be there." He thought for another moment and then snapped his fingers. "I got it. Help me find Corporal Kirby."

They searched again until they found the corporal. He looked younger than the others, dark hair cropped so close it was little more than a shadow over his scalp. Using both hands, Stephen turned the soldier's head to one side. The neck was covered in bruises. "Report said his neck broke when he fell off the Humvee, but he didn't have any burns, either. Since it doesn't look like he magically healed, that can only mean—"

"He fell off before the explosion," Melinda said, finishing his thought.

"Or he was thrown off."

The bruising was consistent with impact, and too dense to look for signs of any other pathology. But the eyes told a different story.

"Splinter hemorrhages." Stephen released his breath in a low whistle. "He was choked, like Herrera."

"Can you tell if his vertebrae were crushed?"

"Not without a scan or opening him up. So, let's presume this was a criminal strangling investigation. We would need something to identify the killer. And Corporal Kirby has something Herrera doesn't." He lifted the soldier's arms, now stiff with rigor mortis. "Two hands."

"His fingernails." Melinda's eyes widened. "If he fought back, there'd be DNA evidence."

"Bingo. Get the extraction kit while I check for any other trace evidence."

As Melinda scurried off to find the kit, Stephen scanned the soldier's uniform, from his sleeves up to his chest and shoulders. Maybe he was way off base. It was like he wanted to believe Greenwood had killed these soldiers, so he could justify examining them after Reaper ordered him to leave them alone. Was it because of what Tom had told him? Or could he simply not ignore his curiosity?

"Here you go." Melinda set the kit on a metal tray stand and opened it. "How long do we have to soak the nails?"

"Long enough for the digestion buffer to work." Stephen dipped the soldier's fingers into a tray filled with solution. "It'll take the DNA Identification Lab a good week to analyze this. I wish we had something we could run now."

"If wishes were rainbows."

Stephen shot her a confused look. "Isn't it supposed to be 'If wishes were horses'?"

"Maybe, but I like rainbows better." She countered with a lopsided smile. "Not a fan of horses."

Shaking his head, he kept holding the digestion buffer in place. "When we're done with this, we'll put everything back the way we found it and go back to working on Herrera. Maybe there's something there we missed."

His phone chirped.

"Can you hold this?"

Melinda took over holding the tray while he de-gloved and dug his phone out of his pants pocket. He unlocked it and discovered a message on his WhatsApp. That was odd. Sharon had convinced him to install the app, but he never used it. When he opened it, he found a ten-second-long voicemail from Sharon. He could barely hear anything, just a hissing noise and background conversation. The sound kept fading in and out. He played it again. This time he heard the words "gas" and "Anja."

He puzzled over it. Sharon must have butt-dialed him, though that seemed unlikely, as she'd have to open the app first. Maybe the transport van had stopped for gas. But who was Anja?

"Everything okay?" Melinda asked.

"I'm not sure." Stephen shut down his phone and stuck it back in his pocket, reminding himself to call Sharon later. He took the tray out of Melinda's hand and dumped the solution into a vial, which he sealed and stuck in his pocket. "Let's put him back."

"Actually," a new voice said from the doorway, "you can leave him there."

Stephen and Melinda turned to find Special Agent Wade standing at parade rest with hands clasped in front. The officer motioned for a group of four flight crew members to enter.

"They're here to take these soldiers home," he said, and then held up the GoPro. "And I'm here to ask you about what we found on this camera."

19

Something hummed in the darkness.

No, more like buzzing. A million angry bees.

The back of Sharon's head throbbed in time with the vibrations undulating from one side of her skull to the other.

She forced her eyes open, fighting against the invisible weight dragging her eyelids down. Dim, orange light filtered in. She blinked, trying to find form in the void, but all she could make out were swirling gray and black shadows. An amber blob hung suspended in midair above her head.

One shadow moved closer. It blurred and morphed, stretching and compressing, like a lava lamp. Sharon wanted to rub her eyes, but she couldn't move her arms. She started to panic.

A shushing sound leaked from the shadow blob. Something pressed down on her shoulder, firmly but gently. It took a moment for Sharon to make out words.

". . . your heart rate up." The voice was deep. Resonant. "We need you relaxed, or the treatment won't work, and . . . well, you'll die."

The buzzing intensified, making it harder to think. Sharon licked her lips, tasting the salt to ground herself. Wherever she was, she was alive.

Who— she tried to ask, but it came out sounding like "Ooo."

The shadow blob rumbled. Sharon realized it was laughing.

"You want to know who I am. You can call me The Controller."

Sharon tried to ask if it was a Nintendo Switch or an Xbox, but her tongue became numb, like her mouth was full of wet socks, and all that came out was a muffled jumble of consonants.

"Don't try to talk," The Controller said. "Soon enough, we'll be connected—intimately connected—and you can ask all you want. But first, they need to prep you for the procedure."

Sharon tried to shake her head but only managed a slight wiggle. She tried to shout, and only a low moan emerged. A prickling heat spread from her toes upward. The buzzing assaulted her from all sides. She pleaded to The Controller with her eyes. *Don't do this. Please let me go.*

The Controller laughed again. The image faded into gray, and then blackness.

"Don't worry," The Controller said, barely audible over the buzzing. "Soon enough, you'll be part of something incredible."

20

Stephen glared at Special Agent Wade as they sat across from each other. The GoPro perched on Stephen's desk near Wade like a Maltese falcon. It took all of Stephen's effort to keep from glancing at it every five seconds. They'd been facing off in silence for what felt like two hours but was more like five minutes. What did this man want? What had he found? Even if Reaper hadn't warned him not to answer any questions, Stephen knew, from years of working in criminal investigations, that volunteering anything was the surefire way to stumble into a trap. So, he waited, holding the investigator's gaze, keeping his hands clasped on his desk.

It was Wade who broke the silence. "You're not going to tell me what's on this?" He indicated the camera.

"You said you wanted to discuss what you found," Stephen said, choosing his words carefully. "Not what you didn't find. That suggests you already know what's on there."

Wade smiled thinly. "You may outrank me, sir, but you're involved in a criminal investigation. You need to respect me as an officer of the law."

"Criminal investigation? What're you talking about?"

"You tampered with evidence."

"I had clearance to perform that autopsy."

"You had clearance from Colonel Restrepo, but I learned General Ross gave you a direct order not to touch those soldiers."

"Colonel Restrepo is in my direct chain of command. The general is not." Stephen dug his fingers into the desk. "He has no authority over forensic investigations."

"There was no forensic investigation." Wade gave Stephen a sidelong glance. "Foxtrot Team was registered as a combat casualty."

"Really?" Stephen leaned forward, injecting authority into his voice. "Then exactly what evidence are you accusing me of tampering with?"

Wade said nothing.

Confidence crept back into Stephen's heart. Clearly, the cop knew there was something fishy about the way those soldiers had died. Whatever reason he had for trying to hide it, Stephen could use that to his advantage.

"We both know I did nothing wrong." Stephen lowered his voice. "Mortuary Affairs was planning to contact Grant's family today, but that was not Sergeant Grant. Had the family of either soldier discovered that the military made such a careless mistake, the lawsuit and bad publicity would've been insurmountable. Not to mention, the real Sergeant Grant is still out there somewhere, maybe dying. Don't you think resources would be better spent trying to find him?"

The corner of Wade's mouth twitched. He looked like the guy in the old sci-fi movie Scanners, right before his head exploded. Wade swallowed. "Pararescue is searching for Sergeant Grant, and we're looking for Corporal Greenwood. In the meantime, all matters pertaining to them are relegated to AFMES at Dover, by order of the Department of Defense. Once you write your report, you are to transmit it to them and delete all local records. Do you understand . . . *sir?*"

A wave of anger washed over Stephen, but he tamped it down. Security Forces had no direct authority over the medical examiner. But Wade was simply the messenger. Someone in the DOD wanted this to go away, and Stephen needed to stay quiet for that to happen. Until he knew why, his best bet was to play along.

"I understand."

Wade nodded and stood, picking up the GoPro.

"You're not going to tell me what you found on that?" Stephen asked.

As if suddenly aware he was holding it, Wade stared at the GoPro for a full two seconds before turning back to Stephen. "Nothing. Our techs couldn't make it work."

"Then why . . ."

"I was hoping you'd tell me. That would've made things much easier."

Without further explanation, Wade pivoted and left the room.

21

When Stephen returned to the autopsy suite, he found Melinda pacing near the table where Sergeant Herrera lay, covered with a blue sheet. She looked up when he approached. "What happened?"

"Not much," Stephen said. "He tried to pin an obstruction charge on me, but he didn't have a leg to stand on. Then he said the DOD ordered us to stay away from all matters involving Foxtrot Team."

"And is that what we're going to do?"

"Officially or unofficially?"

She half smiled. "I should probably only know about the official part."

"You're right." He looked over at the cooler. "They took all of them?"

"And they made me hand over the DNA sample we took from that soldier's fingernails."

Stephen's stomach dropped. "But . . ."

"I dumped some extra fluid into a tube when you were blocking their view."

He erupted into a grin. "I'm scared of you."

"Don't be. I use my powers exclusively for good." She leaned close and whispered, "What do we do with the sample you have, though? We can't send it to the lab if the DOD ordered you to stay away from Foxtrot Team."

Stephen rubbed his thumbs and fingers together as he considered that. She had a good point. Even if they didn't go after him, they'd block him from accessing the results. His gaze fell on the sheet covering Sergeant Herrera, and a plan started to take shape in his mind.

"We use their own game against them." He donned a fresh surgical gown and gloves. "Just like they did with Greenwood."

She frowned, then brightened. "Switch the names."

"You got it. Help me over here."

They uncovered Herrera. Stephen fought back the uneasiness in his stomach as he inspected the mangled torso. This soldier gave his life for his country. The thought that he'd been betrayed by a fellow soldier sickened Stephen. He turned Herrera's head to the side and held a penlight over the soldier's neck. "You can augment fingerprints on skin using cyanoacrylate glue, but the dry climate would've precluded the prints from setting. Maybe there's something else we can find."

"Like what?"

Stephen dug through deeper. His breathing rate increased as he spotted it. "Forceps."

Melinda handed him a set of surgical tweezers. He used them to pluck out a tiny strip of flesh, lighter in color than Herrera's own.

"If Herrera detonated a grenade, the tissue of anyone in proximity would've scattered in various directions, including on Herrera himself." He smiled. "A DNA analysis will confirm whether or not this is from the same person who killed Corporal Kirby."

"So, we send both samples under Sergeant Herrera's name." She screwed up her face. "But that tissue's been there for days. Why does it look so fresh?"

Stephen studied the strip of skin. Son of a bitch, she was right.

"I'll take a closer look at this." He dropped the sample into a test tube. "But first, Sergeant Herrera has done enough for us today. It's time for him to go home to his family."

Thirty minutes later, Stephen set the last stitch in the soldier's chest and studied his work. Not his best, but the morticians would handle the rest. They could reconstruct shattered faces so well, even loved ones hardly noticed the difference.

"Put him back in the fridge." He stripped off his gloves. "I'll run this sample."

"What about that message you got earlier?"

"What message?" He froze, stricken as he recalled the email from Sharon. "Shit. I completely forgot when Wade showed up."

He checked the wall clock. Five after eleven. And he'd promised Reaper he would get a head CT over lunch. But he had to make sure his sister was okay.

"Where the hell is McNiven?" he asked, realizing he sounded like an idiot since there was no way Melinda could know the answer. "Colonel Restrepo said he'd be here to help."

"I don't know, but when he shows up, do you want me to ask him to run that histopath?"

Stephen started to tell her no but thought better of it. It would help to distribute the workload. "Have him prep a slide before sending the rest to the lab. I want to look at it myself under the microscope."

"Yes, sir."

Stephen returned to his office and dialed Sharon. An automated message notified him that the number's owner was not in a serviceable area. He looked up the DSN number for Panzer Kaserne and dialed it. There were two low-pitched ringtones, several clicks, and then three low beeps.

"Garrison Stuttgart," a female voice said. "This is a secure line."

"This is Colonel Englehart at Ramstein. My sister, Major Sharon Englehart, took the shuttle there this morning, but I can't reach her. Can you tell me if she's checked in?"

"Sir, there was no shuttle from Ramstein today."

"What?"

"We had to cancel all shuttles due to yesterday's storm."

"But . . . that doesn't make sense." Stephen opened his email on his desktop. Had he read the message wrong? "She emailed early this morning."

"Are you sure she's stationed here?"

The email app appeared on-screen. Stephen skimmed through the two emails he'd received from Sharon. "Yes, she specifically said Stuttgart."

"Sir, if you give me her date of service, I can search our records to see if she was supposed to arrive today or not."

Stephen gave her the information and waited while the attendant placed him on hold. His heart rate accelerated. First, the Ramstein Inns didn't know anything about Sharon staying there, and now there was no shuttle? What the hell was going on?

"Sir?"

"Yes, I'm here."

"Major Englehart was reassigned to the First Battalion at Baumholder."

"Baumholder?" Stephen's ears pricked. Baumholder was less than an hour from Ramstein. "You're sure?"

"Yes, Sir. SOCEUR is transferring all Special Forces units there."

That still didn't make sense. Why hadn't Sharon told him that in her emails? "Can I speak to your CO?"

"Colonel Thompson is off-post this morning. I can leave him a message."

"All right, please tell him to call me." Stephen gave her his cell number. "Uh, do you have a number for Baumholder?"

The attendant gave him the number. He thanked her and hung up. Two minutes later, as he waited for someone at Baumholder to pick up, his mind raced. Sharon wouldn't confuse Stuttgart with Baumholder, would she? No, he clearly remembered she was originally arriving in Stuttgart. If she was headed to Baumholder, why wouldn't she fly directly into Ramstein right from the start?

"Baumholder Garrison. This is a secure line."

Stephen introduced himself again, explained that he'd been told his sister was traveling there that day, and provided her date of service. He concluded by asking, "Can you tell me if she's in-processed yet?"

"Sir, you said she took the shuttle this morning?"

"Yes. She called it the Super Shuttle."

"We have a shuttle between here and K-Town, but it's not scheduled until this afternoon."

Stephen's mouth went dry. "How is that possible? She emailed me this morning and said she was getting on the shuttle."

"I don't know, sir." The attendant paused. "Did you say she was with the First Battalion?"

"Yes."

"They're not scheduled to transfer here for another three months."

"That's not what Panzer Kaserne told me."

"Sir, they must've been mistaken. A Navy SEAL and a Marine Raider were on the itinerary to arrive today on the shuttle, but we received a message from AMC they were making their own travel arrangements through their hotels."

"Is that common procedure?"

The attendant was silent for a moment. "No, sir, but it does happen. They're helpful in coordinating care for incoming personnel. Perhaps Major Englehart made arrangements through them, also."

"Yeah. Perhaps. Thanks anyway."

As he hung up, Stephen pondered what the attendant had said. Maybe Sharon had gone through the hotel, but if she had, what shuttle did she take? What hotel did she stay at, since she wasn't registered with the Ramstein Inns? And who was Anja?

Stephen was about to dial the local AMC when Melinda poked her head in the door. "Steve—uh, sir—Major McNiven is here."

"It's about time. Did you send him to run those labs?"

"Not yet. He . . ." She looked down at the floor and drew a breath, and then her gaze met his. "I think he should tell you."

Stephen's chest tightened. He'd never seen Melinda look so haunted. He nodded.

Major Michael McNiven entered, blond hair cropped high and tight, wearing his Class A blues and a tense expression that rivaled Melinda's. He stopped in front of Stephen's desk, hands folded in front of him.

"What's going on, Mike?" Stephen tried to read McNiven's face. His face was doughy, eyes bloodshot, as if he'd been . . . crying? "Why were you so late?"

"I was getting the details, trying to make sense of it." McNiven licked his lips. "And I was trying to figure out how to tell you."

"Tell me what happened."

"It's Tom Wilson." McNiven released a long, slow sigh. "He's dead."

22

It took several moments before Stephen could speak. Tom Wilson was dead.

"That's . . . not possible," he said at last, the words sounding distorted, as if they were being filtered through a wormhole from some terrible parallel universe. "He was fine this morning. I mean, he wasn't fine, but he was stable. The ICU doc said he'd be home in a few days."

"He had a humerus fracture." McNiven ran his fingers through his hair. "That led to fat emboli syndrome. There was nothing they could do."

"Fat emboli?" Stephen knew the syndrome involved chunks of fat released from long bone fractures entering the bloodstream and seeding in various locations of the body, including the lungs and brain. He replayed the morning's discussion with Tom in his mind. "But that's associated with cognitive dysfunction. Tom was completely lucid."

"Maybe it didn't reach his brain, but his lungs took a huge hit. He started vomiting and went into respiratory arrest before they could get him to the OR."

Stephen visualized the scene—doctors and nurses rushing to Tom's bedside, giving him rescue breaths and oxygen, intubating him, trying to keep him oxygenated as his lungs shut down. Stephen's throat constricted, as if he were the one who could no longer breathe. He forced the image away. "But FES develops twenty-four to forty-eight hours after injury. He was attacked last night. How could it progress to death so quickly?"

"That's why I didn't come here right away. I was trying to make sense of it." McNiven spread his hands like a worshipper at the altar. "It just shows we don't understand everything."

That was a bullshit excuse, and McNiven should've known better. But there was another problem. "Why were you there?"

"I was on my way to a Mortality and Morbidity meeting with the ICU staff when I heard the Code Blue. I arrived as they were trying one last time to resuscitate him." McNiven shook his head. "It was bad."

"The ICU doc said he'd call me if anything changed. He said Tom would be fine."

"It's not his fault. Your view may be colored by the fact the deaths you see are due to foul play, but not so in my world. At least in the hospital, most deaths, even unexpected, are due to the limits of medical science."

What McNiven was saying made sense on some level, but that inner voice kept whispering to Stephen, *Are you sure? Are you 100 percent sure?*

"They're going to do an autopsy, right?" The words spilled out of Stephen's mouth. Before McNiven could reply, he added, "Let me do it."

"Bad idea." McNiven shook his head. "You're too personally invested. You're looking for things that aren't there. You can be sure I'll do the best—"

"I said, I'll do it." Stephen got in McNiven's face, close enough that he could smell the mint aftershave on the major's cheeks. "I'll talk to Reaper. She'll let me."

McNiven held up his hands in surrender. "If she gives it to you, that's her decision."

Stephen stepped back, letting his hands fall to his sides. "Fine."

The man gave Stephen a hard look. "Be careful, okay? There aren't many of us around here. We can't lose another one."

"What do you mean by that?"

"Nothing." McNiven looked up at the ceiling, as if something more interesting was crawling around up there. "Reaper said you needed coverage while you take care of personal business. What do you need me to do?"

Did McNiven know more than he was letting on? Stephen had planned to stop by AMC instead of getting the head CT, but he suddenly doubted the major would cover for him with Reaper. Tom's last words rolled around in Stephen's head. Don't discuss this with anyone.

Cautiously, Stephen said, "Sergeant Stewart has some tissue samples that need mounting and processing. I'll look at the slides when I get back."

"Sure." McNiven turned for the door and glanced over his shoulder. "You sure you don't need anything else? If you want to take the rest of the afternoon off..."

"I'm fine." Stephen waved him away. "I'll be back in an hour."

After McNiven left, Stephen pulled out a legal pad, grabbed a pen off his desk, and drew three columns on the top page. In the first column, he wrote *Greenwood,* and proceeded to make notes under the header, from the switched body to the dead members of Foxtrot team to the implant. In the second column, he wrote *Herrera,* noting the soldier's crushed neck. Moving on to the third column, he wrote *Tom.* He found it harder to process this one, but he managed to draw strength and wrote down *PSP1986, Brubaker,* and *FES.*

When he'd finished, he skimmed his work. Three separate mysteries—but were they separate? Kirby and Herrera had suffered similar neck injuries. Greenwood had the same PSP1986 tag as the cases Tom had stumbled onto back at Dover. Maybe they were connected.

Slowly, as if moved by an unseen force, his hand drifted to the far right of the page and drew one more vertical line. He hesitated, and then wrote at the top of the column: *Dad*.

22

Thirty-three years earlier

The Red Skull had taken over the small island of Ta-Nehisi, the inhabitants now his slaves, thanks to his modified super-serum. Only one man stood in his way of world domination. Steve Rogers, known to the world as Captain America, was parachuting in from a small biplane..."

"Son?"

Steve yanked his head out of the comic book at the sound of his father's voice. It took him a moment to pull his mind back from the Pacific Islands to his room. He was lying on his bed, wearing a T-shirt and baggy shorts. R.E.M.'s *Superman* blasted from the boom box on his desk. Posters of supermodels and comic book covers papered the walls.

"Yeah?" Steve's initial annoyance at being interrupted melted away at seeing his father's face peeking through the crack in the door. Although Dad had been home for a week, Steve had barely seen him.

Right after he and Uncle Alex had returned from Panama, Dad had been sent off for another eight-day mission. When he came back from that, he had doctor appointments and a promotion ceremony to Captain and reports to write and blah, blah, blah.

Dad turned down the music and sat on the edge of Steve's bed. Steve moved to give him room, noticing that he was hiding something behind his back. Steve leaned around to see what it was. Dad twisted to keep it hidden.

"Your mom told me what happened at school today." Dad glanced up at the posters, his lip curling, and then turned back to Steve. "What's been happening for the past few months."

"It wasn't my fault." Steve glanced away. "Not today, anyway."

"Your teacher said it was."

Steve pretended to wipe a stain off the comforter. "Teacher's a bitch."

"Hey." His father used his thick index finger to direct Steve by the chin to face him. "Language."

Blood rushed to Steve's cheeks. "But she is."

"I know she is." He rolled his eyes. "I could tell on your first day of school. But you must act like it doesn't bother you."

"Why?"

"Because that's how it is. We have to play the game."

"What game?"

"This one."

Dad pulled a long rectangular box out from behind his back and laid it on the bed. The cover bore a picture of a smiling general with a thick white mustache, moving a black game piece across a board. On the side of the box was *Tactico*.

"Never heard of that one," Steve said, his curiosity spiking. It had been a couple of years since the family played a board game together. "Is it any good?"

"Is it good?" Dad snorted. "This is the best game ever invented. I played it with my dad when I was your age. Help me set it up."

They opened the box and laid out the game board. It was easy to understand the layout. Three rows of black pieces on one side. Three rows of white on the other. Dad instructed Steve to set up the pieces wherever he saw fit.

"You're trying to capture my flag, and I'm trying to capture yours," Dad said as he finished placing his last pieces. "Each piece has different rank and ability. You don't know which of my pieces are which until you attack. The one with lower rank loses and is gone from the game. I'll start." He moved a black piece one space. "Now, it's your turn."

Steve scanned the pieces, not understanding the rules. He looked up for help, but his father's face was expressionless. Groaning, Steve moved a white piece showing a soldier with the number 6 next to him one space.

They went back and forth for a few moves, until Steve moved his piece next to one of his father's.

"What do I do now?"

"Attack me."

"Okay. Uh, I attack."

"Flip your piece around."

Steve flipped his piece, and Dad did the same. His bore the number 10.

"My admiral beats your captain." Dad used his piece to knock over Steve's.

Steve banged his fist on the bed. "That sucks. I lost the battle."

"Yes, you did. But think about this. The admiral is the highest-ranked piece. The only one who can defeat him is the spy. Now, you know where my admiral is. If you take him out, and my spy, you can use your admiral to take down all my other pieces."

It took a moment for Steve to process that. "So, by losing that battle, I learned something that can help me win the war?"

"You always were a fast learner." Dad beamed as he stretched his arm to move another black piece into Steve's territory. "But don't get cocky. When you find something out, don't let anyone else know, or they'll use it against you. And don't use that information right away, like you did with your teacher. Wait until the time is right, when they've forgotten all about it, and then spring it on them."

Steve had stopped listening. He was staring at his father's forearm.

"Dad, what's wrong with your arm?"

Dad froze, inhaling through his nose, and then looked down at his arm, rotating his wrist. The veins bulged deep purple. The muscle fibers twitched, making it seem as if roaches were crawling under his skin. He yanked his sleeve lower and hid his hand in his lap.

"It's nothing," he said, avoiding Steve's gaze. "Don't worry about it."

"But Dad—"

"I said, it's nothing!"

His father glared at him, nostrils flaring. And then Steve saw it. What had been wrong with Dad's eyes. The swollen capillaries. The sanguine hue to the sclerae. The hollow darkness in the pupils, which had expanded so much that only a thin perimeter of brown color remained, like twin eclipses. Something was growing inside his father—something frightening.

"I'm—I'm sorry, Dad."

Dad's body lifted off the bed, fists rising, like a cobra about to strike.

And then he stopped. His eyelids snapped shut. He breathed in and out through his nose, pulling his fists close to his chest. The blood vessels flattened and faded. Releasing his breath, he opened his eyes and smiled. The yellow tint was gone. The darkness was gone.

"It's okay, son. Just a little something I've been fighting ever since I got back from the desert. But I'll be fine soon, and I promise I won't be going anywhere for a long while."

Steve returned the smile, but he knew bullshit when he heard it. He caught a glimpse of the Captain America comic book lying half-open on his bed. On the page, the Red Skull had turned one of the denizens of Ta-Nehisi into a grayish monster with bulging muscles. The monster's eyes were dark pits, and it did whatever its master ordered it to do.

Uncertainty swirled in Steve's stomach. Dad looked completely normal now. Maybe he had imagined all of it, his mind running wild from reading too many comic books, like Mom had said. If something was happening to Dad, he should tell someone, but who? Mom was a mess, pretending the rest of them didn't know about her drinking. He'd heard Dad yelling at her about it the other night. Sharon? She was too little. There was nothing she could do about it, and it would only scare her. Uncle Alex? Alex tried to be Steve's buddy, taking him boxing and sharing comic books with him, but he was Dad's supervisor. If Steve told him, Dad might lose his job, and then they'd all be in trouble.

Dad pointed at the game pieces. "Your turn, son. What's your move?"

23

Stephen's thoughts jumbled together in a gigantic tangle as he lay in the CT scanner. Tom had been right about there being similarities between Corporal Greenwood and Captain Isaiah Englehart, but there was more that didn't add up. Even if the military had done something to his dad, that was over thirty years ago. Dad hadn't had a cerebral implant, and he certainly hadn't risen from the dead. There was a piece Stephen was missing, but what?

"Sir?" The CT technician's voice echoed inside the chamber. "We're all done."

Exhaling with relief, Stephen waited while the table slid out of the machine. The tech approached as Stephen stood and brushed off his uniform.

"See anything funky?" Stephen asked, trying to find humor in the situation. He wondered what he would do if they found something wrong, like a subdural head bleed. Or an implant. "My missing keys, maybe?"

The tech, a young senior airman, cracked a smile. "No, sir. Everything looked normal to me, but the radiologist will review it over the next couple of hours."

"Great. Thanks."

After leaving the radiology suite, Stephen considered his next move. His stomach growled, reminding him that he'd skipped breakfast. He still needed to get his treatment, the one he'd been getting weekly since he was twelve, but that could wait. Donating five vials of blood for his annual testing had made him extra hungry.

As he made his way to the hospital cafeteria, his footsteps grew heavy. Try as he might to keep up his jokester persona, he had to face the fact that Tom was dead. True, they hadn't been best friends. But working together for a year, especially in their line of work, created a bond that was hard to explain to anyone outside their specialty. Stephen felt like he was just starting to get to know the real Tom when tragedy struck. And the way Tom had asked Stephen to talk to his parents, it was almost like he'd known what was going to happen.

The cafeteria was crowded when Stephen arrived. He grabbed a sandwich, a soda, and some fries and worked his way to an empty table in the back of the room. As he ate, he thought more about what Tom had said.

You think they'll just let us go?

A chill ran down Stephen's back. Tom's death couldn't have been intentional . . . could it? McNiven had made a good point. Long bone fractures were notorious for causing fat emboli, which were in turn impossible to treat. No anticoagulants could cut through them. The sole way to get rid of them was surgical, and that only worked if the emboli weren't widely distributed. The mechanism of death made sense. So why did it still feel wrong?

"I thought I'd find you here."

Stephen cringed at the sound of the familiar voice. His fingers sank into the sandwich as he curled them into fists, his shoulders tightening. Not now. He couldn't deal with him now.

"Stephen, I'm talking to you."

Gritting his teeth, Stephen lifted his head and made eye contact with General Alex Ross.

The general's white mustache twitched. "You look like crap."

"Is that your way of asking how I'm doing? Because you giving a shit would be something new."

Ross clucked his tongue. "If that were true, you'd have been stuck in a foster home with some alcoholic abuser. You wouldn't have the career you have today. And you'd be in a holding cell right now, awaiting court martial. You violated my direct order."

"I had orders from Colonel Restrepo, and she has direct authority over AFMES." Stephen pushed away his sandwich. He'd lost his appetite. "What's your interest in this? What do you know about those soldiers?"

"That's classified."

"Don't give me that. According to Special Agent Wade, there's reason to suspect foul play. Forensic investigations involving this base are my jurisdiction."

"They didn't die on this base."

"No, but Greenwood killed Tom Wilson. On this base."

Ross was silent. For a moment, only a moment, his eyes softened, and then he looked down at the table. "I'm sorry about what happened to Major Wilson. Horrible way to go."

Stephen knew all about horrible deaths and didn't need to hear it from this man, of all people, but hearing Ross say the words "I'm sorry" was so foreign, he couldn't manage a snarky response. Instead, he said, "Thanks. I'm trying to wrap my head around it."

Still staring at the table, Ross said, "I imagine you want to do the autopsy."

Stephen blinked.

Looking up, Ross half smiled. "Come on, I know you wouldn't trust anyone else to do it as well as you. And the truth is, they probably wouldn't."

Unable to find the words to respond, Stephen continued to stare. Was Alex Ross complimenting him?

"I can talk to Restrepo," Ross continued. "Give her my blessing to have you do it, if only to set your mind at ease that there was nothing anyone could've done to save him."

Still in shock, Stephen managed to say, "That's—that's really kind of you."

"Well, we need every physician on this base at their top game right now. This hospital is under scrutiny. The DOD, and the taxpayers, want to know their money was well spent in building this place." The warmth had faded from Ross's eyes, and he was all business again. "That's why I need to know you'll keep quiet about Greenwood."

Prickly heat crept up Stephen's neck. "You son of a bitch. You don't care about me or Tom. You want me to keep my mouth shut."

"You're missing the big picture, Steve, like you always do." Ross's brow furrowed as he leaned forward and murmured, "If word got out that we sent a man who wasn't dead to autopsy, and then couldn't restrain him when he woke up, there's a good chance they'd shut down your program, if not the entire hospital, until it all got sorted out."

The heat drained from Stephen's face. Ross had a point, in his own arrogant way. "All right, I'll give you that. But you were all over me to stay away from those bodies long before Greenwood turned *Night of the Living Dead*. Why? What was so important about them?"

A muscle ticked in Ross's jaw.

"Did you know one of the bodies was misidentified?"

"Of course not." Ross scowled and glanced over his shoulder. Seeming satisfied that no one was watching, he whispered, "You know how hard it is to make positive ID in the field, especially when there are burn injuries."

"But that's the thing. Greenwood wasn't burned."

Ross's eyes widened. "What?"

"Not a mark on him. He . . ." Stephen stopped himself. He'd been so eager to rub it in Ross's face, to defend himself, he hadn't stopped to think about Tom's warning not to trust anyone. Even if he trusted Ross, he couldn't be sure what a general would do with that kind of information. Hopefully, he hadn't already said too much. "He looked dead, but his body showed no sign of physical injury. That's how we discovered they'd switched the bodies, and why I asked Reaper for authorization to begin identity confirmation."

Ross nodded. "That makes sense. You did the right thing."

Stephen's shoulders relaxed.

"But you didn't stop there." Ross narrowed his gaze. "According to Special Agent Wade, you opened Greenwood's skull. Why?"

Stephen's cheeks cooled. Tom had warned him not to tell anyone about the implant. But did Ross already know?

"We noticed something on Virtopsy. A bright spot in Greenwood's brain."

Ross's face was stonier than a statue, giving away nothing. "What was it?"

It's our only chance of finding out where this all started.

The lie flowed more naturally than Stephen thought was possible. "A chunk of shrapnel. Looked like it had been there for years, which is why we couldn't find any entry path. But it was sitting right on the brainstem. Greenwood must've dislodged it in combat, and it shut down enough critical life processes that he appeared dead. After we removed it, his brain started working again. It's the only thing that makes sense, right?"

Ross peered through Stephen's eyes to his soul. Then he brightened and sat back in his chair. "It does make sense. Thank you for being honest with me. Unfortunately, Greenwood is responsible for killing your friend. When we find him, he'll be sent to Leavenworth to await trial."

The idea that a soldier could be tried for something he had no control over, due to whatever had been done to him, rankled Stephen. But Greenwood was responsible for Tom's death.

"Well, I hope you catch him soon, then." Stephen sipped his soda. "So, you're not going to tell me what happened to his teammates?"

Ross smiled thinly. "Accept a command position and you won't have to ask."

"I'll think about it." The thought of having to interact with Ross on a regular basis twisted Stephen's gut, even though they'd be in different chains of command. Eager to change the topic, he asked, "Hey, have you spoken to Sharon?"

"Last week, when she told me she was headed to Panzer Kaserne. Why?"

"I don't know. She got redirected here due to the storm, emailed me that she was taking an early shuttle to Stuttgart, and hasn't replied since then."

"Well, you know how in-processing goes. She's probably too busy to get to a computer."

"That's the thing. Stuttgart told me she was reassigned to Baumholder, but Baumholder said she didn't show up there."

Ross frowned. "What do you mean, she didn't show up?"

"They told me the shuttle didn't run until this afternoon, and suggested she might've arranged for private transportation, but that doesn't sound like Sharon. She won't even take an Uber."

"I'll talk to the COs at both installations and let you know what I found out."

The gentle tone of Ross's voice surprised Stephen. "Uh, thanks."

Ross gave a curt nod and then indicated the band-aid on Stephen's arm. "That time of the year, huh? Everything's still fine?"

Stephen absently ran a finger over the spot where they'd drawn his blood. His mind drifted back thirty-three years, to a time when Ross had taken him boxing. Stephen had gotten angry at Ross for pretending to be his father while his real father was off saving the world, so angry he attacked him. The older man threw Stephen into the ropes, and the boy's head crashed against the pole. When Stephen woke up again, he'd been in the Lovell General Hospital East for twenty-four hours, where they'd discovered that he had a rare form of leukemia.

Thanks to an experimental treatment, Stephen survived. He'd been in remission for over three decades, but the military doctors continued to insist he get annual labs since the leukemia was so rare, they couldn't guarantee it would stay away forever.

"Yeah," Stephen said. "Everything's fine."

"You know, whatever you may think, I care about both of you." Ross tilted his head. "And I'm proud of you. Both of you."

Stephen was flabbergasted. Who was this man masquerading as Alex Ross? "Thanks. Uh, listen, I need to get back to work. It was . . . kind of nice talking to you."

A smile spread across Ross's face. "Same here."

As Stephen walked away, he resisted the urge to look over his shoulder and see if Ross was watching him. It had taken his last reserves of willpower to keep from telling the general about the implant. Maybe he'd misjudged the man all those years, but he was still part of the military machine, and there was something Ross wasn't telling him. If he was going to keep secrets, so was Stephen.

24

For the second time, Sharon awoke to the sound of buzzing. The orange light was gone, but now she was in a sea of gray and white. Her head pounded worse than before.

As she forced herself to focus, she started to see shapes. Metal walls. Hospital beds. Medical equipment. IV bags on poles. There was someone in the bed next to hers: the Navy SEAL from the shuttle. He was asleep, but not resting. His body jerked. Sweat streamed down his cheeks. He started to cry.

Sharon reached for him. Something yanked on her arm. Pain bit into her flesh. An IV needle connected to a tube that ran up to a near-empty bag of amber fluid.

"Hello?" she said, her voice sounding weak. "Nurse? Doctor?"

No one answered.

She dragged herself into a sitting position. Her head spun.

Then her eyes focused on the fluid bag. She'd taken advanced Combat Casualty Care training in honor of her mother and was familiar with most of the common resuscitation medications and solutions, but this one was new to her.

Where the hell am I?

She squinted into the gloom. There. A doorway, on the opposite side of the room.

Biting off a pained howl, she ripped out the IV. Blood trickled from her wrist.

She managed to stand. Her knees buckled. Slowly, she took a step.

Her leg collapsed. She stumbled, catching herself on the bedframe. The throbbing in her head became a roar. White spots floated on the edge of her vision.

You can do this. Put one foot in front of the other.

Step by step, Sharon started to cross the room, holding on to beds as she went.

A third of the way there. She had to keep going.

The soldier in the next bed moaned. She froze. He took a few ragged breaths and then settled back into deep sleep. Releasing her breath, Sharon started moving again, bare feet slapping against the stone floor. She paused to listen after every two steps.

Still, no one came.

She moved faster, three steps at a time. Her muscles seemed stronger now. She could feel the fibers twitching, propelling her forward.

Over halfway to the door. She smiled to herself. She was going to make it.

Pain knifed through her skull. Everything turned white. She staggered and clutched the nearest bedpost.

No. I need to keep going.

More pain. Jagged. Electric.

She fell, pulling the bedsheet with her. Her palm struck a sharp rock protruding from the ground. She barely registered this new pain over the pulsating agony in her brain.

Sharon rolled onto her back. Blood streamed from a deep gash in her palm. The throbbing continued. She noticed the sheet in her other hand and followed it up toward the bed. Then she gasped.

A young man stared back at her with lifeless eyes. His face was frozen in a mask of pain and horror. His skin bubbled, in some places charred.

You're not going anywhere yet, a voice commanded. It was the one who'd spoken earlier. The Controller.

She looked around wildly. The other soldiers remained asleep. No one else in the room.

Indoctrination will start soon.

The voice resonated inside her head. Sharon panicked.

You're not going crazy. All will be clear in time. But you must comply.

Another lightning bolt of pain, stronger than the last. Her body convulsed, and she blacked out.

25

Soldiers in and out of uniform milled around the Ramstein Inn's lobby, reading newspapers, watching last week's boxing match on the big-screen TV, or checking their itineraries. At the base's largest temporary living facility, it was common to find personnel in transition, with nowhere to be until they finished in-processing. But today it seemed exceptionally busy.

Stephen made his way to the check-in counter. A young woman smiled as he approached.

"Checking in?" she asked with a hint of a German accent.

"I called earlier about my sister, who told me she stayed here last night. Sharon Englehart."

"Yes, you spoke to me. You still haven't found her?"

"Not yet, but maybe you can help. Was there a shuttle to either Stuttgart or Baumholder this morning?"

She tapped her chin. "There is a scheduled shuttle to Baumholder, but it's not until this afternoon."

"Could she have gotten a private shuttle?"

"Sometimes our guests make their own arrangements."

"This would've been early. Around five."

"That was before my shift. I can check the logs. Please, wait here."

As Stephen waited, he skimmed through Sharon's emails again. *Where did you go, sis?* He reread her last words: *Will call when I get a working phone. Church out.* But then she *had* tried to call, and he'd been too busy to answer.

The clerk returned, wearing a puzzled look.

"What's wrong?" Steve asked.

"The overnight clerk recorded a shuttle this morning at five."

Finally, some good news. "Great, can you tell me how to contact them?"

"That's the problem. I've never heard of this company, Bundesfahrer." She shook her head. "We always recommend Kleinbusse or Martz. This company would have to be arranged by someone who knew of them personally."

Stephen's mind raced. *Someone who knew of them* ...

"Is there an employee here named Anja?" he asked.

"No."

"How about a guest?"

"What's her last name?"

"I don't know."

"Even if I could share our guests' personal information, I can't search our registry by first name." She looked sincere. "I'm sorry I can't help you more."

"It's all right. I understand." He decided to try one last attempt. "What about the overnight clerk? Can you ask them what they know?"

"Unfortunately, Monika left for a week's vacation in Austria this morning. She won't be reachable until she returns."

Stephen deflated. He'd hit a complete dead end. "You don't have any contact information for this Bundesfahrer, do you?"

"Sorry, no."

Stephen's phone rang. He thanked the clerk and answered.

"You should get back here. Now."

"Melinda? What's going on?"

"Colonel Restrepo's here." Her voice sounded tense. "She said you can do Major Wilson's autopsy, but you only have until the end of the day to do it."

26

The moment Stephen entered his office, he spotted Reaper leaning over his workstation, scrolling through his laptop. The computer was facing away from him, so he couldn't see what she was reading, but the thought of her snooping through his files sent a surge of irritation through him. He stormed over and closed the lid on the laptop.

She snapped her head up and furrowed her brow. "What are you doing?"

"How did you unlock my computer? I never gave you my password."

"No, you didn't." She straightened her back. "I have admin access to everyone's accounts."

He was taken aback. "Since when?"

"Ever since they discovered a potential leak from hospital records." She snorted. "*Your* computer. *Your* password. Don't be naive. You know everything in this building is government property. Including you."

Stephen's cheeks burned. He caught sight of Melinda poking her head out from his office, watching the exchange. He surreptitiously waved her away.

"That may be true," he said, fighting to keep his voice level. "But you could've asked first."

The colonel studied him, squinting, and then half smiled. "You're right. May I please snoop through your files?"

He made a mock flourish. "By all means."

Politely, she pushed away the closed laptop. "That's not why I'm here. First, I want to tell you how sorry I am about Major Wilson. His death is hard on all of us, but I imagine it's doubly so for you."

"I'm handling it. McNiven's helping."

"Yes, and he can stay down here as long as you need, until AFMES can send a replacement." She puffed out her cheeks. "I also heard you wanted to do the autopsy personally."

"The ICU doc said he was going to be fine. I owe it to Tom to find out what happened."

"I understand." She gave him a hard look. "But this is a medical autopsy. Not a forensic one. There was no crime, other than being assaulted by Greenwood."

The tone of her voice sent a chill down Stephen's back, like she could read his mind. "I still remember how to do medical autopsies.

But why are you only giving me until the end of the day? Did General Ross make a deal?"

"What? No. I didn't talk to him." She sighed. "It's a direct order from Colonel Agarwal. He wants Tom's remains shipped stateside tomorrow."

"Why?"

"He didn't tell me, but I imagine the order came from the DOD."

"But what about root cause analysis? If there was a preventable error, the hospital should . . ."

"They want to make this go away." The sharp tone of her voice cut off any further argument he could muster. "Greenwood. The attack. All of it. That means burying everything connected to it before we have any more leaks—in this case, literally burying it. So, do what you must to make yourself feel less guilty, and then get back to work."

"Yes, ma'am." Stephen knew he should leave it at that, but he couldn't resist asking, "What if I find something to indicate foul play?"

The colonel's eyes cooled. "Then I trust you to make the right decision."

Inside the autopsy suite, Stephen found Melinda already gowned and masked, standing at attention next to an exam table covered with a blue sheet. He could make out the form of a human body under the sheet.

Stephen sucked in his breath as he approached. Without moving his eyes from the sheet, he told Melinda, "At ease."

"Are you okay?" she whispered.

Nodding absently, he pulled back the sheet. His throat swelled. Tom Wilson lay on the table, right eye closed, left eye still bandaged. If Stephen hadn't known better, he'd think Tom was sleeping, or playing a prank, waiting for the right moment to jump up and shout, "Surprise!" Stephen wished he would.

But he didn't.

Stephen replaced the sheet and crossed the room to gown up. Questions tumbled around in his mind as he pulled on a scrub cap and mask. How could Tom have died so suddenly when he'd been stable? And had he known something was going to happen to him?

"What studies did they run in the ICU?" he asked when he returned to the exam table.

"Blood gases only." Melinda handed him the reports. "He crashed so unexpectedly, they didn't have time for anything else."

"Low oxygen partial pressure and increased alveolar-arterial gradient, progressing to metabolic acidosis. I can see why they thought fat emboli." Stephen thumbed through the reports. "You're right. That's all they ran. Why didn't they at least send a blood count and bleeding studies in case it was a clot instead of fat?"

Melinda shrugged.

"Sorry, I don't expect you to know what they were thinking." Stephen donned a pair of gloves. "Let's run a Virtopsy scan first. Since they didn't even do a chest x-ray, we may be able to confirm the cause of death without opening him up."

They ran the body through the scanner. When the machine finished, Stephen scrolled through the images. "Pulmonary edema . . . some cerebral edema . . . Wait. This can't be right."

"What can't?"

"Spleen and liver both show signs of failure. If he died of primary cardiorespiratory arrest, there might be some multisystem damage, but not to this extent." Stephen zoomed in on the liver. "The blood vessels are congested, suggesting hemolytic anemia."

"I sort of know a little about that, but could you explain it?"

"It's when the blood cells rupture, caused by certain drugs, infections, and autoimmune or genetic predispositions, though Tom didn't have any of those."

"Can a blood transfusion cause it?" Melinda asked, studying the ICU reports.

"Yes, a severe enough allergic reaction could. Why?"

She held up the report. "He got two units of blood when they first brought him in."

The heat drained from Stephen's face. "Oh."

Setting the report aside, Melinda stepped beside him and whispered, "I know how badly you want to make sense of this, and in your mind the sole explanation is that someone had evil intentions, but maybe that's not the case this time. It's okay to just . . . cry. Or punch the wall. Whatever you need to do."

Stephen stared at the computer screen, breathing in and out through his nose. He appreciated Melinda's support, and he understood what she was saying. What Reaper had said. Even what Ross had said. Part of him wanted to believe it. But Tom's words kept coming back to him, over and over: *If anything happens to me…*

"How much time do we have left?"

"Fifteen minutes."

He shut off the monitor. "Let's draw labs. Toxicology. Autoimmune panel. Heavy metals. I want to find the cause of death. The *real* cause of death."

Melinda gave him a look that said *You're crazy, and I'm only doing this because I must—and because I care about you.* She nodded. "Yes, sir."

The tension in her voice was palpable. It was clear she didn't know whether to speak to him as a lover or a boss. They needed to figure it out together. He respected her too much to make that decision for her.

"Hey." He leaned close enough for her to hear him whisper. "Let's talk tonight, okay? I'll go to you."

She didn't look at him as she drew blood. "Are you sure that's a good idea? You've got a lot on your plate."

"Even more reason. I'll make sure no one sees me." He took a deep breath. "I promise I'll be there."

Her lips twitched, and then she gave a slight nod.

Someone knocked on the door. Stephen and Melinda both flinched.

"Sorry to interrupt, sir," a senior airman said from the doorway. "We're here to transport Major Wilson's remains."

Stephen checked the clock. "We still have five minutes."

"We were told to come now, sir."

"All right." He whispered to Melinda, "Finish drawing the labs, while I distract them."

Stephen stripped off his gloves and marched over to the airman. "Let me see those orders."

The tech handed him a sheaf of papers. Stephen scanned them. The transfer order was signed by Colonel Agarwal, with no other signatures. That itself seemed odd. Typically, every order went through a chain of command, even for a simple purchase order for soap. There was no good reason for Agarwal to act unilaterally. Unless he wasn't.

"Everything in order, sir?"

The airman was young and tall, with ash-blond hair and striking brown eyes. In another light, she might've been a dead ringer for Sharon. The thought of his sister made Stephen's tongue numb. Sharon was a big girl and could take care of herself, but he couldn't shake the feeling that something had happened to her. *Gas... Anja...* What did it mean?

"Sir?"

He shook off his reverie and handed back the orders. "Yes, it's fine. Sergeant Stewart, can you help Airman . . . uh, Milgrom . . . transfer Major Wilson?"

"Yes, sir." Melinda came up behind him and slipped him the test tubes, then approached the airman. "Let's make sure you've got the transfer case prepped properly."

As the two headed for the door, Stephen squeezed the sample tubes. There was one person who could give him answers, and Stephen needed to find him.

27

The moment Stephen stepped inside the Gartenschau conference center, clutching his attendee bag stuffed with flyers and free comics, he felt giddy. When Edmund Brubaker had insisted on meeting somewhere public, it was like Stephen had been offered the key to Heaven. Superhero cosplayers stood at the entrance, passing out goodie bags and posing for photos. Vendor tables from local comic bookstores lined the event hall. People of all ages milled around the enormous room, some wearing street clothes, others wearing costumes of varying quality. A massive banner hung from the ceiling: *Wilkommen zu Kaiserslautern Comic-Con!*

Although his comic book collection was small, mostly Captain America runs and a few other titles, Stephen read online issues as a way of escape from the everyday routine. He no longer believed in real superheroes and villains. It was up to the average person to embody the principles of superheroes, to save themselves. Still, embracing the fantasy sent a thrill through his body.

"Herr Englehart?"

Surprised by the husky voice behind him, Stephen turned to find a scrawny young man wearing a headband over spiky blond hair, a black-and-orange windbreaker, and orange warmup pants. He'd painted what looked like whiskers on his cheeks.

"Edmund?"

The man nodded.

"How'd you know it was me?"

Edmund scoffed at Stephen's jeans and hoodie. "You may as well wear a sign on your back that says *Amerikaner*."

Stephen decided not to waste time pressing the issue. "Tom put a lot of faith in you. He said you could help me."

"Herr Wilson was very kind." Edmund shook his head sadly. "He always brought me MREs."

Stephen wrinkled his nose at the thought of the prepackaged Meals Ready-to-Eat soldiers took with them on missions. "You like those?"

"Yes, especially the chili and beans. Our restaurants always add sauerkraut." He made a sour face. "*Schrecklich*."

Stephen couldn't help but smile. "Well, I can get you all the MREs you want if the information you have is useful."

"For Herr Wilson, I would help you anyway, and I assure you, the information is quite useful. He told you what I do?"

"Not really. He said you were outside the system."

Edmund snorted. "You could say that. I am . . . how do you say? A hooker."

"Hooker?" Stephen scratched his head. "You mean hacker?"

"Yes. Hacker. I am well-known on the dark web for sneaking past the chancellor's firewalls and publishing her secret plans to cut assistance programs to refugees. Perhaps you've heard of this?"

"No."

Edmund looked disappointed, but he brightened quickly. "No matter. What's important is whether Herr Wilson told you what we were investigating."

Stephen hesitated. Could he trust this kid? What choice did he have? "He said my father was part of a military project that was abandoned thirty years ago."

Edmund nodded. "Project Super-Patriot."

"Don't bullshit me. I know we're surrounded by superheroes and . . . what the hell are you supposed to be, anyway?"

"Naruto Uzumaki."

"I don't know who that is."

"He's a famous manga character. "

"I don't read manga."

"He has his own anime series." Edmund moved into a fighting stance and said, "*Dattebayo*!"

Stephen stared at him.

"Really? Nothing?" Edmund pouted. "I thought you were a comic book fan."

"Yeah, Marvel. Some DC. Maybe a little Dark Horse." Stephen waved his hands. "It doesn't matter. You expect me to believe the US military created something that sounds like it was ripped out of a Captain America comic?"

Edmund straightened his back. "Yes, that is what I expect you to believe, because it's true. Back in the eighties, the US military was less—how shall I say?—concerned about ethics in their race to end the Cold War. They wanted super-soldiers, and they looked to comic books for inspiration. Even recently, they tried to create an armored suit based on Iron Man."

"That one I'd heard about, but I thought it looked more like a cross between a Tusken Raider and Snake Eyes from G.I. Joe."

"Yes, I thought that, also. That project failed. So did Project Super-Patriot, but I believe, as did Herr Wilson, that someone wanted it revived."

He's crazier than the Joker, the voice whispered in Stephen's mind. *Let's get out of here before he convinces you the military used a gamma bomb on Dad.*

Something about what Edmund was saying clicked with Stephen, however, and he blocked out the voice. After seeing Greenwood rise from the dead and heal a gaping wound in seconds, he couldn't afford to take anything for granted. "What makes you think that?"

"A series of code numbers Herr Wilson found in old autopsy reports."

"PSP1986. I know . . ." Stephen froze. "PSP. Project Super-Patriot. You're kidding me."

"As I said, it's the truth, and the fact Herr Wilson told you about it leads me to believe you've uncovered proof we were right."

Stephen pressed his lips together. Everything that passed through AFMES was confidential. Sharing with a non-US citizen could be considered an act of treason. But Wilson had said Edmund was the only one Stephen could trust.

"All right." He lowered his voice. "But if you leak a word about this to anyone, I'll drop an anonymous tip to the chancellor's office. Are we clear?"

Edmund smiled thinly. "*Kristallklar*."

Stephen told him about Greenwood waking up during autopsy and that he was tagged with the PSP1986 code. "And he had a cerebral implant."

Edmund's eyes widened. "Really?"

Casting another glance over his shoulder, Stephen pulled a free comic book out of his attendee bag and then bent down as if to tie his shoe. He withdrew the test tube from his sock and wrapped it inside the comic before handing it to Edmund. "It's burnt out, but Tom thought you could get something useful from it."

Edmund cradled the package as if it were a baby. Stephen half expected him to start cooing at it.

"Yes." Edmund dropped the bundle in his own attendee bag. "It may take several days, but as soon as I find something, I will call you."

"Thanks. I'll look forward to it."

After saying goodbye, Stephen started weaving through the crowd for the door. As he did, his phone vibrated. His heart jumped when he checked it. There was a message from Sharon.

Shuttle ran out of gas. Had to hitch a ride. At Baumholder now. Will update you later. Love you.

A flurry of emotions ran through him. Relief she was safe. Mild irritation over her abbreviated explanation—why hadn't she called him to pick her up? And puzzlement over that last line. She always signed off with the same phrase: *Church out.* When was the last time Sharon had written *Love you?*

He reminded himself she was probably exhausted, and maybe being so far from home was making her nostalgic for family. That had to be it. Quickly, he typed back. *Glad you're safe. Miss you.*

As he pocketed his phone, he got a creepy sense of being watched. Trying to be casual, he slowly turned his head and looked to the side.

A tall man twenty or so feet away, wearing a cheap Batman mask, turned away to peruse a booth for a German imprint.

Stephen's chest tightened. "Batman" was too far away to have overhead his conversation with Edmund, but he was clearly spying. Stephen considered trying to duck out without the man seeing him, but that wouldn't give him answers about who the man was or what he wanted. Then again, maybe he was wrong, and Batman hadn't been watching him after all.

He clenched and unclenched his fingers. What would Steve Rogers do?

Making up his mind, he resumed his exodus but pulled out his phone and turned on the camera, as if he were recording the convention for posterity. After nine steps, he continued to hold the phone in front of him and switched to the rear-facing camera. Five paces behind him, Batman veered to the left, picking up his pace.

Stephen spun around and jogged back to where the man had been. He spotted Batman trotting to the end and ducking into an exhibition hall. Stephen chased after him and turned into the same hall.

He came to a halt.

The room was dark, illuminated by various spotlights and glow sticks to recreate the atmosphere of the Batcave. Cases displayed Batman memorabilia, from a replica of Adam West's Batmobile to collector's edition comics and posters. Everyone in the room was wearing a Batman mask or costume of some kind.

Stephen searched for his pursuer. It was too dark. He filtered through the room, trying to peer past masks, but managed to gain only a few dirty looks.

There was an open door at the back of the room. He pushed his way to it and ran through, finding himself outside in an alley. He looked up and down, but it was no use. Whoever had been following him was gone.

27

Sharon awoke to a piercing headache. She jammed her palm against the side of her head, but it kept digging at her. Grating. Penetrating through her entire skull.

No, it wasn't a headache. It was . . . something else.

Voices.

That wasn't right, either. Not voices. *A* voice.

. . . time to wake up, soldier, it was saying.

The Controller. Inside her head.

Wonderful. Now she was going crazy.

You're not going crazy. The Controller's words echoed in her mind. *Merely fulfilling your duty. Now, open your eyes.*

Sharon did as the Controller ordered. She was still in the same underground chamber. The other beds were empty.

Get up.

Sharon considered resisting, but the sooner she found out what the hell was going on, the sooner she could get out of there.

Get dressed.

She was wearing a hospital gown. Her uniform lay spread out on the bed.

She hesitated, searching the room. No cameras on the ceiling, but they could be hidden.

I can only see through your eyes. Dress quickly, before the others arrive.

Shaken by the word "others," Sharon stripped off the gown and yanked on her uniform, glancing over her shoulder at every opportunity. She laced up and tied her boots, then assumed a fighter's stance.

"Where am I?" she said aloud, unsure she wanted anyone to answer.

Think of this as Officer Candidate School cubed. You are part of something bigger than you, bigger than the Army. You will serve your country in a way few have ever done. There was a long pause. *Assuming you survive.*

Footsteps thudded behind her. She whirled.

A fist crashed into her cheek. Her head jerked to one side.

Pain resounded in her head. Sharon staggered. She tried to block out the throbbing ache.

It was the Navy SEAL from the shuttle. His name tag read Byrne. His face was expressionless, eyes vacant.

"What are you doing?" She wiped blood from her mouth. "I'm not going to hurt you."

"I'm sorry." Regret rimmed his eyes. He launched himself at her, fist raised.

This time, she blocked him with her left hand, twisted, and punched his gut with her right.

The man recoiled. He snatched a broken shard of glass off a table and leaped at her.

Sharon twisted out of the way and kicked at him. He dodged, then sliced with the glass shard. She blocked again. This time, the glass sliced through her palm.

She yelped. The pain made it hard to concentrate.

You're no longer a slave to pain, the voice said. *Just say "Relief."*

"What?" She ducked. The broken glass whizzed over her head.

Say it. Relief.

"Relief. Relief!"

Ice rushed through her body, as if someone had injected menthol into her veins. The pain was gone. She could think clearly again.

Byrne was winding up for another attack.

Sharon leaped onto the bed and rebounded off it. She grabbed the SEAL by the neck and dragged him to the ground. The glass slipped from his hand and slid away across the floor.

He clawed at her hands, but she held tight.

"Stop fighting," she said through gritted teeth. "I'm not your enemy."

"You. Are." His words came out between ragged gasps. "Controller. Said."

The voice assumed a steely edge. *Finish him.*

Sharon's cheeks cooled. "Are you crazy?"

He failed. You must finish him.

"No."

Sharon released the boy and shoved him off. They both rolled to their feet.

"I'm not playing this sick game," she said. "I'm done."

Then you both lose.

Electrical current jolted through her skull. She fell to her knees. Byrne collapsed next to her.

Sharon fought back until darkness consumed her.

28

Stephen parked his BMW SUV a block away from Melinda's house, as usual. Although base housing was cheaper, living on the economy had its advantages. On base, everyone knew your business. The local Germans kept to themselves and couldn't care less what the Americans did, so long as they paid their rent and didn't have loud parties.

Once he crossed the intersecting street, he proceeded to the second house on the right and, with a glance around to ensure no one was tailing him, turned up the short driveway to a simple white block house. A plain mat lay in front of the door, welcoming in English.

A half minute after Stephen rang the bell, Melinda opened the door. Her hair was down, delicately framing her face. She wore cotton shorts and a loose-fitting USAF T-shirt that fell off one shoulder. Despite the weary expression on her face, she looked incredible. It was all Stephen could manage not to grab her right there on the stoop.

"You made it," she said flatly, her eyes never leaving his face. "I wasn't sure you would."

"I said I would."

"Yeah, well, that doesn't mean anything."

She wasn't going to make this easy. "Can I come in?"

Melinda stepped back and held the door, then shut it once he was inside.

"So, what do you . . ." She stopped and looked up at him, brow furrowed. "What's wrong? You look nervous. Did something happen to your sister?"

"No, she texted me. She's fine. It's . . ." He searched for the right words and decided to be straightforward. "Someone followed me earlier."

"What? Who?"

"I don't know. And I'm not sure why. But if someone is spying on me, then we're at higher risk than ever of being caught."

"You want to break it off."

He didn't answer. He should. It was for the best.

She flipped her hair off her shoulder and inched closer. Stephen could smell her perfume, a blend of lilac and ginger. "Are you sure that's what you want?"

"Melinda . . ."

She shushed him, touching his lips, sending jolts through his cheeks. She grazed the back of her hand over his chin.

"It's . . ." he began, but whatever he was going to say escaped him. The only thoughts that filled his mind were of her body, the feel of her nipples against his chest, the warmth of her thighs around his waist. "We need . . ."

Her lips met his. He drank in the taste of her mouth. Holding her hips, he pulled her close. Her tongue slid along his. They embraced each other for what seemed like an eternity.

Their lips parted. Melinda pulled back her head, smiling, eyes twinkling. "What do we need?"

Thoughts of implants, conspiracies, and spies vanished. He wrapped his arms around her waist and smiled back. "This."

They walked hand in hand upstairs. She opened the bedroom door and led him inside. Releasing his hand, she crossed over to the bed and lay down.

As he was removing his hoodie, a creeping sensation traveled down his neck, like he was being watched. He stopped and turned to the window, pushing aside the curtain

All he saw was the gray sky.

"You coming or what?" Melinda had removed her T-shirt and now stretched out against the pillows with her arms behind her head.

Stephen glanced once more at the window, then shook his head and let the curtain fall back into place. He was just jumpy because of what had happened at the convention center. What he needed was something to take his mind off his paranoia. And, lucky for him, it was right there in front of him.

With a leer, he ripped off his hoodie and shirt and jumped onto the bed.

29

The classical theme to Tim Burton's *Batman* filtered from a beat-up boom box. Stephen hummed along to it as he typed up a report on field endotracheal tube placement errors. He felt better than he had in a long time. Things with Melinda had been going strong the past week ever since the day of the Comic-Con. The sex was even hotter than before, their relationship intensified now that they were sharing their feelings with each other, and their secret was safe. McNiven had proven to be a godsend—his work ethic was better than Tom's, and he had a sharp eye for details that others might have missed. Reaper had promised he could stay until they found a replacement, which was taking longer than expected, but Stephen didn't mind. The best part was that Special Agent Wade had left them alone. If he'd found Corporal Greenwood, Stephen didn't know—and frankly, he didn't care so long as the man stayed out of Stephen's life.

As he reviewed what he'd written, his cell phone rang.

"May I speak to Colonel Englehart, please?" a female voice said.

"Speaking."

"This is Monika."

"Okay…?"

"I'm the night clerk from the Ramstein Inns. Bettina gave me your number."

Stephen sat up straighter in his chair. "Oh, right. I forgot."

"I only returned last night. Bettina said you were trying to find your sister."

"Yes. I mean, I was, but I've already heard from her. She texted me again yesterday, in fact, to tell me she was preparing for deployment next week."

"Oh, that's wonderful to hear. I remember your sister. Very tall and strong. Like an Amazon."

Stephen smiled. "That's her, all right. But Bettina told me she wasn't registered at your hotel."

"She wasn't. She stayed with one of our regular guests, Frau Wagner."

So, his first instinct had been right. Maybe that was why Sharon had been so cagey about where she was staying, although she wasn't one to be easily embarrassed about her sexual escapades. "Well, I'm glad someone kept her out of the storm. Thank you for calling me."

"Thank you for telling me she was okay. When Bettina told me she was missing, I became immediately concerned. First Frau Wagner, and then your sister…"

"Hold on. Frau Wagner's missing?"

"Maybe missing is the wrong word. But she left the day your sister departed and never returned to check out."

Warning klaxons sounded in the back of Stephen's mind. "Monika, would Frau Wagner's first name happen to be Anja?"

"Yes. How did you know?"

"Did Anja arrange Sharon's shuttle?"

"Yes." There was a pause. "Is something wrong? I thought you said your sister was okay."

"Yeah, I did. But now, I'm not sure." Stephen tapped his finger against his chin. "Bettina said she'd never heard of the Bundesfahr shuttle service. Have you?"

"No, and I'd never seen the driver before. But I assumed they were a new company that Frau Wagner knew about through her work."

"Why? What does she do?"

"She works for AMC."

The muscles in Stephen's neck tightened as pieces started to click together. "Thank you, Monika. You've been a big help."

After hanging up, Stephen flipped his thumb back and forth over the phone's lock screen. Whatever had happened to Anja didn't matter now. Sharon was fine. Wasn't she?

Biting his cheek, he called the number she'd texted him from.

Three tones sounded, followed by a female voice saying, *"Kein Anschluss unter dieser Nummer."* Number not in service.

The muscles in his jaw clenched. Maybe she'd gotten a new phone for deployment and forgot to tell him? He opened his email browser and sent a message: *Hey, let's talk before you ship out. Call me.*

After sending the message, he leaned back in his chair. He drummed his fingers on his desk. He checked his email. No new messages.

She's probably in the middle of exercises. She's not going to reply instantly.

He nodded to himself, toyed with his phone, and then called Baumholder.

"Major Englehart has already deployed," the tech told him after initial greetings.

"What? But she wasn't supposed to deploy for another week."

"It appears there was a change in her orders, sir. She left this morning."

"Whose orders?"

"Colonel Laskaris, sir."

"Let me speak to Colonel Laskaris."

"He's overseeing an off-post training operation, sir."

Heat flushed Stephen's face. "When will he back on post?"

"Uh, this afternoon."

"Great. Thanks."

He hung up before the tech could say anything else, and before Stephen said something he'd regret later.

Melinda appeared in his doorway. Seeing her made the madness more bearable. He smiled and started to give her a warm greeting but stopped when he saw the worried look on her face. "What's wrong?"

"The lab sent the results on Major Wilson's blood samples."

"And?"

She handed him a sheath of papers. He flipped through them, skimming over the normal labs, until he saw the one abnormal value. He looked up at her. "Is this verified?"

Melinda nodded.

His chest tightened. Things were worse than he'd thought.

According to the lab report, Major Tom Wilson had been exposed to toxic levels of arsenic.

30

What does this mean?" Melinda asked as Stephen logged in to the computer system. "I thought people got arsenic poisoning from contaminated water."

"Chronic poisoning, yes, but arsenic has no taste or odor, so a victim could ingest it without realizing it." Stephen's hands trembled as he typed. Right when he'd finally accepted Tom's death as an unpreventable complication of his injuries, this happened. He forced himself to maintain composure as he pulled up the man's inpatient records. "To cause the extensive systemic damage we saw, in such a short time, it would have to be administered in a way that bypassed regular filtering systems. Intravenous would be the fastest."

Melinda's eyes widened. "You think someone injected it into his bloodstream? But why would they want to kill Tom?"

"Isn't it obvious? He'd already gotten punished once for digging into…"

Stephen stopped talking. Someone had to know that Tom was investigating Project Super-Patriot. Special Agent Wade had said they couldn't get any information off the GoPro, but maybe he was lying. His team could've hidden a bug somewhere while they searched his office. Stephen had to be careful what he said.

"His conspiracy theories," he said at last. "And what happened with Greenwood might've shed some unwanted light on those theories. The better question than why is who?"

"What are you looking for?" Melinda leaned against his chair.

"I'm not sure yet." He skimmed through the ICU progress notes. After initial stabilization, the doctors had documented Tom's condition as stable with good prognosis. No mention of fat emboli. Tom was blood type AB+, so the risk of a transfusion mismatch was low. There were other minor blood components that could sometimes cause reactions, but not as severe as what Tom had experienced. "No one recorded any hives or itching within the first few minutes of transfusion, but then an hour later, Tom went into what looked like anaphylactic shock."

"Is that common?"

"Transfusion anaphylaxis is extremely rare. And I already checked Tom's outpatient records. He had a transfusion five years ago after a car accident and had no problems with it." Stephen clicked through the ICU records again. "They pretreated him with antihistamine just in case."

Stephen could feel Melinda's breathing rate increase. This was too much for her. He had no right to involve her in any of it.

"Hey." He turned around to face her. "Why don't you—"

"Could someone lace the donor blood with arsenic?"

The idea took root in his mind. "Yeah, they could. The blood products would carry the heavy metal to every organ, and it wouldn't get picked up on screens. How did you think of that?"

"It seemed easier than trying to sneak into his room and inject it into his IV. It gets crazy in the ICU. Everyone's running around, not paying attention to what others are doing. Whoever did it could've tainted the blood bag and passed it on without anyone noticing."

Stephen wanted to grab her by the shoulders and kiss her. "You're brilliant. If we find the lot number for the blood Tom received and trace its course to see who had their hands on it, we can figure out who did it." He searched through the medical records. "It looks like two technicians in the blood bank prepared the blood. They both cleared it on all screens. Then it was signed out for delivery to the ICU by . . ." He stared at the screen. His heart started pounding.

"By who?"

Afraid to say the name out loud, he pointed at the screen.

Colonel Agarwal. The hospital commander.

"Why would he pick up blood for a patient?" Melinda asked, following Stephen's cue to avoid saying names.

"Good question." Stephen searched through the EMR again. "He wasn't even involved in Tom's care."

"What should we do?" A worried look passed over her face. "Tell Colonel Restrepo? Call security?"

He shook his head. "We do nothing yet."

"Nothing?"

"We don't have proof he did anything. He could've been passing through the ICU when Tom coded and offered to help. For all we know, one of the technicians tainted the blood bag."

Melinda demurred. "So, what do we do?"

"First, we figure out where they could've gotten that much arsenic. Oncologists use low doses of arsenic trioxide to treat acute myeloblastic leukemia. Since cases of AML here would be rare, it shouldn't be hard to track a large amount signed out. Talk to the pharmacy. And ask McNiven to follow up on the DNA samples we sent last week."

"Where will you be?"

Stephen adjusted his uniform. "I need some answers about Sharon."

31

When Stephen arrived at the AMC desk at the Ramstein AB passenger terminal, there was a crowd waiting to check in. Families had luggage carts overflowing with bags and suitcases. Pet kennels contained barking dogs and sleeping cats. With that many disgruntled passengers, he wouldn't have much time to ask a lot of questions, so he needed to be concise and direct. He ticked off the main points in his head and stepped forward as soon as there was an opening.

"Where are you traveling today?" The clerk was a young airman with a buzz-cut. He looked bored. Or tired. Or bored and tired.

"I'm not. I'm trying to find someone." Stephen slipped a photo of Sharon out of his wallet and laid it on the counter. "Do you remember seeing this woman come through here?"

The clerk glanced at it for the smallest fraction of a second possible and shook his head. "Hundreds of people pass through here every day."

"This would've been a week ago. Her flight was rerouted due to the storm."

The clerk shuddered. "Don't remind me of that day. I was afraid for my life."

"Why?"

"This guy had a breakdown and pulled a gun on me. If it weren't for this soldier with the sickest moves I've ever seen . . ." He stopped and looked at the picture again. His eyes widened. "Hey, that's her."

"You recognize her?"

"Yeah, she was like Wonder Woman or Black Widow, you know?"

Stephen smiled. He did know. "Do you remember what she did afterward?"

"The other clerk assisted her while I talked to security."

"Was the other clerk Anja Wagner?"

"Yeah!" The airman side-eyed him. "How'd you know that?"

Stephen's fingertips tingled. "Can I talk to Anja?"

"She was a temp. Gone the next day."

"Do you know any way I can contact her?"

The airman scratched his scalp. "I think she said she usually works out of Baumholder."

"Baumholder?" Bells dinged in Stephen's mind. "You're sure?"

"Yeah, I'm pretty sure she works in Central Processing." The clerk frowned. "Why all the questions? Is she in some kind of trouble?"

"I don't know yet. But I think something may have happened to my sister." Stephen wrote *Bundesfahr* on a paper slip. "Have you ever made arrangements with this shuttle company?"

The clerk squinted at it. "Never heard of it."

"All right. Thanks." Stephen handed the clerk a business card. "If you hear from Anja, please have her call me."

As he walked away from the desk, Stephen dialed Baumholder. When the attendant answered, he asked to speak to Central Processing. It took a few minutes, but he eventually got a live person on the line. He explained who he was and that he needed to speak to Anja Wagner.

"I'm sorry," the technician said. "She's away from her desk."

"Can I leave her a message?"

"I'm afraid I can't connect anyone to her without authorization from the commanding officer."

Frustration bubbled up Stephen's gullet. Since when did he need authorization to speak to a Human Relations representative? "Who's the CO?"

"Colonel Laskaris."

Again with Colonel Laskaris. Stephen didn't even bother asking if he could speak to him on the phone. He already knew the answer. "All right, thanks."

Stephen headed for the airport exit. He knew where he had to go, and fortunately it wasn't a long drive. With any luck, he'd be back before anyone missed him at work.

His phone chirped as he unlocked his car.

There was a text message from a local number. He opened it.

I've got answers, it read. *Meet me at my house. EB.*

Stephen read the message twice more as he climbed into the driver's seat. EB. Edmund Brubaker. It had been a week since he'd given the implant to the German hacker. While it was important, as was finding Tom's killer, his sister took top priority.

He sent a quick reply to Edmund. Tonight.

Then he stuck the phone in his pocket, started his car, and began the drive to Baumholder.

32

As Stephen drove toward Garrison Baumholder, his thoughts meandered back three decades to the time before everything changed. With Dad gone so much, and Mom getting drunk in his absence, it had been up to young Steve to keep things running and to keep his little sister safe. Once, on Halloween, Sharon had insisted on taking a shortcut to where the richer houses were so they could get better candy. They'd only been in Worcester for half a year, ever since Dad got assigned to Fort Devens, and didn't know the area that well, but she'd rushed blindly ahead and stumbled across a group of teens who'd been smoking cigarettes in the woods. If Steve hadn't shown up in time to chase off the bullies right as they'd been closing in on her, who knew what might've happened to her?

A thin smile crossed his lips. That was Sharon, always shooting from the hip, while Stephen was the careful one, stopping to assess his surroundings. And yet how many times had he missed the obvious? His mother, a strong Polish woman, had hated all the time he spent boxing with Uncle Alex while Dad was gone.

"At least Alex has been here," young Steve had said defensively, bitter about Dad's recent deployment on yet another mission. "That's more than I can say for Dad."

Anger flashed in Mom's eyes, and for a moment, Steve thought she might hit him, something she'd never done before. But instead, she broke into tears.

"Your tata loves you," she said, touching Steve's cheek. "Remember that. No matter what he says or does, even if it's beyond forgiveness, never forget that he would do anything for you and your sister. Promise me?"

It had felt like spiders were crawling along Steve's back. "Why are you saying all this, Mama?"

"Promise me."

"Okay. I promise."

"Good." She'd squared her shoulders. "No more time with Alex Ross."

"But he said he'd take me to Awesome Con next week. They're supposed to have a sneak peek of the Batman movie."

"No."

"But—"

"Z choinki się urwałaś?"

Steve stared blankly at her. "Huh?"

"It's Polish. It translates to 'Did you fall out of your tree?' It means you're missing the obvious, and it shows. Ross may seem like a friend, but there's something about him I don't trust." A dark shadow passed over Mom's face. "He's putting the wrong ideas in your head with all those Captain America comic books. All that fighting. Problems aren't solved by fighting."

"But Cap is about patriotism."

"There are more important things than patriotism," she'd said. "Like family."

Now, as Stephen took the exit off the Autobahn for Baumholder, his mother's words bounced around in his head. Family was more important than anything. He'd learned that the hard way, after his parents were gone. Sharon was the only family he had left, and he wouldn't let anything else happen to her.

"Can you be less aggressive on those turns?" a rough voice said from the rear cabin.

Stephen jumped. He turned to look back.

"Face forward. Don't do anything stupid."

Adrenaline rushed through Stephen's body as he imagined who was in his car. Tom's killer? A spy? His best bet was to cooperate until he knew what he was up against.

"What do you want?" He kept his eyes on the road.

"I need your help." The voice sounded familiar. "I've been watching you. You're the only one not working for them who has a clue what's going on."

"Working for who?" Stephen fought the urge to turn around despite the warning. "I don't know what you're talking about."

"I heard you talking about your dad. He was like me. Wasn't he?"

A chill ran down Stephen's back. "Greenwood?"

"Guess I never thanked you and your buddy for waking me up, did I?"

Bile surged up Stephen's gullet. "My buddy's dead thanks to you."

Greenwood was silent for a moment. "I didn't want to hurt him. I lost control."

"You lost control?" Stephen spat the words. "Is that what happened to your teammates?"

"Yeah, it is. It's gotten harder over the past few months. But you wouldn't understand, would you?"

That struck a chord with Stephen. He saw his father's face, eyes bulging with rage, blood on his hands. He remembered his own anger for months afterward, all the trouble he'd caused until his therapist taught him to control it.

"Try me," he said.

"No time for that. I need to find Sergeant Grant, and you need to help me."

"Grant? Your team leader?"

"Yeah."

"Why do you need him? To finish him off?"

"If I wanted to kill anyone—especially you, with the way you're pissing me off—I'd have done it by now." Greenwood grunted as they rolled over a speed bump. "He knows where to find The Controller." He added stress on the word, as if it was a name, not a title. "The one who pulls the strings. He's the reason for all of this. When I find him, it all ends."

Stephen tightened his grip on the steering wheel. Greenwood didn't sound crazy or animalistic anymore. He sounded like a cold-blooded killer.

"Is Grant like you?" Stephen asked, turning onto a one-way street.

"No."

Stephen waited for Greenwood to say more, but he didn't.

"Who is this Controller?" he tried. "Is he Army? Air Force?"

"I don't know. Not even sure he's a *he*. We hear his voice in our heads, never see him. I assumed he's male, but he could be a tough-as-nails woman."

An image of Colonel Restrepo popped into Stephen's mind as he steered through a roundabout. She fit the description, and she disappeared for long periods of time. He shook it off. That was ridiculous. Reaper could be difficult to work for, but she was hardly the mastermind type. Although, she did say she'd worked with DARPA, and she'd quickly dismissed the idea that they were involved in implants or regeneration.

"Hey!"

Greenwood snapped his fingers sharply enough to make Stephen lose control of the wheel. The SUV swerved onto the curb. Stephen jerked the wheel the other direction. The vehicle veered back onto the road.

"What the fuck?" Greenwood barked. "Are you trying to call attention to us?"

"No, I was trying to process." They were nearing the garrison. There would be guards out front. Stephen could alert them, and they'd handle Greenwood. That was the smart thing to do. Except he'd seen what Greenwood could do. More likely, he'd rip the guards in half and then finish off the one who ratted him out. Stephen swallowed hard. "You're wasting your time. I don't know where Sergeant Grant is, or how to find him."

"You don't have to. Give me back the implant and I'll track him myself."

"I don't have it."

"Bullshit. I know you kept it."

"No, I didn't. I turned it over to the SPs."

Greenwood gnashed his teeth. "Why are you lying to me?"

Because you're insane, Stephen thought. He couldn't risk Greenwood harming Edmund to get that implant. "I can try to find out where Grant is."

"How?"

"Leave that to me." Stephen slowed as the front gate came into view. A line of cars waited to enter. Stephen pulled over to the curb and stopped. "As soon as we get back to Ramstein. Deal?"

Greenwood's breathing was heavy, like a bear's. "Hey, I know where we are. Why are we at Baumholder?"

"I have something to take care of. It doesn't involve you."

The man grabbed Stephen by the collar and dragged him around to face him. There wasn't a scar on his face, nothing to indicate his frontal bone had been removed, or that his jaw had been broken and dislocated. His eyes were twin glaciers rimmed by amber.

"All bases are at Force Protection Condition Bravo," Greenwood said, his voice a thunderous rumble. "They'll be conducting ID checks and random vehicle searches. How do you plan on getting me past them?"

"I don't," Stephen said. He unlocked the passenger rear door. "You're going to wait here."

Greenwood's face reddened. "You want me to hide out in the woods?"

"From the way you smell, I'm guessing that's what you've already been doing for the past week." Stephen bit his tongue. His snark helped him stay calm, but he didn't need to antagonize a soldier who could kill him with his bare hands. "As soon as I'm done, I'll come back for you. Trust me, it's the only way."

Greenwood's lip curled as he stared at Stephen for an uncomfortably long time before saying, "You better not tell anyone about me. You saw what I can do. I'll crush them, and then I'll come after you."

Stephen fought back another wiseass retort. He'd pushed it enough already. "As long as you stay out of sight, you don't have to worry. This is family business."

Greenwood's gaze burned into Stephen for several more heartbeats, hot breath flowing over his face. He wore dirty jeans and a stained black T-shirt, probably stolen from a dumpster. At last, he let go of Stephen's collar and sat back on his haunches.

"All right. But if you're not back in thirty minutes, I'm coming in after you."

Stephen nodded. He waited for Greenwood to slip out of the car and scramble into the woods before driving to the garrison's front gate, adding finding a way to get rid of Greenwood to his ever-growing list of problems.

33

The command building was simple and sparsely decorated. An American flag hung from a pole next to the yellow, black, and red stripes of the German national banner. Photos of former commanders lined the hallway. The wooden floors creaked as Stephen walked down the hall. Odors of pine and bleach filtered into his nostrils.

Stephen proceeded down the hallway, trying to hatch a plan to deal with Greenwood. There was a sliver of truth to the soldier's story that made Stephen want to help. On the other hand, the man had admitted to killing his teammates, and that was before he'd been reanimated. Who knew what he was capable of?

By the time Stephen reached the commander's suite, he was less than sure about anything. But first things first, he needed to find his sister. The rest would have to wait.

"Can I help you, sir?" The receptionist was somewhere in her forties, with dark, shoulder-length hair and too much makeup. Her mood was ten times brighter than the overhead light.

"I need to speak to Colonel Laskaris," Stephen said, trying to sound official.

"Do you have an appointment?"

"No, but it's urgent. I drove from Ramstein to talk to him."

"I'm so sorry." Her fake smile beamed, while her deadpan eyes suggested she wasn't the least bit sorry. "But the colonel has a full schedule today."

Stephen puffed out his chest, hoping she would catch the AFMES patch on his uniform. "I'm here about a recent death at Ramstein. Unless he'd rather speak to the inspector general."

The woman's eyebrows lifted like they were attached to balloons. Her eyes rolled around for a moment, and then she held up one finger before rising and entering the room behind hers.

As Stephen waited, he wondered if Laskaris would call his bluff. He had no reason to believe the colonel had anything to do with Tom's death, but he hoped Laskaris cared enough about appearances to be willing to avoid taking chances of being implicated.

A moment later, the woman reappeared, looking sheepish as she reclaimed her chair, while a man half a head shorter than Stephen emerged wearing Army service dress. Silver eagles adorned his shoulders. His close-cropped silver hair accentuated the unusual oblong shape of his skull. The man stopped next to the receptionist's desk and surveyed Stephen with cold hazel eyes, creases deepening around his nose and mouth.

"I'm Colonel Laskaris." His voice carried an accent Stephen couldn't place. "Peggy says you need to discuss something that couldn't wait."

"Yes," Stephen said, managing to feel intimidated despite having a height advantage. "That's right."

Laskaris nodded and turned back to his office, calling over his shoulder, "Come on in."

The inner office was far more ornate than the antechamber, with lush Turkish tapestries, a heavy redwood desk, and a plush leather office chair that reminded Stephen of a throne. A framed photo of Incirlik Air Base hung on the wall behind the desk. Laskaris swept through the room like a dervish and plopped into his chair, motioning for Stephen to take a far less comfortable wooden chair.

"Let's cut through the bullshit," Laskaris said before Stephen's butt touched the chair. "You're not here on AFMES business, are you?"

"Why would you say that?"

"You're Alex Ross's kid." When Stephen reacted, Laskaris laughed. "Don't act surprised. He talked about you when he pushed for funding to expand the regional medical examiner program here."

Stephen winced. "I can imagine."

"He said you're a hell of a pathologist. If we had five more of you, there'd never be another unsolved murder."

For two seconds, Stephen was too stunned to speak. "He said that?"

"He did." Laskaris took a sip of water. "He also said you're a workaholic. The only times you leave your office are when you need food, sex, or answers." He smiled thinly. "And I don't keep food in my office."

Stephen shifted in his seat. Something about Laskaris unsettled him. Maybe it was the eerie tone of his voice, making everything he said sound like a question. Or the way he rarely blinked, his gaze knifing into Stephen's mind.

"You're right," Stephen said after clearing his throat. "I'm looking for—"

"Your sister."

"How did you—"

"Like I said, Ross likes to talk. About both of you." Laskaris leaned back in his chair. "I was ecstatic when I saw orders for Sharon Englehart to take command of the First Battalion. I'd heard incredible things about her. She's a real warrior."

"That's her."

A strange look crossed Laskaris's face. "Too bad she turned out to be such a disappointment."

Stephen blinked. "What do you mean?"

"She disappeared before deployment." He snapped his fingers. "Vanished. CID is still investigating, but—and I'm telling you this out of respect for your uncle and not because you bullied your way in here—if she doesn't turn up in the next eight hours, she's officially AWOL."

The blood drained from Stephen's' face. A soldier being declared Away Without Leave was devastating. If enough time passed and they considered her a deserter, she could be arrested on sight. It didn't make sense. Where Stephen bucked authority, Sharon always played by the rules, even when they were kids. She'd never go AWOL, unless something had happened to her.

"Why didn't anyone contact me? I'm her next of kin."

"Actually, you're not. I guess you weren't aware she listed General Ross as her PADD."

Stephen started to feel lightheaded. The Person Authorized to Direct Disposition determined what to do with human remains if a service member died. "She what?"

"The Army European commander apprised Ross of the situation three hours ago." The corner of Laskaris's upper lip curled back. "I'm surprised he didn't already tell you. I guess you two aren't as close as he claims."

Stephen's fingertips dug into the wooden arms of the chair. He and Ross hadn't spoken since their cafeteria conversation a week ago. After Stephen received the message from Sharon that she was okay, he'd forgotten to inform Ross. Was this payback?

"No," Stephen said at last. "Maybe not."

"Well, at least you saved our investigators a phone call. Maybe you can shed some light on your sister's actions." Laskaris leaned forward, hands clasped together on the desk, brow furrowed. "When you last spoke to her, did she give you any indication she was planning to desert? Did she mention any conversations with religious extremists?"

This discussion wasn't going the way Stephen had expected. He'd planned to ask the questions, not the other way around. "No. Nothing like that. We didn't even talk. I—I was busy working and forgot to drive her to the airport."

Laskaris's cheek twitched. "So, she was mad at you. Does she tend to be irrational when angry?"

"No, the opposite. She doesn't let anger or fear control her actions. If anything, she channels those emotions into ingenuity. And she follows her own moral code to guide her actions."

"So, what would cause her to violate that code?"

Stephen stared at Laskaris. Was he imagining it, or had the colonel grown an inch while they were talking? He shook his head, both in answer to the question and to shake away the ridiculous thought.

"Only if she thought she had to, in order to save someone else. Once, before our parents died, she lied to Mom, saying she broke a lamp that I'd broken. She didn't believe in lying. But she did it because she knew I'd get a whupping for it, and she just got sent to her room."

Something clicked in Stephen's mind. "Is anyone else MIA? Maybe Sharon is trying to help them."

"That's a lovely, romantic thought. But no. No one else is missing."

"Are you sure? When I called last week, they told me there were others who missed the base shuttle. Did they show up when they were supposed to?"

The snarky grin slid away from Laskaris's face. His gaze sharpened. "I don't like your tone."

"And I don't like being stonewalled." Stephen sat up straighter. "Last week, no one at Baumholder or Stuttgart had any idea where Sharon was, each insisting the other was responsible for her. Then today I found out she was being deployed a week early, under your orders. Isn't it possible, Colonel, that Sharon didn't disappear, but someone under your command made a mistake? Maybe she's on another base and they forgot to log her in correctly."

Laskaris's eyes continued to burn into Stephen. "It's possible. We're still in transition, and half of the support staff is cross-training. I'll investigate it."

Stephen felt a rush of adrenaline. He'd managed to redirect the tide and get a CO to admit the military machine wasn't perfect. Maybe he could press his luck a little more. "There's a woman working here who I believe arranged the private shuttle for Sharon. Her name is Anja Wagner."

Laskaris frowned. "Miss Wagner no longer works for us."

"But I called Central Processing this morning. They said she was away from her desk, and I needed clearance from you to speak to her."

"That's because she was packing up to ship out. She was caught manipulating personnel files for personal gain. I'm afraid I can't go into more detail than that."

The room seemed to tilt off-kilter. "If she was altering files, couldn't she be responsible for misdirecting Sharon? I need to talk to her."

"Impossible. She's in Frankfurt, being detained by the Bundespolizei for questioning. Their process is ten times slower than ours, if you can believe it."

I don't believe it. Laskaris seemed too eager to get rid of him. Maybe it was because he didn't want to deal with the matter, or maybe he was hiding something. There didn't seem to be anything to gain by pointing fingers, though, not when Greenwood was waiting outside the gate for his return. He stood and held out his hand. "Well, please have someone call me directly if you find out anything about Sharon. Thank you for your time."

Laskaris stared at Stephen's hand like he'd been offered a pile of dog shit. Then he stood and squeezed it hard enough that the small bones ground together. In a low voice, Laskaris said, "We'll find her. But, if she is a deserter, she'll face the maximum penalty under the Uniform Code. And your uncle won't get her out of it."

Laskaris released Stephen's hand and then sat back at his desk to read through a report without another glance up. Massaging his hand, Stephen turned to go. As he did, he noticed a four-by-six framed photo on the colonel's desk of a stunning dark-haired woman. He was about to ask about her when his phone rang.

It was McNiven. "You need to get back here."

"Did you find something in the DNA report?"

"No. Well, sort of, but not what you were expecting."

"What do you mean?"

"It doesn't matter. Reaper wants to talk to you."

Stephen lowered his voice as he left the command office. "Why? What happened?"

"She won't say, but she's pissed off." McNiven paused. "I think you're in big trouble."

34

Forty minutes later, Stephen knocked on Reaper's door even though it was wide open, then stood outside, waiting at attention. He'd never felt forced to follow strict military protocol in any of his other duty assignments, but Reaper demanded it. And until he could be certain she wasn't this Controller he'd been told about, he needed to avoid painting more of a target on himself than he already had.

Reaper sat at her mahogany desk, back straight while she typed on her computer. An American flag perched overhead in a wooden frame.

"Enter," she said without looking up.

He stepped inside and started for the empty chair nearest him.

"Close the door."

The skin behind Stephen's ears tightened as he complied. Reaper always made a big deal about her open-door policy.

"Sit."

She continued typing silently as he sat. Tension rushed up the back of his neck. Did this have to do with the DNA samples he'd sent? Did she know he'd tested Corporal Kirby without authorization?

"What's going on?" he asked. "McNiven said—"

Her hand shot out, palm forward. When he closed his mouth, she lowered her hand and returned to typing.

Stephen's heart thudded. Reaper was sweating him out. But what did she want? A confession? No, there was something else. Besides the computer, the only other object on her desk was a picture of her kids: a lanky, mop-headed boy in his late teens and a freckly ginger girl who appeared to be middle-school-aged. They smiled at the camera as if enjoying the best time of their life, but something about their eyes suggested that it was a lie, that they were putting forth appearances while covering up something darker.

Stephen dabbed a fingertip at the corner of his eyes and looked again. Now, they looked sincerely happy. Had he imagined their secretive looks? Or was he projecting his own feelings?

Reaper rotated the photo away and then typed a single key on the keyboard. Rich orchestral music filtered through speakers mounted on the four office walls: deep cellos and light violins.

"Samuel Barber's 'Adagio for Strings.'" Reaper turned to face him. "Made popular by the movie Platoon. One of my favorites. You don't want to miss this part."

She touched her keyboard again. The volume shot up. Cello strings reverberated. The violins wailed, assaulting Stephen's ears.

Reaper crooked her finger. He leaned forward.

"This room is bugged," she said, loudly enough for him to hear. "Don't react to what I have to say, or I'll shut off the music and say it anyway. Nod if you understand."

Stephen bristled but nodded.

She tapped her index fingers together, a habit that always got under Stephen's skin.

"You've been digging into Major Wilson's death against my orders. Why?"

There was no point in denial. "Virtopsy showed signs of hemolytic anemia that didn't fit the proposed mechanism of death, so I ran additional studies. They came back positive for arsenic."

"It could've been a lab error."

"That would mean the lab seriously fucked up."

"True, but that's better than what you're implying. Do you have a suspect?"

Stephen bit his inner cheek. How could he tell her that Colonel Agarwal, the base commander, was a suspect? But then, so was she. "Not yet, but I asked Melinda to see if anyone requisitioned arsenic trioxide in the past month."

Reaper stopped tapping her fingers. "Smart. But you didn't tell anyone else about this?"

"No."

"You didn't think to come to me?"

He hesitated. What could he say? That he didn't trust her?

She waved her hand. "Never mind. I want you to drop your investigation."

His gut clenched. "But I—"

"That's not a request." She opened a folder on her desk and shuffled through a ream of loose papers. "I distinctly remember ordering you to stay away from anything dealing with Foxtrot Team, yet you violated that order. Didn't you?"

Stephen reattempted a look of confusion. "Of course not."

She rolled her eyes and held up a paper. "Do you think I'm an idiot? You sent fingernail samples from a soldier whose hands were burned off."

Stephen's cheeks grew hot, but he said nothing.

"Well," she continued, "your efforts were fruitless. It came back classified. You've got nothing."

The news deflated Stephen, but he didn't let it show on his face. Besides, what he had was an enhanced super-soldier stowed away in his basement. Deciding he was better off keeping Greenwood where he could keep tabs on him than leaving him to his own volition, Stephen had stopped at his house on his way back from Baumholder, leaving the corporal with clean clothes, food, and a television until he figured out what to do with him. Stephen had questions about Project Super-Patriot he hoped Greenwood could answer once he'd taken care of other business. Stephen had hidden his laptop in his SUV, fearing Greenwood might use it to search official websites and trigger alarms, or worse, find something in Stephen's personal files to use against him. True, if Greenwood wanted to hurt him, he could've easily done something already, but the idea of housing someone so dangerous left Stephen uneasy.

Worse was the thought that Reaper was behind it. If she was the Controller that Greenwood had talked about, it would be both in her interest and a simple matter to block access to DNA records. Rather than discouraging him, it made him more curious about what those files contained.

"Besides," she continued when he didn't respond. "You've got more going on in your personal life that should take precedence, don't you? I understand your sister is missing."

"How—?"

"You should've come to me right away," she said without answering his unfinished question. "I still have connections. I can have them trace everywhere she went, from the moment she arrived, to the time she disappeared. Is she the type who would desert her post?"

"Not at all. She's the most dedicated soldier you've ever seen."

"So, she follows orders without question?"

"No, she believes in taking down bullies and defending those who can't defend themselves. That's what's driven her ever since we were kids, after our parents . . ." Alarms sounded in his head. "Why are you asking me questions about Sharon's personality?"

The corner of her mouth drifted upward into the barest hint of a smile. "You think I'm so distracted by political affairs that I have no idea what goes on here, don't you? A self-removed leader. Isn't that what you called me?"

Stephen's tongue swelled. "I never said—"

"I know I haven't been around much. Maybe I have been relying on you to take the reins. That's what a leader is supposed to do. Train. Delegate. Groom a deputy to one day take over as commander."

Stephen bit down on his back teeth.

"Except that's not what you want, is it? You have no intention of accepting promotion. You're counting the days until you can get the hell out of Dodge."

Stephen swallowed. Had he been that obvious?

"That's why I don't understand why you're doing everything you can to jeopardize your retirement. Tampering with classified information, running your own unauthorized investigations to satisfy some personal vendetta..."

"Vendetta? I'm not looking for revenge. I want to stop this guy before he hurts anyone else."

"But, as I said, that's not your job. You're a pathologist. A damned good one. Which is why I don't want to see you throw away your career over this."

Her tone of voice made Stephen's skin crawl. "What do you mean?"

She removed an envelope from a desk drawer and slid it in front of Stephen. Puzzled, he searched her face for some giveaway of what he was about to find as he opened the envelope and slid out a glossy photograph. His chest tightened.

He recognized Melinda's white furniture set, the pink floral bedspread in a heap on the floor. There was a reflection in the image, as if shot through a window. On the bed, he could make out Melinda, lying underneath Stephen.

"Where—where did you get this?"

"That's not really your question, is it?"

He looked up at her again. Her expression seemed chiseled from stone, giving away nothing, but her eyes shifted from side to side, searching for his reaction.

"How long have you known?" he asked.

"Four months. As my children can tell you, I know everything that happens in my house."

He tightened his fists as if he could grasp some last vestige of control over the situation. "What are you going to do about this?"

"Nothing. At least, not if you drop this Melvillian quest for information about something you neither understand nor have any reason to know about." She folded her hands together again. "So, Stephen, what's your move?"

35

Thirty-three years earlier

A monitor beeped nonstop.

Three weeks into treatment for what the military doctors had some complicated name for but was just cancer, Steve barely even noticed it anymore. It meant his IV line was clogged, or the battery in the pump was low, or sometimes it didn't mean anything at all. Eventually, a nurse would come turn it off. Steve continued reading the latest issue of Captain America Uncle Alex had dropped off.

"Whatcha reading, son?"

Steve looked up at the sound of his father's voice. He blinked several times, unsure whether it was really Captain Isaiah Englehart standing in the doorway, wearing a black T-shirt and jeans, or if it was another one of the hallucinations he'd had since starting the treatment.

"Dad?"

"I got here as soon as I could."

"Soon as you could?" Steve scowled. "I've been here six weeks."

"I know. I wanted to come earlier, but—"

"But you had to finish your mission." Steve tossed aside the comic book and crossed his arms. "It's always about the mission."

Dad frowned. "What I'm doing is important."

"Aren't I important?"

Dad winced.

"The doctors say I'm getting better," Steve said. "But these treatments make me feel like I'm burning on the inside. I don't know how much more I can take."

"You'll get through this."

"And what if I don't?" Tears crept under Steve's eyelids. He fought them back. "What if I die, and you're not here? Will your mission be *worth it?*"

Dad's eyes flared. His skin took on a purplish tint. Steve tensed, remembering all the times that Dad had gotten so angry, he seemed close to knocking down a wall with his bare hands.

But instead, the man closed his eyes and took a deep breath. The purple faded from his skin. He crossed the room to dig under a pile of clothes. When he returned, he laid a box on Steve's bed. It was the Tactico game.

"Let's play, son."

Steve used the strategies his father had taught him. Dad countered at every turn. Steve tried attacking with one of his high-ranked pieces, but Dad easily defeated him. Steve tried to lure him into a bomb, but Dad dodged it.

Frustration bubbled under Steve's skin. His veins flooded with lava. He wanted to smash the game board and everything in the room.

But then, as he studied the board, he realized he still had one move, a dangerous one he hadn't tried. His father was watching him, silently, his expression giving away nothing. The anger ebbed. Steve picked up his general and used it to attack one of his father's pieces. His father's eyebrows drifted upward as Steve captured a miner.

"That was careless." Dad picked up another piece and attacked Steve's general. "My admiral beats your general."

Steve smiled but didn't move.

"Why are you smiling?" Dad asked.

Instead of answering, Steve turned around the piece that had been next to his general. The spy.

"My spy captures your admiral." Steve's grin widened. "And I still have my admiral."

Dad stared at the game board. Then he laughed. "See? I told you: you can handle yourself. How did you plan that?"

Steve shrugged. "It was the only move I had left."

Nodding, Dad said, "Desperation sometimes calls for heroic measures. But don't count on Hail Marys. There's always time to strategize." He clapped Steve on the shoulder. "Remember to look at the whole game board. And never give up."

36

As Stephen drove off base and turned onto the main road through Kaiserslautern, checking his rear-view mirror every thirty seconds to ensure no one was following him, he replayed his conversation with Reaper. He'd made a deal to stop asking questions about Foxtrot Team and to end his relationship with Melinda. In exchange, she would lock the photos away and keep his policy violations secret. It was a simple play, pretending to go along with the program, but Stephen had made a point of not saying anything about Greenwood or the implant.

Questions buzzed in his head as he drove. Who had taken the photos of him and Melinda? Did Reaper have a spy? Why was she so curious about Sharon? Everything felt wrong, but there was one person who could help him find answers.

When he arrived at the small town of Erlenbach, Stephen hoped he was making the right move. He'd been more careful now, checking under his car for bombs or tracking devices, glancing in mirrors and windows for tails, and scanning ceilings for hidden cameras and microphones. If someone was spying on him, he needed a spy of his own.

He pulled into the long driveway of a small farmhouse, behind a beat-up pick-up truck. As he got out of his car, the stench of manure struck his nostrils, making his stomach heave. He covered his nose with his arm and rushed to the front door.

An old woman cracked the door open. Stephen took a step back in surprise.

"Ja? Können ich Sie helfen?"

"Uh, Ich . . . Kennen Sie..." Stephen fumbled. Had he gotten the address wrong? The German words escaped him, so he gave up and spoke in English. "I'm looking for Edmund."

The woman nodded and opened the door, waving him in silently. He stepped into a hallway painted a bright lemon yellow, lined with black-and-white photos. Most were of a child with wild hair and an impish grin. In some, the child was building robots and working on computers. As Stephen reached the more recent portraits, he recognized Edmund's face.

The hallway ended at a T-intersection. The old woman pointed at a door on the right and then disappeared into what Stephen assumed by the aromas of pork and cabbage to be the kitchen.

Stephen opened the door and walked down a flight of stairs, his footsteps thudding on the hard pine. The air smelled musty, with a trace of ozone.

"Hallo," Edmund called from a workbench, where he was soldering what looked like a computer board. "I see you met Mum."

"Yes. She seems . . . nice."

Computers of varying age and model lined the basement, interspersed with devices and gadgets Stephen couldn't identify. The monitors all had the same screen saver: rotating screenshots from the movie *Wargames*.

"How are you able to do what you do from here?" Stephen asked, inspecting a computer stack that looked better suited for a military intelligence operation than a small-town hacker. "I'm surprised you even have internet."

Edmund chuckled as he set down the soldering iron and took a swig of Spezi. "There is a radio station not far from here. I spliced into their DSL to boost my own signal. It also helps to mask my IP address. But my download speed is, like most of the country, pathetically slow. Do you have what I requested?"

Stephen slid the backpack off his shoulder and set it on the workbench. He unzipped it and pulled out several brown-wrapped packages.

"*Wunderbar*." Edmund hugged the packages to his chest. He sifted through them, and his face fell. "Really? The chicken fajita? Are you trying to kill me?"

"That was all I could find in the storage room. They haven't restocked since the last mission."

Edmund tossed the chicken fajita package in a trash can. "At least you got two chili and beans. You want me to show you what I've found?"

"Actually, I have another favor to ask first."

Edmund's eyebrows rose. "The first help paid a debt to Herr Wilson. Anything else will cost you."

"What's your price?"

"Five thousand euros."

"Five thousand?" Stephen stared at him. "Are you nuts?"

"If you don't like it, you can find someone else."

Haggling had never been Stephen's strength. And he had enough squirreled away for his retirement—if he didn't get court-martialed. "Fine."

"Good. What do you need?"

"Access to the Armed Forces DNA registry. I need the results of some tests that came back classified."

Edmund scoffed. "Why can't you request this information yourself?"

"Someone doesn't want me to have it." Stephen made sure his tone of voice carried the seriousness of the situation. "I believe the soldiers involved are part of Project Super-Patriot."

After a moment of silent staring, Edmund turned away and dug through a pile of technical equipment. He picked up a bulky, box-shaped object, studied it, tossed it aside, and rifled through the pile some more.

"I'll get you the money as soon as you get me the information," Stephen said, hoping Edmund's attention span hadn't moved onto something else.

"Keep it. Aha!" He pulled out a pinky-sized black rectangle and handed it to Stephen. "Insert this into any workstation at your DNA registry for one full minute. It'll install a backdoor protocol that will allow me to search their directories without restriction. The only way they can discover it is if they know to look for it, but by then, the software will have self-destructed. You need to tell me as soon as it's installed. I'll have a two-hour window to work."

"You don't want to get paid?"

"Of course I want to get paid. But if this is part of exposing Project Super-Patriot, then it still falls under my debt to Herr Wilson." Edmund crooked his finger and headed to the far end of the workbench. "That is the highest priority."

"What exactly did Tom do for you?" Stephen asked as he followed Edmund.

"That's a long story that I will tell you someday." The man picked up a small metal box. "But first, I need to show you this."

"What is it?"

Edmund opened the box, revealing the cerebral implant Stephen had removed from Greenwood's brain.

"I already know what that is," Stephen said. "I gave it to you."

"Patience. Look here."

The young hacker plucked it from the box with two fingers and flipped it upside down. Using a thin pair of tweezers, he removed a tiny plate, exposing the inner circuitry.

"What am I supposed to be looking at?"

"Not that. This."

Edmund held up the plate and rotated it. Now, Stephen could see something written on the inner cover.

"A serial number," Edmund said before he could ask. "I tracked it to a biotech company in Wolfstein called Avant-garde Intelligente Medizin."

"That's great." Stephen felt a rush of hope. "Let's contact them and find out what this is."

"We can't."

"Why not?"

"Because the company burned to the ground three years ago. Someone didn't want the technology out there."

"So it's a dead end."

"Not necessarily. I found a buried news brief that the company had signed a contract with DARPA six months before the lab was destroyed."

Stephen's cheeks cooled. "So DARPA was involved. You think they destroyed the lab and stole the technology?"

"The company never announced they were working on cerebral implants. The only ones who could've known were employees and contractors affiliated with them." Edmund took another sip of Spezi and offered it to Stephen, who declined. "If we knew someone at DARPA, or another biotech company, we could open a backdoor into their network and trace these serial numbers, find out if they were being used anywhere else."

"I know someone who used to work at DARPA," Stephen said, "but she may be behind the current iteration of Project Super-Patriot."

Edmund gave a look like Stephen had announced he was an alien in disguise. "You know who's behind Super-Patriot?"

"That's not what I said."

Stephen explained to Edmund what Greenwood had told him about the mysterious Controller and about Reaper's threats. Edmund drank it in as if listening to the story of Creation. When Stephen finished, Edmund polished off his Spezi in one gulp and tossed the bottle into the trash. He stuck his hands in his pockets and stared at the floor for what seemed to be an interminable amount of time before asking, "She told you to stop investigating Herr Wilson's death?"

"Yes."

Silently, Edmund walked over to one of his monitors. He unlocked the screen saver and opened a dialogue window. With a few keystrokes, he pulled up a series of images.

"What's this?" Stephen asked, moving closer. They were black-and-white photos of a hallway from an aerial view. A gurney was parked on one side.

"Security footage from your base hospital," Edmund said. "The day after Herr Wilson died, I broke into the system and copied the data to my hard drive. It's good that I did, because the following day, it had all been erased. This is the hall outside Herr Wilson's ICU room." He pressed a key and then pointed at the screen. "Watch."

Nurses and doctors raced on- and off-screen. The movement made Stephen dizzy.

"Here you are leaving the ICU." Edmund pointed at the screen as an image of Stephen scurried down the hall. Moments later, a woman in uniform marched up the hallway. Edmund froze the screen. "Do you recognize her?"

"Yes. That's Colonel Restrepo. She never told me she'd visited Tom."

"Perhaps there is much she hasn't told you." Edmund pressed a key, and the video began playing again. Reaper left Tom's room. A minute later, another figure approached, wearing civilian clothes. Edmund hit pause. "What about him?"

"That's Special Agent Wade."

Edmund pointed at the screen. "Watch."

The video moved forward. Within seconds, nurses and doctors ran into the hall, heading to Tom's room. Stephen spotted McNiven as he sprinted down the hall to join them, recalling the pathologist saying he'd tried to help. Moments later, Wade slipped into the hallway and slinked away.

Stephen's stomach fluttered. Wade and Reaper had both visited Tom moments before he went into shock. Either of them—or both—could've been responsible.

"Colonel Agarwal wasn't there," Stephen said, mesmerized by the screen. "So why was his name on the blood bag requisition?"

Edmund's brow furrowed. "I don't understand."

"Never mind. Can you do background checks on Restrepo and Wade? If they had criminal records, they would've been expunged before they joined the military, but maybe there's something that would give us a lead."

"Of course. I'll let you know what I find."

Edmund snapped a photo of the implant's serial number with his phone and an external macro lens, and then another of the implant. His finger flew across the touchscreen. A moment later, Stephen's phone beeped. An on-screen message asked him to accept a file from Edmund. When he did, the images of the implant and its serial number filled the screen.

"Show your boss those photos." Edmund snapped the metal cover back onto the implant. "If she is not dirty, she can help us find answers from DARPA."

"And if I'm right about her?"

"Then you won't be telling her anything she doesn't already know."

"But then she'll know I know."

"And you'll know she knows you know." Edmund waved his hand. "It's very confusing, but you know she has someone spying on you. You must assume she has everywhere bugged—your workplace, your home, your girlfriend's home. Which means she already knows everything you know, except what we've discussed here." He handed Stephen a small black device. "Use this to scan your house for listening devices. If you find any, bring them to me."

"If I tell her about the implant, it'll confirm I know about Project Super-Patriot."

"Yes, but it also suggests you trust her. Play dumb. Make her believe you're nothing more than an *Einfaltspinsel*—a patsy, I think you say—who stumbled onto something big and needs her help to make it go away. The fact she showed you those photos instead of eliminating you like Herr Wilson suggests she is hoping this is the case."

Stephen boggled. "How do you know so much about espionage?"

Edmund indicated a stack of German-edition paperbacks. "I read many Vince Flynn novels. Which reminds me . . ."

The hacker crossed the room and shoved aside a file cabinet, revealing a hidden door. He opened it and reached inside. "This house was used as part of the resistance in World War II. I've managed to uncover some, but not all, of its secrets." He withdrew a small package wrapped in burlap, set it aside, and then concealed the door again. "Herr Wilson gave me this for safekeeping. I believe he would want you to have it."

"What is it?"

"You tell me. I never opened it."

Puzzled, Stephen unwrapped the package to find a set of glass microscope slides. A chill ran down his back. The date on the top slide was from 1989.

"Jesus, Tom," he murmured. His friend must've stolen the slides from Dover. If Stephen got caught with them, he wouldn't have to worry anymore about early retirement—he'd face court-martial.

"What about you and your mom?" Stephen asked. "You're risking a lot getting in the middle of this."

"I have many ways to conceal my location." Edmund gave him a stern look. "And I trust you to keep my secret."

37

Stephen was on full alert as he strode into the hospital the next morning. Every eye seemed to be watching him, every ear listening, as his boots clacked on the polished tile floor. When he'd arrived home, he discovered Greenwood was gone and hadn't even left a note. It was just as well, since Stephen had forgotten his promise to look for Sergeant Grant. The thought of a bloodthirsty super-soldier wandering the streets sent a shiver down Stephen's back, but if he contacted the authorities, he'd be the one behind bars for harboring a fugitive. And he had other things to deal with, anyway.

Edmund's bug-sniffer had worked as promised. Stephen found listening devices in his living room and kitchen. He neutralized the living room one by leaving his TV on, and carefully deactivated the kitchen one, which he kept in his SUV for now. His cell phone, at least, was clean. The thought of his privacy being invaded rankled him, but he didn't have time to brood over it. Now that he knew Tom had been right all along, he needed to find the truth so his friend's death wouldn't be in vain.

When Stephen arrived at the AFMES office, carrying a manila folder, McNiven was at the main computer terminal, reviewing Virtopsy images. Melinda was running inventory. Reaper was nowhere in sight. McNiven looked surprised to see Stephen. Melinda fidgeted in her chair.

"I didn't think you were coming in." The major switched off the monitor. "Restrepo said you were taking personal leave."

"Did she?" Stephen wondered what other lies Reaper was telling about him. "I changed my mind. Work helps me think more clearly."

"Sorry about those reports," McNiven said. "That's the first time I've ever been denied access."

"Same here." Stephen forced a grin. "Maybe we stumbled onto alien DNA from Area 52."

"I heard you read too many comic books," McNiven said. "Well, is there anything else I can help you with?"

Stephen turned to Melinda. "Sergeant Stewart, did you find out anything from the pharmacy?"

"Only that they ran out of arsenic trioxide two weeks ago," she replied without looking up from her work. "And it's still on backorder."

"Arsenic trioxide?" McNiven's eyebrows lifted.

"Tom's labs came back with high levels of arsenic," Stephen said.

"And you think someone poisoned him?"

Stephen nodded.

McNiven eyed him. "Who do you think did it?"

"I don't know yet." Stephen squeezed his fists, hoping he was doing the right thing by disclosing this to the major. "It would help if we could figure out who had access to both Tom and a supply of arsenic trioxide."

"I'm on the hospital's Environmental Standards committee," McNiven said. "I've got full access to data tracking heavy metal exposures and medical use. I could see if anyone's used arsenic within the past two months."

"That'd be great. Thanks."

After McNiven left, Stephen scanned the ceiling for spy devices. His heart jumped as he noticed a half-dome light. Had that always been there? He tried to remember. Yes, he thought it had, but he wasn't sure. He couldn't take chances.

"Sergeant Stewart." He held out the manila folder, keeping his voice firm and direct. "I need you to run this requisition to the lab. We need more lab slips in case of computer failure."

She tilted her head as she accepted the folder, giving him a questioning look, but a second later her eyebrows rose, and she tucked the folder under her arm. "Yes, sir. Right away."

After she left, Stephen avoided looking at the ceiling and went to the small lab. Thank goodness Melinda had followed his lead. The note he'd stashed inside the folder would explain what he needed her to do with the attached flash drive. He hated sticking her in such a risky position, but if she got caught, she could say she was following orders, giving him time to come up with a better story.

He pulled an envelope out of his pocket and withdrew a glass slide labeled IE, 1989. His chest tightened. IE. Isaiah Englehart.

As he positioned the slide under the microscope, he struggled to breathe. Reviewing his father's autopsy report had been difficult enough. To see the actual histopathology felt like opening a window into a part of his father's life he'd never dreamed he would find. Forcing himself to stay calm, he peered through the eyepiece and adjusted the focus.

The cells showed similar changes to those he'd seen in Greenwood's brain tissue: larger size, thicker walls, and denser mitochondria. But no sign of cell replication.

His cell phone rang. He jerked his head back in surprise and banged his forehead against the eyepiece. Cursing, he rubbed the sore spot and picked up the phone.

"Don't hang up."

Stephen recognized the gruff voice. Greenwood. Careful not to mention the soldier's name, he said, "Where are you?"

"Doesn't matter. I need you to do something for me."

"I'm not doing—"

"Go to the ICU."

"What? Why?"

"Because I need you to visit a patient." Greenwood grunted. "Sergeant Gardner Grant. He's been here the whole time."

38

Stephen kept his head down and tried to act casual on the way to the ICU. His mind raced to process his phone conversation with Greenwood.

"What do you mean he's here?" Stephen had asked.

"He's been in a coma with no ID. He awoke today and told them his name. I can't get on base, so I need you to talk to him. He'll know where to find The Controller."

"Why would he know when you don't?"

"I remember telling him during the mission, but I can't remember what I told him. My memory's still spotty."

As calmly as he could muster, Stephen asked, "Do you remember killing your teammates?"

"No, but I can't stop picturing their faces. I know I killed them, and the pain won't go away. The only way it'll stop is by taking out The Controller."

"Revenge won't bring you peace."

"What kind of soldier do you think I am? Yeah, I want The Controller to pay, but this is about keeping him from hurting the others."

"What others?"

"Right before the last mission, he told us we were the first wave of recruits. When we returned, there would be more. A lot more."

Stephen's mouth went dry. More recruits meant more potentially psychotic super-soldiers. "How was he going to recruit them?"

"Same way he got us. Make them disappear in transit to their new duty assignments so it looked like they went AWOL."

AWOL. The word bit into Stephen's mind. His heart stopped beating for a full second.

Sharon.

That had been all Stephen needed to agree to Greenwood's request. If Sharon was in The Controller's grip, he would do whatever was necessary to save her. But now, as he approached the ICU and spotted the SP standing guard outside Grant's room, he regretted not coming up with a more solid plan.

The guard squinted as Stephen held out his ID badge. "AFMES?"

"Armed Forces Medical—" Stephen began.

"I know what it means, sir. What business do you have with Sergeant Grant?"

"Four of his teammates died last week. I have reason to believe the sergeant can provide details to clarify the cause of death."

The guard scowled. "I'll have to clear it with Special Agent Wade."

No way would Wade okay his talking to Grant. Stephen puffed out his chest and projected as much authority as possible. "Airman, I have five more cases awaiting me, but I took the time to come and save OSI the trouble of obtaining a statement from Sergeant Grant. Now, if you want to waste time calling Wade, you can, but you'll be delaying a vital death investigation."

The guard's expression wavered, his eyes darting from side to side, then he waved Stephen forward. "Go ahead, sir."

When Stephen entered the room, he found a young man sleeping. One side of his face was covered in burn scars.

Stephen laid a hand on the sergeant's shoulder. "Sergeant Grant?"

Grant's hands flew up to protect his face, balling into fists. He thrashed and shouted, "Get away, you monster!"

"Easy, easy." Stephen spoke in hushed tones. "You're safe. You're at Ramstein Medical Center."

The confusion bled from the sergeant's eyes. He blinked several times as he tried to focus on Stephen's face. His gaze dropped to Stephen's hospital ID.

"Sorry, Doctor." Now that Grant was calm, Stephen heard the hint of a Kentucky drawl. "I thought I was still in the desert."

"You've been in a coma for a week."

Grant's face contorted, and then he looked up with wide eyes. "My team. I need to help them."

"I'm afraid they're dead."

The sergeant slumped against his pillow. "I was their team leader. I was supposed to take care of them."

"Can you tell me what happened?"

Grant side-eyed him. "What kind of doctor did you say you are?"

"Medical examiner."

"Aren't you supposed to wait until I'm dead?"

"I'm investigating what happened to your team. There were . . . unusual findings." Stephen cleared his throat. "I hoped you could shed light on them."

Grant stared at the bedsheets, slowly breathing in and out through his nose, and then he looked back at Stephen. "You mean Greenwood."

Stephen nodded.

"I knew he was trouble from the moment he joined us." Grant shook his head. "Deodato and I served two tours together, and Kirby and Romita had been in the same unit on one of those tours. This was going to be my first mission as team leader, and we'd been training together for two weeks, until . . ."

"Until what?"

"Until Lance Corporal Miller got caught buying hashish from a local merchant." Grant groaned. "Can you believe it? We had ourselves a real-life Lance Corporal Schmuckatelli."

Stephen smiled inwardly at the familiar term for an enlisted service member who made a bonehead mistake. "So, Corporal Greenwood replaced him?"

"Yeah, but it was weird." A dark cloud passed over Grant's face. "He appeared out of nowhere. No troop transports in or out for nearly two weeks, and suddenly he's there."

"Maybe he was already there?"

"None of the other guys ever saw him, either." Grant shook his head. "A guy like that would be hard to forget. He always seemed to be looking through us. And he never slept. The night before the mission, I caught him awake, cleaning his rifle. He said he was keeping sentry, but I swear he was watching us sleep."

"Was he just creepy? Or did he do anything else that seemed . . . off?"

"Off?" Grant erupted into choking laughter. "Everything about him was off. He kept wandering away on his own, ignoring me, claiming he was following someone else's orders. We caught him talking to himself a dozen times."

Stephen recalled Greenwood trying to reach The Controller through the implant. "Any unusual . . . abilities?"

"Not right away, but on the mission . . ." Grant swallowed hard. "Yeah."

"Tell me about it."

"It was supposed to be simple recon. Scope out an abandoned airfield to see if we could use it as a forward operating base and report back. Easy-peasy. In and out." Grant exhaled. "But we were ambushed by insurgents. They hammered us with mortars and bullets. Took out the tires on our Humvee. Clipped Kirby in the side, but he stayed up top, manning the M2 cannon. I called in for a raptor to extract us, but Greenwood had other plans."

"What did he do?"

"Rushed in on his own. Outright disobeyed my order to hold back and didn't tell us. Ended up getting caught by Cassaday's SSW40 shell." Grant wet his lips. "I don't know how the hell he survived that. The explosion should've incinerated him. Instead, he reappears, half of his uniform charred, and starts picking us off one by one with his bare hands. He was a rampaging monster."

Unbidden images of Stephen's father flooded his mind. Yellowed eyes. Swollen, purplish veins. Unimaginable strength. "Sort of like . . . the Hulk?"

"Yeah. If I hadn't shot him with the SSW40 at point blank range, you'd be autopsying me right now." His voice grew quiet. "He's dead, right?"

Stephen shook his head.

Grant paled. "Oh, shit. What the hell is he?"

"That's what I'm trying to find out, but I need your help. Who assigned Greenwood to your unit?"

"Captain Simon was our platoon leader. He reviewed Greenwood's orders and told me he'd be joining us." Grant pressed his fingertips against his temple. "I'm starting to get a headache."

"Captain Simon never said who issued the orders?"

"No, but there was . . . something else. When we were in the Humvee, Greenwood was talking to himself again, only this time, I heard him say a name."

"What name? Who was he talking about?"

"I'm . . . trying to remember. It's getting fuzzy." Grant lolled his head back. "I don't feel good."

"I'll get the nurse." Stephen reached for the call button.

"No." Grant grabbed his wrist. His eyes had a haunted look. "I remember. It wasn't a who. It was a *where*. Tawergha. He said, 'This better not end up like Tawergha.'"

"Do you know what he meant by that?"

"A mission in Tawergha last year went bad. Eighteen dead."

Stephen's lips went dry. "How have I never heard about this?"

"It was black ops. Only reason I know about it is my buddy sent his fiancée an email the night before, saying where they were headed. He said he had a bad feeling and wanted her to know he loved her, in case . . ." Grant trailed off and shook his head. "If he'd survived, he would've faced serious charges for violating protocol. Sometimes, I wonder if they killed him on purpose, in retaliation."

A knot formed in Stephen's gut. "What happened in Tawergha?"

"No idea, but someone didn't want anyone to find out. And I'd guess Greenwood and whoever he was talking to were there."

Stephen mused over this new information. Could whatever happened in Tawergha have been important enough to kill simply to cover it up?

"Greenwood said he told you about someone called The Controller," Stephen said, hoping the sergeant's memory was intact. "Do you remember?"

Grant touched his forehead and squinted his eyes shut. "It's kind of fuzzy. I remember something, but the name . . ." His eyes flew open. "What do you mean, Greenwood told you? You talked to him?"

Uh-oh. "He, uh, I mean—"

"Jesus, does he know where I am?" Grant scrambled for the nurse call button. "I have to get out of here."

"Wait, I can explain."

"Yes, please do." Special Agent Wade stood in the doorway, hands on his hips. "Starting with why you're violating DOD orders."

39

You're not supposed to be here, sir," Wade said to Stephen, his voice barely a hiss. "I warned you to stay away from Foxtrot Team. You're interfering with an active investigation."

"And you're interfering with mine." Stephen leaped to his feet. Wade took a step back. "I'm the only one on this base with authority to confirm identity of decedents and determine cause of death. This young man has information that could provide answers to the deaths of several service members, including Dr. Tom Wilson, so I need—"

Sergeant Grant vomited onto himself.

"What the hell?" Wade's eyes widened.

The sergeant's face was ashen, and he clawed at his throat. The overhead cardiac monitor started beeping. Grant's heart rate jumped to 120.

"Can't . . . swallow," Grant whispered. Each intake of breath was accompanied by a harsh whistling sound. "Can't . . . breathe."

"How long ago did they extubate him?" Stephen asked.

"Huh?" Wade cocked his head.

"He was on a ventilator for a week. Sometimes after pulling the endotracheal tube, there's so much edema the windpipe closes off." Stephen grabbed a non-rebreather mask off the wall and strapped it over Grant's face, then turned on the oxygen. To Wade, he said, "Go get help."

"Uh, right." The special agent ran out of the room.

"Hang in there." Stephen laid a hand on Grant's forehead as he tried to recall how to treat respiratory distress. "We'll take care of you."

Grant's hand clamped around Stephen's wrist, surprising the medical examiner with his strength. The sergeant looked him in the eye. "I . . . remember."

"Remember what?"

"Controller . . ." Grant gasped. "Who . . . he is."

"He? You're sure it's a man?"

"I should've . . . known it . . . was him." Grant's eyes bulged. His chest rose and fell. "He . . . sent us."

"Who?" Stephen's heart pounded. "Who is he?"

"He's . . ." Grant sucked in breath. "He—"

"Out of the way!"

Two men and a woman stormed into the room, wheeling a crash cart.

"I'm Dr. Epting," the woman said while one nurse prepared syringes and another slipped a pulse ox on Grant's finger. "What happened here?"

"I think he has post-extubation edema," Stephen said. "He went into distress."

Epting bounced her gaze between Stephen and Grant, then shoved Stephen aside and began listening to Grant's chest with a stethoscope.

"Sat's down to 85," a nurse said, looking up at the monitor.

"He's crashing." Epting pulled a plastic kit out of the crash cart. "Draw up fentanyl and rocuronium for rapid sequence intubation and find me a size 3 Miller laryngoscope blade."

"Is he going to be okay?" Wade asked, poking his head in.

"We need to clear the room." Epting positioned herself behind Grant's head and began pumping breaths with a bag valve mask as the nurse injected medications into the IV. "You'll have to wait outside."

"But he's vital to an investigation . . ." Wade began.

"Outside." Epting shot a glance at Stephen. "Both of you."

In the hallway, Stephen leaned against a wall while Wade paced, squeezing his fist. The security guard remained at attention.

"What did he say to you?" Wade stopped in front of Stephen. "Did he tell you where Greenwood is?"

Anger danced in the man's eyes, together with fear. Why was he so nervous? Stephen considered the possibilities and then shook his head. "He said they were attacked by insurgents, and Greenwood suffered a head injury. He has no idea where the corporal is now."

Wade's brow wrinkled. "That's all he said?"

If Grant contradicted Stephen's story, he'd be in deeper trouble, but he'd have to take that chance. He nodded. "That's it."

A moment later, one of the nurses poked his head into the hallway. "He's back on a ventilator, but he's stabilized. We'll call you if anything changes."

Wade and Stephen held each other's gaze, neither giving away anything. At last, the agent adjusted his sleeves. "Stay out of this. Sergeant Grant has nothing to do with Major Wilson, and what happened to his teammates is not your concern. I wouldn't want to see you suffer any repercussions for interfering." He gave Stephen one last pointed look. "Sir."

40

Stephen fingered the scar on his shoulder as he stormed back to his office. Sure, Wade could've been following orders, but it felt like more than that, like the OSI officer had a vested interest in keeping Stephen in the dark. Why?

The office was empty when he arrived. His pulse quickened. Melinda and McNiven should've already returned. If either had been caught in their missions, especially with Wade patrolling the hospital . . .

He ran to his desk and bent over his computer. The screen saver was off. Tension crept up his neck. Had someone been using his system? He hit the Return key. The screen lit up with the hospital's lock screen displaying the Department of the Air Force seal. His tension ebbed. The monitor must have powered down.

If Grant was right, Reaper wasn't The Controller, but that didn't mean she wasn't involved. She'd already admitted to spying on Stephen and had blocked him from investigating Foxtrot Team. He tapped his finger on his desk, replaying Edmund's words in his head: *Make her believe you're nothing more than a patsy who stumbled into something big and need her help to make it all go away.*

Sucking in his breath, he dialed Reaper's cell phone.

"Englehart?" Her voice was laced with suspicion, or maybe Stephen was projecting his own feelings. "Why aren't you using the DSN phone?"

"Because someone may be listening. I need to—"

"I had an unpleasant visit from Special Agent Wade," she said, cutting him off. "I thought I ordered you to stay away from anything and anyone involving Foxtrot Team."

"You did, but . . ."

"What's going on with you? What are you not telling me?"

"Remember that implant I told you about?"

"Yes."

"Well, when I said it was missing, that wasn't entirely true . . ."

When Stephen finished explaining, Reaper released her breath and said quietly, "You want to know if DARPA created these monsters?"

"Underneath, they're American soldiers, but someone's controlling them. And I'm afraid they're trying to turn Sharon into one of them."

Reaper was silent again, but Stephen could hear her tongue clicking. At last, she said, "You're barking up the wrong tree. I already told you—DARPA wasn't working on anything like this."

"But they could've been doing it without your knowledge—"

"I said, they weren't involved. Trust me on this." She cleared her throat. "But their contractors are a different story. You're sure the implant is safe with your German friend?"

"Safer than on base."

"Okay. I'll let you know when I find something. Try to stay out of trouble until then."

Relief washed over Stephen for the first time that day. "Yes, ma'am."

"Hey," Melinda said from the doorway.

Stephen clutched his chest and hung up the phone. "You almost gave me a heart attack."

"Sorry." She sat down opposite him. "So, I talked to Tina on the sequencing team. Did you know she's a cancer survivor?"

"No."

"She's got an amazing story. No chemo, just diet, meditation, and supplements. I can't even imagine how strong she had to be."

Stephen struggled to stay patient. "Yes, she's Kryptonian. What happened?"

Melinda pouted. "You don't have to be rude, sir. My mother survived breast cancer."

"I'm not . . ." He clenched his fists. "I'm sorry. I didn't mean to be rude."

"Thank you." She nibbled her lower lip. "I told her I wanted to cross-train into sequencing. She showed me how everything works, where they log in their data, and so on."

"You want to cross-train into sequencing?"

"Yes." She gave him a look that told him to stop asking questions.

Stephen inhaled through his nose. "That sounds fascinating."

"I asked her if she had any sequencing guides I could read, and if she could copy them onto my flash drive." She laid the manila folder on his desk. "They were big files, so it took several minutes to copy everything, but I'm sure they'll be worth the read."

A burst of gratitude rushed through him as he understood the significance of what she was saying. Finally, something was going right. If he didn't think someone might be watching, he'd kiss her.

A knock at the door made them jump. McNiven stood in the doorway, glancing between them. "Am I interrupting something?"

"No." Stephen nudged the manila folder into a desk drawer and locked it. He'd have to find a better hiding place for Edmund's flash drive later. "I was telling Sergeant Stewart we need more blood spot kits. We go through them like toilet paper."

"Yes, sir," Melinda said, standing. "I'll get right on it."

McNiven watched her leave before turning to Stephen. "You're lucky. Our tech still can't tell a bone saw from a sternum saw."

"Yeah, I am lucky. What did you find out?"

"Nothing that makes sense." McNiven dropped a printout on Stephen's desk. "The only order for arsenic trioxide within the past year was six months ago, by Colonel Agarwal."

Stephen had forgotten the wing commander was a board-certified oncologist. "I didn't think he still did procedures."

"Not often, but this was a special case." McNiven's mouth twitched. "Reaper's daughter."

"Her daughter had acute promyelocytic leukemia?"

McNiven nodded.

Thoughts swirled through Stephen's mind. How had he not known that the pathology director's daughter had a rare form of leukemia? Now all of Reaper's odd habits made sense: sneaking off at random times, carefully put together one minute and looking like she'd crawled out of bed the next, and her volatile mood. Stephen had been too busy thinking about his affair and retirement to notice what was really going on with her.

"How much arsenic did he order?" Stephen asked.

McNiven shook his head and whispered, "There's no way Agarwal killed Tom. He has zero motive."

Unless he's The Controller. "I'm not saying he did. But if he ordered more than he used, someone else could've acquired the leftover."

For a moment, McNiven remained silent, lips pressed together. "He ordered a gram—way more than he would need to treat a ten-year-old."

"Did he return the rest to the pharmacy?"

"I'll have to talk to them to find out."

Stephen's cell phone started ringing. He checked the caller ID and recognized the local German number. "Do that and get back to me. And thanks."

As McNiven left, Stephen answered his phone. "Edmund, I was about to call you. It's all set—"

"I've already obtained the information you requested. I'm emailing it to you now." Edmund's voice hitched. "But you need to get out of there."

"What?" Stephen leaped to his feet. "Why?"

"The soldier you visited is dead. I saw it on the security camera feed."

"That's impossible. He was back on a ventilator but stable."

"I can access only video, no sound, so I don't know for certain what happened, but his hospital room is now teeming with investigative police, acting out a scene from CSI."

Stephen's skin grew cold. "Are you telling me he was murdered?"

"Someone did not want him to talk." Edmund sucked in air. "And though I'm not an expert lip-reader, I believe Special Agent Wade thinks that someone was you."

41

The gleaming white corridor walls seemed to constrict around Stephen as he fled the medical examiner's office, trying to act casual so as not to alert the other mortuary staff. Melinda and McNiven had both given him odd looks as he excused himself and ran out the door, but with any luck, Stephen would be long gone before Special Agent Wade arrived.

As he rounded a corner, he stopped short and ducked his head back before peering out into the mortuary lobby. Colonel Agarwal was standing by the memorial wall, cursing into a cell phone. Stephen held his breath. The hospital commander could order a lockdown at any minute. Even if he didn't, he'd be suspicious of his medical examiner sneaking out during duty hours. Stephen held his position and listened with bated breath.

Agarwal gesticulated wildly and started pacing, his voice fading in and out as he circled the memorial wall. Stephen was only able to make out "You need to fix this mess," and "You should've come to me sooner."

Stephen's gut twisted. Was Agarwal dirty? Was he The Controller?

The hospital commander stopped on the other side of the memorial wall. He continued to talk into his phone, the wall muffling his conversation. He remained directly in the path to the exit.

Biting his tongue, Stephen backtracked up the hall to an intersection and then turned right, continuing past the Personal Effects room. At least so far, the SPs weren't storming the building. But Stephen had to find a way out before they did.

As Stephen was passing the EOD room, the heavy metal doors swung open. Master Sergeant Booker emerged with two enlisted personnel in tow. Stephen kept his chin high and gave the sergeant the curtest of nods as he continued past them.

"Sir?"

Stephen stopped, his hands tightening into fists. He could feel the others' eyes on his back.

Slowly, keeping his face as expressionless as possible, he turned around. Booker's head was tilted, brow furrowed. The other two stood at attention.

"Yes, Master Sergeant?"

"You seem like you're in a hurry, sir."

Stephen swallowed hard and jerked his thumb down the corridor in the direction he'd been headed. "Colonel Restrepo asked me to locate the personnel files for the decedent that came in yesterday from Camp Lemmonier."

Booker's gaze narrowed. He cocked his head in the opposite direction. "Personnel Files is that way."

Stephen's eyes widened. He fumbled for a response.

Booker burst out laughing, and the other two joined in. "I'm messing with you, sir. You AFMES folks only leave your office for Groundhog Day. You really should get to know the rest of the facility layout." He pointed down the hall. "Third door on the left."

His cheeks cooling, Stephen thanked him and strolled down the hall, listening for the others' footsteps to fade away. When they disappeared around the corner, he accelerated his pace, passing the Personnel Files office and continuing to the opposite end of the hall, where a sign read Departures.

There was no one in the warehouse-sized chamber when he entered. A stack of casket lids stood off to the side, illuminated by the hallway fluorescents peeking through the doorway. This was where the Fallen, after being fully processed and autopsied, awaited transport to their final destinations. The departure ceremonies were much smaller than the arrivals, but equally solemn, as uniformed service members saluted the caskets on their way to the flight line. Stephen had never attended one, even after Tom's death. Maybe it was because of the finality those ceremonies represented, the reminder that this was the last goodbye, that they were gone forever.

Gone forever.

Stephen shook off his reverie and hustled toward the center of the room. He didn't bother turning on the lights. There wasn't anything in there he needed, just the way out.

As he jogged toward the massive roll-up door, big enough for an eighteen-wheeler to pass under it, he nearly tripped over a casket in the center of the chamber. The Stars and Stripes were neatly draped over it. The hairs on the backs of his arms stood on end. There weren't any scheduled departures.

Sucking on his teeth, he lifted back the flag and undid the casket latches. He paused to listen for signs that anyone was searching for him. The hallway remained empty.

With a grunt, he opened the casket.

He gasped.

Inside lay Colonel Luiza Restrepo.

42

Once more, Sharon awoke to pain. Her head pulsated, like two giant hands were repeatedly crushing her skull, over and over. She opened her eyes and wished she hadn't. She was still in the same damned metal room, only now all the beds were empty except hers.

She squeezed her hand, the one Byrne had cut, into a fist. When she'd awoken after the fight, she'd discovered that it had completely healed. She had no idea how long she'd been asleep but assumed it had been for days. There had been little time to think about it, for in the next moment, two more soldiers had attacked her. She'd easily beaten them both, and again The Controller's voice in her head ordered her to kill them. When she refused, electricity racked her brain and she fell unconscious once more.

The same thing happened three times after that. She'd wake up, feeling healthy but with no idea of how much time passed. Soldiers attacked. Sharon fought them off. The Controller ordered her to kill them. She refused. Zap.

This last time, one of the other soldiers had rammed a metal pole into her thigh. It had sunk deep into her muscles. She'd roared in pain until she uttered "Relief," and then, with the sensation miraculously gone, she'd knocked her assailant out with her fist. Now, there was a bandage wrapped around her thigh, but the pole was gone. She gently prodded the area.

It didn't hurt at all. She unwrapped the bandage.

Not a mark. Her thigh was completely healed.

Sharon rubbed her forehead. How long had she been asleep this time?

Not as long as you think, Major.

Blood congealed in Sharon's veins. That voice, so cold, reverberated in every corner of her mind.

"What do you want with me?" She searched the cavern for hidden cameras, feeling like a rat in a cage, waiting for someone to throw her a bit of cheese and then force her to find her way out. "I'm getting tired of this game."

As I said, you're a soldier. All you need do is follow orders.

"Whose orders? Why don't you show yourself?"

In due time. First, you need to prove your loyalty.

She scoffed. "I am loyal to my duty, my honor, and my country. I serve the United States Army. I will follow the orders of my commanding officer, not whoever the fuck you are."

Eerie laughter reverberated in her head. *I am your commanding officer. And you will follow my orders. Without question. Without hesitation.*

The pain seared inside her skull. She staggered but didn't fall. This time, it only lasted a few seconds.

"You . . . can hurt me . . . all you want," she said between ragged gasps. Her fingers gripped the nearest bed as she forced herself to stay upright. "You won't . . . make me your slave."

I don't want a slave. I want loyalty. Unfortunately, the kind of loyalty I demand often requires some encouragement. You're far more resilient than most. But everyone has a breaking point. And, as it so happens, I know yours.

A door opened. Two male soldiers entered, dragging a third behind them. Sharon's heart jumped. She recognized the Ranger from the shuttle, but the other, wearing a Green Beret patch on his shoulder, she knew well. Deshaun White. They'd trained together. And slept together.

The soldiers' eyes were vacant, their faces expressionless. They stopped four feet away from Sharon and hoisted up Byrne. His face was beaten and swollen. Blood streamed from his nostrils, and duct tape covered his mouth.

Deshaun approached Sharon, leaving the other to hold Byrne upright. He showed no sign of recognizing her. He held out a Sig-Sauer M18, handle first.

Take the gun.

Sharon hesitated. What sort of trick was this?

No trick. This is your one chance to escape. Take the gun.

Cautiously, Sharon took the pistol. Deshaun returned to stand next to the other two. She checked the magazine. Fully loaded.

Now, shoot them.

Sharon's throat swelled. "No."

Shoot them. Or he dies.

The Ranger slid a knife out from his belt and held it under Byrne's chin. The blade grazed the man's neck, leaving a thin, scarlet streak. Byrne winced.

"Stop it." She aimed the pistol at the Ranger. Her hand remained steady, but her voice wavered. "Deshaun, you're better than this."

Deshaun stared blankly ahead.

Major White knows how to follow orders. They will kill this young man if you don't shoot them first. So, what will it be?

Sharon's hand started to tremble. She aimed the pistol at the Ranger's head, then slid over toward Deshaun's. She had an easy shot. One, two. She could take them both out before they could reach her. But the way they stood there, emotionless, she knew they weren't in control. She'd be killing them in cold blood.

The Ranger dug the knife into Byrne's flesh. Blood started to drip onto the floor. Byrne cried out, but his voice was muffled by the tape.

"You've made your point." Sharon closed her eyes. "I'll do whatever you want. Just let him go."

You still don't understand. I don't want your promises. Words don't win wars. Actions do. Shoot them, and the boy goes free.

Sharon's heart pounded. She couldn't do this. She was trained to kill, but not like this. These men had done nothing wrong. There had to be a way to save them, too.

Tick-tock, tick-tock. Time's running out.

Deshaun slid a knife from his belt and pressed it against Byrne's abdomen below the sternum. Byrne shook his head, screaming through the duct tape.

"No!"

In one fluid movement, Sharon redirected the gun at DeShaun's forehead and fired. She shifted her aim, targeted the Ranger, and fired again.

Both soldiers crumpled to the ground.

Sharon fell to her knees. She opened her mouth, but no sound would come out.

Byrne lay on the ground, writhing, trying to unbind his hands behind his back, tape still covering his mouth. He looked up at her, eyes pleading.

She glanced at Deshaun's unmoving body, fighting back the urge to vomit.

Well done, Major. You've saved the day.

Sharon's fingers tightened around the pistol. She told herself that she'd done what she had to do. But she couldn't quite believe it. She should've found another way. Wasn't that what Stephen had told her once? Heroes always find another way.

Your brother's a fool. There's only one way. My way.

She heard movement. She whipped around and lifted the gun.

DeShaun sat up.

Sharon's jaw dropped. She lowered the gun. "DeShaun? But . . . I killed you."

The Ranger coughed and rolled over onto his side.

Byrne struggled against his bonds.

"I don't understand. How . . ."

I told you. You're part of something greater now. This wasn't a test solely for you, but for them, as well.

DeShaun and the Ranger climbed to their feet. DeShaun rubbed his forehead as if he'd simply bumped it on a desk. Blood streamed from the Ranger's hairline, but the hole in his scalp closed before her eyes. The bullet lay at his feet.

Sharon's stomach flip-flopped. "What . . . what have you done to us?"

Helped you reach your full potential.

DeShaun exchanged looks with the Ranger. Both nodded as if they'd heard something Sharon had not. They turned and paced over to Byrne, who screamed against the tape covering his mouth. Their hands reached out for him.

The fear in his eyes struck Sharon to her soul.

She raised the gun again and squeezed the trigger three times in rapid succession.

Click. Click. Click.

Her cheeks cooled. The ammo cartridge was still half full.

Remote lock. The Controller laughed. *You've already passed your test, and you've earned your reward. Petty Officer Byrne will be returned to the others.*

DeShaun and the Ranger dragged Byrne, kicking and screaming, out of the room.

"You're . . . sick," Sharon said to the empty room, certain The Controller could still hear her. "You made me shoot them . . . for your . . . stupid game."

I didn't make you do anything. You chose to shoot them to save this boy, whom you know nothing about. For all you know, he could be a rapist. Or a serial killer. The voice hardened, accusing. You are a soldier. You cannot follow your personal code on the battlefield. That's how good people die. If you're to be of any use to me, you need to follow orders. Without question.

Sharon flinched at the way The Controller said those last words. "If you want me to blindly follow orders, why not control me, like you did them?"

You think I controlled them? Technology can do many things—relieve pain, allow wireless communication, monitor your vital signs and movements—but it can't turn you into a puppet.

Sharon's tongue swelled. "But Deshaun . . ."

Deshaun returned and stood at attention, eyes front, mouth a thin line. Sharon understood. He hadn't been controlled. He'd known what he was doing all along.

The only way to survive, to complete the mission, is to follow orders. Your loyalty will be rewarded. Although Sharon couldn't see The Controller's face, she was certain whoever he or she was, they were smiling. *Let's begin.*

43

Blood surrounded a hole in Reaper's chest, directly through the ribbon rack on her class A uniform. One of the silver eagles on her lapel was smeared with crimson. Reaper's eyes were open, her mouth twisted defiantly. Stephen held two fingers over her carotid artery. The moment he touched the cool skin, he knew it was futile.

A wave of revulsion washed over him. Someone must have overheard his conversation with her. They killed her because of what she knew. And now, if they caught him, they would do the same.

Noises from the hallway alerted him. He froze, listening, like a hunted fox.

Were those footsteps? He held stock still.

Nothing.

Releasing his breath, he closed Reaper's eyes, replaced the casket lid, and haphazardly draped the flag. He didn't have time for ceremony. The best he could do was delay someone else from finding the body and sounding the alarm.

Stephen ran to one side of the rolling door and jammed the heel of his palm against a red button.

The door slid open.

The casket transport truck sat outside, empty. He pressed the red button again and ran to the truck as the rolling door dropped behind him. He tried the driver's door handle. It swung open, and he jumped inside.

After a search of the truck's cab, he cursed. The driver had been careless to leave it unlocked, but he hadn't left the key. Stephen's pulse quickened. Any moment, Wade and his goons could appear, or Agarwal could lock down the gates, trapping Stephen on base. He didn't have time to waste.

His hands fumbled under the dashboard until he found the wires leading from the ignition. He uttered a thank you to any god listening. To save money after building the new hospital, the Air Force had continued to employ outdated transport vehicles manufactured before the switch to keyless ignition. He yanked the wires down and into view.

The last time Stephen had hotwired a car, his parents had still been alive. He hadn't gotten far before the police caught him. With any luck, he'd make it farther this time. It took him three tries, but he managed to spark the transport to life. He shifted the truck into Drive and pulled away from the hospital. The entrance gate wasn't far away, just minutes along the main road. He was going to make it.

Blue lights flashed in front of him.

Stephen's chest tightened. Two patrol cars were headed right for him.

He gripped the steering wheel and pressed down on the accelerator. The truck was only lightly armored, but it could withstand a collision with a police cruiser or two. He hoped.

The patrol cars got closer.

Stephen fought to keep the wheel steady. Mud bordered the road on the right. If he swerved, the truck would get mired for sure. He set his jaw.

The cruisers whizzed past, sirens blaring.

Releasing his breath, Stephen kept driving until he reached the gate. No barricades on the exit.

As Stephen drove off base, his mind raced. He had to find somewhere to hide, somewhere whoever killed Grant and Reaper wouldn't find him, at least until he figured out a plan to fight back. But where?

The answer came to him in a flash. He headed for the autobahn toward Erlenbach.

44

The moment Stephen arrived at the little house in Erlenbach, he sensed something was off. The dilapidated truck remained in the same spot, a small oil patch blossoming on the ground underneath it. The air felt heavy despite the cold. A crow cawed from a tree and then flew off.

Cautiously, Stephen approached the front door. It was closed. He tried the handle. Locked.

He rang the bell. After a full minute passed, he rang it again. Nothing.

Checking over his shoulder, he turned around and mule kicked under the doorknob. The door flew open.

The smell hit him before he'd made it halfway down the hallway. It was a smell he knew all too well—the smell of death.

Stephen glanced into the kitchen and spotted the old woman lying face-down in a pool of blood. Even though he knew it was pointless, he ran over and checked her carotid. No pulse.

His gut flip-flopping, he backed away from the woman and made his way to the basement. The stairs creaked as he took them one by one. With each step, he prepared for someone to leap out at him, but no one did.

Three steps from the bottom, he saw Edmund slumped at his workbench. Two small bullet holes dotted the back of the chair. Stephen scanned the rest of the workbench. The computer monitors had been smashed in. Edmund's broken tech lay strewn all over the floor.

Whoever had done this wasn't worried about being caught. They hadn't even tried to make it look like a botched burglary. They were looking for something specific.

Stephen's heart thumped as he spotted the metal box on its side on the floor, the lid next to it. It was empty.

His mouth went dry. The implant. That was what this was all about. And now they had it. Whoever they were.

His gaze fell on Edmund. The boy's head was turned at an awkward angle. Eyes wide open, mouth agape in frozen shock. Anger burned up the back of Stephen's neck. The ones responsible had gone too far. Stephen needed to find them and rescue Sharon before anyone else died.

He pulled a pair of nitrile gloves out of his pocket and donned them. Frantically, he searched through the debris, hoping Edmund had left something they hadn't taken. The background checks on Reaper and Wade. Information about the implant. Something.

After six minutes of digging through the wreckage, he sat back on his knees and grunted. It was all gone. They'd taken everything.

He followed Edmund's lifeless gaze and spotted the stack of novels. Stephen shook his head. All those Vince Flynn stories, and Edmund had ended up the victim of a terrorist plot.

The books. Edmund had made a point of telling Stephen about his love for those books.

He dug through the German titles and found one in English by a different author: *Under Occupation* by Alan Furst.

Stephen opened the cover, skimmed the title page, and then flipped through the next few pages. It was a spy novel about the Underground Resistance in France during World War II. If there was a clue for him hidden in the story, he had no idea where to look.

He riffled through the rest of the book, half thinking the hacker might've hollowed out the middle and stashed the implant there. No such luck. But as he was about to give up, he felt the pages near the back sticking together. He flipped through more slowly. Sure enough, two pages were adhered with a thin strip of tape. Stephen removed the tape and spread open the pages.

Nestled between them was a single sheet of paper. At the top, typed in English, was *Defense Advanced Research Projects Agency* and a date—*October 2, 1989*—followed by the title, *Project Super-Patriot.* A red stamp read: *Top Secret.*

Stephen's heart pounded as he read through the fact sheet. It described a classified operation to develop a serum that could alter a subject's cellular structure to make aerobic metabolism more efficient, multiply fast-twitch muscle fibers, and heighten reflexes. Effectively, it granted the subject what the researchers termed super-strength and super-speed. They'd tested fifty subjects, all military personnel. Only twenty survived, the rest suffering massive cardiac infarction. The project was deemed a success—until the survivors began to exhibit uncontrollable rage attacks, resulting in several tragedies requiring exceptional effort by the military to cover them up.

The rest of the report described DARPA's failed attempts to reverse the transformation. In the end, the military decommissioned the subjects and ordered DARPA to abandon all further efforts at developing Project Super-Patriot.

Stephen drew in a low breath. Decommissioned. A fancy way of saying terminated. But that would mean Dad hadn't killed himself. Stephen had always felt there was someone else there that day, that someone had killed his parents, but no one believed him. The paper crumpled in his hands. Now, he knew for sure.

He stopped crumpling the paper. There was a business card taped to the back. He removed it and flipped it over. *Friedrich Gersch, PhD. Biotech Researcher, University of Basel.*

The name nipped at Stephen's memory. Where had he heard it?

Before he could place it, he heard sirens in the distance.

His body tensed. They were too far out in the middle of nowhere for it be a coincidence. He listened more closely. Yes, they were getting nearer.

Cursing, he stuffed the paper and the business card into his pocket. There wasn't anything in the basement to paint him as the killer. But that would change if the authorities found him there.

The sirens were close. Less than a mile away.

No time to escape out the front door. Stephen was trapped.

Memory struck Stephen like a lightning bolt. He dashed over to the wall and shoved aside the filing cabinet Edmund had moved earlier, finding the hidden door. He opened it, revealing a small tunnel.

He heard radios squawking upstairs. Someone shouted in German to come out peacefully. The Polizei. They'd be downstairs soon.

Stephen stuffed himself into the hole and slid the wall panel back into place, hoping the police wouldn't notice it, at least not until he could get away.

He pulled out his cell phone and turned on the flashlight. The tunnel was narrow, intended for someone much smaller than he. That meant he'd have to use both hands to clear away dirt. He stuck the phone in his mouth and started crawling.

When he stopped to catch his breath, he checked the clock on his phone. He'd been scrambling for eight minutes. The tunnel was deathly silent. So far, no one was following him. Dirt tumbled onto his back. Visions filled his mind of being buried alive. He saw the faces of every casualty he'd autopsied, grinning at him, laughing. *Now you know what it feels like,* they chanted. *This is eternity.*

Shaking off the images, he pushed himself onward. His palms stung as rocks bit into them. His lungs burned from the limited oxygen. But he couldn't give up. He had to escape. For Sharon.

After what felt like hours but, according to his phone, had only been sixteen minutes, he ran up against solid rock. Panic clutched his chest. He clawed at the stone, trying to find an edge. At last, he found a crevice big enough to slip three fingers into and felt a click. He pulled the wall down toward him until it touched the floor. Spitting the phone into his hand, he reactivated the flashlight and inched forward.

He swung the light around, illuminating the curved rock walls of an old, dried-up well. There was no ladder, no rope.

A glint caught his eye. He moved closer and ran his hands over the wall. Some of the stones jutted out farther than the others, creating narrow steps. He groaned. Rock climbing had never been his thing, but he didn't have a choice.

His back screamed as he dug his fingertips into the crevices, planted one foot at a time onto a step, and dragged his weight upward. Every few steps, he stopped and listened. Nothing from above, nothing from below.

At last, he reached the top of the wall. Sweat dripped from his cheeks. His clothes clung to his body, wet and sticky, as he crawled over the lip of the well and tumbled into a bed of dry leaves. He was in a wooded area. He could see the back of Edmund's house a short distance away.

Trying not to step on branches or crackly leaves, he scrambled to the side of the house, crept along the wall, and peered out into the driveway.

Two green-and-white police cars were parked, lights flashing. A single uniformed officer stood by the transport truck, calling in the license plate.

Stephen didn't want to hurt anyone, especially a police officer doing his job. But even if he took the cop down, it wouldn't take long for the remaining police officers to contact the base and learn the truck had been stolen. They'd have roadblocks at all the main intersections between there and Ramstein.

Glancing aside, Stephen spotted the pickup parked a few yards away.

The police officer continued to talk into his radio. His gun was holstered.

Stephen didn't even know if the truck was operational. It would be far easier to knock out the cop and take his car. Assuming the other officers didn't come running outside at that very moment. And assuming the cop didn't get the drop on him first.

With a grunt, he scrabbled over to the truck. The cop's back was still turned. Stephen opened the driver's door and slid inside. He eased the door closed until he heard a faint click, then scanned the cabin. Damn. He'd hoped Edmund had left the keys in the ignition, but no such luck. He reached under the steering console. Hot-wiring two vehicles in one day would be a new record for him.

On second thought, he checked the glove compartment. Bingo. He grabbed a keyring holding two keys and a tiny replica of the Millennium Falcon. He inserted the larger key into the ignition, crossed his fingers, and turned.

Nothing.

Stephen's heart thumped. He checked the driveway again.

The cop was gone.

Blood drained from his cheeks. Had the cop gone inside? Or had he spotted Stephen? He looked in all directions. The woods were still empty.

Heart pounding, Stephen looked again at the truck's simple dashboard. No onboard computer. No fancy fingerprint locks. What was he missing?

Then he noticed the gearshift. Standard transmission. Holding his breath, he held down the clutch with his left foot, shifted into first gear, and tried the key again.

The truck sputtered and then roared to life. Stephen hit the gas, and it barreled forward.

Off to the left, he saw the cop run outside, reaching for his gun. Stephen cut the wheel hard to the left. The truck veered and lumbered straight toward the cop.

Panic struck the officer's face. He forgot about grabbing his gun and dove back into the house. Stephen swerved in the other direction. The truck barely missed clipping the side of the police car.

Over the rattle of the engine, he heard shouting behind him. He upshifted and slammed the pedal to the floor. The truck rocketed down the dirt road, until soon the little house was out of sight.

45

The engine whined as the truck rattled along the winding road to Landstuhl. Stephen lowered the window to let in fresh air since the air conditioner was broken. The stench of manure from passing farms made him gag, but he forced himself to keep driving, keep going, keep running. Every five minutes, he checked the rearview for flashing blue lights. So far, nothing.

The only ones who knew about Edmund were Melinda and Reaper. No, that was crazy. He trusted Melinda.

He chewed the inside of his cheek. But Reaper's phone might've been bugged, or she might've told someone about Edmund before they killed her. And they might go after Melinda next. Stephen tightened his grip on the steering wheel. Damn it. He knew he shouldn't have involved her.

Steering with one hand, he pulled out his phone and dialed. A moment later, he heard Melinda's voice.

"Stephen? Where are you? What's going—"

"Are you okay?" he asked.

"Yeah, Colonel Agarwal sent everyone in Pathology home early. They think you killed Colonel Restrepo."

Stephen's gut clenched. "I didn't."

"I'm sure you didn't, but they're looking for you. You can't go back on base." She paused. "You can hide here."

"I don't want to endanger you—"

"I'd rather be in danger with you than not know if you're okay."

The truck shuddered as he accelerated. He realized he felt the same. "All right. Don't answer the door unless it's me."

Gritting his teeth, he spun the wheel and took the next exit.

When he arrived at her neighborhood, he parked two blocks down, as usual. Dark clouds were creeping in, casting ominous shadows. Stephen tried to look casual as he strolled down the sidewalk. When he was three houses away, he slowed his pace and pulled out a pair of binoculars he'd found in the truck. The sole car in the driveway was Melinda's. He scanned the trees and rooftops. All clear.

Carefully, he made his way to her front door and checked the lock. No sign of forced entry.

He rang the bell.

After two minutes, the door opened. Melinda stared up at him with wide eyes.

"Oh my God," she whispered. "What happened to you?"

He pushed past her and entered. "Close the door."

She complied and turned around. "Tell me what—"

He grabbed her and pulled her close, pressing his lips against hers. She stiffened at first but quickly melted into his embrace.

After a passionate moment, he pulled back, panting. "I'm glad you're okay."

"I am, too. But why are you covered in dirt?"

"I went to see Tom's friend Edmund." Stephen scrubbed his scalp. "He's dead."

Melinda's hand flew to her mouth. "Fuck."

"It's my fault for going to them for help."

"Don't talk that way." Melinda rested her hands on his shoulders. "You did what you had to do. You couldn't have known."

"Couldn't I?" He barked a scoffing laugh. "Tom was right. I'm in way over my head. I'm trying to take down the admiral with a lieutenant."

Melinda screwed up her face. "What does that mean?"

"Tactico. You know, the game . . ." He shook his head. "Never mind."

"You need to call him," she said.

Stephen knew who she meant. "No."

"He's the only one with enough power to bypass the surveillance. If you explain to him—"

"I'm not dragging him into this. Bad enough you're involved. I need to handle this myself."

"Why? To prove to him you're stronger than he thinks?"

Stephen winced. "That's not—"

"I know how he treated you, Steve. You talk in your sleep." Melinda pushed a lock of hair behind her ear. "You were the troublemaker, the one he had to fix. He always treated you differently than he did your sister. You tried to convince yourself you didn't care, but you did. You spent way too much time as a teenager trying to prove yourself to him, to make him respect you. But you're still doing it, aren't you? You're still trying to win his love."

The back of Stephen's neck burned. She was right. He lived in the shadows of others. No matter what he did, no matter what he accomplished, it wasn't enough. He would always be the student, never able to surpass his teacher.

"Why would he help? If anyone found out, his reputation would be tanked."

She touched her hand to his chest. "He'd do it for Sharon."

Stephen considered that. "But he'd call every commander in Europe and demand they find and release her. Hell, he'd send in the Marines to storm the countryside."

"And that'd be a bad thing?"

"If what Greenwood says is true, this so-called Controller has tendrils in every area of the military. He'll see it coming. If he spooks and runs, we'll never find them."

Melinda chewed her bottom lip. "Then you need to call the shots. Don't give too much information. I know you hate the idea of being in command, but now you don't have a choice. You need to take charge."

Stephen let that sink in, once again wondering what Steve Rogers would do. Resolutely, he dialed a number he knew by heart and waited.

The phone rang four times, and then he heard a click and a "Hello?"

After taking a deep breath, Stephen said, "Uncle Alex, I need your help."

46

Thirty-two years earlier

As his mom pushed the wheelchair through the hospital double doors to the sidewalk, Steve closed his eyes and drank in the fresh air. After three months of treatment, surrounded by sterile white walls and the bitter tang of antiseptic, feeling the winter sun on his face and neck again was like entering Heaven. He flexed his arms, strength flowing through them. Yeah, much better.

"I'm so proud of you," Mom said as they reached the curb. "You never gave up. You kept fighting."

"Like I had a choice," he said. "Those doctors pumped me full of that junk whether I wanted it or not."

A dark cloud passed over her face. "I don't want to hear talk like that coming out of your mouth again. That medicine saved you."

Something crawled under Steve's skin, like a worm creeping from the back of his hand through every muscle to his heart. He shuddered at the thought of having to take that medicine every month for the rest of his life to keep the leukemia at bay. "Yeah, I guess you're right."

Mom glanced away. When she turned back, she was smiling as if he'd said nothing. "Anyway, I have a surprise for you. Here he comes now."

The family sedan pulled to a stop at the curb in front of them. The door opened. A thrill ran through Steve's chest as the driver stepped out.

"Dad!"

He jumped out of the wheelchair, threw his arms around his father, and hugged tight.

"Hey, son." His father clapped him on the shoulder. "It's good to see you."

A tear formed in Steve's eye. He squeezed his father and then pulled back, turning his head so Dad couldn't see him crying. "What are you doing here? I thought you were in the desert somewhere."

Dad's lips pressed together seriously, but then he winked. "They let me out early for good behavior. Come on, let's get you home."

For that entire first week home, Dad seemed atypically calm. No yelling. No fits of rage. He was himself again. Steve even wondered if whatever had been happening to him had finally gone away. Sharon didn't seem to notice it—she was too young. But he did.

One day, during a surprise winter storm that forced them to stay inside, Dad pulled out the Tactico game and started setting up the board on Steve's bed. Steve joined him, choosing locations for the most critical pieces the way Dad had taught him. Dad barely looked at him, only making eye contact each time Steve captured one of his pieces. All the while, Steve noticed Dad's lips parting every so often, like he wanted to say something and was then stopping himself. He wore the same look he had the first time he went away, before The Change. What did it mean? Was he going away again?

"Pay attention, Steve," his dad said, breaking the silence as he captured one of Steve's captains. He removed the piece from the board and lay it on its side, then cast a disapproving look. "You need to always keep your head in the game. No matter how much you're hurting. No matter how much you want to be somewhere else."

"Sorry, Dad," Steve said, avoiding the man's stare. He hated the disappointment, but even worse would be if his father asked him what he was thinking about.

As if reading his mind, Dad rested his hand on Steve's shoulder. Steve looked up at him.

"No." Dad's eyebrows lifted. "I'm sorry."

"For what?"

"For everything. You deserve better. So do your mom and sister." He sat up straight, throwing back his shoulders. "That's why tomorrow I'm tendering my resignation."

Steve's jaw slackened. "You're . . . quitting the military?"

"I won't get full retirement benefits, but there's a job opening at Paragon Security Systems downtown. I already talked to them, and they could use someone with my background." The corner of Dad's mouth quirked. "How do you feel about it? No more moving every three years. And you'll have to put up with me evenings and weekends. All the time."

Instead of speaking, Steve threw his arms around his father and squeezed. Tears streamed down his cheeks.

"Yeah," Dad whispered as he hugged him back. "That's what I thought."

47

Icy rain pelted the frozen yard of Melinda's townhome, the sky dark and ominous. Stephen flinched as a chunk of ice struck the window he was staring through, thinking back to the day his father had told him he was leaving the Army. The weather had been the same, a foreshadow of what was to come. Traveling on a day like this was dumber than dumb, but his chances of helping Sharon dwindled with every moment he delayed. And the horrible weather would be useful in covering his tracks.

He looked down at his phone for the third time that morning, trying to make sense of the email from Edmund, the hacker's final message to him. It contained an unredacted lab report. The DNA sample from Kirby's fingers had come from Corporal Greenwood as he'd expected, but the DNA in the skin tissue he'd found on Sergeant Herrera matched a Green Beret named Richard Purcell. The soldier's hooded eyes in the AFDIL file photo sent a chill down Stephen's back, but that was nothing compared to what he read. According to the report, Purcell had died a year ago. In Tawergha.

"Hey."

He turned to find Melinda watching him from the bed, a sheet wrapped around her torso. She half smiled, but worry lingered around her eyes.

Forcing a smile in return that he hoped was reassuring, he tucked away his phone in his pocket, sat on the bed, and took her hands in his. "Hey."

"Do you have to do this?"

"Yes." He slid his thumb back and forth over the stretch of skin between her thumb and forefinger. "I do."

Her chest rose and fell under the sheet. "Let me go with you."

"No."

"Please, Stephen. I can help."

"Look, it's going to be hard enough to find where they're hiding Sharon, even with Uncle Alex's help. Involving you will be more dangerous."

She withdrew her hands from his and looked down, twisting the sheets between her fingers. "I'm afraid something's going to happen to you. I don't want to lose you." She sniffled and dabbed at her eyes. "I love you."

Hearing those words from her lips sent a cold rush through Stephen's body as he realized he didn't want to lose her, either. He opened his mouth to answer her, but no sound came out.

Her face lifted, her eyes, rimmed with tears, meeting his.

"Come here." Stephen pulled her into his arms. She squeezed him, shuddering with sobs. He caressed her back and made shushing sounds. "This is going to end soon. I promise."

Something scuffled downstairs.

"Did you hear that?" Stephen asked, holding Melinda at arm's length.

"Hear what?" She frowned. "I didn't hear anything."

Stephen touched his finger to his lips.

Another soft scuffle.

Stephen jumped up and grabbed a lamp off the nightstand, ripping the cord out of the wall.

Melinda's eyes widened. "What are you doing?"

"Protecting you." Stephen crept toward the bedroom door. "Stay here."

"You're joking."

"Unless you've got an assault rifle stashed in here, I'm not." He clutched the lamp as he opened the door as quietly as possible. "If you hear gunshots or the sound of fighting, call 112."

Before she could argue, he slipped into the hallway.

He paused at the top of the steps. Silence.

Holding the lamp like a bludgeon, Stephen started down the stairs, hugging the wall with his back to relieve weight from his feet, allowing him to creep down the steps with minimal noise. Stopping to listen every two steps, he made it to the bottom.

His fingers throbbed as he clutched the lamp. He loosened his grip.

Something rustled in the kitchen. Stephen crept along the wall. Muscles taut, he nudged open the kitchen door.

A weasel sat on the counter, digging through a box of cereal.

Stephen slumped against the wall and lowered the lamp. The weasel's head snapped in his direction. It stared at him for a second, then bolted out the back door.

He froze. Why was the door open?

Stephen spun too late to dodge the chair rushing toward him. He twisted his torso. The chair crashed into his shoulder instead of his head. He dropped the lamp.

Through the pain, he saw a figure dressed in black turning to run down the hallway. Stephen lowered his head and charged like a bull. He tackled the man face-down onto the stone floor. A gun dropped to the ground, and Stephen snatched it up.

He held the struggling assailant down with one hand and aimed the gun, a military-issue M18, at the back of his attacker's head. "Who are you?"

The assailant stopped fighting. He turned his head. Stephen's stomach dropped.

It was Major Michael McNiven.

48

"What are you doing here?" Stephen pressed the gun barrel against McNiven's head. "Who sent you?"

The major pressed his lips into a thin line.

"Son of a bitch." Stephen connected the rest of the pieces. "You killed Reaper, didn't you?"

"You need to stop talking," McNiven said. "You're making things worse."

"I'm making things worse?" Stephen's mind raced. "You killed Sergeant Grant, too. And Edmund, because he must've seen you on the security camera. And . . ." Stephen's chest tightened. "Fuck. You took the arsenic from Colonel Agarwal. You killed Tom."

"Steve, you need to walk away from this right—"

Stephen smashed his fist into McNiven's nose. Bone crunched.

The man spat out a wad of blood. "Look, you're making a mistake—"

Stephen punched him again, across the cheek. "You took the photos, didn't you? That's how you knew to find me here. It was all you. Why?"

When McNiven didn't answer, Stephen hit him again. And again. Blood dripped from his knuckles. Rage streamed through his own blood. He wanted to break every bone in this man's body, the way McNiven had broken Stephen's life.

Then, like flipping a switch, he stopped the rage.

"You couldn't have done all this by yourself. Who do you work for?"

McNiven stared back at him, one eye black and swollen, but said nothing.

Stephen punched him in the jaw. "Who is The Controller?" A jab to the nose. "Where do I find him?" A direct blow between the eyes. "Where the fuck is my sister?"

Coughing up blood, McNiven murmured, "I . . . don't know."

Stephen stood and dragged the man to his feet. He pressed the gun against McNiven's head. "Tell me or you're dead."

He croaked what might've been a laugh. "You . . . won't kill me. I . . . planted enough evidence . . . to frame you for Grant's . . . and Reaper's deaths. I'm . . . the only one . . . who can clear you."

Stephen's heart sank. McNiven was right. Stephen needed him alive.

Gritting his teeth, Stephen slid the gun barrel along the major's scalp, stopping at his ear. "Maybe that's true, but I don't need you in one piece."

McNiven's eyes widened.

"See," Stephen continued, "I know just the right angle to blast off your ear without the bullet entering your skull. You won't be able to hear from that side or wear sunglasses ever again, but that's fine with me."

"All right, all right." McNiven raised his hands in a show of surrender. "I'll tell you . . . what you want. Just . . . put the gun down."

"No way." Stephen pressed the barrel more firmly against McNiven's scalp for emphasis. His mind shifted back to playing Tactico with Dad. He'd exposed the spy. Now he could use him to find The Controller. "I'm not letting you out of my sight."

McNiven laughed, seeming to have regathered his strength. "You idiot. Like you said . . . I couldn't do it all myself. While you're toying with me . . . did it ever cross your mind . . . to check on your girlfriend?"

Stephen's cheeks went cold. Melinda. He'd left her alone upstairs.

Before he could stop himself, he turned his head to listen.

McNiven's fist crashed into Stephen's cheek.

Stephen staggered and tried to recover, but the major landed a kick in his chest. He flew backward, the back of his head ramming against the wall.

Colors swirled around him. Rubbing his scalp, he fought to see clearly. He spotted McNiven running out the back door.

"Shit!"

Stephen bolted outside into the icy rain. As he rounded the corner of the house, he heard a loud snap.

He stopped dead in his tracks.

Corporal Greenwood was holding McNiven by the arm. The pathologist's body hung limp, his head twisted at an impossible angle.

"What did you do?" Stephen asked, barely able to form the words.

Greenwood looked at Stephen, then down at the body. "I heard everything. This fucker killed Grant. He was going to escape."

"He was our only connection to The Controller." Stephen jammed his fists against his temples, still clutching the M18. "He could've cleared my name. Fuck!"

Stephen aimed the gun at Greenwood.

The corporal tilted his head. "You're joking, right?"

Anger made it hard to hold the gun steady. "How did you find me?"

"I've been following him, hiding under his vehicle." Greenwood jerked his head at McNiven's corpse. "I was too late to stop him from killing the German kid and his mom. I wasn't sure what he was doing here until I heard your voice."

Freezing rain bounced off Stephen's cheeks. "Why didn't you do something earlier?"

"I thought you had it handled."

"Yeah. I did. Until . . ." Stephen's gut knotted up. "Melinda."

"Huh?"

"Do something with him. We're both wanted for murder. We don't need another dead body lying around." Stephen ran for the back door without waiting for Greenwood to respond.

He dashed up the stairs, praying that he would be in time.

"Melinda!" he shouted as he barged through the bedroom door, gun in hand.

He stopped short.

Melinda wasn't there.

49

After searching the entire upper floor of the little house, Stephen had to accept that Melinda was gone. He found no sign of forced entry, but the people he was dealing with knew how to cover their tracks. If he had time, he might've been able to find some trace evidence, but time was against him.

He ran down the stairs two steps at a home and bounded outside. Maybe Greenwood had found something or remembered more. Maybe if Stephen pressured him about Richard Purcell and Tawergha, it would trigger a memory.

Greenwood was gone. So was McNiven's body.

"Shit." Stephen ran around to the front of the house and searched for some sign of where the soldier could've gone. Nothing. He retreated to the front entrance and paced, thinking up a plan. He could wait a few minutes, see if Greenwood returned, but then he'd have to act.

Five minutes later, he gave up. He'd eliminated the spy, but he still had no idea where The Controller was hiding. If he called General Ross again, explained what happened…

His chest tightened. McNiven had showed up a short time after he'd called Ross. His adoptive uncle knew where he was, knew his plan.

Stephen struggled to breathe. Was Uncle Alex The Controller? That didn't make sense—Ross wouldn't hurt Sharon. But he could've been involved, and that meant Stephen couldn't trust anyone in US military command. Where else could he turn?

Another thought struck him. Edmund had left that document about Project Super-Patriot to warn him about the depths the military might go to cover up their failed experiment. But he'd also left him something else.

Stephen searched through his wallet until he found the business card from the University of Bern. He dialed the number and waited. It rang three times before he heard a voice say, "Hallo?"

"Is this Professor Friedrich Gersch?"

"Ja. Who is this?" The professor's soft Germanic accent was subtle, most apparent in the way he pronounced "this" as "zis."

"Stephen Englehart. I'm the medical examiner at Ramstein Air Base."

There was a pause, and then, "You work with Doctor Wilson, ja? I helped him with the Virtopsy machine."

"I . . . used to. There's been . . ." He searched for a better way to say it, and decided the direct route was best. "He's dead."

"I'm sorry to hear that. He was a good man, but I didn't know him that well. This isn't the reason you're calling me, is it?"

"In a way, it is." Stephen cleared his throat. "Were you helping him investigate something called Project Super-Patriot?"

A tense pause. "I'm afraid you've made a mistake. I don't know what you're talking about. Goodbye, Doctor."

"Wait! I need your help."

Silence from the other end, leaving Stephen unsure if Gersch had hung up or was simply waiting for him to continue. He assumed the latter. "This is a secure line, free of unwanted listeners. I promise I'm not working for anyone but myself. I just need answers."

"You sound desperate, Doctor. Are you certain you're not under duress? If you are not, tell me the model number of your Virtopsy machine."

The biotech researcher sounded like a spy. "I'm not under duress, and I have no idea what model number we use. But I am in trouble, and so is my sister if I don't find her soon, so please, tell me you know something that can help me."

"Not over the phone. Do you have access to transportation?"

"Yes."

"Drive to Inzlingen. When you reach the border, find another way across. Walk or take a bicycle. Once in Schweiz, make your way to the Viktoriahaus at the Botanical Gardens. I will meet you there at nine, when they open, but come alone. If I suspect someone is with you, you will never see me."

This sudden power shift threw Stephen for a loop. He'd planned to set the rules, to make Gersch prove his trustworthiness, but the researcher had turned that plan on its head. He wanted to search for Melinda but had no idea where to start. Gersch was his only chance. "All right, but how will I find you?"

"You won't. I'll find you."

"But what if—"

The line went dead.

Stephen grumbled as he stashed the phone. A trip to Switzerland hadn't been in his plans for the week, but then neither had being a fugitive.

50

As Sharon opened her eyes, she tried to remember what day it was. Had she been there for weeks? Months? Years?

Groaning, she sat up. The others were still asleep. She stripped off her T-shirt. She'd long gotten over the fact that she had no privacy. If one of them had enough willpower remaining to ogle her, let them. It wasn't like any of them would ever have sex again, not with Big Brother lurking in their minds.

She pulled on her uniform and jumped to her feet. The Controller would expect her to go through her routine of calisthenics, so that was what she did. Then, when the others awoke, they would train. Rinse, wash, repeat.

Except today would be different. Today, she was going to get the hell out of there.

As Sharon stretched, she purposefully kept her eyes from looking at the pantry, where their breakfast trays awaited, wrapped in aluminum foil. She'd noticed The Controller's voice seemed dimmer when she was removing the foil. It seemed crazy, but she had the idea that if she created a makeshift helmet out of the foil, it might block whatever signal The Controller was using to communicate with them. An image of people in the 1960s wearing tinfoil hats popped into her head, and she nearly laughed. Except this was no laughing matter. If she could stop the pain, she could fight her way out.

As if summoned by her thoughts, electricity shot through her mind and body. She convulsed. White light flooded her skull.

Then, just as suddenly, it stopped. She crumpled to the ground.

As her thoughts started to coalesce, she heard someone crying. She fought to lift her head and look at the other beds. DeShaun was curled into a fetal position, sobbing. So was Reinhardt. And Yacoub. They were all crying. Sharon reached up to her face and found it wet with tears.

The door hissed open. A stranger staggered into the chamber, hands behind his head. He was big, somewhere around six feet tall, with the build of a heavyweight boxer. His face wouldn't have impressed anyone, but it was his eyes that caught Sharon's attention. Hazel, ringed with red. Vacant, but something lingering around the edges. Fear? Anger?

Good morning, class. Sharon winced as The Controller's voice filled her mind. *Say hello to Richard Purcell. He's an earlier graduate. But he's been a bit of a disappointment.*

Purcell drew his elbows inward. His face twisted. It was obvious he could hear The Controller's voice. And he didn't seem happy about what he heard.

Children, this is a lesson about what happens when you don't follow orders. Thanks to this Dick, the project nearly got shut down. To make matters worse, he disappeared. I had to expend unnecessary time and resources to track him down. And by now, you should know how much I detest wasting resources.

A chill ran down Sharon's spine. She glanced around the room and could tell that the others shared the same feeling.

"What did he do?" Deshaun asked out loud.

He betrayed the mission. He failed to eliminate a target as ordered. He thought he was being benevolent, sparing a child. The Controller's voice became bitter. *That child detonated a bomb concealed underneath his clothes. Killed four Navy SEALs and fourteen civilians in Tawergha. Would've killed Dick, too, if not for his gift.*

Sharon felt a pang of sympathy for Purcell. Even after the indoctrination, all the torment The Controller had put them through, she found it hard to believe that, placed in a similar situation, she wouldn't make the same choice. Some orders were too cruel to be followed.

You think my order was unfair, don't you? Even after all my teaching. You still don't understand.

Sharon pressed her lips together. She'd been certain The Controller couldn't actually read their minds, so long as they didn't form their thoughts into words. But now she wasn't sure. If he did know what they were thinking, did he know her plan? Was that why he was doing this?

After he recovered from the bomb, Dick went rogue. He killed a group of civilians on a bus without provocation. He insisted he was following orders, but I never issued that order. You may think he was a man faced with an impossible choice, but he wasn't. Underneath that façade lies a cold-blooded killer. The same that hides in each of you. The process awakens that killer. That's the reason for the training. For the implant. With great power comes great insanity. I am all that stands between you and madness. That is why you must follow my orders, without question. That is why you must obey.

Purcell lowered his arms. Now Sharon could see a syringe in his shackled hands. The soldier grimaced, as if fighting against some unseen force, and then plunged the syringe into his chest and depressed the plunger.

The soldier shivered and convulsed. He fell to his knees and vomited.

"What. Did. You. Do. To. Me?" he whispered.

You've proven yourself unworthy of your gift. The Lord giveth, and the Lord taketh away.

Purcell's eyes bulged. He ripped open his shirt, exposing the spot where he'd jabbed the needle. Blood drained from an open wound that was already starting to fester.

Sharon's chest tightened as she understood. The Controller had taken away his healing power.

"He's lying to you!" Purcell shouted. He struggled to stand. "I followed every order without question. He made me attack that bus. And it wasn't filled with civilians. They were ISIS. I saw them!"

Sharon glanced at DeShaun, arching her eyebrows in question. He shrugged.

"Don't let him fool you." Blood was flowing from the wound in Purcell's chest now. His breathing became ragged. "We're not working for the government. We're stooges for a terrorist organization. That's why he doesn't want you to question his orders. They're turning us into weapons against our own people!"

Sharon's stomach twisted. It was the same thought she'd had but didn't dare voice. Whom did they really serve? If they were part of an official military study, why the subterfuge? Why did The Controller hide himself?

"The Controller isn't real!" Purcell shouted. "He's something they created to control us. That's why we never see him. He's just a—"

His voice cut off, replaced with gurgles and chokes. His eyes bulged. Blood streamed from his mouth. He started to turn and collapsed to the floor.

Standing behind him was a man of modest height and build. He wore Army BDUs in desert camouflage print. Black eagles adorned both lapels. His pale eyes bore deep into Sharon, awakening a long-buried memory.

It had been the day of her graduation from Officer Candidate School. The brand-new butter bars on her epaulets demarking her as a second lieutenant were already melting from her excitement. Stephen hadn't been able to attend due to a licensing board exam, but Uncle Alex had been there, and he'd brought a friend: an Army major heading up an antiterrorism taskforce who leered at Sharon with pale eyes in a way that made her feel like he'd sucked the life out of her body. The same man who stood before them now.

"I'm the Controller," the man said, wiping blood from a long hunting knife with a white cloth. He sheathed the knife in a leather scabbard on his belt and stuffed the cloth in his pocket. He surveyed Sharon and the others with a cold, domineering gaze. "As you can see, I'm quite real. This man suffered delusions, hallucinations, and uncontrollable rage. Somehow, he slipped past our screening, a mistake that will not happen again. You should believe nothing he said. Trust only what I tell you. Follow orders, and you will be rewarded. Defy me . . ." His lip curled as he indicated the lifeless heap on the floor. "Well, you've seen what will happen. Now, get ready. You're going on your first field mission."

Sharon stared at the dead soldier. Something buzzed in her ear. She swatted it away, just as she wished she could dispel this feeling of dread, that something horrible was about to happen.

"What's our mission?" one of the other Rangers asked.

The Controller's jaw set grimly. "To find and eliminate the last threat: Corporal Mark Greenwood."

51

The latest song by one of the Jonas Brothers, Stephen could never remember which one, played on the radio as he pushed the pickup to its top speed of eighty miles per hour on the autobahn. Each time a car came up behind him, he tried to see inside, but without fail, they veered to the left and zoomed past before he could get a good look.

As he steered with one hand, he patted his bulky ski parka until he felt the reassuring bump of the gun he'd taken from McNiven. The outfit he'd purchased at a Peek & Cloppenberg on the way screamed tourist—blue jeans, white socks, and sneakers—but he was better off not trying to blend in and instead portraying himself as an American on holiday, ignorant of the local rules and customs. Unless Special Agent Wade knew where he was going and had already sent Swiss authorities his photo, he shouldn't have any problems.

Nevertheless, as the music faded to crackling static and the number of cars on the highway thinned, Stephen's chest tightened. If he was walking into a trap, he wouldn't be able to fight his way out alone with only a pistol. He'd never be able to clear his father's name. Never be able to save Sharon or Melinda.

Gritting his teeth, he pressed the accelerator as far down as it would go. Failure was not an option. He was going to get answers, and he was going to save his sister.

Twenty minutes after entering Inzinglen, he reached an intersection. The main street continued to the left. His GPS urged him to go that way until he reached the border. Instead, he veered right. After another ten minutes, the road became a dirt path. The truck bounced over rocks and bumps past farmhouses and abandoned machinery. He hadn't even realized he'd crossed the border until his GPS announced he was now in Switzerland. He smiled inwardly. So far, so good.

It took another half hour to reach Basel's city center. Once he crossed the Rhine River, he found a parking garage to stash the truck, and then continued on foot until he arrived at the botanical gardens. The receptionist gave him a once-over but said nothing as she waved him in. He kept his stocking cap low over his ears and brow as he trudged along the path.

He walked until he reached the Viktoriahaus and entered. A gardener was watering plants on the opposite side, but otherwise the dome was empty. Stephen pretended to be interested in an array of giant water lilies.

Moments later, he heard a rush of air as the door opened. A man entered, a few inches taller than Stephen and at least twenty pounds lighter. A fedora topped his head, and a jacket far too light for the weather hung from his lanky frame. A small gray mustache covered his upper lip. As he moved closer, Stephen saw that he had vivid blue eyes, which sparkled with life.

The man crossed over to stand next to Stephen. In a low voice, he asked in English, "Was the gardener here when you arrived?"

"Yes," Stephen replied.

"Has he shown an interest in you?"

"No."

"Let's wait."

They stood silently, appearing enraptured by the blooming flowers. Stephen's pulse throbbed at his temples. He kept his hand on his belt, near the butt of the pistol, in case it was a trap.

After two minutes, the gardener coiled up his hose and, without so much as a glance at the patrons, left the building.

"I believe it's safe to talk." The man turned to Stephen. "I'm Friedrich Gersch."

Stephen shook his hand, noting the firmness of the older man's grip. "You seem pretty familiar with the cloak-and-dagger stuff."

"Biotech consulting is not my singular passion. But, like all Swiss, I do not take geopolitical sides. I care about what is right. Any secrets you wish to share are safe with me." He grew serious. "For instance, you mentioned you needed to find your sister. What happened to her?"

"She's been missing for over a week. I think she's been conscripted into a dangerous experiment."

"Project Super-Patriot." When Stephen looked at him in surprise, Gersch clucked his tongue. "Don't seem so stunned. You're the one who recklessly blurted out that name over the phone. I assume your sister is a soldier."

Stephen nodded.

"Then it doesn't take a doctorate degree to put two and two together. Tell me what you already know about the project."

Stephen chided himself for again letting Gersch take control of the conversation. He'd expected to be asking the questions, not the other way around. His fingertip grazed over the gun handle.

"You don't trust me." Gersch shook his head. "Please remember, you contacted me. But if you need further proof . . ." He reached into his pocket and withdrew a photograph, which he handed to Stephen.

It was an old Polaroid, faded around the edges, the colors bleeding into orange-yellow. The photo was of a room full of soldiers, all male, wearing olive tank tops and BDU pants. They were looking at something off-camera. Stephen held the photo closer. There was a shadow on the wall that didn't belong to the others. It was huge. Distorted.

"This is from Project Super-Patriot?" he asked.

Gersch nodded.

"How did you get it?"

"That's not the question you should be asking." Gersch pointed a bony finger at the photo. "What else do you see?"

Stephen scanned the photo. His chest tightened. He recognized a face he saw in his dreams every night, the face of a man he revered more than anyone else.

"Dad," he whispered.

He ran a shaky fingertip over the image, imagining the smooth, clean-shaven skin. The lingering scent of Old Spice. The throaty laugh when Stephen beat him at Tactico. Only Dad wasn't laughing in this photo. He looked scared. Like he knew something bad was about to happen.

"You don't seem shocked," Gersch said. "I assume Doctor Wilson told you?"

Pressing his lips together, Stephen nodded.

"What did he tell you about the project?"

"Not much." Stephen unfolded the document he'd found in Edmund's basement and handed it to the researcher. "But this answered a lot of questions."

Gersch's eyebrows knitted together as he started reading. He glanced at Stephen several times before he finished, and then he released his breath in a whoosh. "So, DARPA was trying to create a real-life Captain America."

Stephen's jaw slackened.

"Come now, ever since the first movie came out, even us poor Europeans know all about your star-spangled superhero." Gersch gave Stephen a wry smile. "Truth be told, I've been a fan of the comic books for years."

"Yeah. Me too." Stephen reclaimed the document and stuffed it in his pocket. "Whoever is behind this new incarnation must've been part of the original project. The new ones can regenerate."

"I'm sorry. Did you say regenerate?"

"Small wounds heal instantly. I saw a soldier come back from the dead."

Gersch mumbled in German. He scratched his forehead and stared at the ground.

"What?" Stephen asked. "What is it?"

"I thought it was a rumor. An inside joke. But, clearly, it's true."

"What's true?"

"In Switzerland, several biotech companies have been studying single-cell freshwater polyps with unique regenerative properties. If you cut them in half, or even tear them apart, they regrow. The hope is that one day, we will understand these creatures well enough to apply their unique properties to human organs. We could regrow a heart or liver, maybe more."

"How close are these companies to finding that answer?"

"On the record, decades away." Gersch pursed his lips. "But my sources tell me one company made a breakthrough three years ago. They succeeded in regenerating a canine leg. It was as if the leg had never gone missing."

"I can't believe that wasn't all over the news."

"It might have been, but before the company could begin human trials, they suffered an unfortunate accident. An explosion. Some say a gas leak, others say a chemical fire. Either way, it decimated more than half of the building—and all the research hidden inside."

A feeling of dread crept over Stephen. "Is that what you believe happened?"

"I believe you have stumbled upon something very dangerous. What you describe sounds like someone is conducting their own research. If American soldiers are the subjects, then someone within the military is behind it."

"You mean DARPA?"

Gersch snickered. "Everyone looks at DARPA as the evil scientists bent on world domination. But I've checked every current project, including the top-secret ones. There is nothing evil going on there. No, the ones behind this have their own agenda."

"You know who they are?"

"I have my suspicions."

When Gersch said no more, only squinting at the morning sun reflecting off the reservoir, Stephen tightened his fists. "You're not going to tell me who?"

"I'm in a tenuous position, Doctor. I need the trust of your military leaders to continue my work unhindered. If you were to make accusations that proved to be unfounded, and word got back to them that I had supplied information to you, it would destroy everything I've built." Gersch looked Stephen up and down. "I am not yet sure I can trust you to be prudent."

Stephen's cheeks flushed. "I took a huge risk coming here."

"Yes, I appreciate that, which is why we are having this meeting at all. If what you've told me is true, and this group is sending unstable human subjects into the field, then we are all at risk. That is why I will do what I can to help, but you must not mention my name to anyone. No one must know I am anything more than a biotech consultant."

"Isn't that what you're doing now? Consulting?"

A thin smile appeared on Gersch's face. "I like you, Dr. Englehart. But I need more than congeniality to trust you."

Stephen toyed with the idea of walking away and finding another solution, but he was out of options. He showed Gersch the digital photo of the implant and the serial number. "These super-soldiers have cerebral implants. I pulled this out of the one I autopsied. He woke up minutes later. I think the implant shorted out and stopped his brain from regenerating."

Gersch's eyes glistened as he studied the image. "What does it do?"

"Best guess? It monitors the subject's vitals, allows them to block pain, and provides near-telepathic communication with whoever's in charge."

"A few years ago, an article claimed the government was staging accidents so they could implant a chip in the brains of unsuspecting civilians. But the implants were faulty. It was considered a hoax." Gersch rubbed his chin. "May I see the implant? I might be able to find out more if I study its inner components."

Stephen felt the sharp bite of remorse. "The wireless technology must have tracking capabilities. They followed it back to Edmund Brubaker, killed him and his mother, and took the implant."

Darkness clouded Gersch's face, making it seem like he was mourning the hacker, but then he said, "Long-range wireless telecommunication has a maximum range of thirty kilometers. Where did your sister disappear?"

"On the way to Baumholder."

"Then their base of operations is somewhere between there and Ramstein." As Gersch handed the phone back to Stephen, he studied the star-spangled shield logo on the case. "You said you're a comic book fan."

"Yes."

"Then you'll appreciate the irony of the serum's origins."

A feeling of dread crept into Stephen's chest. "What do you mean?"

"That polyp I told you about, the one with regenerative properties. You probably studied them at some point in your training." He leaned forward. "They're called hydra."

Stephen stared at Gersch. "You're kidding."

"I wish I was."

"You know who's behind it, don't you? Who?" Stephen grabbed Gersch's lapel. "Tell me."

"I looked you up, after you called me." The researcher stared back at Stephen fearlessly. "You know. You've always known. You've chosen to ignore the truth."

"I don't know."

"You do."

Gersch jerked his chin, indicating the Polaroid Stephen still clutched in his other hand.

Slowly, as if waking from a dream, Stephen lifted the photo and studied it. He found it hard to breathe as he scanned the soldiers' faces again, lingering on the face of his father. The old man couldn't mean him. He was dead. He'd been dead for a long time.

No, not his father. His stomach lurched. He'd been so focused on the look of fear in his father's face, he hadn't noticed the one man in full uniform off to the side, partly obscured in shadows. Bronze maple leaves adorned his shoulders. Unlike the others, who looked either afraid or angry, he was grinning like a hyena beneath a bushy white mustache.

Alexander Ross.

52

Stephen's mind raced as he trudged back through downtown Basel. It was so obvious now. Everything had started when Ross came into the picture. Every time his father came back angrier, Ross never seemed fazed. When his parents died, it was Ross who took them in—for their protection, or to keep under his thumb? Why hadn't Stephen put the pieces together earlier?

Because you didn't want to believe it.

It seemed like years since Stephen had heard that nagging voice, even though it had been mere days. But it was right. Despite all the arguments, despite all the subterfuge and misdirection, Stephen clung to the desperate belief that his adoptive uncle loved him in his own way. That made him blind to what was really going on. Well, no longer. Whatever it took, he'd make the general tell him where to find his sister.

He fished in his pocket for the small key ring as he entered the garage. It would be impossible to get back onto base, or any military installation, especially in Edmund's rust bucket. He needed a plan. Maybe he could lure Ross to a cafe somewhere, set up a trap.

As he approached the truck, he reflected on the last thing Gersch had said to him: *If you find the serpent's den, they will strike back with all the venom they have. There will be no bargaining. No reasoning. Even for your sister, it may be too late. Are you prepared to do what must be done?*

Stephen had weighed the question before answering. *Thirty years of my life have been a lie. I'll do whatever it takes to make them mean something.*

He stuck the key in the lock.

Cold metal pressed against the back of his neck.

"Hello, Doctor," a feminine voice, thick with a German accent, purred in his ear. "I hear you've been looking for me."

Muscles taut, Stephen continued to face the truck, right hand raising the key over his head while the other slipped to his belt.

"Uh-uh." The gun barrel jammed harder against his neck. "Hand me the pistol. Slowly."

Stephen gnashed his teeth but complied. Once she had the M18, the woman said, "Now, turn around. Keep your hands behind your head."

Taking small steps, Stephen pivoted to face her. She wore a black pullover, jeans, and boots. Her raven hair fell past her shoulders. Blue eyes with gold flecks bore into Stephen with a cold edge that sent a shiver down his back. In another time and place, he would've found her incredibly attractive. But the gun pointed at him made that impossible. Something stirred in the back of his mind. He'd seen her before. But where?

"So," she said before he could make the connection. Her lip twisted into a leer. "You're her brother. I see it in your cheekbones. A pity. What fun the three of us could've had together."

Realization struck him. "You're Anja Wagner."

"Of course I am. Do I look like Angelina Jolie?" She shook her head. "Where is the implant?"

"What implant?"

She swung the pistol and fired.

Searing pain bit into Stephen's shoulder. He cried out and staggered back against the truck.

"The next bullet will be far more painful." She stepped closer, grabbed his jacket, and pressed the gun against his forehead. "Tell me where it is."

Stephen struggled to block out the fire in his shoulder and focus on what she was asking. Didn't she know the implant was gone?

As he started to answer, he stopped himself. He was still alive was because she believed he knew where the implant was. He needed to keep the advantage.

"Hidden." He lifted his chin, injecting as much authority into his voice as he could muster. "I'm the only one who knows where. I can take you there if you tell me where to find Sharon."

Her brow furrowed. "You're in no position to make demands."

"I think I'm in the perfect position. You need me alive, and it's not just for the implant, is it? I'm valuable to someone." He studied her face, and then it clicked. She was the woman in the photo on Colonel Laskaris's desk. "You work for Laskaris, don't you? Or are you his lover? That's why he made up that crap about you being detained by the Bundespolizei, right?"

"Don't be gross." She made a sour face. "He's my father."

"But—"

She pointed the gun between his eyes. "Stop asking questions. Knowing my father won't save your life."

"Maybe not, but knowing General Ross might." Stephen knew he was gambling with his life—for all he knew, Uncle Alex was the one who sent Anja--but he needed information. "Unless you want to piss off my uncle."

Her gaze narrowed as she studied his face. He remained passive.

She's buying it. All she needs to do is drop her guard for a second, just enough for me to get a punch in...

Her face twisted into a scowl. "You bore me. I'll tell The Controller you tried to escape, and I had no choice but to kill you. He'll believe me. He always does."

She aimed for his forehead again.

He'd have to try to dodge. But he knew he wasn't fast enough.

Her finger slid toward the trigger.

Something moved in the flatbed behind Stephen. Anja's gaze shot upward, over his shoulder. Her eyes widened. Her aim drifted to the side.

Stephen turned to see what was happening.

A massive fist shoved him out of the way. He flew to the ground. His knee smashed against the pavement. Pain flared and shot up his leg.

He rolled onto his back and stared in shock.

Corporal Greenwood had Anja in a headlock. His bulging biceps compressed the side of her face. She clawed at his arms, but he tightened his grip. Color drained from her cheeks.

"Stop!" Stephen shouted, ignoring the pain in his knee and shoulder, using the truck to haul himself into a standing position. "Don't kill her."

"She was going to kill you," Greenwood growled.

"I know, but we need her." Stephen staggered toward them. He paused to stoop and pick up both pistols she'd dropped. Hers was a USP Tactical favored by the German military. The heft felt good. He stuck McNiven's M18 in his belt and held onto the USP. "She's going to tell us how to find The Controller."

Greenwood glared at Stephen, still grappling Anja by the neck, and then he loosened his grip. The woman coughed. Her gaze locked onto Stephen.

"Go ahead and kill me. I won't tell you shit." She spat at him.

"Yeah, you will. Because, if you don't, we'll hand you over to the Bundespolizei. For real this time."

"Is that supposed to scare me?" She scoffed, but Stephen caught a flicker of fear in her eyes.

"You're not born German, are you? I saw Turkish stuff in Colonel Laskaris's office. He was stationed at Incirlik. That's where he met your mom, right?" Stephen felt more confident as he saw the fear in her eyes deepen. "I'm betting you took the last name Wagner to fool the immigration office. Germany has been cracking down on Turkish immigrants over the last few years. All it takes is a phone call and you'll be back in the hands of Turkish authorities. And, from what I hear, they don't treat defectors kindly."

Anja glared at him, eyes smoldering. At last, she looked down at the ground. "All right. I'll tell you where to find your sister."

"Great." Stephen nodded at Greenwood.

The soldier gave him a puzzled look.

"Release her."

Greenwood stared for another moment and then unwrapped his arm from the woman's neck.

Stephen approached Anja, who had begun to massage her throat, and then cracked the butt of her pistol across the back of her head. She crumpled to the ground.

"What the fuck?" Greenwood gaped at him. "Why'd you do that?"

"Anything she told us would be a lie." Stephen searched Anja's pockets and found a black key fob. He pressed a button. The headlights flashed on a cherry-red Porsche parked at the other end of the garage. Stephen nodded approvingly. Since he needed to ditch the truck, at least he was making a substantial upgrade. "Use the ropes in back and tie her up."

"But what was all that about her being Turkish?"

"I'm sure she is Turkish. But her dad's a US colonel. Even if she's illegitimate and he helped her enter through unofficial channels, there's no way he'd allow her to be deported. The fact she went along with it confirmed she was acting."

Greenwood grunted as he bound Anja's hands together and hog-tied them to her already bound ankles. "So, why are we letting her live?"

"Insurance." Stephen found his phone and pulled up Google Maps. "When we get to the hidden base, she's our ticket inside."

"But we don't know where it is."

"Actually, we do." Stephen showed Greenwood a map of the area between Baumholder and Ramstein. "In order for The Controller to direct the implant, he had to be operating within a thirty-kilometer radius. It's just over forty klicks between the two bases. That means the base must be somewhere here." He used his index finger to indicate a circular area. "You told me it was underground. The Heilingen Tunnels are a short distance east, and there are some tunnel branches that were closed off by the German government."

"Which means the base could be hidden in one of those branches." Greenwood grunted in what Stephen took to be a sign of respect. "Good thinking. But how will we know where the entrance is?"

"That part is easy."

Stephen typed a name into the app. A red dot appeared on the map halfway between the two bases.

"What's that?" Greenwood asked.

"That is the spot where Avant-garde Intelligente Medizin once stood, before it was destroyed." Stephen gave Greenwood a knowing smile. "And where they created the implant."

53

Major," the scientist snapped as he pressed down on Sharon's arm. "Please hold still."

Sharon startled, his voice disrupting her reverie. She stared at him as if waking from a dream. She'd been thinking about the day she got orders for Stuttgart. She'd called Stephen with the good news, grateful that they'd be on the same continent for the first time in nearly ten years. After hanging up, she'd admired how calm her brother was, always in control.

Except that hadn't been invariably true. When Dad kept getting deployed, Stephen was always acting out, getting in trouble, driving Mom crazy. And then, after he got sick, he'd changed. He was angry. Primal. Like there was a monster growing inside him, clawing its way out.

Then, when their parents died and Uncle Alex put them in counseling, he'd changed again. He became mild-mannered, a jokester, like the beast had been exorcised from his body. As she prepared to relocate to Germany, she'd wondered if she'd imagined it, or if Stephen had, even for a moment, suffered from the same darkness as their father.

And that was when it hit her. It hadn't only been when Stephen got sick that he seemed different. It had been after he went boxing with Uncle Alex.

The scientist cleared his throat. He studied her with rheumy eyes, lip curled under a bulbous nose, reminding her of an unpleasant Mister Bean.

"I'm sorry... what?"

"I need to draw blood and you keep moving."

"Oh. Right." She shook her head and held her arm steady. "Why do you need my blood?"

He plunged the needle into her vein. She winced.

"We need to monitor your enzymes and biomarkers. You're not showing any signs of compromise, so we need a negative control for comparison." He filled one vial with blood and grabbed another. "That's all I can tell you."

"Yeah, fine. Whatever."

As the tech continued to draw blood, Sharon couldn't stop thinking about that memory. Uncle Alex was the common denominator. Stephen had gotten sick when he started hanging out with Alex, and then he'd started changing. Dad had changed when he started working with Alex. And now the Controller had her, and she was changing. Oh God.

"All done." The tech removed the needle. A rivulet of blood ran down Sharon's arm.

"Don't I get a Band-Aid?" she asked.

"You'll heal in a minute. No reason to waste resources."

Anger bubbled in her chest as she curled and uncurled her fingers. There were four coolers with frosted glass doors. Through them, she could see racks of test tubes. She presumed some were blood samples, some were the super-serum, and some were the neutralizer the Controller had demonstrated on Purcell. If she could get her hands on a few vials, she'd have enough proof to expose the operation once she found a way out. And, if anyone hurt her along the way, she'd eventually heal. She spied the metal clipboard where the tech had been writing notes. His back was turned as he affixed labels on the tubes.

"How about a lollipop, then?"

The tech scoffed and began arranging supplies on the counter. Sharon recognized the bag of amber fluid they'd pumped her with when she first arrived. "Go back to your holding room. We need this area secure for the next procedure. "

"Let me help you clean up."

His head turned in her direction.

Sharon smashed the clipboard against his nose. He staggered backwards.

She swung again, parallel to the ground. The clipboard sliced across his cheek.

He yelped and grabbed at his face, but she didn't give him a moment to recover, kneeing his groin.

He fell, the back of his head striking the counter. He crumpled.

A lightning storm racked her body. She collapsed to her knees.

Stupid, stupid, stupid, The Controller said after the current ceased. *The spike in your vitals alerted me to your plan. You can't take any action against me without my knowledge.*

She dug her fingers into the desk and dragged herself to her feet. "Let me go . . . I know . . . what you did . . . to my brother."

Laughter echoed off the walls of her mind.

I've done nothing to him. I never even met him until the other day. But, thanks to your actions, if he tries to come here to save you, I will destroy him.

"Hurt him . . . and I'll kill you."

Something happened to you two, something you've forgotten. I can sense it.

"What the hell are you talking about?"

Thanks to the serum, it should take just a little electric stimulation . . . ah, right here.

A jolt, much smaller than the last, lit up her brain. Sharon clutched the counter for support. Lights and sounds and smells popped up in her mind like stars swirling together, coalescing into memories.

The scene replayed over and over, stuck in a never-ending loop, revealing the truth that had been buried for over thirty years. An inferno ignited inside her.

Ah, that's it. He did more than fail to sound the alarm, didn't he? He tore your family apart. You understand now what needs to be done, don't you?

Lava flooded her veins. Her hand tightened around the nearest fluid bag, the squishiness stoking her rage. "Oh, I understand."

So, tell me. For what do you fight?

For most of her life, Sharon had fought for something. Her place in the family. Her identity. The rights and security of others. Respect. And holding on to her fragile relationship with her brother. All built on lies.

"I fight for myself and for the American way of life," she said at last, through bared teeth. "And for you, Controller."

54

As Stephen floored the Porsche down the autobahn offramp toward Wolfstein, he glanced at the back seat. Anja snored loudly. She'd woken once on the two-hour ride, and it only took a rap on the head by Greenwood to knock her unconscious again. The big man squirmed in the tiny back seat, looking as comfortable as an elephant in an elevator.

"We almost there?" Greenwood asked. "I gotta piss."

"I'm sure your friends will be happy to let you use their restroom." Stephen snorted and veered onto a dirt road. "We're heading into the woods. You can find a tree when we stop."

"Anyone ever tell you you're an asshole?"

"All the time, starting with my kindergarten teacher."

Stephen grinned as Greenwood fell silent, but the mirth quickly washed away. His jokes wouldn't be enough this time. Even with the brute's help, he was about to take on far more than he could handle. If it weren't for Sharon, he'd be driving to Slovenia to hide in the mountains. But he couldn't abandon his sister, especially knowing the one man he'd trusted to help find her was involved.

During the drive, Greenwood had explained how the implant worked, not only allowing communication and monitoring, but delivering a bioelectric shock if a soldier failed to follow orders. When Stephen asked him about Richard Purcell, Greenwood told him that although the Green Beret had blown up in the Tawergha explosion thanks to the serum, he'd regenerated. But he wasn't the same after that. The Controller had deployed him to Achin. Something went wrong, and he'd disappeared. Now, what had happened to Sergeant Herrera made sense. Everything made sense.

A sloping mountain rose over the horizon ahead as Stephen headed for a wooded thicket. So far, no one had tried contacting Anja. That was good, as he hadn't needed an excuse for why she wasn't answering her phone, but bad in that either The Controller trusted her to get the job done, or she'd missed a check-in. Stephen hoped for the first option, because the latter meant there'd be a welcoming party waiting for them.

He parked beneath a towering fir tree and shut off the engine. The two men climbed out of the Porsche, Greenwood hefting the sleeping assassin over his shoulder, and trudged toward the mountain in silence. There wasn't much either could say. All too soon, one way or another, their partnership would end, most likely in death. The last lingering question was whose death.

When they crested the hill, they spotted the ruins at the mountain base. A chain-link fence cordoned off the perimeter. A sign proclaimed in German that the property had been condemned as an environmental threat and that trespassers would face imprisonment.

Stephen scooped up a handful of snow and tossed it at the fence. Nothing. At least it wasn't electrified.

"Set her down there and help me," he said.

Greenwood gave him an odd look at being ordered but complied without a word. Stephen mused on the fact that, even though the corporal had far more field experience, Stephen was Greenwood's superior officer. Not that that mattered much now. Even if they succeeded in stopping the project, they would both be equally court-martialed. Stephen rubbed his hands together before opening the sack he'd salvaged from the truck and pulling out a pair of wire cutters. He could tolerate prison time if he knew his sister was safe.

They worked quickly, Stephen clipping the chains and Greenwood peeling them back. Not a word passed between them. Stephen's thoughts were filled with Sharon and what he would say when he saw her. He could only imagine what Greenwood was thinking about. Probably something violent.

After a few minutes, they had an opening large enough for Greenwood to crawl through. The soldier went back for Anja while Stephen stuck the wire cutters back in the sack. He pulled out the M18, checked the magazine, and then returned it before drawing the USP out of his belt and repeating the process. Two guns against a squadron of super-soldiers. Greenwood could hold off a few, but eventually he'd lose. There was one solution, and the big guy wasn't going to like it.

"You ready?" Greenwood asked, carrying Anja over his shoulder.

Stephen nodded and stuck the USP back into his belt.

The ground was frozen hard on the other side of the fence and littered with debris. They picked their way toward the ruined building.

Most of the lab was a charred husk. No footprints in the snow except theirs.

"It's coming back to me," Greenwood said when they were still a good twenty yards from what remained of the building's entrance. "There are security cameras there and there." He stopped walking and pointed at a spot ahead of them and another off to the right. "Twenty more feet and we'll be in range. Somewhere there's a hidden entrance that's unmanned and unmonitored. I think it's that way, to the left. We should try to find it."

Stephen shielded his eyes from the sun's glaring reflection off the white snow as he studied the points the corporal had indicated. "You're right. You should try to find it."

Greenwood turned to face him. "You mean, we."

Shaking his head, Stephen drew the USP. "Set her down."

"What're you doing, Doc?" Greenwood's voice lowered to a rumbling growl.

"If they spot you, they won't take chances. They'll come at us with full force. If it's just me, they'll think I'm a desperate man trying to find his sister. They'll underestimate me."

"They'll kill you."

"That's why we brought her."

Stephen crouched next to the sleeping woman. He slapped her cheek.

Anja's eyes flew open. A string of curses in German mixed with Turkish spewed from her mouth.

"Sharon always had a thing for dirty talk." Stephen motioned to Greenwood. "Throw me the duct tape."

Greenwood tossed him a roll. He snapped off a strip of tape and pasted it over Anja's mouth. The woman's muffled yells continued as she thrashed and fought against the ropes binding her limbs. Stephen pulled out a hunting knife and slashed the hog-tie rope but made sure the restraints binding her wrists remained intact. Anja tried to scramble away, but he grabbed her arm with one hand and pressed the USP against her side with the other. Her eyes simmered, but she stopped fighting.

"This is crazy." Greenwood looked Stephen up and down. "You think you're Captain America, don't you?"

Stephen stared back at him, asking himself that same question. He didn't even have an unbreakable frisbee with which to defend himself. Did he really think he could be a superhero?

He recalled one day, three decades earlier, reading the latest issue of Captain America, where Cap had just fought against another superhero vigilante to save the lives of criminals.

"Dad," he'd asked as he put down the comic book. "What makes someone a hero?"

His father had scratched his chin. "That's a tough question, son. There are more heroes out there than you think, and most don't wear capes or masks. It's about doing what's right, no matter the cost. It's about helping others for no other reason than because it's the right thing to do. That's why Steve Rogers doesn't follow orders blindly, even though he wears a uniform. A hero doesn't only do what they can do. They do what they *should* do."

The boy thought about that and then he looked up at his father again. "Can you teach me to be a hero?"

Dad flinched, as if a mosquito bit him. Then he smiled and tousled his son's hair. "It's not something you can teach. It's something inside you."

"Is it inside me?"

"For sure. You have a hero's heart." Dad had touched his chest then. "When the time is right, you'll know what to do."

Now, Stephen wondered if that was true, or if his father had been bullshitting him. There was so much his father hadn't told him. Dad had been a patriot, but like Mom had said, there were things more important than patriotism. Like family. Stephen tightened his grip on the pistol. That was what he was going to do. He was going to fight for his family.

55

You sure about this?" Greenwood asked as they stood outside the abandoned, snow-covered lab. For the first time since they'd met, Stephen heard a hint of respect in the soldier's voice.

Stephen wasn't sure at all, but he nodded before he could convince himself it was a bad idea. He forced Anja to stand and urged her forward, keeping the pistol trained on her back, making sure to leave enough distance for sufficient reaction time if she tried anything. He glanced once over his shoulder to ensure Greenwood had moved out of sight, and then didn't look again.

When they reached the entrance, Stephen scanned the rubble. He couldn't see any way inside. He nudged Anja, who had finally stopped protesting.

"How do we get in?"

She glared at him.

He ripped the tape off her mouth. As she worked her jaw, he said, "I'm sure you've been here at least once. How do we get in?"

Silence.

Stephen surveyed the scene again, knowing that with every second that passed, it was more likely they would find him first.

Time to use that big brain. Visualize the scene. Find what's not supposed to be there.

Concrete slabs lay against shattered shelving units and research equipment. Wind puffed a snow flurry through a gaping hole in the roof. Dust swirled in a small eddy on what remained of the shattered linoleum floor and then settled again. No footprints. Nothing to indicate anyone had been there in years.

Maybe this is the wrong place.

The dust swirled again. Stephen watched the little dervish dance and then dissipate once more. It was staying in one spot, as if the wind wasn't coming from above, but below.

Using the gun barrel as a prod, he nudged Anja forward. She tensed. It took another shove to get her moving. They approached the spot where the dust devil had been. He spotted a gap between two large tiles.

"Open it," he ordered.

She gave him a hard stare for two heartbeats and then bent over, fumbling to move the larger tile with her bound hands. She managed to lift it, exposing a hole. A stone staircase descended into the darkness.

"Let's go." He waved the gun toward the staircase. When she didn't move, he drew the M18 with his other hand and aimed both at her chest. "Ladies first."

He followed her down the steps. When they reached the bottom of the staircase, lights flicked on. They were old rock tunnels, but Stephen could see the glint of metal ahead. He nudged Anja onward with his foot.

The hiss of escaping air echoed off the rock walls. Footsteps approached.

Stephen held his ground, keeping both guns trained on Anja's back.

Three soldiers wearing Marines fatigues appeared in the tunnel and stopped five or six feet away. Their hands were empty. The two in front were half a foot shorter than Stephen, but the one in the back was half a head taller. Their faces were expressionless.

"That's far enough," said the short one on the left. His name patch read White. "You're not authorized to be here. Hand her over and we'll let you walk out of here."

"I've got a better deal." Stephen raised the USP higher, so it was more visible. "Release Sharon Englehart, and I won't kill Ms. Wagner."

The soldiers remained motionless. No exchanged glances. No discussion. They stood stock still, like robots. Stephen's skin crawled.

"You're in over your head, boy," the one named White said at last. His voice sounded different, like someone else was speaking through him. "If Anja's your only bargaining chip, you've lost. She knows the price of failure."

Before Stephen could react, a gun appeared in the tallest soldier's hand, aimed at Stephen.

Stephen shoved Anja aside and fired the USP.

The large man's head jerked to the side. Blood spattered the wall next to him. He crumpled to the ground.

The other two soldiers rushed Stephen. He fired three shots with each pistol.

The soldiers shuddered as bullets ripped into their chests. They stumbled forward and collapsed at his feet.

Stephen stared down at the bodies. He'd killed three men in cold blood. He'd never killed anyone before. He should've felt something, anything, but he didn't. It almost felt . . . familiar. A cold vacuum spread through his body. It took all his strength to shake it off.

"Come on." Stephen grabbed Anja by the arm and dragged her past the bodies down the tunnel. It couldn't be that easy. He didn't dare look back over his shoulder.

About twenty feet ahead stood a metal door. Keeping the M18 jammed against Anja's side, he pushed her onward while holding the USP in his line of sight. He wasn't sure what he intended to do once inside, but that didn't matter. All he knew was, if he had any hopes of survival, he needed to get out of the tunnel. He had to see The Controller face-to-face. He had to demand his sister. Whatever happened after that, he'd improvise.

They were less than ten feet from the door when it swung open. Three more soldiers emerged.

"Controller!" Stephen shouted, hoping the man could hear him. "Call off your guard dogs. I know how to fix your problem with the serum. Free Sharon and I'll tell you how."

The soldiers froze in place like robots with their power shut off. They stared blankly ahead, sending creeps along Stephen's skin.

One soldier opened his mouth and said, "He's bluffing. Kill him."

Stephen fired four shots. Two of the soldiers staggered backward. The third surged at him.

Dragging Anja to the floor, Stephen twisted around and fired straight up. The bullet caught the soldier in the chin. His eyes rolled back, and he collapsed.

As Stephen reached for Anja, another shot rang out. Anja's eyes widened. Blood gushed from a hole in her chest.

Stephen turned. Another gunshot.

Pain ripped into the side of his head. A horrible ringing sound filled his ears. He barely heard a third gunshot, and then a fourth. The pain in his arm and gut were less, but only because of the wool blanket covering his senses. He crumpled to the floor.

Gray rimmed his field of vision. He managed to roll onto his back and look up. The last thing he saw before blacking out hurt far more than the bullets.

Sharon was holding a smoking gun.

56

A humming sound burrowed its way through the silent blackness. It branched out, rooting through every dark corner, carrying with it flashes of light.

Stephen forced his eyes open. He saw shadows and murky shapes at first, and an amber light suspended over him. His body felt numb, as if he were floating on a cloud.

Am I dead? He should've been panicked, but he felt no rush of fear, no bounding pulse, no tingle of adrenaline. That would make sense if he was dead.

Then, as he tried to move his arm, excruciating pain shot up his shoulder. He winced, fighting the urge to cry out. No, not dead.

Slowly, the pain subsided. Holding as still as possible, he focused on the shadows, willing them to take shape. They coalesced into what seemed to be a makeshift hospital room. Empty stretchers lined metal walls, surrounded by monitors and IV poles. He lifted his head enough to look down at his other arm. An IV ran from the back of his hand along the side of the bed and up into a bag of what looked like blood. A piggyback connector led to a smaller bag of clear liquid.

"A mixture of propranolol and lorazepam," a reedy voice said. A shadowy figure stood in the doorway. "Need to keep you calm, so you don't rip your sutures."

Stephen recognized the voice. The reveal of his opponent felt almost anticlimactic after everything he'd endured. It took a moment for his mouth to work, but he was able to whisper, "Where's . . . my sister?"

Colonel Laskaris approached, the amber light casting eerie shadows on his face. His ACU was heavily starched and ironed. His features were chiseled into a severe look, like an ancient Greek statue.

"You should be dead." Laskaris slid a finger along the IV line. "She was aiming for your forehead. I had to force her to shoot areas that were more likely to heal properly."

The recollection that it had been Sharon who shot him struck Stephen with full force. The image of her standing over him, holding a smoking gun, played over and over on a loop in his mind. Her face expressionless—no, not completely. There was a gleam in her eye.

Stephen forced himself not to think about it. Whatever Sharon had done, it was the fault of this man standing before him. The amber light flickered, making Laskaris look even more like the devil he was.

"Why . . . would you . . . save me?" Stephen said, his voice still hoarse, but growing stronger. "Afraid . . . of my . . . uncle?"

Laskaris winced. Stephen smiled inwardly. Good. He'd struck a nerve.

"Your uncle doesn't know you're here." Laskaris started walking around the perimeter of the bed, keeping his face turned away from Stephen. If he was lying, it was hard to tell. "You're alive because of what you said in the tunnels. You claimed to know how to fix the serum."

A small thrill of satisfaction ran through Stephen. He'd shouted the comment as a last-ditch play, but apparently it had worked. Fortunately, it wasn't an empty promise. "I do."

Laskaris stopped pacing. His head whipped toward Stephen. His eyes were of cold steel. "You're a coroner. Why should I believe you figured out what eight of my best scientists could not?"

"Because your scientists are idiots," Stephen jeered. "But they're only as good . . . as the idiot who hired them."

The colonel's cheeks reddened, appearing almost black in the amber light. He drew a pistol from a belt holster, rushed to the bedside, and pressed it against the side of Stephen's skull. "Don't think you have unlimited immunity. One more wrong answer, I'll kill you right now, and the hell with your uncle."

Stephen had no doubt Laskaris would keep his promise. But he'd gotten the reaction he'd wanted. Laskaris was desperate. If he wasn't, Stephen would already be dead. All he had to do was dole out a little more bait, and he could lead the colonel right to the trap. "Your scientists have been looking at it the wrong way. The problem's not with the serum."

A flurry of emotions danced over the man's face. He lowered the pistol. "What do you mean?"

"The serum does what it's supposed to do: stimulate cell replication and tissue regeneration. But they were lazy. They used the old super-serum as a base, to improve mitochondrial metabolic efficiency. I saw the same cellular changes in Greenwood as in the samples from the original subjects."

The puzzled look on Laskaris's face confirmed that he didn't understand half of what Stephen was saying. No wonder the project was failing. Laskaris understood military command, but he didn't know a thing about science.

"Those cellular changes create a feedback loop, triggering catecholamine overproduction, resulting in explosive rage," Stephen continued, hoping the more jargon he used, the easier it would be to enthrall his opponent. "That's what made my—I mean, the original soldiers lose control. This diluted version you're using does the same thing, but at a much lower level. They get a small boost of strength and speed, not enough to trigger a full catecholamine cascade."

Laskaris frowned. "Then why did I lose control over Greenwood?"

Now Stephen understood. For Laskaris, it wasn't about the project or the mission. He wasn't concerned about the damage Greenwood had done, or the innocents who died. He was just pissed that Greenwood had broken free. And that was his biggest mistake.

"The implant," Stephen said.

"The implant is what keeps them under control."

"Maybe that was the intent," Stephen said. "But you didn't test it."

"We ran plenty of field tests. It took us a while to quiet some hiccups, but the current product works."

"I'm sure you did. I heard about your 'field tests'—staging accidents so you could try the implant on unsuspecting civilians. And I'm sure you tested the serum. But did you test them together?"

Worry lines marred the colonel's forehead. "Why would you ask that?"

"The implant must be programmed to respond to specific tissue types and to modulate certain neurotransmitters. That's what allows it to deliver a bioelectric shock." Stephen bristled at the thought of Sharon and the others being tormented at the hands of this madman. "But what if that tissue is altered? Greenwood suffered traumatic brain injury. I'd guess the same happened to Richard Purcell. Their cerebral tissue regenerated, but at least briefly, it was a mass of stem cells, unrecognizable to the implant. The implant's processor can assume only one thing: it's been forcibly removed."

Laskaris's eyes widened. "So, it delivers shock after shock."

"The shock destroys the surrounding brain tissue, which regenerates, triggering another shock. Eventually, the tissue can't keep up. The soldier's cognitive processes break down."

"They become uncontrollable beasts." Laskaris stared at the ground. "Just like the originals."

Stephen winced at the implication that his father had been an uncontrollable beast. "The implant shorted out Greenwood's brain stem. He kept trying to regenerate, but the implant kept zapping him. When I removed the implant, his restorative abilities were able to work, but the damage had already been done."

Laskaris's head jerked up. "What do you mean?"

"His brain is fried," Stephen lied, hoping he sounded convincing. "He's alive, but he can barely speak, and whatever he says is gibberish."

"So he can't tell anyone what happened to him."

"No, he can't." Stephen swallowed against the bile rising in his gullet. "Your secret is safe."

Laskaris nodded as he inspected the IV line again. "Why are you telling me this?"

"I know you gave my sister the serum, and I'm assuming she has the implant." Stephen licked his lips. "I can help you solve the mismatch problem if you release me and promise to treat her first. All I care about is seeing her safe."

Laskaris leaned close enough for Stephen to see the pores on his skin. "What makes you think I need you? You've already told me the problem. My scientists can find a solution."

"Without me, you wouldn't even have figured out what the problem was." Stephen coughed. His chest was burning. "And even if my uncle doesn't know I'm here, I don't think you want him to find out you let me die."

Laskaris continued to glare at Stephen, his face wrinkled like he'd drunk spoiled milk. Then a thin smile spread across it. "You're right. I can't let you die. So, I'm going to give you the serum."

Stephen recoiled. "What?"

"This is the third blood transfusion. Our surgeon already closed off the severed arteries, but several of your internal organs went into shock from blood loss. I'm afraid it's a matter of time before they fail altogether." His grin turned vicious. "Unless you can regenerate."

"I don't want it."

"The propranolol will keep your heart rate down to allow the serum to work. Then, once it's in your system, we'll give you the implant."

Stephen's mouth went dry. "But I just told you—"

"I don't trust you, Doctor Englehart. If you're lying to me, you'll be another soldier under my control. And, if you're telling the truth . . ." He shrugged. "Well, you'll be even more motivated to fix the problem, now won't you?"

Stephen wanted to scream, to leap off the bed and attack the colonel, but the sedative cocktail dulled his senses. He could only glare.

Laskaris turned toward the door, stopped, and looked back. "Oh, and I think I'll have someone special deliver the serum to you, so she can tell you to your face how much she loathes you. Think of it as a reminder of who's in command."

A low, gurgling growl was all that came out of Stephen's mouth.

With a final sneer, Laskaris said, "Goodbye, Doctor," and walked out.

57

Sharon watched Anja lying in a hospital bed, eyes closed, dark hair fanned out on a pillow, skin ashen, breathing shallow and labored. Bandages covered her chest. An IV tube ran to her arm from a bag of amber fluid. A monitor beeped every few seconds, reflecting the on-screen heart rhythm. Heart rate fifty-five. Blood pressure eighty over forty.

Sharon knew enough to know that was low. Too low, but not low enough. She gripped the bed rail, wanting both to caress the woman's cheek and snuff out her life at the same time.

"She is beautiful, isn't she?"

Sharon whirled around to see Laskaris standing a few feet away, arms folded across his chest. His expression was set in granite, his gaze sharp but directed at Anja, not Sharon.

"I didn't know she was your daughter when we . . ." She trailed off, unable to say the words to him. "You know."

"Of course you didn't." He still wore that creepy grin, but it seemed softer as he watched Anja's chest rise and fall.

"Did any of the others volunteer?" she asked. "Or did you entrap them, too?"

For a moment, he said nothing, as if gathering his thoughts, long enough to make Sharon suspect he was going to spew some bullshit. But then he spoke. "The first few did. Purcell. Greenwood. They understood right off the bat what we were doing here. But they weren't enough. We needed more, and it's not like we could send out flyers." He sniggered at his own joke. She didn't join in. "That's when we reached out to training officers and commanders who had . . ."—he made air quotes—"'blemished' records. They were willing to trade us information about their top candidates in exchange for help clearing their names."

Blood drained from Sharon's cheeks. "That's how you found out about me."

"Oh, no, my dear. I wanted you from the moment we met, when your uncle introduced at your graduation fifteen years ago." When she flinched, he shook his head. "Not in that way. I could see your potential, even when you were still so young. I kept track of you over the years, waiting for the time when you would be ready. I'm sorry about the subterfuge to get you here, but the very qualities I sought—determination, decisiveness, dedication to a cause—they would've kept you from volunteering. Would they not?"

She kept her voice level. "You're correct."

"That's why I'm not mad about what you did to my daughter." He slid his hand through Anja's hair, letting it fall between his fingers. "Your moral compass has deterred you from reaching your apex. Thanks to the training you've received here—and the serum—you've learned to follow orders. I told you we needed to stop your brother at all costs, and you did what needed to be done. Even if that meant shooting an unarmed prisoner."

Sharon's body grew cold.

"Don't worry," he continued, grazing the back of his hand across Anja's cheek. "The serum will take longer to work due to the extent of her injuries, but it will work. She'll be better than ever soon enough. But there's a matter we must handle before then."

"My brother."

"I've made a deal with him."

Her stomach lurched. "You what?"

"He's figured out the fly in our ointment, so to speak. In exchange for his help solving the problem, I agreed to release you."

"But—you said—"

"Let me make that clear. I said I'd release you." He simpered. "But as I've stressed many times, I don't control you. I'm not ordering you to do anything. You're free to decide whether to stay or go. I only ask you to do one thing first."

"What's that?"

"Get an IV bag of serum from the lab and bring it to him."

She reeled. "You want to give him the serum?"

"I told him I would. But I'm going to leave the decision up to you. If you believe him, if you think he's telling the truth, then give him the serum. If not . . ." He grinned viciously. "Do with him as you please."

58

Twenty minutes or so after Laskaris left—Stephen could only estimate by counting the drips in the IV line—a door hissed open. Boot heels clopped on the stone floor. His head turned slowly, until he saw an Amazonian woman in combat gear approaching. His chest tightened.

Sharon stopped at the bedside and stared at him. She was holding a bag of amber liquid.

"Sharon." Stephen's voice came out weak and dry. "Don't do this."

She gave him a long, hard glare, and then moved to the IV pole. She slid the roller clamp to stop the flow into the tubing. "You shouldn't have come here."

"I know you're not in control. I know you're still in there, the same little girl who stood up to Mom to help her big brother. And I know you won't let anything happen to me, just like I couldn't let anything happen to you. That's why I'm here."

Her gaze turned diamond hard. "Then you're a bigger idiot than ever."

Stephen's heart sank. It had to be a trick. She didn't know what she was saying.

"You think I'm a mindless zombie doing whatever The Controller orders?" She leaned close to the bed, tiny veins bulging at her temples. "You thought you could big brother me back to sanity? I've got news for you. I'm not insane. The Controller isn't controlling me. He didn't change me. He showed me who I am. Who I really am."

"But . . . the implant . . ."

"Is flawed." Her eyes danced. "I know. But you're going to fix it, right? Once you get a taste of the power. It's there, buried deep inside you. You think you know who you are, but you have no idea. They made sure of that. *Z choinki się urwałaś?*"

The sudden use of the Polish expression their mother had taught them so long ago caught Stephen off guard. He stared at her, unable to speak.

She slapped the bag onto the IV pole, connected the tubing, and leaned close to check the IV site. As she did, she whispered, "Remember the boxing incident."

He managed to turn his head slightly, enough for their eyes to meet. He could see it now. That glimmer in her eye. It wasn't anger or hate, or her raw power. It was her using her beautiful mind. He stopped himself from smiling and tried to look horrified. She winked and then stepped back, twisting her expression into one of disgust.

"You're worthless." Turning on her heel, she marched out of the room.

After she disappeared, Stephen struggled to understand her clues. *Z choinki się urwałaś. "You're missing something important, and it shows."* Was there something about the boxing incident that was obvious to everyone but him? That had been decades ago, when Uncle Alex got in a lucky hit and...

Realization struck harder than his uncle's blow. When Alex tossed Stephen, the back of his head had crashed against the post, hard enough to knock him out. So, why did he have a scar on his shoulder?

A cold finger ran down his spine. The scar wasn't from the boxing injury. They'd done something else to him. When he was still a kid. Was that what his parents' fight was all about? Not Mom's drinking. Not Stephen getting in trouble at school. Not Dad's deployments. It was because Ross had used Stephen as a guinea pig.

And Dad had let him do it.

Stephen felt sick to his stomach, and he wasn't sure if it was the serum kicking in or his revulsion at what he'd realized. His Dad hadn't been a hero, after all. The games, the extra attention—it wasn't him trying to reconnect. He'd been trying to make up for what he'd allowed to happen.

Magma bubbled through his veins. Questions bounced around in his head. What had they done to him? Why experiment on a child? And what kind of parent would let them?

Fire seared white-hot behind his eyes. Worms burrowed under his skin.

He lifted his hands. His veins were purple. His skin was jaundiced.

His heart pounded. He glanced at the IV. The bag was empty. He focused on the label. *Epinephrine.* Also known as adrenaline.

His forearm muscles swelled. He clenched his fists and swung his arms outward. The leather straps snapped like they were tissue paper.

Stephen bounded off the bed. The stone floor cracked as his feet thudded onto it. His body had grown twice in size. Incredible strength flowed into every muscle. His senses had heightened into overdrive. He could hear the stone dust settling onto the floor. He could smell traces of blood in the IV as he ripped it out of his hand. He could feel his skin cells knitting back together as the wound closed. Whatever internal injuries he'd had were gone. His body had fixed itself. But his mind was caught in a torrent. Every thought drowned in pain. He wanted to scream. To run. To smash.

One single thought managed to float above the rest: Sharon. She had tried to save him. And now, he had to save her.

Slowly, the anger subsided. His body shrank back to its normal size. He could still feel the power surging through his blood vessels, but he could control it. So long as he concentrated on what mattered.

His guns were gone, but he didn't need them. He balled his hands into fists and headed for the door.

59

Cold wind blew on the back of Stephen's neck as he made his way down the tunnel. He wasn't sure where he was going, but he could smell molten solder at the other end, along with human sweat. So far, he hadn't run into any guards. Maybe they hadn't figured out yet that he'd escaped, but that wouldn't last long. At least there were no interior surveillance cameras. Laskaris probably didn't think he needed them, since everyone there had implants to track their movement.

The stone gave way to a metal corridor. Stephen tried to move silently, but each footfall reverberated like gunshots in his ears. He could only hope it was because of his heightened senses and not because he was really plodding along like an elephant. When he reached the end of the hall, he found a metal door with a glass window. Inside, he could see four men in white lab coats using robotic equipment. One was soldering what looked like a circuit board. Another was using a taser to test various electrical voltages.

A keypad was mounted on the wall next to the door. Stephen had no clue what the access code was. He could smash the panel or the door itself, but even with his newfound strength, he wasn't sure he could hold up against an army of regenerating super-soldiers if the scientists set off an alarm.

Well, if he couldn't use his brawn, he'd have to use his brain. He rapped on the window.

The scientists looked up in surprise. He waved at them.

They glanced at each other nervously. One of them approached the window.

"I'm here for my implant," Stephen shouted, gesticulating. "The Controller ordered me here so I can help you. I know how to make it compatible with regenerating brain tissue."

The scientist's eyes widened. He reached for an access panel and stopped. He looked back at the others, who shook their heads.

Frowning, the scientist pressed a different button. His voice transmitted from a speaker somewhere overhead. "You're supposed to be sedated for surgical implantation."

Stephen tried to look offended. "What kind of pussy do you think I am? Just jam it in me."

The scientist looked confused. "I'll—I'll have to check with The Controller."

"Yeah, you do that. He loves being interrupted in the middle of preparing for the next mission. It's not like he has a short temper."

Now, the scientist looked anxious. He turned back to the others. They shrugged.

Quickly, the man punched a code on the access panel. The door slid open.

"See? Much faster." Stephen stepped inside. The door slid closed behind him. He grinned. "So, how do we do this? The easy way or the hard way?"

The scientists glanced at each other.

"What?" one asked.

"Hard way, then," Stephen said, and punched the nearest in the face. Before the others could react, he spun and kicked another in the abdomen. A third charged at him. He let the man get close, then grabbed his arm, twisted it around, and put him in a headlock. The scientist clawed at his arm, but as Stephen squeezed he went limp.

Something bit into his neck. Something hot.

He jerked around, swinging his fist. He connected with what felt like a jaw.

The fourth scientist staggered back, clutching the soldering iron. His face was a frozen mask of fear.

Stephen swatted the tool out of the man's hands and raised his fist.

The man shrank against the wall. He covered his head with his hands and cowered.

Stephen hesitated. These men weren't trained fighters. He didn't want to hurt them. But they weren't innocent, either. They were part of this mad science project. They had to pay.

Heat surged through his body. The veins on his arm had started to swell, turning purplish. He needed to stop them. To smash them.

He lowered his fist. No, he didn't. He could control this.

His veins flattened again, and he took a deep breath.

The scientist peeked up at him, hope dancing in his eyes. Stephen grinned at him. Then he punched him in the face.

He ripped the ID badge off the unconscious man and picked up the taser before leaving the room. Cautiously, he poked his head out the door. No one coming. So far, so good. He jogged back up the corridor and stopped at a junction. Which way? He sniffed the air. The smell of sweat and body odor was stronger to the left. He turned right.

The tunnel grew wider as he proceeded, the lights brighter. Up ahead, he could see it opening into a sort of chamber. He spotted various combat dummies and gear. Some sort of training arena.

Quickly, he backtracked down the tunnel. As he started to turn the corner, he heard two sets of footsteps approaching. There was nowhere to hide. He flattened himself against the wall and braced for a fight.

The footsteps grew closer.

He tightened his grip on the taser and held his breath.

The footsteps stopped.

"Understood," a deep voice said.

"Proceeding to investigate." The second voice was huskier.

Stephen listened but didn't hear anyone else speaking or the sound of a radio. After another pause, the footsteps receded in the opposite direction. One of the researchers must have sounded an alarm. That gave him mere minutes to act.

He listened again. No sound of movement.

A metal door stood at the end of the short hall. A card scanner was built into the wall next to the door. Stephen swiped the scientist's ID card through the scanner. The light over the door turned from red to green.

Once inside, Stephen scanned the room. Monitors lined the walls, each one displaying a set of vital signs including heart and breathing rates, blood pressure, and what Stephen assumed was EEG activity. He glanced at each one in succession until he found Sharon's. Her heart rate was elevated.

He turned to the center of the room, where a computer panel stood, with a set of controls and a thin white microphone. That had to be where Laskaris overrode the automated systems.

Stephen ran over to inspect the controls. Activate the microphone, select a specific subject or all subjects, boost radio transmission, and so on. There were two he wasn't sure of. Both had lightning bolt symbols. He guessed one administered shock and the other was an emergency shutdown, but he wasn't sure which was which. If he hit the wrong one, he would end up shocking all the super-soldiers, including his sister, and giving away his location in the process.

He glanced again at the monitors. Each represented a human life. A victim. No matter what else they might've done, that was what they were.

Holding his breath, he jabbed a button.

Nothing happened.

He checked the monitors again. All vital signs remained stable. He hadn't administered a shock. But he hadn't deactivated the machine, either. What the hell had he done?

"You really don't have any respect for command, do you?"

Stephen's head whipped up in time to catch a fist with his jaw. He staggered, prepared to fight back, and heard a click.

His blood cooled.

Laskaris was pointing a gun at him.

60

Stephen rubbed his cheek, the burn of embarrassment at being caught off-guard worse than the actual injury. On either side of Laskaris stood a soldier with ham-hock fists.

"Did you think you were the first to try this?" The tone of the man's voice was harsh but betrayed amusement. "I disconnected the shutdown control months ago. I'm the only one who decides if—and when—this project ends." He tilted his head. "Just like I decide whether you live or die."

Stephen spat blood onto the floor. He'd had one shot at stopping Laskaris, and he blew it. If he couldn't shut down the system, he had no way of disconnecting the super-soldiers from the colonel's network. He'd lost.

Don't waste time on the small targets. Draw in his big guns and let them blow themselves up.

The bomb in Tactico. He smiled inwardly. He wasn't out yet.

"What are you going to do?" he said. "Shoot me? Thanks to you, I'll regenerate."

Laskaris's smile faltered, and then he puffed out his chest. "True, but without the implant to suppress the pain, you'll wish you could die."

"I've been through worse. But that's not why you haven't shot me yet. You need me."

"I don't need you. You're only a smart-mouthed coroner."

"Medical examiner."

"Excuse me?"

"Medical examiners are physicians. Coroners are elected positions and aren't required to have a medical license. It's a common mistake."

Laskaris scowled. The soldiers on either side of him stared ahead blankly. "Whatever. My scientists are already working on a way to suppress the noradrenaline surges, so—"

"Epinephrine."

"What?"

"Both are involved in the fight-or-flight response, but adrenaline, or epinephrine, has more widespread effects, whereas noradrenaline works primarily on the blood vessels and makes you more alert. The serum causes a surge in epinephrine, not noradrenaline."

Laskaris blinked. "Right. I knew that."

"No, you didn't. You said noradrenaline."

"I didn't . . ." Laskaris inhaled through his nose, releasing his breath through his mouth. He wagged the gun at Stephen. "What the fuck are you doing?"

"What do you mean?"

"You're stalling. Trying to confuse me." Laskaris turned his head, glancing in every direction. "What did you do?"

"Honestly, I have no idea what you're talking about," Stephen said. "And how would I have had time to do anything? A few minutes ago, you had me strapped to a table."

The features on Laskaris's face melted together. "Yes, you were strapped down, weren't you? How did you escape? Your sister?"

Stephen feigned a wince. "She'd never help me. Not thanks to you. For that, I owe you a great deal of pain."

Laskaris scratched at his chin. He glanced at the monitors, then rubbed his temples, eyes closed.

"What're you doing?" Stephen asked.

The colonel turned toward his guards, opened his eyes, and stared at them, one by one. Wordlessly, they turned and began searching the room.

"You froze the shutdown control because you don't need it," Stephen said, the pieces clicking together. "You have an implant."

Laskaris glared at him but remained silent.

"But yours doesn't receive. It transmits. I'm right, aren't I?"

The guards continued checking the equipment. Laskaris kept the pistol trained on Stephen's chest. Slowly, the colonel shook his head. "My scientists aren't responding. What did you do?"

"Me? Nothing."

"Don't give me that bullshit." Laskaris lurched forward, pressing the gun barrel against Stephen's sternum. "You're smart. I'll give you that. And maybe I do need you alive. But I can kill you and bring you back, kill you and bring you back, over and over and over. And it'll hurt. It'll hurt bad. Every damned time."

Anger started to work its way down Stephen's back. No, he had to hold it together a little longer.

"Or, maybe that's not the only way to hurt you," Laskaris continued, spittle spraying Stephen's face as he spoke. "Even if your sister hates you, you still love her. I can cause her unbearable pain. And I'll make you watch."

Rage boiled in Stephen's gut. "Don't. You. Touch. Her."

Laskaris glowered. "Tell me what you did."

"I didn't do anything."

Laskaris cracked the pistol across Stephen's jaw. Stephen shook his head, dazed. He managed to stick his hand in his pocket.

"Don't lie to me." Laskaris grabbed Stephen by the neck and pressed the pistol against his chin. "Tell me the truth, or I'll blow your head off and see whether or not it regenerates."

Stephen pulled the taser out of his pocket. He jammed it against the side of the colonel's head and fired.

Electric current danced over Laskaris. His eyes rolled back. His body shook. He crumpled to his knees.

The monitors flickered and went dark.

Stephen tossed aside the exhausted taser. The two guards teetered, heads tilted, and then they looked at each other in confusion.

"I've cut you off." Stephen scooped the pistol off the floor and aimed it at Laskaris's head. "It's over."

"Not quite."

Stephen stiffened. The voice was one he knew all too well.

He turned to find General Alex Ross wearing his Class A service dress, silver stars glistening on their epaulets. Stephen's chest tightened. Ross had one arm tight around Melinda Stewart's neck.

"You really fucked things up here, Steve." Uncle Alex clucked his tongue and jammed a gun against Melinda's cheek. "Now, you're going to fix them."

61

Stephen could barely restrain his loathing for Alexander Ross, the man who'd been a surrogate father most of his life. The man whom he'd both hated and loved at various times. The man who'd betrayed him long ago, and Stephen had never known. He kept his pistol trained on Laskaris's head, bargaining that the colonel was important enough that Ross wouldn't risk his life. "Let her go. She's got nothing to do with this."

"I thought you abhorred the idea of taking command." Ross sneered. "And yet, here you are, thinking you can give me orders. Hand over your gun."

Stephen lowered his gaze to make eye contact with Melinda. She trembled as Ross's hand clamped over her mouth. Guilt racked Stephen's body. The last thing he'd wanted was for her to be in danger because of his mistakes. "Did he hurt you?"

She shook her head.

"What's she doing here?" Stephen demanded from Ross.

"When I figured out where you were going, I decided to bring insurance." The general glared at Laskaris, who appeared dazed but awake. "If I'd been informed you were already here, I would've arrived much sooner."

Laskaris dragged himself upright, his eyes red-rimmed. "I had it handled."

"Yes, I can see that." Ross wrinkled his nose and turned back to Stephen. "Unless you want to say goodbye to your little Jezebel, you will do exactly as I say, starting with handing over that gun."

Melinda pleaded with Stephen through her eyes. His resolve wavered. Laskaris needed to be stopped. Ross needed to pay. Sharon needed to be free. But did any of that matter with Melinda's life on the line?

"Shoot her already." Laskaris still looked stunned from Stephen's assault, but he was starting to regain his bravado. He glanced over his shoulder at the two soldiers standing stock still. "We don't have much time. In a few minutes, their failsafe will kick in, and they'll all make their way here. I need to regain control before then."

"You're not doing anything to them." Stephen jabbed him with the gun barrel. "They're free."

"They're not free." His eyes smoldered. "If I don't restore the connection, their implants will fire random impulses and they'll run amok. No one will be safe."

Stephen hesitated. There was a chance Laskaris was telling the truth.

"Poor Steve," Ross said, clucking his tongue. "Still trying to be the hero, but once again you end up lost. Maybe that's because you're not really trying to save the world, are you? You're not even trying to save her. You want revenge."

"Shut up." Stephen fought back the urge to rip off Ross's face.

"You think we abused your old man. Tortured him. Turned him into a monster. Well, guess what?" Ross grinned wickedly. "He volunteered. Even when the serum was ripping him apart. Even when he could barely think straight, he kept coming back. You think he was going to quit that day before he lost it?" Ross shook his head. "He wanted a stronger dose."

Stephen didn't want to believe it. But after what he'd learned, how could he not?

"He wanted to be strong," Ross continued. "No matter what it took. I didn't turn your daddy into a monster, Steve. He already was a monster."

"Don't act like you were innocent." Stephen suppressed the urge to spit at him. "I know you experimented on me. I know Dad let you. He didn't stop you, but you did it. And you covered it up, made me forget."

"I needed to know if the serum would be more stable in a developing brain. And it was. To a certain extent."

Stephen frowned. "What does that mean?"

"The serum granted you limited regenerative abilities, something it hadn't done for anyone else. Didn't you ever wonder why you never got sick after you went into remission? Never had another broken bone after that boxing injury?"

Stephen stared. He hadn't paid attention, but Ross was right.

"Sure, you acted out now and then, but nothing like your father's rage attacks." Ross wrinkled his nose, causing his mustache to dance over his lip. "At least, until your father pushed you over the edge."

The words burrowed a hole in Stephen's chest. "What are you talking about?"

"You think I had your parents executed, don't you?" He snorted. "Don't be ridiculous. I'd never waste military resources like that. Are you sure it is my voice, and not your conscience?"

Stephen blinked. Something flickered in the back of his mind. "What?"

"It's a quote from Sophocles's *Antigone,* spoken by the sentry to Creon. It's also a challenge phrase your therapist implanted as a sentry to your fractured mind. There's something we buried, but it was always there, lingering in the dark. Regenerating would've restored those memories." Ross's eyes glittered. "It's time to remember."

62

Thirty-two years earlier

Ice granules clung to Steve's gloves as he rolled a snowball bigger and bigger, until it was the right size for the snowman's head. Cold wind nipped at his exposed wrists. His toes were numb from the melted snow leaking through his sneakers, but he didn't care. Sharon cheered, jumping up and down, as he set the head atop the snowman's body. She bounced like Tigger, laughing and giggling. It was the first time he'd seen pure joy on her face since they'd moved to Worcester. It was also the first time Steve had felt he could breathe easily. Dad was going to separate from the military for them. No more deployments. No more time away. No more arguments. They could be a family again.

"Oh no," Sharon said, her little face drooping as she searched her pockets. "I can't find the buttons for the eyes."

"Don't worry." Steve stooped to dig through the snow. "We can use a couple of rocks."

"You can't use rocks." Sharon put her hands on her hips and drew out her words, sounding like one of those annoying teenage girls in the romantic comedies Mom liked to watch. "It has to be buttons. Don't you know anything?"

"All right. Fine. I'll go get them." He turned toward the house and wagged his finger at her. "But don't talk like that ever again."

"Like what?"

"You know what."

"No, I don't."

"Forget it."

Steve shook his head and started walking. If he'd kept going, it would've turned into an argument, and there was no way anything was going to spoil this perfect day.

The moment he stepped inside, he knew something was wrong. It was quiet. Too quiet.

"Hello?" he called out. "Mom? Dad?"

"Steve!" Mom's voice burst from the living room. "Run! Get out!"

"Shut up!"

Ice crept through Steve's chest at the sound of the voice. It was his father, he was certain, but he sounded different. Fierce, more animal than human.

"Steve, please go." Mom sounded like she was crying. "Get your sister somewhere safe."

"You think he's not safe with me? Huh?" The last was punctuated by a loud, sickening crack.

Steve's stomach twisted. He ran to the living room. "Guys, what's going..."

He froze. Couldn't speak. Couldn't breathe.

There, in the middle of the living room, was Dad. Well, it looked like Dad. It had Dad's face. But it wasn't Dad. It couldn't be.

Its muscles bulged to the size of beach balls. Its eyes glowed yellow, darting around like popping corn. Saliva dripped from its lips as it bared its teeth. Purple veins popped out everywhere.

One bloody fist was raised over its head. The other hand clutched a fistful of cloth from Mom's favorite Ralph Lauren blouse. Suspended inside the blouse, neck rolled back, arm bent at an impossible angle, eyes staring lifelessly at the ceiling, was Mom.

Steve's body went numb.

Blood streamed from her mouth and spattered on Steve's copy of Captain America #230 on the coffee table, staining the cover image of a massive green fist smashing Cap's shield.

"Mom?" Steve whispered, unable to believe what he was seeing. This couldn't be happening. It had to be a bad dream. Any moment, he would wake up. He had to wake up.

The beast's gaze shifted in his direction. What might've been awareness of what it had done, maybe even regret, passed over its face. Its mouth started to move, to say something. Whatever it was, Steve didn't want to hear it, unless it was to say April Fool's, even though it was still February, but that would be okay because it would mean none of this was really happening.

"Steve?"

It was Sharon's voice. She was in the kitchen.

The beast's head jerked in that direction. Its nostrils flared. Its breathing sounded like a locomotive, harsh and ragged. Mom slipped from its grasp and slumped onto the floor. The creature let out a low growl.

"No!" Steve lunged, grabbing the creature's arm. Somewhere in the back of his mind, he asked himself what the hell he thought he was doing, what he could possibly do against this monster that looked like Dad but wasn't, not anymore—but he shut it all out. One thought stuck in his mind. He had to save Sharon. "Leave her alone!"

The beast whirled. One arm lashed out and caught Stephen in the gut. He flew backward into the coffee table. The glass shattered. Comic books tumbled to the floor. Glass shards sprayed across the room. One jagged piece sank into his arm. Steve cried out.

Grunting, the creature turned toward the kitchen.

"No!"

Anger surged through Steve's body. He could feel his muscles swelling, getting stronger. His heart pounded, pumping blood to every fiber. He could smell the creature's anger. He could taste its fear.

With a roar, Steve leaped to his feet and charged at the beast. The creature's eyes widened in surprise. It moved into a defensive position, but Steve tackled it. He pounded on its back with both fists.

The beast jerked its head back. Its skull crashed into Steve's mouth. He fell onto his back, spitting out a wad of blood.

Then the monster rushed at him. He rolled into a crouch and punched at its kneecap. Howling, it stumbled and fell onto its rear. Steve pounced and wrapped his legs around its waist. He punched its face again and again.

A shriek cut through the air.

Steve stopped and looked over his shoulder, dreading what he saw.

Sharon stood in the doorway, hand over her mouth, eyes wider than vinyl records. Her pink Puppy Surprise doll dangled from her fingers.

"Sh... Sharon," the beast murmured, the words coming in ragged bursts. "Go 'way... honey. It's... okay."

Tears flooded Sharon's eyes. Her lip trembled. "Daddy?"

"Shhh." The beast smiled warmly, the yellow in its eyes fading. "Daddy and Steve... are just dealing with some... issues. Go back in the kitchen... okay? I... love you."

Sharon's mouth hung open, her eyes searching for understanding.

Steve nodded.

Hugging her doll, she turned and ran into the kitchen.

Steve sat back on his haunches and dropped his hands by his sides. His father's face was a bloody mess—lip swollen on one side, a jagged cut under his left eye.

"Dad." The rumble in his voice made it sound like it belonged to someone else. "I'm sorry. I didn't—"

"Finish . . . the job, son."

"What?"

"Finish. The. Job." His father gave him a hard look, one eye drifting outward. "You and . . . your sister aren't safe around me. No one is. Only you . . . can make sure I don't hurt anyone else."

Shaking his head, Steve said, "I can't, Dad. I can't . . . I can't lose you, too."

An uneven smile crept across Dad's face like a gash from a knife. He lifted a mangled hand and caressed Steve's cheek, the skin as rough as sandpaper. "You'll never . . . lose me. But the monster inside me . . . it wants full control. And, after what I did . . . to your mother . . ." He looked down and bit his lip. Tears welled in his eyes. "I'm sorry, Steve. I'm so sorry."

"Dad . . ." It was all Steve could say. He couldn't forgive him, but he didn't want to see him suffer either.

"There are only two other outcomes. If you retreat, the military will take me away. Dissect me. Turn me into a weapon more dangerous . . . than the atom bomb." He coughed. "Or I run. Let the beast take over . . . and disappear. Neither is an acceptable option. I'll always be . . . a threat. End this now, so you can remember me . . . as I was, not what I've become."

"No, Dad." Steve sobbed. "Please."

"Stephen Englehart, do as I say right now. Do it!"

Steve lifted his hands and studied the blood trailing down his fingers. He couldn't.

His father's hand shot out, clamped around his wrist, and squeezed.

"Then," the beast said, eyes glowing, teeth bared, "I'll make Sharon do it."

"No!"

Steve's hand doubled in size. He swung. His fist connected with the monster's cheek. Teeth and blood sprayed the furniture.

He smashed again.

Again. And again.

At last, he stopped, panting. He stared at the crumpled, unmoving heap on the floor.

He couldn't breathe. Couldn't think. Then he heard a whimper, and he spun around.

Sharon was huddled in the doorway, watching him. Her eyes widened when he turned toward her. She screamed and scrambled against the door jamb.

"It's okay." He reached out for her. "I won't hurt you."

"You-you-you—" She wet her lips. "You k-k-killed Dad. Did you kill Mom, too?"

"No! I didn't." Steve shook his head vigorously, trying to make it all go away. "That was Dad. I had—I had to—"

"What are you?" Her voice sounded small, timid. Her eyes were wet, cheeks stained with tears. "What was Dad? What happened to you?"

"I don't know." He studied his hands. They looked normal now, but he knew the beast lurked under his skin, waiting for him to release it. "We need—we need to do something about them."

"I called Uncle Alex. He'll know what to do."

"Alex?" Images flashed in Steve's mind, connecting like Legos. He reached for Sharon's hand. "No, Sharon. We need to get out of here."

"No, we have to stay here." She yanked her hand away. "Dad always said if anything happened, we should wait for Uncle Alex, and he would take care of everything."

"Uncle Alex is the one who did this to me." The growl crept back into Steve's voice. "We can't trust him."

"Then who can we trust?" she shouted, with enough force that he recoiled. "We don't have anyone else, Steve. Our parents are dead, thanks to you."

"But I didn't—"

"Maybe you didn't kill Mom, but this is all your fault. They were fighting about you. They always fought about you." Tears streamed from her eyes anew. "Why couldn't you just be happy?"

Steve stood in shock. He'd never known how Sharon felt about him, how what he did affected her. He wanted to tell her he was sorry, that he would make it up to her. But as he looked down at the bloody mess on the floor, he knew there was no way he could ever make it up to her.

Blue lights flashed outside. Steve fell into a crouch, coiled to flee.

"We have to go. Now."

"No. We're waiting for Uncle Alex."

"But—"

A hand gripped Steve's shoulder. He whirled around, drawing back his fist.

"Easy, son." The man stepped back, raising both hands by his head in surrender. It was Uncle Alex. "It's me. Are you two all right?"

Steve stood with fists raised. He wanted to wipe the smug look off the man's face. But no matter what he'd done, Steve couldn't kill him. He couldn't hurt another person. Slowly, he lowered his fists but said nothing.

Sharon began to sob.

"You're coming with me," Uncle Alex said. "Go pack your things."

Sharon turned, but Steve stopped her. To Alex, he said, "We're not going anywhere with you."

Alex's face darkened. "Listen, you little shit. You've destroyed everything. Everything! Do you understand that? But we're going to fix this. I'm getting you into therapy."

"Therapy?" Steve held out his hands. "Therapy won't fix this."

"Excuse me, sir." A uniformed officer glanced at the kids and then turned to face Alex. "The coroner's asking questions. I think he may figure out . . ." He glanced at Steve again, his face turning ashen. "Uh, you know."

Sharon started to whimper.

Alex rolled his eyes and shoved the officer away. "You idiot. Go deal with him. Make up something about drugs. I don't care."

After the officer scurried away, Alex shook his head. "This is how it's going to work. From now on, you do as I say, without question, and all of this will go away. I'll take care of you, like I promised your dad I would, and I'll make sure nothing like this ever happens again. Understand?"

Sharon looked up at him, sniffling, and nodded.

"This is never going away," Steve said, unable to believe what he was hearing. "This monster inside of me—"

Alex grabbed his wrist and yanked him close. His hot breath fell on Steve's face.

"You're not going to say anything about this night to anyone. Either of you." He gave Sharon a pointed look. "Ever. Do you understand?"

"But . . ." Sharon began.

"I will protect you, but I can't do that if you go around flapping your jaws. How do you think your parents would've felt if you got locked up for what happened?"

Steve stared at him. Was he worried about Steve, or his own skin?

"Good," Alex said, even though neither child had answered him. "The therapy will keep your demons at bay. And, after a while, this will all seem like it never happened." He pulled them into an awkward hug. "You're both destined for great things. Let's not let tonight alter that."

63

Stephen stared at the general, his heart pounding and fingers numb. It all made sense now. Why he'd always felt responsible for his parents' death. Why his therapists made him never let his anger go unchecked.

"You erased our memories," he said, each word echoing in his ears. "To cover up your project and your own ass."

"No, I *changed* your memories. And it was for your benefit."

"*My* benefit?"

"If I hadn't, the rage would've overpowered you eventually, as it did your father. Only by making you forget and teaching you to keep your anger reined in could you get where you are today." He sniffed. "You should be thanking me."

"You did this to me. I never had leukemia, did I?" Stephen thought about all the monthly screens and injections. "Those treatments were to keep my power in check, while you drew samples to develop more serum. You son of a bitch!"

Stephen started for the general but stopped as Ross tightened his grip around Melinda's throat. He remembered gazing into those eyes while they lay together, naked, feeling her soft skin against his. He remembered kissing those full lips. Something stirred in his chest, a mishmash of guilt and affection. This was his fault. She shouldn't have been caught up in this mess at all. If she died, it would be because of him, because he made the choice to let her die.

"Let her go" he said, "and we can settle this one-on-one. She's not a part of this."

Ross pursed his lips. "Hand over your gun."

Stephen hesitated, steeling himself. He couldn't surrender, not when there was still a chance to save Sharon and himself.

Melinda's eyes pleaded with him. The wall he'd built around his heart crumbled. He couldn't have her blood on his hands. He cared too much about her, more than he'd let himself admit.

Slowly, Stephen de-cocked the pistol and held it out to Ross, handle first.

"Noble move." Ross accepted the gun and released Melinda. "Not a very smart one, but noble, in any case."

To Stephen's shock and horror, Ross handed Laskaris's gun to Melinda. She straightened her back, her lips pressing into a hard line. She checked the magazine, cocked the gun, and aimed it at Stephen's forehead.

"Melinda?" he whispered.

"Sorry, babe. I got a better offer. But thanks for saving me." The corner of Melinda's mouth crept upward. "My hero."

64

The room wobbled and shifted around Stephen. He half expected a time-traveling supervillain to materialize and laugh maniacally while claiming to have altered Stephen's timeline in horrifying ways. There was no other explanation for why Melinda would be aiming a pistol at him now, siding with the man who'd destroyed Stephen's life.

"Melinda," he said when he found the ability to speak. "If he's got you under some kind of mind control..."

She laughed bitterly. "Is that what you think? God, you're so dense."

Stephen's head spun. He'd chosen saving Melinda over revenge, over freeing himself and his sister, and for what? It had all been a trick. He was too drained to get mad, to power up. Everything he'd done had been for nothing.

"We don't have time for this." Laskaris pushed past Stephen to search the control module. "The rest of the subjects will be here any moment. Once they arrive, the implants will deactivate, and they'll be out of my control."

"How long before you can reestablish a link?" Ross asked.

"Too long. When he shorted out my remote, he sent a feedback loop that fried the main relays. All we can do is cull the herd."

"What's that supposed to mean?"

"It means we eliminate the ones who are not loyal." Laskaris glared at Stephen. "And I know who to start with."

"You son of a bitch," Stephen said, catching the undertone in Laskaris's voice. He wanted to rip the man's arms off, but Melinda had the gun trained on his head. There was no point in trying. He was trapped.

"Save it." Ross gave Stephen a pointed look and then turned to Laskaris. "You fucked this up as much as he did. From here on out, I'm calling all the shots."

Laskaris seemed about to say something but choked it back. He nodded. "Yes, sir."

To Melinda, Ross said, "Keep an eye on him while the colonel and I prepare for the subjects."

"Yes, sir," she said, more forcefully and eagerly than Laskaris.

As the two men worked on the other side of the room, Stephen studied Melinda's face. Had she been working with Ross all along? Was that how Ross had always kept two steps ahead?

"Melinda," he whispered. "Why are you doing this?"

"Shut up. No talking."

"You helped me hack into the DNA lab. Why would you do that if you were working with them?"

"I said, shut up."

He remained quiet, but his mind kept running, continuing the conversation without her. Maybe it was because Stephen hadn't said he loved her back. No, she couldn't have been that petty.

He swallowed hard. "Ross showed you the GoPro video, didn't he?"

Her sharp intake of breath confirmed his suspicion.

"That was bullshit," he said. "I wanted Tom to think we had a brief fling so he wouldn't tell anyone about us."

"It seemed more like the one time you told the truth."

"I get that you're hurt," he said. "But working with Ross? This isn't you."

"You don't know the real me. You never did." She clucked her tongue. "But I know you. I know everything about you. I know you can't leave a mystery unsolved. That's why I'm not going to tell you why I'm doing this."

Stephen's muscle fibers tensed. She was tormenting him. Had he hurt her so badly that she was the one now pursuing revenge? Or was there another reason?

"Come on, Melinda."

She didn't answer.

A terrible thought entered his mind. "Please tell me you're not screwing him."

She kept quiet, one eyebrow lifting.

The idea made his gut spasm. He choked back to keep from vomiting.

"They're coming," Laskaris said, glancing at the door. "Listen."

From the corridor, Stephen heard tramping boots. A lot of them.

"Take this." Laskaris tossed a black bundle to Melinda. "Put it on."

"What is it?" Stephen asked, his curiosity overpowering the order to stay quiet.

Melinda unwrapped the bundle, revealing a gas mask. She shot Laskaris a quizzical look.

"That's an order, Sergeant."

Melinda glanced at Stephen, then slipped the mask on. Laskaris and Ross did the same.

"I don't get one?" Stephen asked. "What, you're going to poison me and the others? Afraid to get your hands dirty by shooting me?"

"You were always overly dramatic, Steve," Ross said. "I didn't raise you for thirty years only to kill you. Or your sister. Isn't that right, Basil?"

Laskaris glared at Stephen, the gas mask making him look like an insect.

"Basil!"

Laskaris's gaze lingered on Stephen before he turned to Ross. "Fine. We'll keep them both alive. For now."

A pit formed in Stephen's stomach. Sharon would survive, and so would he. But for what? There was no escape. Ross had made sure of that. The siblings would be kept alive to play a part in the general's mad plan for conquest, and there was nothing Stephen could do to stop it.

The first super-soldiers marched into the room. Their eyes were vacant, like the guards'.

"It's working. See?" Laskaris gloated at Stephen, or possibly Ross. "They're coming home. They're still loyal to me."

"You said your homing beacon would draw them here, and it has," Ross said. "That's obedience, not loyalty."

"What's the difference? We demand compliance from our troops. It's what boot camp is all about. If they follow our orders, what do you care?"

"I care because I want soldiers who can adapt and think for themselves. If I wanted robots, I would've built robots." Ross jabbed a finger at Laskaris. "You promised me they would still have free will. What good is it to me if they only obey you? What if you die?"

The colonel's grin was almost visible through the mask. "Well, I guess it's up to you to ensure that doesn't happen."

Ross's eyes widened. "You son of a bitch."

"Uh-uh." Laskaris wagged a finger. "Now's not the time to piss me off, Alex. I've been happy to let you pretend to be in charge, but you need me far more than I need you."

"Could you boys please stop comparing dick sizes?" Melinda said. "I don't care who's in charge. Whatever we're going to do, let's do it fast, before these soldiers shake off their daze."

More soldiers entered the room and stood in formation. Stephen's chest tightened as he spotted Sharon. He thought she glanced in his direction, but then he realized her head was tilting this way and that, like a bird's, as if she was trying to process her surroundings. He felt the rage burning through his veins but couldn't transform. Whatever last vestige of hope remained inside him vanished. There was nothing he could do now. He wasn't a hero. He was a patsy.

"She's right." Laskaris gathered up his materials. "Now that they're all here, we need to get out of the chamber. We can watch what happens from the monitors. Whoever survives, we can sedate and reprogram."

One of the soldiers laughed. Laskaris whipped around. His jaw dropped.

Corporal Greenwood leaped from the center of the pack. He grabbed Laskaris by the throat, dragged him to the ground, and began punching him in the face.

Melinda shot at Greenwood. Bullets ripped through his back.

The other soldiers blinked at each other.

Greenwood recovered and cracked his neck. He looked over his shoulder, a wicked grin appeared on his face. "That all you got?"

Stephen smiled to himself, hope blossoming in his chest. Greenwood must've found the back entrance and followed the others there. If the soldier hadn't given up, maybe Stephen shouldn't, either.

Ross ran for the door.

Sprinting, Stephen tackled him. The general's head banged on the metal floor.

"You asshole!" Ross shouted.

The gun handle connected with Stephen's jaw. White pain clouded his field of vision. He fell backward, rubbing his cheek.

As the white faded to gray, he heard shouting and fighting. He managed to focus enough to see Ross standing over him. The gun was pointed at his head.

". . . killed you so many times, boy," the general was saying, brow furrowed. "Your dad was like a brother to me. I kept you safe out of respect for him. Even when so many times, you came close to screwing everything up for me."

"You didn't keep me alive to repay a debt," Stephen said. "I was your golden goose. All those blood draws you made me do, saying I had leukemia. You were collecting my blood to make your super-serum."

"And you wanted to retire early. You would've ruined everything, cutting off our pipeline. That's why I enlisted Melinda to give you reason to stay in. But even she wasn't enough. You had to keep digging." Ross's cheeks reddened. "I'd kill you right now if you wouldn't simply regenerate. But I can make you feel pain."

He turned toward Sharon, who was rushing toward them.

"No," Stephen whispered.

Ross fired.

The bullet caught Sharon in the chest. She staggered backwards.

"No!" Stephen tackled Ross. The gun fell from the general's hand.

Stephen flipped him onto his back and straddled him. He wrapped his hands around the general's neck. Ross glared up at him, eyes burning, digging his fingernails into the backs of Stephen's hands. Stephen clenched harder, the pain jolting through him. Waves of anger washed over his body. He was due revenge. For his father. For Sharon.

Ross choked. His cheeks turned purplish. His eyes bulged. He laughed.

He *laughed.*

Confused, Stephen released his grip. Why the hell was Ross laughing?

"Look . . . at . . . you," Ross whispered. "Just . . . like . . . your old man. A . . . monster."

Stephen looked down at his hands. Purplish veins bulged.

He was losing control.

Stephen released Ross and sat on his heels, staring at his hands.

Something bit into his back. He jerked from the impact. The bullet ripped through his chest.

Another shot. Pain. Stephen reeled and toppled backwards.

Melinda stood over him, the gun barrel aimed at his head.

"I'm really sorry," she said, though her face didn't show a trace of regret. She stared into his eyes. "But I need you out of this fight."

Stephen's muscles tightened. He needed to stop Ross and Laskaris, and to do that he had to get past Melinda. But if he attacked her, he might kill her. He couldn't control himself, like Dad couldn't control himself. He stayed there, supine, frozen with indecision.

"I always knew you didn't have the heart," Melinda said. Her finger slid along the trigger.

An Amazonian yell cut through the air.

Melinda turned. Her eyes widened.

Sharon steamrollered her. Melinda twisted as she fell, firing wildly at the woman.

A bullet caught Sharon in the abdomen. Her eyes blazed. She grabbed Melinda's wrist and snapped it backward.

Bones cracked. Melinda screamed.

Another soldier attacked Sharon. They both tumbled to the ground. Melinda took the opportunity to retreat, clutching her injured hand.

Stephen struggled to his feet. He looked this way and that. Ross was gone.

He turned to the center of the room. Greenwood was fighting four of the super-soldiers and winning. He'd been without the implant longer than they had. He'd adapted. They hadn't.

Past Greenwood, Laskaris was huddled against the far wall, fumbling with some kind of secret panel.

Stephen spotted tiny nozzles mounted to the ceiling.

His throat closed off. He knew what Laskaris was doing.

65

The sounds of Greenwood fighting off the super-soldiers faded into the background. Time slowed to a crawl. Laskaris was preparing a final failsafe, one that would eliminate everyone and everything. Mere moments remained to stop him. Everyone else was embroiled in battle. Stephen was the only one free to act.

He scanned the area and spotted the bag Ross had been holding. He sprinted toward it.

A hand grabbed his ankle, tripping him, making him fall. Melinda clung to his foot, her beautiful features twisted into a mask of hate and anger.

"If I die," she spat, "you're going with me."

Rage bubbled under his skin. He used his free foot to kick her in the face.

She yelped and released him.

He scrambled over to the bag and opened it. Empty. Panic caused his heart to race. Ross must've grabbed the masks before fleeing.

Stephen searched the chamber. There was too much chaos with the soldiers fighting each other.

There! On the floor near the door, what looked like a mask.

He glanced at Laskaris. Greenwood had almost reached him. But it looked like Laskaris had nearly finished repairing the wires.

Stephen dove across the floor and found two gas masks.

He pulled one over his face. He spotted Sharon, raced over to her, and strapped the other mask over her head.

Something hissed. Loud.

Gas sprayed from the overhead nozzles. The soldiers stopped fighting as it filled the room. They stared at each other in confusion.

Then, one of them started to quiver. He fell to his knees, screaming.

Another followed. Then another. Within seconds, all of them, including Greenwood, were writhing on the ground.

A timer began beeping from somewhere overhead.

Stephen, still holding Sharon, made eye contact with Laskaris.

"You did this!" Laskaris shouted, picking up a gun off the floor. "All my work, for nothing."

"You're killing them!"

Laskaris laughed bitterly. "It's not a nerve gas. It counteracts the serum. They're in pain because their cells are losing their plasticity. In a few minutes, they'll be normal again. No regeneration. No heightened metabolism. Just normal."

Stephen spotted Greenwood. The big man was doubled over, muscles in his back spasming.

"I've already activated the self-destruct. No one will ever know what happened here." Laskaris marched toward them, aiming the gun. "But I can't have you two telling them."

He fired. A bullet whizzed by Stephen's ear.

"Is he insane?" Sharon asked. "He can't kill us."

"No." Stephen pressed on the back of Sharon's head, nudging her to duck down. "But he can if he destroys the masks."

Melinda's pistol lay eight feet away, protruding from under a writhing soldier.

Laskaris fired another shot. This time the bullet pinged off the floor inches from Stephen's foot.

There was no way Stephen could reach the other gun in time, not while helping his sister.

Something roared behind Laskaris. He whirled, surprised.

Greenwood attacked. His fist crashed against Laskaris's ear.

The colonel yelled in pain and retreated, holding his ear with one hand and gripping the gun with the other.

Stephen goggled at Greenwood. The soldier was off kilter, not quite as fast, but he otherwise seemed unfazed by the gas.

"We need to go!" Sharon shouted in Stephen's ear. "Now!"

She was right. The other soldiers were starting to recover. Some might remain loyal to Laskaris despite his treachery, the way beaten dogs limp back to their masters. Stephen and Sharon needed to be long gone before that happened. He glanced over. Greenwood was lunging at Laskaris. The colonel fired two shots. Greenwood recoiled as the bullets tore into his shoulder and abdomen. Blood spurted from the shoulder wound. He wasn't healing.

If Greenwood fell, Stephen and Sharon would be next. Stephen had to get the gun. He turned toward it.

It was gone.

He heard a click. His chest tightened as he turned around.

Melinda was aiming the gun at him. Her leg was twisted. Blood stained her face. Her nose looked swollen and bent, probably broken, but her hands were steady.

"You should've killed me when you had the chance," she said.

"I still have a chance," Sharon said, and chopped Melinda's arm. She caught the gun as it fell, whirled, and shot Melinda in the chest. The smaller woman's eyes widened. She clutched her chest, where a dark stain was appearing.

Sharon kicked her in the face. Melinda fell to the ground and stopped moving.

Stephen stared at the body, questions about why she'd done what she did milling inside his mind.

"Let's go," Sharon said, pulling his arm.

Stephen was prepared to run with her, but then he glanced over his shoulder once more. The soldiers had stopped writhing. Those who were still alive sat on the ground, staring at each other in confusion.

The timer continued to beep.

He looked toward the center of the room and froze.

Greenwood, despite the blood streaming down his neck, despite the deathly pallor to his skin, had somehow managed not only to stay upright, he'd wrestled the gun away from Laskaris and was now beating him to a pulp. The older man struggled, but each blow stole a bit more of his fight.

Time came to a complete stop. Greenwood's thirst for revenge had been so powerful that, even without the serum, he was able to channel his rage into strength. He was going to destroy Laskaris, even if it meant his own death. In some way, Stephen understood. If he managed to escape, if he found Ross, he would exact the same revenge. He still had the serum coursing through his veins. Maybe this was all he was meant to be. A monster.

Laskaris landed a blow to Greenwood's chin. The larger man's head jerked back. Instead of toppling over, he grabbed the colonel with both hands and . . . made eye contact with Stephen.

Greenwood's face showed no sign of rage. No hate. No vengeance.

A thin smile appeared on his face. Greenwood shifted his gaze toward the other soldiers, and then he jerked his head toward the door.

You have a hero's heart. When the time is right, you'll know what to do.

The timer beeped. Time restarted.

"We need to get them all out," Stephen said to Sharon, realization overtaking him. "We need to save them. The scientists, too."

"Are you crazy? This place is going to blow any second."

"That's why we have to move fast. They don't deserve to die."

Sharon slapped her forehead. "I don't believe it. You're trying to be a superhero? I've been with these men for the past two weeks. Even without the implant or the serum, they're dangerous. If we turn our backs on them for a second, they'll kill us. Why would you risk your life for someone like that?"

Stephen inhaled through his nose. "Because it's the right thing to do."

Sharon held his gaze for a moment longer. "All right."

They rounded up the soldiers and ushered them to the door. The timer beeped.

As they got the last one out the door, Stephen looked back.

Greenwood had Laskaris pinned to the ground. He made eye contact again with Stephen. Digging his knee into Laskaris's chest, Greenwood lifted one hand and saluted.

Stephen returned the salute, turned, and ran.

He jogged down the corridors. As he rounded a corner, he stopped. The soldiers and researchers were jamming the hall.

"What're you doing?" Sharon shoved them aside. "We need to keep moving."

"The way's blocked," one of the soldiers said slowly, as if waking from a dream. "Door."

Stephen craned his head over the crowd. A blast door had closed off the passage. Part of Laskaris's contingency plan.

"Is there another way out?" he asked.

"Only the access tunnel," a scientist said. "But it's on the other side of the control room. We'll never get there before detonation."

Stephen's mind raced. He couldn't have come this far to fail now.

"There must be an override near the control room," he said. "Laskaris wouldn't take any chances of being trapped on the wrong side."

"I saw an access panel that wasn't part of the schematics," another scientist said. "We weren't allowed to touch it."

"Where is it?"

The scientist gave Stephen instructions.

"Okay, I got it. Sharon, get them out."

"Steve, you don't know what else Laskaris rigged. There could be more gas. Even if you survive the explosion—"

"I know the risks. I came here to do one thing." He grabbed her wrists and looked into her eyes. "Please, let me save you."

She held his gaze, tears welling in her eyes. At last, she nodded. He released her, smiled weakly, and then ran back the way they came.

He reached the control room and located the panel, right where the scientist had said it would be. He had no tools, but he didn't need them. Gripping the panel at opposite corners, he tugged and pulled. Power flooded his body. With a roar, he ripped the panel off.

Inside was a maze of wires and relays. If he disconnected the wrong one, he'd shut down the power, trapping them all inside. He ran a finger along a white wire he guessed was the main relay. Red crossed blue; blue crossed green.

Whispering a prayer, he ripped out the green wire.

The timer continued to beep, but in the distance, he heard what sounded like cheering. At least, he hoped he'd heard it.

Stephen ran. His footfalls echoed as they clanged on the floor.

An explosion boomed behind him. He ran faster, as fire roared down the passage.

He wasn't going to make it.

"We did it, Dad," he whispered, pushing himself to run a little more. "I'm a hero."

The world went white.

66

As Stephen repositioned himself in the hospital bed, a monitor beeped, aggravating his aching head. To make matters worse, the young German doctor standing at the foot of the bed was at least six feet tall, blond, and displayed the all the compassion of a loaf of Bavarian pumpernickel.

"... a mild concussion," the doctor was saying as he jotted notes on an electronic tablet. He peered at Stephen over a pair of reading glasses. "You should be more careful around our mountains. You're lucky your injuries weren't more severe."

"I know." Stephen rubbed his leg under the sheet. It didn't hurt anymore, but he didn't want to give the doctor reason to examine it again. "That's what I get for trying to climb alone. Next time, I'll stick with my group."

The doctor nodded and made more notes. "Is there anyone we should contact?"

"No, they headed back this morning. I'll catch the ICE train after you discharge me." He hesitated. "You are planning to discharge me, right?"

A thin smile appeared on the doctor's lips. "We still need to observe you overnight. I've never seen such quick recovery, but that may not be a good thing. Sometimes with head injuries, there is a honeymoon period of lucidity, followed by rapid decompensation."

"Precautions. I get it." Stephen slumped against his pillow. He held up the TV remote. "Do you get any American stations on here?"

"I believe you can find FOX News on channel sixty-eight."

"Pass." Stephen tossed aside the remote. "I guess I'll take a nap."

"I'll have the nurse check on you. Please use the call button if you feel more pain." The doctor nodded curtly and departed.

Stephen exhaled, thankful he hadn't asked more questions. Not that he planned to provide many answers.

A few minutes later, he heard a knock on the door. "Come in," he said, hugging the pillow as he lay on his stomach.

He heard the door close.

"Steve?" a familiar voice asked.

He rolled over onto his back. His jaw dropped.

"Sharon?"

Sharon pushed away a hoodie and threw her arms around her brother. Stephen hugged back, stunned.

"Thank God you're okay." Sharon held him tighter. "When you didn't show up after the explosion . . ."

"The blast door started to close again after you escaped but got stuck halfway. I managed to duck behind it." He shivered, recalling the flames rushing past, licking his skin. "I blacked out when the door dislodged and fell on my head. When I woke up, I'd suffered second-degree burns to my legs and broke my arm, but I was able to drag myself out of the tunnels. I hid inside what was left of the research lab, making sure no one else made it out."

"You mean Greenwood and Laskaris."

Stephen nodded. "I was the only one."

Sharon drew in a breath and released it. "Good."

"What about the other soldiers, and the scientists?"

"They're all on board a transport back to Baumholder." Sharon half smiled. "The battalion commander's going to blow a nut, especially with Laskaris gone."

Stephen studied Sharon's face. So much like their mom's but stronger, more determined. And something else. "Why didn't you go back with them?"

"I wasn't going anywhere until I found you. First, I checked the rubble from the explosion. When I couldn't find a body, I started checking hospitals."

"How did you find me?"

She blew raspberries. "Seriously? You registered as Jerry Siegel. Cocreator of Superman? It wasn't hard."

Stephen stretched out on the bed. "Well, they're discharging me tomorrow. At least we can travel back together. You're going to do a hell of a job as unit commander."

She averted her gaze. "Yeah, uh, about that . . . I'm not going back."

"What?"

"I've been AWOL for two weeks. Even if they don't court-martial me, they'll insist on full medical evaluations to figure out what was going on in that base, and to prove we're not a threat to the public. The other soldiers are safe now that they're normal. But me?" She shook her head. "I'm done being a lab rat."

"But where will you go?"

"When I went back to get her, Anja was gone. Laskaris gave her the serum. She's more dangerous now than before." She bit her lower lip. "And Uncle Alex is still out there. If I have to search the entire planet, I'm going to keep hunting until I find him and make him pay for what he did to us."

Stephen's chest tightened. "This isn't you. You don't have to seek revenge."

"He ruined us. He destroyed our family. He used us and lied to our faces every day of our lives." Her eyes blazed. Stephen recoiled, expecting to see yellow eyes and swollen purple veins. But she didn't have the rage mutation like he and Dad did. This was something different. This was fear. "They changed me. Not only my physical abilities, but inside. If you hadn't shown up when you did . . ." She looked away. "I fought back as hard as I could, but eventually they would've broken me. I can't return to a job where others trust their lives in my hands, where they rely on me to do the right thing. Not when I don't trust myself."

Stephen drew in a deep breath. "Listen, all heroes go through a period where they hit rock bottom. Once, Wonder Woman killed this villain Max Lord, and—"

"Stop." She touched her fingertips to his lips. "Thank you for trying to save me. Again. When I figure things out, I'll make you proud. I promise."

He nodded. Sharon always kept her promises.

"What about you?" she asked. "All of this must've soured your view of the military even worse than before."

"Actually, I've decided to accept a command position."

"What? I just told you—"

"All I need to do is get hold of the treatment Alex used to suppress my powers for over thirty years. When they go to test me, they'll see I'm only a normal human who did what he had to in order to save his sister."

"Okay, but . . . command? You?"

"Restrepo is dead. Someone has to take over the Pathology division. And whoever they appoint to take Ross's position is going to need close monitoring to make sure they don't follow the same dark path he did." He flashed her a toothy grin. "Besides, who better to oversee examination of the dead than someone who can't die?"

"You're a mess, brother." She grinned. "And you're going to be amazing."

"Thanks." He lowered his gaze. "But I'm worried."

"About what?"

"I have control over the rage now." He studied his hands. "But what if I lose control? What if I turn into Dad?"

"You're not Dad." She laid her hand on his shoulder. "You put the needs of others before your own, even when they didn't deserve it. You have a hero's heart."

They hugged again, the last time for who knew how long. For once, Stephen wasn't worried about her. She would find herself. She would be a hero again. And he would change the military machine. He would fix things. Because it was the right thing to do. He would be a hero, too.

So long as he could contain the monster within.

EPILOGUE

Church Hill Cemetery
Framingham, MA
Two weeks later

A cold wind blew, kicking up dried leaves off the ground. Light mist fell on Stephen's shoulders as he stood at attention in front of the tombstones, clutching a pair of lily bouquets. Colonel Agarwal had insisted Stephen use some of the leave time he'd saved up to recuperate, probably picturing a tropical island or a cruise somewhere, not a gravesite in the middle of Massachusetts. But for Stephen, it wasn't a spa vacation he needed.

Physically, he felt better than he ever had. The concussion, the burns, everything had healed. But inside, his emotions were covered by a massive clot that could break off with the slightest nudge, causing years of anger, pain, and loss to ooze out. Everything he knew about his life had been turned upside down. When he'd exposed the secrets of his past to the light, he'd found far more than he expected. And now he had a new secret, one he needed to hide from everyone, even those closest to him.

The last time he'd stood in this cemetery had been on this very day, over three decades ago. Normally, a soldier killed in the line of duty would be buried at Arlington alongside his brothers in arms. But the military had wanted nothing to do with Isaiah Englehart after the way he'd died, and now Stephen understood it went much deeper than that. They'd wanted to erase him altogether. So, Isaiah and his wife had been buried in the family plot here in Framingham. Less dignified, perhaps, but at least they were surrounded by people who'd given a shit about them.

Stephen sniffled as he bent his knee to lay the bouquets one by one in front of the two tombstones. As a pathologist, he knew death. He understood it. But where he'd once thought of death as final, now he knew that not everything remained buried. He wiped a tear from his eye before facing his mother's grave. "Hi, Mom. I'm sorry for the way I made your life hell. I guess that's what kids are supposed to do, but I could've made your last days a lot easier. I'm sorry I didn't pay enough attention…"

Mucus clogged his throat. He coughed, choking back a sob. Straightening his shoulders, he turned to his father's grave. "And Dad, I understand now why you did what you did. All that time, you thought you were protecting us by following orders, and it turns out

Mom was right all along. A hero knows what's important. And family is more important than service."

His tongue seemed to swell too big to speak. He swallowed hard, wiping his nose with the back of his hand. "I want you to know..." His voice cracked. He barely managed to groan, "I forgive you," before shuddering grief overtook him. Stephen had thought he'd gotten past the shock of discovering that everything he knew about his childhood had been a lie, but being there now, confronted by the permanent reminder, he knew he'd been wrong.

He went to massage the scar on his shoulder, seeking his old source of relief. He stopped when he remembered that it, too, had healed. Damn it. A chill wind bit into his bones. He hugged himself and shivered.

"Excuse me."

Stephen looked up to find a stunning, dark-haired woman in her midthirties standing next to the grave. She was wrapped in a stylish overcoat. Her brown eyes were filled with concern.

Wiping his eyes, Stephen fought to keep his voice steady. "Yes?"

"I'm sorry if I disturbed you." She twisted her full lips. "But I was wondering if there was anything I could do to help."

"Help?" The word pinged inside Stephen's head before he fully registered it. "How do you plan to help? This is a cemetery."

"Yes, I know, but—"

He jumped to his feet. She tensed and moved into a defensive posture. Stephen had the odd feeling she could take him down in seconds despite her small frame. He held up his hands. "I'm not going to hurt you. I just want to know why you'd approach a stranger at a cemetery."

"At first, I thought you were grieving someone who recently died, but then I saw the dates on the tombstones." She pointed at the date on each stone. "They're your parents, aren't they? You lost them both on the same day."

He narrowed his gaze at her. "How do you know that?"

"I lost my parents the same way. Well, sort of." She scratched behind her ear. "I recently learned they weren't who I thought they were."

Something stirred in Stephen's chest. "I know the feeling."

"They're buried over there." She indicated a nearby plot. "I came here in the hopes that seeing them again would provide answers, but instead it raised more questions. Do you know what I mean?"

Stephen nodded. "I do."

"I thought you did. I sensed that about you."

He arched an eyebrow.

"I'm not a psychic, and I'm not coming on to you." She handed him a card. "If you ever need a good listener, I offer free consultations."

Stephen read the name on the card and looked up at her. "You're a psychiatrist?"

"Yes. I specialize in memory and amnesia."

"Well, thanks, but I'm only in town for a few days." He tucked the card into his pocket. "If I suddenly develop amnesia, I'll give you a call—if I remember, of course."

She half smiled. "Of course. It was nice talking to you."

"You, too."

As he walked back to his rental car, Stephen knew he wouldn't need the help of a memory specialist. For the first time in forever, he knew exactly who he was.

Author's Note

As you've probably guessed by now, I've always been a bit of a comic book geek. When I was 11 my parents got me a subscription to the Amazing Spider-Man and Incredible Hulk series—an amazingly incredible time to jump on as it was right as the Hobgoblin first appeared in the comics. Spidey and the Hulk have remained my favorite characters: one a smart-mouthed teen with a deep-rooted sense of responsibility to help others even at his own personal risk, and the other a genius unable to control the personification of his own raw emotions. Although I wasn't originally a Captain America fan, it was Mark Waid's "Man Without a Country" run, with Cap framed and exiled yet still doing what he felt was right, that sold me on the character. When I started writing Heroic Measures, I knew I wanted it to be a twist on the Super-Soldier project, a What If? tale where the subjects were victims, but I also wanted to bring my two other favorite characters into play somehow.

There is no AFMES at Ramstein AB. A $970 million contract to build a new hospital was signed but the completion date has been pushed back to 2027. As far as I know, there are no plans to include a mortuary and medical examiner office there, but to me it made sense that they might want to have something closer to the Middle Eastern theaters of operation. I originally planned to set this novel at the Port Mortuary in Dover with scenes set at DARPA, but getting access to details without having actually set foot there proved near-impossible. So, since I'd spent three years stationed at Spangdahlem AB, only an hour away from Ramstein, I felt comfortable enough with the landscape to predict what the new facility might be like. It also gave me opportunity to pull in some of my own experiences living in Germany.

I'm a developmental-behavioral pediatrician, not a medical examiner. The only time I've dissected a cadaver was in medical school. I owe a great debt to my colleagues in the field who answered my questions about how things might work, what's available in the morgue and what's not, and how medical examiners think. I hope you find Stephen and Tom as realistic as they are entertaining.

I also never set foot on the battlefield, spending most of my time on base or on humanitarian missions (for which I was trained to use an M9 pistol), so I had to rely on colleagues who did to visualize those combat scenes. But what I did experience firsthand is military bureaucracy. There are bad eggs in every field, from medicine to politics to the military. Even though this book centers on corruption in military leadership, I wanted to honor those who serve in every branch, fighting to protect our freedoms, as well as their families who sacrifice so much to support them. As General Norman Schwarzkopf said, "It doesn't take a hero to order men into battle; it takes a hero to be one of those men [or women] who goes into battle."

You may have noticed many homages to superhero comic lore, as well as references to creators and artists who've worked on Captain

America over the years. If you didn't, go back and look for them! This book has been the most fun to write, and I hope you enjoyed reading it as much as I enjoyed writing it.

Oh, and if you're curious about that mysterious character in the epilogue, be sure to read The Memory Thieves series. And keep reading for a sneak look at my next book, Spontaneous Remission, releasing in 2025 and featuring none other than Professor Friedrich Gersch. All will be revealed in time.

As Jack Kirby, the creator of Captain America, once said: "Our dreams make us large."

Keep dreaming.

Joel Shulkin, February 7, 2024

Acknowledgements

There are so many people I need to thank I'm sure I'm going to miss someone, and I'll end up writing an apology in the next book, but here we go. First and foremost, thank you for reading this book! Whether you bought it or won a copy or got it as an ARC reader or a reviewer or whatever, I appreciate your taking a chance on a relatively new author. There are so many new books launched into the world every day, but I hope you found this one unlike anything you've read before.

Thank you to **Captain Craig Mallak, USN (retired)**, former head of AFMES, for answering my endless questions and helping me get my facts straight. And thank you to **Gregory Stancel, MD**, for fact-checking my manuscript and answering even more questions about pathology at Ramstein/Landstuhl.

Huge thanks to my agent, **Lynnette Novak** of the Seymour Agency for being such a champion of this book and of me as a writer that she encouraged me to take a chance on indie publishing so I could share this story with the world. And thank you to **Nicole Resciniti** and the rest of the Seymour Agency for helping spread the word, as well as to my agency suspense siblings for being such incredible supporters.

Special thanks to **Ralph Walker** and **Christine Clemetson**, my fantastic critique partners, for keeping me on my toes and getting the story shaped and kinks worked out.

Also thank you to **Edward Farmer** as an early sensitivity reader; even though I ended up changing direction with the characters, his insight was extremely helpful.

Thank you to my editor, **Dylan Garrity**, for doing such a marvelous job weeding out the typos and catching a few key plot holes that had been previously missed.

And thank you to **Abigail Simmons** of the Killion Group for designing that kickass creepy cover.

As I mentioned earlier, I'm not a pathologist, so thank you to medical examiner-authors **Judy Melenek** and **DP Lyle** for their insights and tidbits that helped round out the story.

Thank you to the crime fiction community for their ongoing support and education on cool things like poisons, firearms, and police procedure.

Thank you to the indie publishing community for helping me figure out how to get this book in your hands without it looking like I printed it at home on a dot matrix printer.

And, as always, thank you to my amazing wife, **Geiza Shulkin,** for supporting me through this whole roller coaster ride, and to our wonderful girls, **Valentina** and **Isabella**, who can't wait to see "Daddy's book make lots of money—like maybe even a hundred dollars".

COLONEL STEPHEN ENGLEHART WILL RETURN IN

EXTRAORDINARY MEASURES

AND SHARON RETURNS IN

NO WONDER

Releasing October, 2024 as an Amazon short

Preorder at https://www.amazon.com/dp/B0CXMNWPTC/

SNEAK PEEK OF

SPONTANEOUS REMISSION

FRIEDRICH GERSCH RETURNS!

Coming in 2025 by Joel Shulkin, MD

Clearwater, Florida

Against the torrential rain battering the Spanish tile roof, the Sisters of Mercy women's shelter stood defiantly, as if to say: *You can beat me all you want but I will never break.* As Betsy Daniels cowered under the flimsy umbrella her home health nurse held over her wheelchair, raindrops slipping under and splattering against her fragile skin, she recalled that once, long ago, she possessed a similar strength. Now she feared it had all but drained away.

Learning your death is imminent can do that to you.

The nurse, a woman in her late thirties named Rebecca, turned to her, and said, "Miss Betsy, are you sure you don't want to go home?"

Replaying the conversation that she'd had with her rheumatologist earlier that day and the dire news he'd delivered, Betsy wiped a tear from her eye and then squared her shoulders as best she could and pretended it had only been a bit of rain. Setting her jaw, she shook her head. "Home's the last place I want to be right now."

Rebecca's lips twisted and she stared at Betsy for a moment longer than would be comfortable in other circumstances, but she turned to the weathered oak door, where a sign proclaimed in ancient script: *I was a stranger, and you welcomed me. Matthew 25:35.*

Shivers ran down Betsy's back. She was no stranger to the owner of this shelter, and with the unthinkable demand she was about make of her pious friend, a demand to help her die on her own terms, Betsy might not be welcome there any longer.

Rebecca rang the doorbell. A light chime sounded inside.

After a minute, the door opened and a woman in her early fifties appeared. Tight curls of raven hair clung to her scalp, the short haircut accentuating the crow's feet edging her eyes as her lips drew back into a toothy grin.

"Betsy!" the woman said in a throaty alto with a hint of Southern twang. "This is an unexpected pleasure. What are you doing here?"

Betsy wet her lips, feeling insubstantial in the glow of Clara Jones's radiant joy. "I needed to talk to someone, Clara. I was hoping if you weren't busy..."

"Busy?" Clara laughed, light and airy. "Never too busy for my oldest friend, sweetheart. Come in, before you catch a cold."

As Rebecca pushed the wheelchair inside, Betsy took note of the changes to the shelter since her last visit some five months ago. Clara had repainted the walls, hung inspirational paintings by artists Betsy didn't know, and bought new leather couches on which several women now sat, watching a game show on a flat-screen TV. The room still felt too small for the number of women who sought protection there, but at least the ones in attendance didn't seem to mind.

"Can we talk in private?" Betsy asked, eyeing the women. They were glued to the television, their shoulders sagging as if the weight of their lives threatened to squash them, but Betsy couldn't risk one of them overhearing her request.

"Of course." Clara motioned for Rebecca and Betsy to follow as she crossed the room. "Let's go to my office."

Clara's office was as cramped and spartan as Betsy remembered, little more than a handful of wooden chairs, a simple writing desk, and a bookcase stuffed with religious and inspirational tomes. Whatever windfall allowed Clara to upgrade the rest of the shelter hadn't extended to the director's private sanctum. Or, more likely, Clara hadn't allowed it.

"Rebecca," Betsy said as the nurse wheeled her into the center of the office and applied the brake. "Could you please wait outside?"

Rebecca glanced at Clara, who nodded and said, "There's tea and coffee in the kitchen. Help yourself."

After the nurse left, Clara sat behind her desk and folded her hands together. "Now, what's going on, Betsy? You look as though you've foreseen the return of the great plagues."

Despite her burgeoning despair, a smile threatened to creep across Betsy's face at her friend's quaint melodrama. She drew in her breath and said, "Nothing like that. But I got some bad news."

Clara's brow furrowed. "How bad?"

"Real bad." Betsy dipped her head, unable to elevate it long enough to meet her friend's gaze. It took all her effort to gasp out the words, "I'm dying."

Silence stretched between them, with only Betsy's pulse filling her ears, until at last, Clara shook her head and said, "Who told you a ridiculous thing like that?"

"Dr. Amin, my rheumatologist at Jacksonville Medical Center. We were there this morning." Betsy dug her closely trimmed fingernails into the arms of her wheelchair and drew in as deep a breath as she could manage against her restrictive chest wall. "My labs confirm my kidneys are failing again."

"So, you need another transplant."

"The transplant committee refused to give me another one."

"How can they do that?" Clara's forehead crumpled. "You don't drink or smoke."

"Dr. Amin said my scleroderma has advanced too far. It's not only my kidneys that are damaged. Most of my organs are working at half their capacity, attacked by my own antibodies. And if he increases my immunosuppressant dosage, it'll cause even more damage." The stifling air in Clara's office wrapped around Betsy like plastic wrap, trapping in the heat and blocking out the air. Her fingers had turned blue, as they often did when she was stressed or cold. They were also numb, but so was the rest of her body, down to her heart. Speaking had grown more difficult over the past few months, and saying the next words drained every ounce of reserve she had left. "He said there's nothing they can do."

Clara wiped at her mouth and seemed to study the surface of her desk before looking up and saying, "I'm so sorry. Have you told Saul?"

"Not yet. He'd been confident for months that my doctors would cure me, even when I'd lost hope." Tears welled in her eyes, but she lacked the strength or dexterity in her hands to wipe them away. Instead, they trailed down her cheeks, rolling past her lips and down her throat. She choked on the salt. "I don't know what to say to him."

"The truth, Betsy." Clara leaned forward. "The truth shall set you free."

Betsy bit off a bitter retort. Clara was her oldest friend, ever since seventh grade when Betsy was the new girl and Clara, the cool girl who was good at everything from singing to playing basketball, took Betsy under her wing and taught her to believe in herself. Betsy always wondered what it was about her that attracted Clara's attention, but she never asked. Maybe it was because she feared the answer was Clara was drawn to broken women like a bee to pollen, and there was no woman more broken than Betsy.

"Easy for you to say," she said at last.

"Not as easy as you think." Clara steepled her fingers. "You remember the old me? The famous defense attorney, representing the worst of the worst and making bank all the way? When my doctor told me I had cervical cancer and only a year to live, I didn't want anyone to know. The only one I told was you."

Betsy nodded. "I remember."

"But I defied the odds. Ten years later, I'm in full remission. And I realized I'd dedicated too much of my life to things that didn't matter. That's why I left law and opened this shelter. You must focus on what's important, Betsy. Be honest, and Saul will understand."

More salty tears clogged Betsy's throat. She mustered a hacking cough and said, "You make it sound so simple."

Clara stood and stepped out from behind her desk, pulled a wooden guest chair closer to Betsy's wheelchair, and sat next to her. She took Betsy's hand in both of hers and said, "The plans of the Lord stand firm forever, the purposes of His heart through all generations."

Betsy wrenched away her hand, wincing at the pain radiating from her knuckles all the way up her arm. "Don't give me that crap about God's plan. What kind of plan is it to make me suffer for fifteen years, only to face an excruciating death?"

"We can't know or understand His will," Clara continued, seeming nonplussed by Betsy's outburst. "His ways are higher than our ways, and His thoughts higher than our thoughts."

"Damn it, I didn't come here to listen to you recite a bunch of nonsense!"

Clara withdrew, eyes wide.

"I don't need a preacher," Betsy said in a hushed voice, unable to meet Clara's gaze. She regretted her curse from the moment it had left her lips, but she could hold back her feelings no longer. She watched an ant crawl across the carpet, following its predetermined course, unaware that, at any moment, it could be snuffed out by a human foot or a wheel from Betsy's chair. Tightening her jaw, Betsy said, "Right now, I need a friend."

Clara's brow furrowed. For a moment, Betsy thought her friend might show a ripple in her ever-serene demeanor, that she might lose her shit. But then Clara tilted her head and smiled. "Betsy, my dearest, I'll be whatever you need."

"Thank you." Betsy pressed her palms together, ignoring the renewed bite of pain the movement brought with it, and touched her fingertips to her lips. This next part was going to be tough. There was a high chance that, friend or not, Clara would refuse. But she had to try. "Because what I need, only you can help me find—or, rather, only you know where to find the man who can provide it."

The smile fell away from Clara's face. "You can't mean—"

"I do." Betsy wet her cracked lips. "I need you to call Frank."

"No."

"He'll make it look like an accident, so it doesn't void the insurance policy."

"I said no."

"You also said you'd be whatever I need." Betsy straightened her back as much as she could manage. "And I need you to be my facilitator. I know Frank owes you a few favors."

"More than a few, but that's not the point." The lines on Clara's forehead deepened. "You only have a short time left. Why not spend it with your husband?"

"Do you have any idea how painful it is when your kidneys completely shut down?" Betsy clenched her fists. "These paltry days I have left aren't going to be filled with pleasant strolls through the park and romantic snuggles in bed. They're going to be a living hell. I am going to suffer."

Clara stared at her wordlessly.

"And Saul will suffer." Betsy swallowed bitter tears. "He won't let go. He'll never let go unless I cut him free."

"But that's not your decision to make. Only God decides—"

"God failed me!"

Clara's expression twisted into a look of shock that was almost comical.

"I did everything I was supposed to do." Betsy's voice crackled with anger. "I went to church. I was a good, loyal wife. I gave to charity. And when I got diagnosed and my body began to fall apart, I prayed, even when I could no longer remain upright in the church pews, even when my spirit shriveled each time a child gawked at me in terror like I was a monster. Every goddamn day I prayed."

"Betsy, please—"

"I thought I needed to be patient. That if I kept praying, if I kept believing, God would see to it that one of my doctors would find a cure. That by some miracle I would get better because I had faith." Betsy shook her head. "But there are no miracles."

Clara opened her mouth as if to speak but shut it again. She stared at the floor for several beats, and then slowly lifted her head. A look of serenity passed over her face, calmer than a sunset over the Gulf of Mexico.

"You think you've lost faith, but you haven't." The crow's feet around Clara's eyes radiated outward. "If you had, you wouldn't be here now."

"I'm here," Betsy began, "because I need—"

"You knew I wouldn't send Frank to you. No matter how much you pleaded or appealed to my guilt, you knew there was zero chance I would agree." Clara took her friend's hand again. Betsy flinched but didn't pull away. "But your faith is challenged. Maybe a greater challenge than most face in their lifetime. Certainly, more than you deserve."

Betsy stared at her, at a loss for words.

"You can meet that challenge. You can fight this." Clara stroked the back of Betsy's hand, tracing over the stiff joints with her fingertips, though Betsy could feel nothing through the thick layer of scar tissue. "Make peace with your fears. Accept that God has a plan, and that while we are not privy to it, He will ensure it serves us all. Once you do that, He will heal your soul."

A heavy weight bore down on Betsy's chest, threatening to crush her. She struggled to breathe as she squeezed Clara's hand. "What if. . .what if I can't?"

Clara bowed her head and kissed Betsy's knuckles. "Pray, as I'll pray for you. Believe with all your heart in God's plan. If, after one month, you remain in despair, unable to see the light, then I will send Frank to you."

Betsy blinked. "But you said—"

"I have faith that you won't need him." Clara's eyes twinkled. "And I pray you will, too."

FEEDBACK

If you enjoyed this book and would like to leave a review (always appreciated but never expected), please visit:

https://www.goodreads.com/book/show/207691554-heroic-measures

https://www.amazon.com/dp/B0CVBFVJZN?ref_=pe_93986420_775043100

https://www.bookbub.com/books/heroic-measures-a-jaw-dropping-forensic-thriller-with-unbelievable-twists-and-gripping-military-and-superhero-themes-death-benefits-book-1-by-joel-shulkin-md

WANT MORE HEROIC MEASURES?

As a thank-you for reading this book, I'd like to gift you an exclusive bonus scene. Simply go to https://BookHip.com/JZFDVSB to download it; by doing so, you'll also join my monthly newsletter & get all the news delivered straight to your inbox.

ABOUT THE AUTHOR

Joel Shulkin, MD is the author of *Adverse Effects* and *Toxic Effects*, the first two novels in the Memory Thieves series, and he has penned award-winning short stories and poetry. A developmental-behavioral pediatrician and United States Air Force veteran with a master's in public health, Joel lives in Florida with his wife, two daughters, and two puppies.

Visit him at https://authorjoelshulkin.com

Milton Keynes UK
Ingram Content Group UK Ltd.
UKHW020837200924
448515UK00006B/34

9 798990 018815